Praise for *The Human Division*

"*The Human Division* is not just John Scalzi at his best,
it is science fiction at its best."
> —Jamie Todd Rubin,
> *Orson Scott Card's InterGalactic Medicine Show*

"Immensely entertaining."
> —*RT Book Reviews* (4½ stars, Top Pick!)

"Featuring the author's trademark humor, clever dialog,
and a hefty dose of action, this is a wonderful addition
to Scalzi's Old Man's War universe."
> —*Library Journal*

"Entertainingly exemplifying the maxim that 'all diplomacy is a continuation of war by other means,' *The
Human Division* is the type of intelligently crafted and
inventive military-political science fiction that reminds
us that though we might be able to pinpoint a genrc's
takeoff point, nobody can predict how far it will fly."
> —Paul Di Filippo,
> *The Barnes & Noble Review*

TOR BOOKS BY JOHN SCALZI

THE HUMAN DIVISION

John Scalzi

Tor Publishing Group
New York

This is a work of fiction. All of the characters, organizations, and events portrayed in this novel are either products of the author's imagination or are used fictitiously.

THE HUMAN DIVISION

Copyright © 2013 by John Scalzi

"After the Coup" copyright © 2008 by John Scalzi

All rights reserved.

Edited by Patrick Nielsen Hayden

A Tor Book
Published by Tom Doherty Associates/Tor Publishing Group
120 Broadway
New York, NY 10271

www.torpublishinggroup.com

Tor® is a registered trademark of Macmillan Publishing Group, LLC.

ISBN 978-0-7653-6955-0

Our books may be purchased in bulk for promotional, educational, or business use. Please contact your local bookseller or the Macmillan Corporate and Premium Sales Department at 1-800-221-7945, ext. 5442, or by email at MacmillanSpecialMarkets@macmillan.com.

First Edition: May 2013
First Mass Market Edition: March 2014

Printed in the United States of America

20 19 18 17 16 15 14 13 12 11

Contents

Contents

Acknowledgments

Writing this particular installment of the Old Man's War universe came with its own unique set of challenges, not in the least was writing thirteen separate episodes that had to work as their own stand-alone stories while at the same time functioning as a novel when they were all stacked together. It was a hell of a lot of fun, but it was also a hell of a lot of work.

To that end, my first acknowledgment here is to my editor, Patrick Nielsen Hayden, whose confidence in the book from the day I first suggested it through to the end of the process helped me considerably, especially on the days I sat there wondering what it was I had gotten myself into. His ability not to panic is a marvelously reassuring thing, and I thank him deeply for it.

Likewise, thanks to Irene Gallo for managing the art side of things, which for this project (especially the electronic version) was far more intensive than it usually is. Irene is the best art director in science fiction and possibly all of publishing, and I am always indebted to her work on my behalf.

Cover artist John Harris's contribution to *The Human Division* is significant enough that I have codedicated the entire book to him, but I want to acknowledge again his spectacular work for the book and for the individual episodes. It was a joy to see all the art for the first time, and a greater joy to get to show it all off to you. The book would not be the same without his efforts.

The copyediting of this particular book was an undertaking of its own epic scale, and for that thanks are in order to Sona Vogel. Thank you for catching my many errors. Also thank you to Heather Saunders for book design, and to Alexis Saarela and Patty Garcia and all of Tor's publicity department for getting me out there in front of folks.

The Human Division was not only released as a print book but also electronically, by episode. This was new territory for Tor and for Macmillan, who went out on a limb to try a new way of getting stories to readers. For getting out on that limb, I am indebted to Tom Doherty, Linda Quinton, Fritz Foy, Dan Schwartz, and Brian Napack.

There are always people I should thank at Tor whom I miss. I hope they will accept my apologies and know I am glad they do the work they do for me and other authors.

Over at Audible, who handled the audiobook version of *The Human Division*, many thanks are in order to Steve Feldberg and William Dufris.

Thanks as ever to Ethan Ellenberg and Evan Gregory, my fiction agents, and I wish them good hunting in selling this overseas. Also, this is a good time to thank my film/tv agent, Joel Gotler, and also the folks involved with the *Old Man's War* movie project: Wolfgang Petersen, Scott Stuber, Alexa Faigen, David Self, and Chris Boal. I'm cheering you guys on.

The electronic edition of *The Human Division* featured dedications for each individual episode. The people to whom those individual episodes were dedicated to were (in order of episode dedication) Brad Roberts and Carl Rigney; Alex Seropian, Tim Harris, Hardy LeBel, and Mike Choi; Alexis Saarela, Patty Garcia, and Tor Publicity; Paul Sabourin and Greg DiCostanzo; Glenn Reynolds; Jonathan Coulton; the SFWA 2012–13 Board of Directors; Diana Sherman; Jared Cloud and Joanna

Beu; The Webb Schools of California Class of 1987; Rena Watson Hawkins; Megan Totusek and Jesi Pershing.

As I was writing *The Human Division* I was also touring for *Redshirts* (my previous novel) and doing a staggering amount of travel. Trying to keep my head in the novel while at the same time doing everything else I was doing was a dizzying experience, to say the least. Friends who helped keep me sane through all of this include (in no particular order) Karen Meisner, Deven Desai, Mary Robinette Kowal, Joe Hill, Kyle Cassidy, Doselle Young, Wil Wheaton, Bill Shafer, Kate Baker, Pat Rothfuss, Natasha Kordus, Robert Lawrence, Jenny Lawson, Pamela Ribon, Lorraine Garland, Neil Gaiman, Paolo Bacigalupi, Hiro Sasaki, Dave Klecha, Yanni Kuznia, Karen Healey, Justine Larbalestier, Adam Lisberg, and Daniel Mainz. Thank you all for putting up with me while I was at loose ends. I am forgetting people. I am sorry. My brain, it is still recovering. Forgive me.

Thanks also to the board of the Science Fiction and Fantasy Writers of America, for putting up with me essentially falling into a hole for the month of October while I was finishing up the novel: Jim Fiscus, Matthew Johnson, Ann Leckie, Lee Martindale, Bud Sparhawk, Cat Valente, and Sean Williams. Sorry, guys. It won't happen again while I'm president. I promise.

And of course, thanks always to Kristine and Athena Scalzi, whom I love more than is entirely sensible and I'm just fine with that.

Finally, thank you. You guys have been asking me to go back to the Old Man's War universe for a while; I wanted to make sure that if I did, it would be worth your time to make the trip. I hope you enjoyed it. I enjoyed writing it for you. Thanks for making it possible.

— John Scalzi
October 27, 2012

THE HUMAN DIVISION

The B-Team,
Parts One and Two

PART ONE
I.

Ambassador Sara Bair knew that when the captain of the *Polk* had invited her to the bridge to view the skip to the Danavar system, protocol strongly suggested that she turn down the invitation. The captain would be busy, she would be in the way and in any event there was not that much to see. When the *Polk* skipped dozens of light-years across the local arm of the galaxy, the only way a human would register the fact would be that their view of the stars would change slightly. On the bridge, that view would be through display screens, not windows. Captain Basta had offered the invitation merely as a formality and was sure enough of its rejection that she had already made arrangements for the ambassador and her staff to have a small reception marking the skip in the *Polk*'s tiny and normally unused observation desk, wedged above the cargo hold.

Ambassador Bair knew protocol suggested she turn down the invitation, but she didn't care. In her twenty-five years in the Colonial Union diplomatic corps she'd never once been on a starship bridge, didn't know when she'd be invited to one again, and regardless of protocol, she was of the opinion that if one was going to issue an invitation, one should be prepared to have it accepted. If her negotiations with the Utche went well, and at this point in the game there was no reason to suspect they would not, no one anywhere would care about this single breach of convention.

So screw it, she was going to the bridge.

If Captain Basta was annoyed by Bair accepting her invitation, she didn't show it. Lieutenant Evans produced the ambassador and her assistant, Brad Roberts, on the bridge five minutes prior to skip; the captain disengaged from her duties and quickly but politely welcomed the pair to the bridge. Formalities fulfilled, she turned her attention back to her pre-skip duties. Lieutenant Evans, knowing his cue, nudged Bair and Roberts into a corner where they could observe without interfering.

"Do you know how a skip works, Ambassador?" Evans asked. For the duration of the mission, Lieutenant Evans was the *Polk*'s protocol officer, acting as a liaison between the diplomatic mission and the ship's crew.

"My understanding of it is that we are in one place in space, and then the skip drive turns on, and we are magically someplace else," Bair said.

Evans smiled. "It's not magic, it's physics, ma'am," he said. "Although the high-end sort of physics that looks like magic from the outside. It's to relativistic physics what relativistic physics is to Newtonian physics. So that's two steps beyond everyday human experience."

"So we're not really breaking the laws of physics here," Roberts said. "Because every time I think of starships skipping across the galaxy, I imagine Albert Einstein in a policeman's uniform, writing up a ticket."

"We're not breaking any laws. What we're doing is literally exploiting a loophole," Evans said, and then launched into a longer explanation of the physics behind skipping. Roberts nodded and never took his eyes off of Evans, but he had a small smile on his face that Bair knew was meant for her. It meant that Roberts was aware he was doing one of his primary tasks, which was to draw away from Bair people who wanted to make pointless small talk with her, so she could focus on what she was good at: paying attention to her surroundings.

Her surroundings were not in fact all that impressive. The *Polk* was a frigate—Bair was sure Evans would know what type specifically, but she didn't want to train his attention back on her at the moment—and its bridge was modest. Two rows of desks with monitors, with a slightly raised platform for the captain or officer of the watch to oversee operations, and two large monitors forward to display information and, when desired, an outside view. At the moment neither display was on; the bridge crew were instead focused on their individual monitors, with Captain Basta and her executive officer walking among them, murmuring.

It was about as exciting as watching paint dry. Or more accurately, as exciting as watching a crew of highly trained individuals do an action they have done hundreds of times before without drama or incident. Bair, who by dint of years in the diplomatic corps was aware that trained professionals doing their thing was not usually a gripping spectator sport, was nevertheless vaguely disappointed. Years of dramatic entertainments had prepared her for something more action oriented. She sighed without realizing it.

"Not what you were expecting, ma'am?" Evans asked, turning his attention back to the ambassador.

"I didn't know what to expect," Bair said, annoyed with herself at having sighed loudly enough to be heard, but hiding it. "The bridge is more quiet than I would have assumed."

"The bridge crew has worked together for a long time," Evans said. "And you have to remember that they pass a lot of information internally." Bair looked over to Evans with an arched eyebrow at this; Evans smiled and pointed a finger to his temple.

Oh, right, Bair thought. Captain Basta and the rest of the bridge crew were all members of the Colonial Defense Forces. This meant that aside from the obvious distinguishing genetically-engineered characteristics of green skin and a youthful appearance, each of them had a computer called a BrainPal nestled up inside their brains. CDF members could use their BrainPals to talk or share data with one another; they didn't have to use their mouths to do it. The murmuring indicated that they still did, however, at least part of the time. CDF members used to be normal people without green skin or computers in their heads. Old habits died hard.

Bair, who had been born on the planet Erie and had spent the last twenty years stationed out of the Colonial Union home planet of Phoenix, had neither green skin nor a computer in her head. But she had spent enough time around CDF members during her diplomatic travels that they no longer seemed particularly notable among the variety of humans she worked with. She sometimes forgot that they were, in fact, a genetically-engineered breed apart.

"One minute to skip," said the *Polk*'s executive officer. Bair's brain popped up a name: Everett Roman. Aside from Commander Roman's notation of the time, nothing else on the bridge had changed; Bair suspected the announcement was for her and Roberts's benefit. Bair's eyes flicked over to the large monitors to the fore of the room. They were still dark.

"Commander Roman," Evans said, and then motioned his head toward the monitors when he had gotten the executive officer's attention. The XO nodded. The monitors sprang to life, one with an image of a star field, the other with a simple schematic of the *Polk*.

"Thank you, Lieutenant Evans," Bair said, quietly. Evans smiled.

Commander Roman counted off the last ten seconds

of the skip. Bair trained her eyes on the monitor showing the star field. When Roman counted zero, the stars in the field seemed to shift at random. Bair knew that the stars hadn't actually shifted. These were entirely new stars. The *Polk* had, without fuss or noise, instantly traveled light-years.

Bair blinked, unsatisfied. If you thought about what just happened in terms of what was physically accomplished, it was a staggering event. As a personal human experience, however . . .

"So that's it?" Roberts asked, to no one in particular.

"That's it," Evans said.

"Not very exciting," Roberts said.

"Not exciting means we did it right," Evans said.

"Well, where's the fun in that?" Roberts joked.

"Other people can do fun," Evans said. "We do precise. We get you where you need to go, on time. Or ahead of time, in this case. We were asked to get you here three days ahead of the Utche arrival. We delivered you three days, six hours early. Here you are, ahead of time twice."

"About that," Bair said. Evans turned his head to the ambassador to give her his full attention.

The deck of the bridge leaped up at the trio, with violence.

Voices on the bridge suddenly became very loud, detailing damage to the ship. Hull breaches, loss of power, casualties. Something had gone very wrong with the skip.

Bair looked up from the deck and saw that the images on the monitors had changed. The schematic of the ship now featured sections blinking in red. The star field had been replaced with a representation of the *Polk* in three-dimensional space. It was at the center of the representation. At the periphery of the representation was an object, heading toward the *Polk*.

"What is that?" Bair asked Evans, who was picking himself up off the deck.

Evans looked at the screen and was quiet for a second. Bair knew he was accessing his BrainPal for more information. "A ship," he said.

"Is it the Utche?" Roberts asked. "We can signal them for help."

Evans shook his head. "They're not the Utche."

"Who are they?" Bair asked.

"We don't know," Evans said.

The monitors chirped, and then there were multiple additional objects on the screen, heading quickly toward the *Polk*.

"Oh, God," Bair said, and stood as the bridge crew reported missiles en route.

Captain Basta ordered the missiles lanced out of the sky and then turned toward Bair—or, more directly, to Evans. "Those two," she said. "Escape pod. Now."

"Wait—," Bair began.

"No time, Ambassador," Basta said, cutting her off. "Too many missiles. My next two minutes are about getting you off the ship alive. Don't waste them." She turned back to her bridge crew, telling them to prep the black box.

Evans grabbed Bair. "Come on, Ambassador," he said, and pulled her off the bridge, Roberts following.

Forty seconds later, Bair and Roberts were shoved by Evans into a cramped box with two small seats. "Strap in," Evan said, yelling to make himself heard. He pointed below one of the seats. "Emergency rations and hydration there." He pointed below the other. "Waste recycler there. You have a week of air. You'll be fine."

"The rest of my team—," Bair said again.

"Is being shoved into escape pods right now," Evans said. "The captain will launch a skip drone to let the CDF know what happened. They keep rescue ships at skip distance for things just like this. Don't worry. Now strap in. These things launch rough." He backed out of the pod.

"Good luck, Evans," Roberts said. Evans grimaced as the pod sealed itself. Five seconds later, the pod punched itself off the *Polk*. Bair felt as if she had been kicked in the spine and then felt weightless. The pod was too small and basic for artificial gravity.

"What the hell just happened back there?" Roberts said, after a minute. "The *Polk* was hit the instant it skipped."

"Someone knew we were on our way," Bair said.

"This mission was confidential," Roberts said.

"Use your head, Brad," Bair said, testily. "The mission was confidential on our end. It could have leaked. It could have leaked on the Utche side."

"You think the Utche set us up?" Roberts asked.

"I don't know," Bair said. "They're in the same situation as we are. They need this alliance as much as we do. It doesn't make any sense for them to string the Colonial Union along just to pull a stupid stunt like this. Attacking the *Polk* doesn't gain them anything. Destroying a CDF ship is a flat-out enemy action."

"The *Polk* might be able to fight it out," Roberts said.

"You heard Captain Basta as well as I did," Bair said. "Too many missiles. And the *Polk* is already damaged."

"Let's hope the rest of our people made it to their escape pods, then," Roberts said.

"I don't think they were sent to the other escape pods," Bair said.

"But Evans said—"

"Evans said what he needed to shut us up and get us off the *Polk*," Bair said.

Roberts was quiet at this.

Several minutes later, he said, "If the *Polk* sent a skip drone, it will need, what, a day to reach skip distance?"

"Something like that," Bair said.

"A day for the news to arrive, a few hours to gear up, a few hours after that to find us," Roberts said. "So two days in this tin can. Best-case scenario."

"Sure," Bair said.

"And then we'll be debriefed," Roberts said. "Not that we can tell them anything about who attacked us or why."

"When they look for us, they'll also be looking for the *Polk*'s black box," Bair said. "That will have all the data from the ship right up until the moment it was destroyed. If they were able to identify the attacking ships at any point, it'll be in there."

"If it survived the destruction of the *Polk*," Roberts said.

"I heard Captain Basta tell her bridge crew to prep the box," Bair said. "I'm guessing that means that they had time to do whatever they needed to to make sure it survived the ship."

"So you, me and a black box are all that survived the *Polk*," Roberts said.

"I think so. Yes," Bair said.

"Jesus," Roberts said. "Has anything like this ever happened to you before?"

"I've had missions go badly before," Bair said, and looked around the confines of the escape pod. "But, no. This is a first."

"Let's hope the best-case scenario is what we get here," Roberts said. "If it's not, then in about a week things are going to get bad."

"After the fourth day we'll take turns breathing," Bair said.

Roberts laughed weakly and then stopped himself. "Don't want to do that," he said. "Waste of oxygen."

Bair began to laugh herself and then was surprised as the air from her lungs rushed the other way, pulled out by the vacuum of space invading the escape pod as it tore apart. Bair had an instant to register the look on her assistant's face before the shrapnel from the explosion that was shredding the escape pod tore into them as well, killing them. She had no final thoughts, other than registering the feel of the air sliding past her lips and the brief, painless *pushing* feeling the shrapnel made as it went through and then out of her. There was a final, distant sensation of cold, then heat, and then nothing at all.

II.

Sixty-two light-years away from the *Polk,* Lieutenant Harry Wilson stood stiffly near the edge of a seaside cliff on the planet Farnut, along with several other members of the Colonial Union diplomatic courier ship *Clarke.* It was a gorgeous, sunny day, warm without being so hot that the humans would sweat in their formal attire. The Colonial diplomats formed a line; parallel to that line was a line of Farnutian diplomats, their limbs resplendent in formal jewelry. Each human diplomat held a baroquely decorated flagon, filled with water brought specially from the *Clarke.* At the head of each line was the chief diplomat for each race at the negotiation: Ckar Cnutdin for the Farnutians and Ode Abumwe for the Colonials. Cnutdin was currently at a podium, speaking in the glottal Farnutian language. Ambassador Abumwe, to the side, appeared to listen intently, nodding from time to time.

"What is he saying?" Hart Schmidt, standing next to Wilson, asked, as quietly as possible.

"Standard boilerplate about friendship between nations and species," Wilson said. As the sole member of the Colonial Defense Forces in the diplomatic mission, he was the only one in the line able to translate Farnutian on the fly, via his BrainPal; the rest of them had relied on translators provided by the Farnutians. The only one of those present at the ceremony was now standing behind Ambassador Abumwe, whispering discreetly into her ear.

"Does it sound like he's wrapping up?" Schmidt asked.

"Why, Hart?" Wilson glanced over to his friend. "You in a rush to get to the next part?"

Schmidt flicked his eyes toward his opposite number on the Farnutian line and said nothing.

As it turned out, Cnutdin was indeed just finishing. He did a thing with his limbs that was the Farnutian equivalent of bowing and stepped back from the podium. Ambassador Abumwe bowed and stepped toward the podium for her speech. Behind her, the translator shifted over to stand behind Cnutdin.

"I want to thank Trade Delegate Cnutdin for his stirring words about the growing friendship between our two great nations," Abumwe began, and then launched into boilerplate of her own, her words delivered with an accent that betrayed her status as a first-generation Colonial. Her parents had emigrated from Nigeria to the Colonial planet of New Albion when Abumwe was an infant; traces of that country's speech overlaid the New Albion rasp that reminded Wilson of the American Midwest that he had grown up in.

Not too long ago, in an attempt to start a rapport with the ambassador, Wilson had noted to Abumwe that the two of them were the only members of the *Clarke* crew who had been born on Earth, the rest of the crew having been Colonials all their life. Abumwe had narrowed her eyes at him, asked him what he was implying and stalked off angrily. Wilson had turned to his friend Schmidt, who was looking on with horror, and asked what he had done wrong. Schmidt told him to access a news feed.

That was how Wilson learned that the Earth and the

Colonial Union appeared to be undergoing a trial separation and were probably headed for a divorce. And learned about who was splitting them apart.

Ah, well, Wilson thought, watching Abumwe wrap up her speech. Abumwe had never warmed to him; he was pretty sure she vaguely resented having any CDF presence on her ship, even in the relatively innocuous form of a technology advisor, which was Wilson's role. But as Schmidt liked to point out, it wasn't personal. By all indications, Abumwe had never really warmed up to anyone, ever. Some people just didn't like people.

Not the best temperament for a diplomat, Wilson thought, not for the first time.

Abumwe stepped away from the podium, bowed deeply to Ckar Cnutdin, and at the end of her bow took her flagon and nodded to her line of diplomats. Cnutdin likewise signaled to his line.

"This is it," Schmidt said to Wilson, and then they both stepped forward, toward the Farnutians, just as the Farnutians slid forward to them. Each line stopped roughly half a meter from the other, still parallel.

As a unit and as they had practiced, every human diplomat, Ambassador Abumwe included, thrust forward their flagon. "We exchange water," they all said, and with ceremonial pomp upended their flagons, spilling the water at what passed for the Farnutians' feet.

The Farnutians replied with a hurking sound that Wilson's BrainPal translated as *We exchange water,* and then spewed from their mouths seawater they had stored in their bodies' ballast bladders, directly into the faces of the human diplomats. Every human diplomat was drenched with salty, Farnutian body-temperature water.

"Thanks for that," Wilson said to his opposite number on the Farnutian line. But the Farnutian had already turned away, making a hiccuping sound at another of its kind as it broke ranks. Wilson's BrainPal translated the words.

Thank God that's *over,* it had said. *When do we get lunch?*

"You're unusually quiet," Schmidt said to Wilson, on the shuttle ride back to the *Clarke.*

"I'm ruminating on my life, and karma," Wilson said. "And what I must have done in a previous life to deserve being spit on by an alien species as part of a diplomatic ceremony."

"It's because the Farnutian culture is so tied to the sea," Schmidt said. "Exchanging the waters of their homeland is a symbolic way to say our fates are now tied together."

"It's also an excellent way to spread the Farnutian equivalent of smallpox," Wilson said.

"That's why we got shots," Schmidt said.

"I would at least like to have poured the flagon on someone's head," Wilson said.

"That wouldn't have been very diplomatic," Schmidt said.

"And spitting in *our* faces is?" Wilson's voice rose slightly.

"Yes, because that's how they cement their deals," Schmidt said. "And they also know that when humans spit in someone's face, or pour water on someone's head, it doesn't mean the same thing. So we devised something that everyone agreed was symbolically acceptable. It took our advance team three weeks to hammer that out."

"They could have hammered out a deal where the Farnutians learn to *shake hands,*" Wilson pointed out.

"We *could* have," Schmidt agreed. "Except for the little fact that we need this trade alliance a lot more than they do, so we have to play by their rules. It's why the negotiations are on Farnut. It's why Ambassador Abumwe accepted a deal that's a short-term loser. It's why we stood there and got spit on and said thank you."

Wilson looked toward the forward part of the shuttle, where the ambassador sat with her top aides. Schmidt didn't rate inclusion; Wilson certainly didn't. They sat in the back, in the cheap seats. "She got a bad deal?" he asked.

"She was *told* to get a bad deal," Schmidt said, looking toward the ambassador as well. "That defense shielding you trained their people on? We traded it for agricultural products. We traded it for fruit. We don't need their fruit. We can't eat their fruit. We're probably going to end up taking everything they give us and stewing it down to ethanol or something pointless like that."

"Then why did we make the deal?" Wilson asked.

"We were told to think of it as a 'loss leader,'" Schmidt said. "Something that gets the Farnutians through the door so we can make better deals later."

"Fantastic," Wilson said. "I can look forward to getting spit on again."

"No," Schmidt said, and settled back into his chair. "It's not us that will be coming back."

"Oh, right," Wilson said. "You get all the crappy diplomatic missions, and once you've done the scut work, someone else comes in for the glory."

"You say it like you're skeptical," Schmidt said to Wilson. "Come on, Harry. You've been with us long enough now. You've seen what happens to us. The missions we get are either low-level or ones where if they fail, it'll be easy enough to blame it on us, rather than our orders."

"Which kind was this one?" Wilson asked.

"Both," Schmidt said. "And so is the next one."

"This brings me back to my question about my karma," Wilson said.

"You probably set kittens on fire," Schmidt said. "And the rest of us were probably there with you, with skewers."

"When I joined the CDF we probably would have just shot the hell out of the Farnutians until they gave us what we wanted," Wilson said.

"Ah, the good old days," Schmidt said sarcastically, and then shrugged. "That was then. This is now. We've lost the Earth, Harry. Now we have to learn to deal with it."

"There's going to be a hell of a learning curve on that one," Wilson said, after a minute.

"You are correct," Schmidt said. "Be glad you don't have to be the teacher."

III.

I need to see you, Colonel Abel Rigney sent to Colonel Liz Egan, CDF liaison to the secretary of state. He was heading toward her suite of offices in the Phoenix Station.

I'm a little busy at the moment, Egan sent back.

It's important, Rigney sent.

What I'm doing right now is also important, Egan returned.

This is more importanter, Rigney sent.

Well, when you put it that way, Egan replied.

Rigney smiled. *I'll be at your office in two minutes,* he sent.

I'm not there, Egan returned. *Go to the State Department conference complex. I'm in Theater Seven.*

What are you doing there? Rigney sent.

Scaring the children, Egan replied.

Three minutes later, Rigney slipped into the back of Theater Seven. The room was darkened and filled with midlevel members of the Colonial Union diplomatic corps. Rigney took a seat at one of the higher rows in the room and looked across at the faces of the people there. They appeared rather grim. Down on the floor of the theater stood Colonel Egan, a three-dimensional display, currently unlit, behind her.

I'm here, Rigney sent to Egan.

Then you can see I'm working, she replied. *Shut up and give me a minute.*

What Egan was doing was listening to one of the midlevel diplomats drone on in the vaguely condescending way that midlevel diplomats will do when presented with someone they assume is below their station. Rigney, who knew that in her past life Egan had been the CEO of a rather substantial media empire, settled in to enjoy the show.

"I'm not disagreeing that the new reality of our situation is challenging," the diplomat was saying. "But I'm not entirely convinced that the situation is as insoluble as your assessment suggests."

"Is that so, Mr. DiNovo," Egan said.

"I think so, yes," the diplomat named DiNovo said. "The human race has always been outnumbered out here. But we've managed to keep our place in the scheme of things. Small, albeit important details have changed here, but the fundamental issues are largely the same."

"Are they," Egan said. The display behind her flashed on, picturing a slowly rotating star field that Rigney recognized as the local interstellar neighborhood. A series of stars flashed blue. "To recap, here we are. All the star systems which have human planets in them. The Colonial Union. And here are all the star systems with other intelligent, star-faring races in them." The star field turned red as a couple thousand stars switched colors to show their allegiance.

"This is no different than what we've always had to work with," the diplomat named DiNovo said.

"Wrong," Egan said. "This star chart is misleading, and you, Mr. DiNovo, appear not to realize that. All that red up there *used* to represent hundreds of individual races, all of whom, like the human race, had to battle or negotiate with any other race they encountered. Some races were stronger than others, but none of them had any substantial strength or tactical advantage over most of the others. There were too many civilizations too close to parity for any one of them to gain a long-term lead in the power struggle.

"That worked for us because we had one advantage other races didn't," Egan said. Behind her, one blue star system, somewhat isolated from the main arc of human systems, glowed more brightly. "We had Earth, which supplied the Colonial Union with two critical things: colonists, with which we could rapidly populate the planets we claimed, and soldiers, which we could use to defend those planets and secure additional worlds. Earth supplied the Colonial Union more of each than it would have been politically feasible to provide itself from its own worlds. This allowed the Colonial Union both a strategic and tactical advantage and allowed humanity to come close to upending the existing political order in our region of space."

"Advantages we can still exploit," DiNovo began.

"Wrong again," Egan said. "Because now two critical things have changed. First, there's the Conclave." Two-thirds of the formerly red stars turned yellow. "The Conclave, formed out of four hundred alien races which formerly fought among themselves, but now acting as a single political entity, able to enforce its policies by sheer mass. The Conclave will not allow unaffiliated races to engage in further colonization, but it does not stop those races from raiding each other for resources or for security purposes or to settle old scores. So the Colonial Union still has to contend with two hundred alien races targeting its worlds and ships.

"Second, there's Earth. Thanks to the actions of former Roanoke Colony leaders John Perry and Jane Sagan, the Earth has at least temporarily suspended its relationship with the Colonial Union. Its people now believe that we've been holding back the planet's political and technological development for decades to farm it for colonists and soldiers. The reality is more complicated, but as with most humans, the people on Earth prefer the simple answer. The simplest answer is the Colonial Union's been screwing them. They don't trust us. They don't want anything to do with us. It may be years before they do."

"My point is that even without the Earth we still have advantages," DiNovo said. "The Colonial Union has a population of billions on dozens of planets rich with resources."

"And you believe that the colony worlds can replace the colonists and soldiers the Colonial Union until very recently received from Earth," Egan said.

"I'm not saying there won't be grumbling," DiNovo said. "But yes, they could."

"Colonel Rigney," said Egan, speaking her compatriot's name but keeping her eyes on DiNovo.

"Yes," Rigney said, surprised at being called on. An entire room of heads swiveled to look at him.

"You and I were in the same recruiting class," Egan said.

"That's right," Rigney said. "We met on the *Amerigo Vespucci*. That was the ship that took us from Earth to Phoenix Station. It was fourteen years ago."

"Do you remember how many recruits were on the *Vespucci*?" Egan asked.

"I remember the CDF representative telling us there were one thousand fifteen of us," Rigney said.

"How many of us are still alive?" Egan asked.

"There are eighty-nine," Rigney said. "I know that

because one of us died last week and I got a notification. Major Darren Reith."

"So a ninety-one percent fatality rate over fourteen years," Egan said.

"That's about right," Rigney said. "The official statistic that the CDF tells recruits is that in ten years of service the fatality rate is seventy-five percent. In my experience, that official statistic is low. After ten years recruits are allowed to leave the service, but many of us stay in." *Because who wants to start getting old again,* Rigney thought, but did not say.

"Mr. DiNovo," Egan said, returning her full attention to her diplomat, "I believe you are originally from the colony of Rus, is that correct?"

"That's correct," DiNovo said.

"In its entire history of more than one hundred and twenty years, Rus has never been asked to supply the Colonial Union with soldiers," Egan said. "I want you to tell me how you believe the colony will respond when it is informed by the Colonial Union that it will require— *require,* not ask—one hundred thousand of its citizens annually to join the Colonial Defense Forces, and that at the end of those ten years seventy-five percent of them will be dead. I want you to tell me how the Rus citizens will respond when they learn that part of their job is to quell rebellions on colonies, which happens more often than the Colonial Union prefers to admit. How will re-cruits from Rus feel about firing on their own people? Will they do it? Will *you,* Mr. DiNovo? You are in your early fifties now, sir. You're not that far off from the CDF recruitment age. Are you ready to fight and very likely die for the Colonial Union? Because you are, in yourself, the *advantage* you say we have."

DiNovo had nothing to say to this.

"I've been giving these presentations to the diplo-matic corps for a month now," Egan said, turning her eyes away from the silenced DiNovo and scanning the room. "In every presentation I have someone like Mr. DiNovo here making the argument that the situation we are in is not that bad. They, like he, are wrong. The Colonial Defense Forces lose a staggering number of soldiers on an annual basis and have for more than two hundred years. Our developing colonies cannot quickly grow themselves to a size sufficiently large to avoid extinction by breeding alone. The existence of the Conclave has changed the math of human survival in ways we cannot yet imagine. The Colonial Union has survived and thrived because it has exploited an unearned surplus of humans from Earth. We don't have that surplus anymore. And we don't have the time to develop a new surplus from within the Colonial Union system and population."

"How bad is it, then?" Rigney heard himself ask. He was as surprised as anyone to hear his own voice.

Egan glanced at him, then drew her attention back to the crowd. "If things continue as they are, based on historical CDF fatality rates, in three years we'll no longer have sufficient forces to defend our colonies from predation and genocidal aggression by other races," she said. "From there, our best estimate is that the Colonial Union as a political entity collapses within five to eight years. Without the overarching protective structure of the Colonial Union, all remaining human planets are attacked and wiped out within twenty years. Which is to say, ladies and gentlemen, that from this very moment, the human race is thirty years from extinction."

The room was dead silent.

"The reason I'm telling you this is not so you can run home and hug your children," Egan said. "The reason I'm telling you this is that for more than two hundred years, the Department of State has been the vermiform appendix of the Colonial Union. An afterthought to the

CU's strategy of aggressive defense and expansion." She stared at DiNovo. "A nice sinecure for mediocrities to be shoved into, where they can do no real harm. Well, all that changes now. The Colonial Union can no longer afford to live the way we've lived. We don't have the resources and we don't have the people. So from this moment forward the State Department has two missions. One: Bring Earth back into the fold, for the advantage of us both. Two: Whenever possible, avoid conflict with the Conclave and unaffiliated alien races. Diplomacy is the best way to make that happen.

"What that means, ladies and gentlemen, is that from now on, the Colonial Union State Department actually matters. And *you*, my friends, now all have to work for a living."

"Do you always squash someone as hard as you squashed DiNovo?" Rigney asked. Theater Seven was now empty; the midlevel diplomats had shuffled out, grumbling to one another. He and Egan were now both standing near the display, which had again shut down.

"Usually," Egan said. "DiNovo was doing me a favor, actually. For every one like him who is stupid enough to open his mouth, there's about fifty of these people who keep their traps shut and plan to ignore what I have to say. This way I get to drive the message home to all of them. Marginally more of them will listen to me this way."

"You think they really are all mediocrities, then," Rigney said.

"Not all of them," Egan said. "Most of them. And certainly the ones *I* have to deal with." She waved at the empty theater. "These people are cogs. They're stationed here, pushing the proverbial paper. If they were any good at what they did, they'd be out there in the universe. The ones out there are the A-teams. Hell, they're the B-teams, too. The ones here are teams C through K."

"Then you're not going to like this," Rigney said. "One of your A-teams has gone missing."

Egan frowned. "Which one?" she asked.

"Ambassador Bair's team," Rigney said. "Along with, I should add, one of our frigates, the *Polk*."

Egan was silent for a moment, processing the news. "When did this happen?" she finally asked.

"It's been two days since there's been a skip drone sent back from the *Polk*," Rigney said.

"And you're only telling me this now?" Egan said.

"I would have told you sooner, but you wanted me to see you scare the children," Rigney said. "And two days without drone contact is our standard alarm raiser. Particularly with missions like this one, which are supposed to be secret. I came to find you as soon as we confirmed two days of dead air."

"What did your recovery mission find?" Egan asked.

"No recovery mission," Rigney said, and caught Egan's look. "We had a hard enough time negotiating a military frigate for the mission. If the Utche show up and see several military ships in the area, none of them with diplomats on them, everything blows up."

"Recon drones, then," Egan said.

"Of course," Rigney said. "Everything's preliminary because the drones have just arrived, but they're not finding anything."

"You sent the drones to the correct system," Egan said.

"Come on, Liz," Rigney said.

"Doesn't hurt to ask," Egan said.

"We sent the drones to the right system," Rigney said. "We sent the *Polk* to the right system. The Danavar system is where the Utche wanted to meet."

Egan nodded. "A system with nothing but gas giants and airless moons. No one will think to look for you there. Perfect for secret negotiations."

"Apparently not so secret after all," Rigney said.

"You're presuming the *Polk* met with a bad end," Egan said.

"Our frigates don't have a history of randomly vaporizing," Rigney said. "But whatever or whoever did this isn't in the Danavar system now. There's nothing there but planets and moons and a big yellow star."

"Have we told the Utche about this?" Egan asked.

"We haven't told anyone about it," Rigney said. "Outside of command, you're the first person to know. We haven't even told your boss that her team is missing. We figured we'd let you do that yourself."

"Thanks," Egan said, wryly. "But surely the Utche have noticed there is no one negotiating a treaty with them."

"The *Polk* arrived three days early," Rigney said.

"Why?" Egan said.

"Ostensibly to give Bair's team time to prep away from the distractions of Phoenix Station," Rigney said.

"And in reality?" Egan asked.

"In reality to make sure we were militarily prepared for an immediate withdrawal if necessary," Rigney said.

"Seems drastic," Egan said.

"You'll recall the Utche have handed our ass to us in three out of the last five military engagements we've had with them," Rigney said. "Just because they came to us for this alliance doesn't mean we trust them entirely."

"And you don't think the Utche might have figured out the CU's trust issues," Egan said.

"We're pretty sure they have," Rigney said. "In part because we let them know we were arriving early. Your boss signed off on the cover story, but we don't assume the Utche are stupid. It was a sign to us of how much they want the alliance that they were willing to give us a tactical advantage."

"You've entertained the possibility the Utche blasted the *Polk* out of the sky," Egan said.

"Obviously," Rigney said. "But they've been as transparent with us as we've been with them, and where they're not transparent, we have spies. This is something we would have known about. And nothing they're doing indicates that they think anything is out of the ordinary. Their diplomatic mission is on a ship called the *Kaligm,* and it's a day out from skip distance."

Egan said nothing to this but instead fired up the display, turning to it. Phoenix Station floated in the display, the limb of the planet Phoenix below it. At a distance from Phoenix Station, CDF and trade ships floated; their names appeared in labels hovering aside them in the display. The image pulled out and both Phoenix Station and Phoenix shrank to a single dot, taking with them thousands of starships arriving at or departing from the Colonial Union's capital. The image pulled farther out and displayed, as dots, dozens of ships, each working its way toward a sufficiently flat spot of space-time to make a skip. Egan began pulling information from a few, crew manifests spilling onto the display.

"Okay, I give up," Rigney said, after several minutes of this. "Tell me what you're doing."

"Ambassador Bair isn't on our A-list," Egan said, still scanning crew manifests. "She's on our A Plus–list. If she was pipped to negotiate, then this mission is an actual priority, not just a top secret diplomatic circle jerk."

"Okay," Rigney said. "So?"

"So, you don't know Secretary Galeano like I do," Egan said, naming the secretary of state. "If I walk into her office, tell her one of her best diplomats and her entire team is probably dead and their mission therefore a complete failure, without a backup plan already in place and ready to implement, things will be very grim indeed. I will be without a job, *you* will probably be without a job simply for being the messenger, and the secretary will go out of her way to make sure that the next posting for both of us will be someplace where our life expectancy will be measured with an egg timer."

"She sounds nice," Rigney said.

"She's perfectly lovely," Egan said. "Until you piss her off." The display, which had been scrolling through ships and crew manifests, suddenly stopped on a single ship. "Here."

Rigney peered up at the image. "What is this?"

"This is the B-team," Egan said.

"The *Clarke*?" Rigney said. "I don't know this ship."

"It handles various low-level diplomatic missions," Egan said. "Its chief diplomat is a woman named Abumwe." The image of a dark and severe-looking woman hovered on the screen. "Her most significant negotiation was with the Korba a few months back. She impressed them by having a CDF officer stationed on the ship fight with one of their soldiers, and lose in a diplomatically meaningful way."

"That's interesting," Rigney said.

"Yes, but not entirely her doing," Egan said, and popped up the images of two men, one of whom was green. "The fight was set up by a deputy, Hart Schmidt. Lieutenant Harry Wilson was the one who fought."

"So why these people?" Rigney asked. "What makes them the right people to take over this mission?"

"Two reasons," Egan said. "One, Abumwe was part of an embassy to the Utche three years ago. Nothing came of it at the time, but she has experience dealing with them. That means she can get brought up to speed quickly. Two"—she pulled out the view to show the *Clarke* in space—"the *Clarke* is eighteen hours away from skip distance. Abumwe and her people can still get to the Danavar system ahead of the Utche and participate in the negotiations, or at the very least allow us to set up a new round of talks. There's no other diplomatic mission that can make it on time."

"We send in the B-team because it's marginally better than nothing," Rigney said.

"Abumwe and her people aren't incompetent," Egan said. "They just wouldn't be your first choice. But right now we're short on choices."

"Right," Rigney said. "You're really going to sell this to your boss, then."

"Unless you have a better idea," Egan said.

"Not really," Rigney said, then furrowed his brow for a moment. "Although . . ."

"Although what?" Egan said.

"Bring up that CDF guy again," Rigney said.

Egan popped the image of Lieutenant Harry Wilson back onto the display. "What about him?" she said.

"He still on the *Clarke*?" Rigney asked.

"Yes," Egan said. "He's a technical advisor. Some of the *Clarke*'s recent missions have had military tech and weapons as part of the negotiations. They have him on hand to train people on the machines we're offering. Why?"

"I think I may have found a way to sweeten your B-team plan to Secretary Galeano," Rigney said. "And to my bosses, too."

IV.

Wilson noted the expression Schmidt had when he looked up and saw him standing by the door of Ambassador Abumwe's conference room.

"You don't have to look *that* shocked," Wilson said, dryly.

"Sorry," Schmidt said. He moved to let other members of the *Clarke*'s diplomatic contingent into the room.

Wilson waved it away. "I'm not usually included this early in the discussion. It's fine."

"Do you know what this is about?" Schmidt said.

"Allow me to repeat: I'm not usually included this early in the discussion," Wilson said.

"Got it," Schmidt said. "Well, shall we, then?" The two of them entered the room.

The conference room was cramped, as was everything on the *Clarke*. The table, with eight seats, was already filled, with Ambassador Abumwe looking owlishly at Schmidt and Wilson as they entered. The two of them took positions against the wall opposite her.

"Now that we're all here," she said, with a pointed glance at Wilson and Schmidt, "let's get started. The Department of State, in its wisdom, has decided that our presence is no longer needed at Vinnedorg."

A groan went up from around the table. "Who are they giving our work to this time?" asked Rae Sarles.

"No one," Abumwe said. "Our superiors are apparently under the impression that these negotiations will somehow magically take care of themselves without a Colonial presence."

"That doesn't make any sense," said Hugh Fucci.

"I appreciate you telling me that, Hugh," Abumwe said. "I don't believe I would have figured that out on my own."

"Sorry, Ambassador," Fucci said, backtracking. "What I mean to say is that they've been having us working on these negotiations with the Vinnies for more than a year now. I don't understand why they want to threaten our momentum by interrupting what we're doing."

"Which is why we're having our little meeting today," Abumwe said, and then nodded to Hillary Drolet, her assistant, who pressed the screen of her PDA. "If you'll access your queues, you'll find the information on our new assignment."

Everyone at the table, and Schmidt, accessed their PDAs; Wilson accessed his BrainPal, found the document in his queue, and streamed the data in the bottom quarter of his field of vision.

"The Utche?" asked Nelson Kwok, after a minute. "Have the CU ever actually negotiated with them before?"

"I was part of a mission to them three years ago, before I took this posting," Abumwe said. "At the time, nothing seemed to come of it. But apparently we've been quietly negotiating with them for the last year or so."

"Who's been the lead?" Kwok asked.

"Sara Bair," Abumwe said.

Wilson noted that everyone looked up at the ambassador when she said this. Whoever this Sara Bair was, she was clearly a star.

"Why is she off the negotiations?" Sarles asked.

"I couldn't tell you," Abumwe said. "But she and her people are, and now we're on it."

"Too bad for her," Fucci said, and Wilson saw there were smiles around the table. Getting this Bair's sloppy seconds were preferable to the *Clarke*'s original mission, it seemed. Once again, Wilson wondered at what fate it was that brought him onto the *Clarke* to join its band of not-that-lovable losers. Wilson also couldn't help but notice that the only person at the table not smiling at the prospect of taking up the Utche negotiations was Abumwe herself.

"There's a lot of information in this package," Schmidt said. He was flicking his PDA screen and scrolling through the text. "How many days before we begin negotiating?"

And it was then that Abumwe smiled, notably thin and humorless though it was. "Twenty hours."

There was dead silence.

"You're joking," Fucci said. Abumwe gave him a look that clearly indicated she had reached the end of her patience with him for the day. Fucci wisely did not speak again.

"Why the rush?" Wilson asked. He knew Abumwe didn't like him; it wouldn't hurt for him to ask the question everyone else wanted to know but was too scared to ask.

"I couldn't say," Abumwe said evenly, looking at him briefly and then turning her attention to her staff. "And even if I could, the reason wouldn't matter for what we have to do now. We have sixteen hours before our jump and then four hours after that before the Utche are scheduled to arrive. After that we're on their schedule. They might want to meet immediately; they might want to meet in a day. We are going to go under the assumption they will want to begin negotiations immediately. That means you have the next twelve hours to get up to speed. After that, we'll have planning sessions before and after the jump. I hope you've gotten enough sleep in the last two days, because you're not getting any more for a while. Any questions?"

There were none. "Good," Abumwe said. "I don't believe I have to tell any of you that if these negotiations go well, then it is good for us. For all of us. If they go poorly, then it will go badly for all of us as well. But it will go especially poorly for whichever ones of you were not completely up to speed and dragged the rest of your team down with you. I need you to be crystal clear on that."

They were.

"Lieutenant Wilson, a word with you," Abumwe said, as the room began to clear. "You too, Schmidt." The room cleared except for the ambassador, Hillary Drolet, Schmidt and Wilson.

"Why did you ask about why there was a rush?" Abumwe asked.

Wilson made a conscious effort not to let the thought *I'm being called on the carpet for that?* show up on his face. "Because everyone wanted to know, but no one else wanted to ask, ma'am."

"Because they knew better," Abumwe said.

"Except possibly for Fucci, yes, ma'am," Wilson said.

"But you don't," Abumwe said.

"No, I know better, too," Wilson said. "But I still thought someone should ask."

"Hmmm," Abumwe said. "Lieutenant, what did it say to you that we have twenty hours to prepare for this negotiation?"

"Are you asking me to speculate, ma'am?" Wilson asked.

"It's rather obvious that's what I'm asking," Abumwe said. "You're Colonial Defense Forces. You no doubt have a military perspective on this."

"It's been years since I've been anywhere near actual combat, ma'am," Wilson said. "I've been with CDF Research and Development for years, even before they lent me to you and the *Clarke* as your tech consultant."

"But you *are* still CDF, yes?" Abumwe said. "You still have the green skin and the computer in your head. I imagine if you dig deeply, you might still have the ability to look at things from a military point of view."

"Yes, ma'am," Wilson said.

"Then give me your analysis," Abumwe said.

"Someone's humped the bunk," Wilson said.

"Excuse me?" Abumwe said. Wilson noted Schmidt suddenly looked paler than usual.

"Humped the bunk," Wilson repeated. "Screwed the pooch. Gone FUBAR. Insert your own metaphor for things going sideways here. You don't have to have military experience to see that; everyone in this room had that thought. Whatever this Sara Bair and her team were supposed to do, they blew it, and for whatever reason the Colonial Union needs to attempt a salvage, so you and your team are the last-minute, last-chance substitute."

"And why us?" Abumwe said.

"Because you are good at what you do," Wilson said.

Abumwe's thin smile returned. "If I want smoke blown up my ass, Lieutenant, I could have your friend here," she said, nodding toward Schmidt.

"Yes, ma'am," Wilson said. "In that case, I'd guess because we're close to jump, which makes us easy to reroute, that you've had at least some experience with the Utche, and that if you fail, and you probably will because you're the last-minute replacement, you're low enough on the diplomatic totem pole that it can be chalked up to your incompetence." Wilson looked over to Schmidt, who looked as if he were about to implode. "Stop that, Hart," he said. "She asked."

"I did indeed," Abumwe said. "And you are right, Lieutenant. But only half-right. The other reason that they picked us is because of *you*."

"I beg your pardon?" Wilson said, now thoroughly confused.

"Sara Bair didn't fail at her task, she disappeared," Abumwe said. "Along with the whole of her diplomatic mission and a CDF frigate called the *Polk*. It and them, gone. No trace."

"That's not good," Wilson said.

"You are once again stating the obvious," Abumwe said.

"How do I matter here, ma'am?" Wilson said.

"They don't think the *Polk* just vanished, they think it was destroyed," Abumwe said. "And they need you to look for the black box."

"Black box?" Schmidt asked.

"A data recorder," Wilson said. "If the *Polk* was destroyed and the black box survived, then it could tell us what happened to the ship, and who killed it."

"And we couldn't find it without you?" Schmidt asked.

Wilson shook his head. "They're small and they don't send out a locator beacon unless they're pinged with an encrypted signal, specific to that ship. It's a military-grade cipher. You need a very tall security clearance for that. They don't just hand those out to anyone, and not to anyone outside the CDF." He turned his attention to Abumwe. "But they don't just hand them out to random lieutenants, either."

"Then we are lucky you are not just a random lieutenant," Abumwe said. "I am told that in your history it seems that you once had a very high security clearance."

"I was part of a team doing research on BrainPal security," Wilson said. "Again, it's been years. I don't have that clearance level anymore."

"You didn't," Abumwe said. She nodded to her assistant, who once again pressed on her PDA. Wilson immediately saw a ping light for his queue in his peripheral vision. "Now you do."

"Okay," Wilson said slowly, and scanned the details of the security clearance. After a moment he spoke again. "Ambassador, I think you should know this security clearance comes with a level of executive authority that technically means I can give orders to the *Clarke*'s crew in the furtherance of my mission," he said.

"I would suggest you not try to exercise that privilege with Captain Coloma," Abumwe said. "She hasn't put anyone on the wrong side of an airlock, but if you gave her an order, she might make an exception for you."

"I will keep that in mind," Wilson said.

"Do," Abumwe said. "In the meantime, as you've no doubt read by now, your orders are to find the black box, decode it and find out what happened to the *Polk*."

"Got it, ma'am," Wilson said.

"It's been implied to me by my own superiors that your finding the black box is of equal or greater importance to me actually successfully concluding these negotiations with the Utche," Abumwe said. "To that end I have detailed you an aide for the duration." She nodded to Schmidt. "I don't need him. He's yours."

"Thank you," Wilson said, and noted that he'd never seen Hart look more pained than just now, when he had been deemed inessential by his boss. "He'll be useful."

"He'd better be," Abumwe said. "Because, Lieutenant Wilson, the warning I gave to my staff goes double for you. If you fail, this mission fails, even if my half goes well. Which means I will have failed because of you. I may be low on the diplomatic totem pole, but I am sufficiently high enough on it that when I push you, you will die from the fall." She looked over to Schmidt. "And he'll kill you when he lands."

"Understood, ma'am," Wilson said.

"Good," Abumwe said. "One more thing, Lieutenant. Try to find that black box before the Utche arrive. If someone's trying to kill us all, I want to know about it before our negotiating partners show up."

"I'll do my best," Wilson said.

"Your best got you stationed on the *Clarke*," Abumwe said. "Do better than that."

V.

"Please stop that," Wilson said to Schmidt, as they sat in the *Clarke* lounge, reviewing their project data.

Schmidt looked up from his PDA. "I'm not doing anything," he said.

"You're hyperventilating," Wilson said. He had his eyes closed, the better to focus on the data his BrainPal was streaming at him.

"I'm breathing completely normally," Schmidt said.

"You've been breathing like a labored elephant for the last several minutes," Wilson said, still not opening his eyes. "Keep it up and you're going to need a paper bag to breathe into."

"Yes, well," Schmidt said. "*You* get told you're inessential by your boss and see how you feel."

"Her people skills aren't the best," Wilson agreed. "But you knew that. And as my *assistant*, I actually do need you to be helpful to me. So stop thinking about your boss and think more about *our* predicament."

"Sorry," Schmidt said. "I'm also not entirely comfortable with this assistant thing."

"I promise not to ask you to get me coffee," Wilson said. "Much."

"Thanks," Schmidt said, wryly. Wilson grunted and went back to his data.

"This black box," Schmidt said a few minutes later.

"What about it?" Wilson asked.

"Are you going to be able to find it?" Schmidt asked.

Wilson opened his eyes for this. "The answer to that depends on whether you want me to be optimistic or truthful," he said.

"Truthful, please," Schmidt said.

"Probably not," Wilson said.

"I lied," Schmidt said. "I want the optimistic version."

"Too late," Wilson said, and held out his hand as if he were cupping an imaginary ball. "Look, Hart. The 'black box' in question is a small, black sphere about the size of a grapefruit. The memory portion of the thing is about the size of a fingernail. The rest of it consists of the tracking beacon, an inertial field generator to keep the thing from floating down a gravity well, and a battery powering both of those two things."

"Okay," Schmidt said. "So?"

"So, one, the thing is intentionally small and black, so it will be difficult to find by anyone but the CDF," Wilson said.

"Right, but you're not *looking* for it," Schmidt said. "You're going to be pinging it. When it gets the correct signal, it will respond."

"It will, if it has power," Wilson said. "But it might not. We're working on the assumption the *Polk* was attacked. If it was attacked, then there was probably a battle. If there was a battle, then the *Polk* probably got torn apart, with the pieces of it flying everywhere from the added energy of the explosions. It's likely the black box probably spent all its energy trying to stay mostly in one place. In which case when we signal it, we're not going to get a response."

"In which case you'll have to look for it visually," Schmidt said.

"Right," Wilson said. "So, again: small black grapefruit in a search area that at this point is a cube tens of thousands of kilometers on a side. And your boss wants me to find it and examine it before the Utche arrive. So if we don't locate it within the first half hour after the skip, we're probably screwed." He leaned back and closed his eyes again.

"You seem untroubled by our imminent failure," Schmidt said.

"No point hyperventilating," Wilson said. "And anyway, I didn't say we *will* fail. It's just more likely than not. My job is to increase the odds of us succeeding, which is what I was doing before your labored breathing started to distract me."

"So what's my job?" Schmidt asked.

"Your job is to go to Captain Coloma and tell her what things I need, the list of which I just sent to your PDA," Wilson said. "And do it charmingly, so that our captain feels like a valued part of the process and not like she's being ordered around by a CDF field tech."

"Oh, I see," Schmidt said. "I get the hard part."

"No, you get the *diplomatic* part," Wilson said, cracking open an eye. "Rumor has it diplomacy is a thing you've been trained to do. Unless you'd like *me* to go talk to her while *you* figure out a protocol for searching a few million cubic kilometers of space for an object the size of a child's plaything."

"I'll just go ahead and go talk to the captain, then," Schmidt said, picking up his PDA.

"What a marvelous idea," Wilson said. "I fully endorse it." Schmidt smiled and left the lounge.

Wilson closed his eyes again and focused once more on his own problem.

Wilson was more calm about the situation than Schmidt was, but that was in part to keep his friend on the right side of useful. Hart could be twitchy when stressed.

In fact, the problem was troubling Wilson more than he let on. One scenario he didn't tell Hart about at all was the one where the black box didn't exist. The classified information that Wilson had included preliminary scans of the chunk of space that the *Polk* was supposed to have been in; the debris field was almost nonexistent, meaning that either the ship was attacked with such violence that it had vaporized, or whoever attacked the *Polk* took the extra time to atomize any chunk of debris larger than half a meter on a side. Either way it didn't look good.

If it *had* survived, Wilson had to work on the assumption that its battery was thoroughly drained and that it was floating, quiet and black, out in the vacuum. If the *Polk* had been nearer to one of the Danavar system planets, he might have a tiny chance of picking up the box visually against the planet's sphere, but its skip position into the Danavar system was sufficiently distant from any of that system's gas giants that even that "Hail Mary" approach was out of the question.

So: Wilson's task was to find a dark, silent object that might not exist in a debris field that mostly didn't exist, in a cube of space larger than most terrestrial planets.

It was a pretty problem.

Wilson didn't want to admit how much he was enjoying it. He'd had any number of jobs over his two lifetimes—from corporate lab drone to high school physics teacher to soldier to military scientist to his current position as field tech trainer—but in every one of them, one of his favorite things to do was to whack away at a near insoluble problem for hours on end. With the exception that this time he had rather fewer hours to whack away on this problem than he'd like, he was in his element.

The real problem here is the black box itself, Wilson thought, calling up what information he had on the objects. The idea of a travel data recorder had been around for centuries, and the phrase "black box" got its cachet with terrestrial air travel. Ironically, almost none of the "black boxes" of those bygone days were actually black; they were typically brightly colored to be made easy to find. The CDF wanted their black boxes found, but only by the right people. They made them as black as they could.

"Black box, black hole, black body," Wilson said to himself.

Hey.

Wilson opened his eyes and sat up.

His BrainPal pinged him; it was Schmidt. Wilson opened the connection. "How's diplomacy?" he asked.

"Uh," Schmidt said.

"Be right there," Wilson said.

Captain Sophia Coloma looked every inch of what she was, which was the sort of person who was not here to put up with your shit. She stood on her bridge, imposing, eyes fixed at the portal through which Wilson stepped. Neva Balla, her executive officer, stood next to her, looking equally displeased. On the other side of the captain was Schmidt, whose studiously neutral facial expression was a testament to his diplomatic training.

"Captain," Wilson said, saluting.

"You want a shuttle," Coloma said, ignoring the salute. "You want a shuttle and a pilot and access to our sensor equipment."

"Yes, ma'am," Wilson said.

"You understand you want these as we are about to skip into what is almost certainly a hostile situation, and directly before sensitive negotiations with an alien race," Coloma said.

"I do," Wilson said.

"Then you can explain to me why I should prioritize your needs over the needs of every other person on this ship," Coloma said. "As soon as we skip, I need to scan the area for any hostiles. I need to scan the area comprehensively. I'm not going to let the *Clarke*'s sole shuttle out of its bay before I'm absolutely certain it and we are not going to be shot out the sky."

"Mr. Schmidt explained to you my current level of clearance, I imagine," Wilson said.

"He did," Coloma said. "I've also been informed that Ambassador Abumwe has given your needs a high priority. But this is still my ship."

"Ma'am, are you saying that you will go against the orders of your superiors?" Wilson asked, and noticed Coloma thin her lips at this. "I'm not speaking of myself here. The orders come from far above both of us."

"I have every intention of following orders," Coloma

said. "I also intend to follow them when it makes sense to do so. Which is after I've made sure we're safe, and the ambassador and her team are squared away."

"As far as the scanning goes, what you need to do and what I need to do dovetail," Wilson said. "Share the data with me and run a couple of scans that I need and I'll be fine. The scans I need to run will add another layer of security to your own scans."

"I'll run them after I've run our standard scans," Coloma said.

"That's fine," Wilson said. "Now, about the shuttle—"

"No shuttle, no pilot," Coloma said. "Not until after I've sent Abumwe to the Utche."

Wilson shook his head. "I need the shuttle before then," he said. "The ambassador told me to find and access the black box before she met with the Utche. She wanted to know whether there is a danger to them, not only us."

"She doesn't have authority on this," Coloma said.

"But I do, ma'am, and I agree with her," Wilson said. "We need to know everything we can before the Utche arrive. It's going to put a damper on negotiations if one of us explodes. Especially if we could have avoided it. Ma'am."

Coloma was silent.

"I'd like to make a suggestion," Schmidt said, after a minute.

Coloma looked at Schmidt as if she'd forgotten that he was there. "What is it?" she asked.

"The reason we need the shuttle is to get the black box," Schmidt said. "We don't know if we can find the black box. If we don't find it, we don't need it. If we don't find it within the first hour or so, then even if we found it we couldn't retrieve it before the Utche show up and you would need the shuttle for Ambassador

Abumwe's team. So let's say that we have the shuttle on standby for that first hour. If we find it by then, once you're confident the area is secure, we'll go out and get it. If we find it after, we wait until after you've delivered the ambassador's team to the Utche."

"I can live with that," Wilson said. "If you'll bump up my scans in your queue."

"And if I don't believe the area is secure?" Coloma said.

"I'll still need to go get it," Wilson said. "But if I know where it is, between autopilot and my BrainPal, I can go get it myself. You won't have to risk your pilot."

"Just the shuttle," Coloma said. "Because that's not in any way *significant*."

"Sorry, ma'am," Wilson said, and waited.

Coloma glanced at her executive officer. "Have Mr. Schmidt here get Neva your information. We have four hours to jump. Sometime in the next half hour will be fine."

"Yes, Captain," Wilson said. "Thank you, ma'am." He saluted again. Coloma returned the salute this time. Wilson turned to go, Schmidt hustling by the captain to catch up with him.

"Lieutenant, one more thing," Coloma said.

Wilson turned back to her. "Ma'am?"

"Just so you know, if you take the shuttle out, any damage you put on it, I'm taking out on you," she said.

"I'll treat it like it was my own car," Wilson said.

"See that you do," Coloma said. She turned away. Wilson took the hint.

"That was a nice touch about the car," Schmidt said, once the two of them were off the bridge.

"As long as you don't know about what happened to my last car, yes," Wilson said.

Schmidt stopped.

"Relax, Hart," Wilson said. "It was a joke. Come on. Lots to do." He kept walking.

After a minute, Schmidt followed.

PART TWO
VI.

"That was XO Balla," Schmidt said. He and Wilson were in an unused storage room, where Wilson had set up a three-dimensional monitor. They had waited out the skip into the Danavar system in its confines. "The *Clarke* sent out a ping using the *Polk*'s encrypted signal. Got nothing back."

"Of course we didn't," Wilson said. "Why would the universe make it easy for us?"

"What do we do now?" Schmidt asked.

"Let me answer that question with a question," Wilson said. "How does one look for a black box?"

"Are you serious?" Schmidt said, after a second. "We're running out of time here and you want to have a Socratic dialogue with me?"

"I wouldn't put this on the level of Socrates, but yeah, I do," Wilson said. "It's the former high school physics teacher in me. And call me crazy, but I think you'll actually be more helpful to me if I don't treat you like a completely useless monkey. I'm going to go on the assumption that you might have a brain."

"Thanks," Schmidt said.

"So, how does one look for a black box?" Wilson asked. "In particular, a black box that doesn't want to be found?"

"Fervent prayer," Schmidt said.

"You're not even trying," Wilson said, reprovingly.

"I'm new at this," Schmidt said. "Give me a hint."

"Fine," Wilson said. "You start by looking for what the black box was originally attached to."

"The *Polk*," Schmidt said. "Or what's left of it."

"Very good, my young apprentice," Wilson said.

Schmidt shot him a look, then continued. "But you told me that the previous scans of the area from the automated drones didn't turn up anything."

"True," Wilson said. "But those were preliminary scans, done quickly. The *Clarke* has better sensors." He dimmed the light in the storage room and fired up the monitor, which appeared to show nothing but a small, single dot at the center of its display.

"That's not the *Polk*, is it?" Schmidt asked.

"It's the *Clarke*," Wilson said. A series of concentric circles appeared, arrayed on three axes. "And this is the area the *Clarke* is intensively scanning, with distance displayed logarithmically. It's about a light-minute to the outer edge."

"If you say so," Schmidt said.

Wilson didn't take the bait and instead called up another dot, close to the *Clarke*'s dot. "This is where the *Polk* was supposed to have appeared after its skip," he said. "Let's assume it blew up when it arrived. What would we expect to see?"

"The remains of the ship, somewhere close to where the ship was supposed to be," Schmidt said. "But to repeat myself, the drone scans didn't turn up anything."

"Right," Wilson said. "So now let's use the *Clarke*'s sensor scans, and see what we get. This is using the *Clarke*'s standard array of LIDAR, radio and radar active scanning."

Several yellow spheres appeared, including one near the *Polk*'s entry point.

"Debris," Schmidt said, and pointed to the sphere closest to the *Polk*.

"It's not conclusive," Wilson said.

"Come on," Schmidt said. "The correlation is pretty strong, wouldn't you say?"

Wilson pointed to the other spheres. "What the

Clarke is picking up is agglomerations of matter dense enough to reflect back its signals. These can't all be ship debris. Maybe this one isn't, either. Maybe it's just what got pulled off a comet as it came through."

"Can we get any closer?" Schmidt asked. "To the one near where the *Polk* was, I mean."

"Sure," Wilson said, and swooped the view in closer. The yellow debris sphere expanded and then disappeared, replaced by tiny points of light. "Those represent individual reflective objects," Wilson said.

"There are a lot of them," Schmidt said. "Which suggests to me they were part of a ship."

"Okay," Wilson said. "But here's the thing. The data suggests that none of these bits of matter are much larger than your head. Most of it is the size of gravel. Even if you add them all up, they don't come close to equaling an entire CDF frigate in mass."

"Maybe whoever did this to the *Polk* didn't want to leave evidence," Schmidt said.

"Now you're being paranoid," Wilson said.

"Hey," Schmidt said.

"No—" Wilson held up a hand. "I mean that as a compliment. And I think you're exactly right. Whoever did in the *Polk* wanted to make it difficult for us to find out what happened to it."

"If we could get to that debris field, we could take samples," Schmidt said.

"No time," Wilson said. "And right now finding what happened to the *Polk* is the means to an end. We still have to be reasonably sure this is what's left of the *Polk*, though. So how do we do that?"

"I haven't the slightest idea," Schmidt said.

"Think, Hart," Wilson said. He waved at the monitor image. "What happened to the *rest* of the *Polk*?"

"It probably got vaporized," Schmidt said.

"Right," Wilson said, and waited.

"Okay," Schmidt said. "So?"

Wilson sighed. "You were raised by a tribe of chimps, weren't you, Hart?" he asked.

"I didn't know I'd be taking a *science test* today, Harry," Schmidt said, annoyed.

"You *said* it already," Wilson said. "The ship was probably vaporized. Whoever did this to the *Polk* took the time to cut, slice and blast into molecules most of it. But they probably didn't cart all the atoms off with them."

Schmidt's eyes widened. "A big cloud of vaporized *Polk*," he said.

"You got it," Wilson said, and the display changed to show a large, amorphous blob, tentacles stretching out from the main body.

"That's the ship?" Schmidt asked, looking at the blob.

"I'd say yes," Wilson said. "One of the extra scans I had Captain Coloma run was a spectrographic analysis of the local neighborhood. It's not a scan we'd usually do."

"Why not?" Schmidt asked.

"Why would we?" Wilson said. "Searching your immediate environment for molecule-sized bits of frigate isn't a standard protocol. Spectrographic analysis is usually reserved for science missions where someone's sampling atmospheric gases. Spaceships themselves typically don't have to be concerned with gases unless we're near a planet and we have to figure out how far out the atmosphere extends. And with systems we've already surveyed, all that information is already in the database. I'm guessing whoever did this probably knew all of that. They weren't concerned that an invisible cloud of metallic atoms would give them away."

"They didn't think we'd see it," Schmidt said.

"And normally they'd be right," Wilson said, and pulled out the view to capture all the other debris fields. "None of the other debris fields show the same density of molecular particles, and what particles there are aren't the same sorts of metals we use to make our ships." He pulled the view in again. "So this is almost certainly what's left of the *Polk,* and it was almost certainly intentionally attacked and methodically destroyed."

"Which means that someone leaked the information," Schmidt said. "This mission was meant to be secret."

Wilson nodded. "Yes, but that's not anything you and I have to worry about at the moment. We're still looking for the black box. The good news, if you want to call it that, is that this narrows down considerably the volume of space we need to search."

"So we go back to the first scan and start picking through those remaining bits of the *Polk,*" Schmidt said.

"We *could* do that," Wilson said. "If we had a month."

"This is where you make me look stupid again, isn't it," Schmidt said.

"No, I'm going to spare you this time because the answer isn't obvious," Wilson said.

"That's a relief," Schmidt said.

"To go back to your suggestion, even if we did go through the earlier scans, we'd be unlikely to come up with anything," Wilson said. "Remember that the CDF wants the black box to be found only by its own people."

"That's why the black box is black," Schmidt said.

"Not just black, but aggressively nonreflective," Wilson said. "Covered with a fractal coating that absorbs most radiation that hits it and scatters the rest of it. Sweep it with a sensor scan and nothing comes back directly. From the point of view of a sensor array, it doesn't exist."

"All right, Harry Wilson, supergenius," Schmidt said. "If you can't see it and can't sweep for it, then how do you find it?"

"I'm glad you asked," Wilson said. "When I was thinking about the black box, my brain wandered to the phrase 'black body.' It's an idealized physical object that absorbs every bit of radiation thrown at it."

"Like you said this thing does," Schmidt said.

"Sort of," Wilson said. "The black box is not a perfect black body; nothing is. But it reminded me that any object in the real world that absorbed all the radiation thrown at it would heat up. And then I remembered that the black box came equipped with a battery to power its processor and inertial dampener. And that the battery is not one hundred percent efficient."

Schmidt looked at Wilson blankly.

"It's *warm*, Hart," Wilson said. "The black box had a power source. That power source leaked heat. That heat kept it relatively warm long after everything else around it entropied itself into equilibrium."

"The battery is dead," Schmidt said. "Even if it was warm, it wouldn't be anymore."

"That depends on your definition of 'warm,'" Wilson said. "The design of the black box means that it has some areas inside of it acting like insulators. Even if the battery's dead, it'll take longer for the black box to reach a temperature equilibrium with space than it would if it were a solid shard of metal. I don't need it to be warm like the inside of this room, Hart. I just need it to be a fraction of a degree warmer than everything else around it."

The display screen flickered and the ghostly blob of attenuated *Polk* molecules was replaced by a thermal map that was a deep blue-black. Wilson gave the thermal map his attention.

"So you're looking for something that's ever so slightly above absolute zero," Schmidt said.

"Space is actually a couple of degrees above absolute zero," Wilson said. "Particularly inside a planetary system."

"Seems like an irrelevant detail," Schmidt said.

"And you call yourself a scientist," Wilson said.

"No, I don't," Schmidt said.

"Good thing, then," Wilson said.

"So what happens if it has entropied out?" Schmidt said. "If it's the same temperature as everything else around it?"

"Well, then, we're screwed," Wilson said.

"I don't love your bracing honesty," Schmidt said.

"Ha!" Wilson said, and suddenly the image in the display pitched inward, falling vertiginously toward something that was invisible until almost the last second, and was an only slightly lighter blue-black than everything around it even then.

"Is that it?" Schmidt asked.

"Let me change the false color temperature scale," Wilson said. The object, spherical, suddenly blossomed green.

"That's the black box," Schmidt said.

"It's the right size and shape," Wilson said. "If it's not the black box, the universe is messing with us. There are some other warmer objects out there, but they're not the right size profile."

"What are they?" Schmidt asked.

Wilson shrugged. "Possibly chunks of the *Polk* with sealed pockets of air in them. Right now, don't know, don't care." He pointed at the sphere. "This is what we came for."

Schmidt peered closely at the image. "How much warmer is it than everything around it?" he asked.

"Point zero zero three degrees Kelvin," Wilson said. "Another hour or two and we would never have found it."

"Don't tell me that," Schmidt said. "It makes me retroactively nervous."

"Science is built on tiny variances, my friend," Wilson said.

"So now what?" Schmidt asked.

"Now I get to tell Captain Coloma to warm up the shuttle, and you get to tell your boss that if this mission fails, it will be because of her, not us," Wilson said.

"I think I'll avoid putting it that way," Schmidt said.

"That's why you're the diplomat," Wilson said.

VII.

The discussion with Captain Coloma was not entirely pleasant. She demanded a rundown of the protocol used to locate the black box, which Wilson provided, quickly, his eye on the clock. Wilson suspected the captain hadn't expected him to locate the black box within the time allotted to him and was nonplussed when he had, and was now trying to manufacture a reason not to let him at the shuttle. In the end she couldn't manufacture one, although for security reasons, she said, she didn't release the shuttle pilot. Wilson wondered, if something bad happened to the shuttle while it was in his possession, what good it would do to have a shuttle pilot on board the *Clarke*. But in this as in many things, he let it go, smiled, saluted, and then thanked the captain for her cooperation.

The shuttle was designed for transport rather than for retrieval, which meant that Wilson would have to do some improvisation. One of the improvisations would include opening the interior of the shuttle to the hard vacuum of space, which was a prospect that did not excite Wilson, for several reasons. He pored over the shuttle specifications to see whether the thing could handle such an event; the *Clarke* was a diplomatic rather than a military ship, which meant it and everything in it had been constructed in civilian shipyards and possibly on different plans from those of the military ships and shuttles Wilson had become used to. Fortunately, Wilson discovered, the diplomatic shuttle, while its interior was designed with civilian needs in mind, shared the same chassis and construction as its military counterparts. A little hard vacuum wouldn't kill it.

The same could not be said for Wilson. Vacuum would kill him, although more slowly than it would anyone else on the *Clarke*. Wilson had been out of combat for years, but he was still a member of the Colonial Defense Forces and still had the genetic and other improvements given to soldiers, including SmartBlood, artificial blood that carried more oxygen and allowed his body to survive significantly longer without breathing than that of an unmodified human. When Wilson first arrived on the *Clarke*, one of his icebreaker tricks with the diplomatic staff had been holding his breath while they clocked him with a timer; they usually got bored when he hit the five-minute mark.

Be that as it may, there was a manifest difference between holding one's breath in the *Clarke*'s lounge and staying conscious while airless, cold vacuum surrounded you and the air in your body was trying to burst out of your lungs and into space. A little protection was in order.

Which is how, for the first time in more than a dozen years, Wilson found himself in his standard-issue Colonial Defense Forces combat unitard.

"That's a new look," Schmidt said, smiling, as Wilson walked toward the shuttle.

"That's enough out of you," Wilson said.

"I don't think I've ever seen you in one of those things," Schmidt said. "I didn't even know you had one."

"Regulations require active-duty CDF to travel with a combat unitard even on noncombat postings," Wilson said. "On the theory it's a hostile universe and we should be prepared at all times to kill anyone we meet."

"It's an interesting philosophy," Schmidt said. "Where's your gun?"

"It's not a *gun*," Wilson said. "It's an MP-35. And I

left it in my storage locker. I don't really anticipate having to *shoot* the black box."

"A dicey risk," Schmidt said.

"When I want a military assessment from you, Hart, I'll be sure to let you know," Wilson said.

Schmidt smiled again and then held up what he was carrying. "Maybe this will be to your liking, then," he said. "CDF-issue hard connector with battery."

"Thanks," Wilson said. The black box was dead; he'd need to put a little power into it in order to wake up the transmitter.

"Are you ready to fly this thing?" Schmidt asked, nodding toward the shuttle.

"I've already plotted a path to the black box, and put it into the router," Wilson said. "There's also a standard departure routine. I've chained the departure routine to the predetermined path. Reverse everything on the way home. As long as I'm not required to actually try to pilot, I'll be fine."

What the hell? Wilson thought. On his shuttle's forward monitor, on which he had pumped up light-source collection to see star patterns over the glare of his instrument panel, another star had become occluded. That was two in the last thirty seconds. There was some object in the path between him and the black box.

He frowned, powered the shuttle into motionlessness, and pulled up the data from the surveys he'd run on the *Clarke.*

He saw the object on the survey; another one of the debris chunks that had been ever so slightly warmer than the surrounding space. It was large enough that if the shuttle collided with it, there would be damage.

Looks like I have to pilot after all, Wilson thought. He was annoyed with himself that he hadn't applied his survey data to his shuttle plot; he now had to waste time replotting his course.

"Is there a problem?" Schmidt asked, voice coming through the instrument panel.

"Everything's fine," Wilson said. "Something in my way. Routing around it." The survey heat data noted the object's size as approximately three to four meters on a side, which made it considerably larger than anything that the standard scans had picked up, but not so large that it required a major change in pathing. Wilson created a new path that dropped the shuttle 250 meters below the object and resumed travel to the black box from there, and he inserted it into the navigational router, which accepted the change without complaint. Wilson resumed his journey, watching the monitors to see the object in his way occlude a few other stars as the shuttle moved relative to it.

The shuttle arrived at the black box a few moments later. Wilson couldn't see it with his own eyes, but after he had first located it he'd run supplementary scans that fixed its location to within about ten centimeters, which was precise enough for what he was about to do. He fired up the final navigational sequence, which made a series of minute maneuvers. This took another minute.

"Here we go," Wilson said, and commanded his unitard to wrap around his face, which it did with a snap. Wilson hated the feeling of the unitard's face mask; it felt as if someone had tightly duct-taped his entire head. It was simply better than the alternative in this case. Wilson's vision was totally blocked by his face mask; his BrainPal compensated by feeding him a visual stream.

That accomplished, Wilson commanded the shuttle to air out the interior. The shuttle's compressors sprang to life, sucking the shuttle's air back into its tanks. Three minutes later, the interior of the shuttle had almost as little open air in it as the space surrounding it.

Wilson cut off the shuttle's artificial gravity, unstrapped himself from the shuttle pilot chair and very gingerly pushed off toward the shuttle door, stopping himself directly in front of it and gripping the guide handle on its side to keep himself from drifting. He pressed the door release, and the door slid into the wall of the shuttle. There was an almost imperceptible whisper as the few remaining free molecules of human-friendly atmosphere rushed out the open portal.

Still holding the guide handle, Wilson reached out into space—gently!—and after a second wrapped his fingers around an object. He pulled it in.

It was the black box.

Excellent, Wilson thought, and released the guide handle to press the door button and seal the interior of the shuttle once more. He commanded the shuttle to start pumping air back into the cabin and to turn the artificial gravity back on—and nearly dropped the black box when he did. It was heavier than it looked.

After a minute, Wilson retracted his face mask and took a physically unnecessary but psychologically satisfying huge gulp of air. He walked back to the pilot's chair, retrieved the hard connector and then spent several minutes looking at the box's inscrutable surface, searching for the tiny hole he could plunge the connector into. He finally located it, lanced the box with the connector, felt it click into position, and waited the thirty required seconds for enough energy to transfer over and power up the black box's receiver and transmitter.

With his BrainPal, he transmitted the encrypted signal to the black box. There was a pause, followed by a stream of information pushed into Wilson's BrainPal fast enough that he almost felt it physically.

The last moments of the *Polk.*

Wilson started scanning the information with his BrainPal as quickly as he could begin opening the data.

In less than a minute, he confirmed what they already strongly suspected: that the *Polk* had been attacked and destroyed in the battle.

A minute after that, he learned that one escape pod had been launched from the *Polk* but that it appeared to have been destroyed less than ten seconds before the black box itself had been launched, cutting out its own data feed. Wilson guessed that the occupant of the escape pod would have been the mission ambassador or someone on her staff.

Three minutes after that, he learned something else.

"Oh shit," Wilson said, out loud.

"I just heard an 'Oh shit,'" Schmidt said, from the instrument panel.

"Hart, you need to get Abumwe and Coloma on the line, right now," Wilson said.

"The ambassador's in her preparatory briefings right now," Schmidt said. "She's not going to want to be interrupted."

"She's going to be a lot more upset with you if you don't interrupt her," Wilson said. "Trust me on this."

"The *Polk* was attacked by what?" Abumwe said. She and Coloma were tied into a conference video, Coloma from her ready room and Abumwe from a spare conference room Schmidt had almost had to drag her into.

"By at least fifteen Melierax Series Seven ship-to-ship missiles," Wilson said, talking into the pilot instrument panel and the small camera there. "It could have been more, because data started getting sketchy after enough systems failed. But it was at least fifteen."

"Why does it matter what type of missiles destroyed the *Polk*?" Abumwe asked, irritated.

Wilson glanced over to the image of Captain Coloma, who looked ashen. She got it, at least. "Because, Ambassador, Melierax Series Seven ship-to-ship missiles are made by the Colonial Union," Wilson said. "The *Polk* was attacked with our own missiles."

"That's not possible," Abumwe said, after a moment.

"The data says otherwise," Wilson said, choosing not to go on a rant about the stupidity of the phrase "that's not possible," because it would likely be counterproductive at this point.

"The data could be incorrect," Abumwe said.

"With respect, Ambassador, the CDF has gotten very good at figuring out what things are being shot at them," Wilson said. "If the *Polk* confirmed the missiles as being Melierax type, it's because it was able to identify them across several confirming points, including shape, size, scan profile, thrust signature and so on. The likelihood of them not being Melierax Series Seven is small."

"What do we know about the ship?" Coloma said. "The one that fired on the *Polk*."

"Not a lot," Wilson said. "It didn't identify itself, and other than a basic scan the *Polk* didn't spend any time on it. It was roughly the same size as the *Polk* itself, we can see that from its survey signature. Other than that, there's not much to go on."

"Did the *Polk* fire back on the ship?" Coloma asked.

"It got off at least four missiles," Wilson said. "Also Melierax Series Seven. There's no data on whether they hit their target."

"I don't understand," Abumwe said. "Why would we attack and destroy one of our own ships?"

"We don't know if it was one of our own ships," Coloma said. "Just that it was our own missiles."

"That's right," Wilson said, and raised his finger to rebut.

"It's possible that we sold the missiles to another race," Coloma said. "Who then attacked us."

"It possible, but there are two things to consider here," Wilson said. "The first is that most of our weapon trades are for higher-end technology. Any one race who can make a spaceship can make a missile. The Melierax Series are bread-and-butter missiles. Every other race has missiles just like it. The second is that these are ostensibly secret negotiations. In order to hit us, someone had to know we were here." Coloma opened her mouth. "And to anticipate the next question, we haven't sold any Melierax missiles to the Utche," Wilson said. Coloma closed her mouth and stared stonily.

"So we have a mystery ship targeting the Colonial Union with our own missiles," Abumwe said.

"Yes," Wilson said.

"Then where are they now?" Abumwe said. "Why aren't *we* under attack?"

"They didn't know *we* were coming," Wilson said. "We were diverted to this mission at the last minute. It would usually take the Colonial Union several days at least to have a new mission in place. By which time these particular negotiations would have failed, because we weren't there for them."

"Someone destroyed an entire ship just to foul up diplomatic negotiations?" Coloma said. "This is your theory?"

"It's a guess," Wilson said. "I don't pretend that I know enough about this situation to be correct. But I think regardless we have to make the Colonial Union aware of what happened here as soon as possible. Captain, I've already transferred the data to the *Clarke*'s computers. I strongly suggest we send a skip drone with it and my preliminary analysis back to Phoenix immediately."

"Agreed," Abumwe said.

"I'll have it done as soon as I'm off this call," Coloma said. "Now, Lieutenant, I want you and the shuttle back on the *Clarke* immediately. With all due respect to Ambassador Abumwe, I'm not entirely convinced there's not still a threat out there. Get back here. We'll be under way as soon as you are."

"What?" Abumwe said. "We still have a mission. I still have a mission. We're here to negotiate with the Utche."

"Ambassador, the *Clarke* is a diplomatic vessel," Coloma said. "We have no offensive weapons and only a bare minimum of defensive capability. We've confirmed the *Polk* was attacked. It's possible whoever attacked the *Polk* is still out there. We're sending this data to Phoenix. They will alert the Utche of the situation, which means they will almost certainly call off their ship. There is no negotiation to be had."

"You don't know that," Abumwe said. "It might take them hours to process the information. We are less than three hours from when the Utche are meant to arrive. Even if we were to leave, we will still be in system when they arrive, which means the first thing they would see is us running away."

"It's not *running away*," Coloma said, sharply. "And this is not your decision to make, Ambassador. I am captain of the ship."

"A diplomatic ship," Abumwe said. "On which I am the chief diplomat."

"Ambassador, Captain," Wilson said, "do I need to be here for this part of the conversation?"

Wilson saw the two simultaneously reach toward their screens. Both of their images shut off.

"That would be 'no,'" Wilson said, to himself.

VIII.

Something was nagging at Wilson as he punched in the return route to the *Clarke*. The *Polk* had been hit at least fifteen times by ship-to-ship missiles, but before any of them had hit, there had been an earlier explosion that had shaken the ship. But the data had not recorded any event leading up to the explosion; the ship had skipped, made an initial scan of the immediate area and then everything was perfectly normal until the initial explosion. Once it happened everything went to hell, quickly. But beforehand, nothing. There had been nothing to indicate anything out of the ordinary.

The shuttle's navigational router accepted the path back and started to move. Wilson strapped himself into his seat and relaxed. He would be back on the *Clarke* shortly, by which time he assumed that either Coloma or Abumwe would have emerged victorious from their power struggle. Wilson had no personal preference in who won; he could see the merit in both arguments, and both of them appeared to dislike him equally, so neither had an advantage there.

I did what I was supposed to do, Wilson thought, and glanced over to the black box on the passenger seat, looking like a dark, matte, light-absorbing hole in the chair.

Something clicked in his head.

"Holy shit," Wilson said, and slapped the shuttle into immobility.

"You said 'shit' again," Wilson heard Schmidt say. "And now you're not moving."

"I just had a very interesting thought," Wilson said.

"You can't have this thought while you are bringing the shuttle back?" Schmidt said. "Captain Coloma was very specific about returning it."

"Hart, I'm going to talk to you in a bit," Wilson said.

"What are you going to do?" Schmidt asked.

"You probably don't want to know," Wilson said. "It's best you don't know. I want to make sure you have plausible deniability."

"I have no idea what you're talking about," Schmidt said.

"Exactly," Wilson said, and cut his connection to his friend.

A few minutes later, Wilson floated weightless inside the airless cabin of the shuttle, face masked, holding the guide handle next to the shuttle door. He slapped the door release button.

And saw nothing outside.

Which is not as it should have been; Wilson's Brain-Pal should have picked up and enhanced starlight within visible wavelengths. He was getting nothing.

Wilson reached out with the hand not gripping the guide handle. Nothing. He repositioned himself, bringing his body mostly outside of the door, and reached again. This time there was something there.

Something big and black and invisible.

Hello, Wilson thought. *What the hell are you?*

The big, black, invisible thing did not respond.

Wilson pinged his BrainPal for two things. The first was to see how long it had been since his face mask had gone on; it was roughly two minutes. He'd have just about five minutes before his body started screaming at him for air. The second was to adjust the properties of the nanobotic cloth of his combat unitard to run a slight electric current through his unitard's hands, soles and knees, the current powered by his own body heat and friction generated through movement. That achieved, he reached out again toward the the big, black, invisible object.

His hand clung to it, lightly. *Hooray for magnetism,* Wilson thought.

Moving slowly so as not to accidentally and fatally launch himself into space, Wilson left the shuttle to go exploring.

"We have a problem," Wilson said. He was back on the conference call with Coloma and Abumwe. Schmidt hovered behind Abumwe, silent.

"*You* have a problem," Coloma said. "You were ordered to return that shuttle forty minutes ago."

"We have a *different* problem," Wilson said. "I've found a missile out here. It's armed. It's waiting for the Utche. And it's one of ours."

"Excuse me?" Coloma said, after a moment.

"It's another Melierax Series Seven," Wilson said, and held up the black box. "It's housed in a small silo that's covered in the same wavelength-absorbing material this thing is. When you run the standard scans, you won't see it. Hart and I only saw it because we ran a highly-sensitive thermal scan when we were looking for the black box, and even then we didn't give it any thought because it wasn't what we were looking for. When I was looking through the *Polk* data, there was an explosion that seemed to come out of nowhere, before the *Polk* was attacked by the ship and missiles we could see. My brain put two and two together. I passed by this thing on the way to black box. I stopped this time to get a closer look."

"You said it's waiting for the Utche," Abumwe said.

"Yes," Wilson said.

"How do you know that?" Abumwe asked.

"I hacked into the missile," Wilson said. "I got inside the silo, pried open the missile control panel and then used this." He held up the CDF standard connector.

"You went on a *spacewalk*?" Schmidt said, over Abumwe's shoulder. "Are you completely *insane*?"

"I went on three," Wilson said as Abumwe turned to glare at Schmidt. "I was limited by how long I could hold my breath."

"You hacked into the missile," Coloma said, returning to the subject.

"Right," Wilson said. "The missile is armed and it's waiting for a signal from the Utche ship."

"What signal?" Coloma asked.

"I think it's when the Utche ship hails us," Wilson said. "The Utche send their ship-to-ship communications on certain frequencies, different from the ones we typically use. This missile is programmed to home in on ships using those frequencies. Ergo, it's waiting for the Utche."

"To what end?" Abumwe asked.

"Isn't it obvious?" Wilson said. "The Utche are attacked by a Colonial Defense Forces missile, and are damaged or destroyed. The original Colonial Union diplomatic mission was traveling by CDF frigate. It would look like we attacked the Utche. Negotiations broken off, diplomacy over, the Colonial Union and the Utche back at each other's throats."

"But the *Polk* was destroyed," Coloma said.

"I've been thinking about that," Wilson said. "The information I was sent by the CDF about the *Polk*'s mission said it was slated to arrive seventy-four hours prior to the scheduled Utche arrival. The black box data stream has the *Polk* arriving eighty hours prior to the scheduled Utche arrival."

"You think they arrived early and caught someone setting the trap," Coloma said.

"I don't know about 'caught,'" Wilson said. "I think whoever it was was in the process of setting the trap and then was surprised by the *Polk*'s arrival."

"You just said these things were looking for the Utche," Abumwe said. "But it sounds like one of them hit the *Polk,* too."

"If the people setting the trap were nearby, it would be trivial to change the programming of the missile," Wilson said. "It's set to receive. And once the thing hit the *Polk,* it would be too busy focusing on that to pay much attention when a strange ship popped up on its sensors. Until it was too late."

"The early arrival of the *Polk* ruined their plans," Coloma said. "Why is this thing still out there?"

"I think it *changed* their plans," Wilson said. "They

had to kill the *Polk* when it arrived early, and they had to get rid of as much of it as possible to leave in doubt what happened to it. But as long as there's enough CDF missile debris among the wreckage of the Utche ship, then mission accomplished. Having the *Polk* go missing works just fine with that, since it looks like the CDF is hiding the ship, rather than presenting it to prove the missiles didn't come from it."

"But we know what happened to the *Polk*," Abumwe said.

"*They* don't know that," Wilson pointed out. "Whoever they are. We're the wild card in the deck. And it doesn't change the fact that the Utche are still a target."

"Have you disabled the missile?" Coloma asked.

"No," Wilson said. "I was able to read the missile's instruction set, but I can't do anything to change it. I'm locked out of that. And I don't have any tools with me that can disable it. But even if I disabled this one, there are others out there. Hart's and my heat map shows four more of these things out there beside this one. We have less than an hour before the Utche are scheduled to arrive. There's no way to physically disable them in time."

"So we're helpless to stop the attack," Abumwe said.

"No, wait," Coloma said. "You said there's no way to *physically* disable them. Do you have another way to disable them?"

"I think I might have a way to destroy them," Wilson said.

"Tell us," Coloma said.

"You're not going to like it," Wilson said.

"Will I like it better than us standing by while the Utche are attacked and then we are framed for it?" Coloma said.

"I'd like to think so," Wilson said.

"Then tell us," Coloma said.

"It involves the shuttle," Wilson said.

Coloma threw up her hands. "Of course it does," she said.

IX.

"Here—" Schmidt thrust a small container and a mask into Wilson's hands. "Supplementary oxygen. For a normal person that's about twenty minutes' worth. I don't know what that would be for you."

"About two hours," Wilson said. "More than enough time. And the other thing?"

"I got it," Schmidt said, and held up another object, not much larger than the oxygen container. "High-density, quick-discharge battery. Straight from the engine room. It required the direct intervention of Captain Coloma, by the way. Chief Engineer Basquez was not pleased to be relieved of it."

"If everything goes well, he'll have it back soon," Wilson said.

"And if everything doesn't go well?" Schmidt asked.

"Then we'll all have bigger problems, won't we," Wilson said.

They both looked at the shuttle, which Wilson was about to reenter after a brief pit stop in the *Clarke*'s bay.

"You really are insane, you know that," Schmidt said, after a moment.

"I always think it's funny when people get told what they are by other people," Wilson said. "As if they didn't already know."

"We could just set the autopilot on the shuttle," Schmidt said. "Send it out that way."

"We *could*," Wilson said. "If a shuttle was like a mechanical vehicle you could send on its way by tying a brick to its accelerator pedal. But it's not. It's designed to have a human at the controls. Even on autopilot."

"You could alter the programming on the shuttle," Schmidt said.

"We have roughly fifteen minutes before the Utche arrive," Wilson said. "I appreciate the vote of confidence in my skills, but no. There's no time. And we need to do more than just send it out, anyway."

"Insane," Schmidt reiterated.

"Relax, Hart," Wilson said. "For my sake. You're making me twitchy."

"Sorry," Schmidt said.

"It's all right," Wilson said. "Now, tell me what you're going to do after I leave."

"I'm going to the bridge," Schmidt said. "If you're not successful for any reason, I will have the *Clarke* send out a message on our frequencies warning the Utche of the trap, to *not* confirm the message or to broadcast anything on their native communication bands, and request that they get the hell out of Danavar space as quickly as possible. I'm to invoke your security clearance to the captain if there are any problems."

"That's very good," Wilson said.

"Thank you for the virtual pat on the head, there," Schmidt said.

"I do it out of love," Wilson assured him.

"Right," Schmidt said dryly, and then looked over at the shuttle again. "Do you think this is actually going to work?" he asked.

"I look at it this way," Wilson said. "Even if it doesn't work, we have proof we did everything we could to stop the attack on the Utche. That's going to count for something."

Wilson entered the shuttle, fired up the launch sequence and while it was running took the high-density battery and connected it to the *Polk*'s black box. The battery immediately started draining into the black box's own power storage.

"Here we go," Wilson said for the second time that day. The shuttle eased out of the *Clarke*'s bay.

Schmidt had been right: This all would have been a lot easier if the shuttle could have been piloted remotely. There was no physical bar to it; humans had been remote-piloting vehicles for centuries. But the Colonial Union insisted on a human pilot for transport shuttles for roughly the same reason the Colonial Defense Forces required a BrainPal signal to fire an Empee rifle: to make sure only the right people were using them, for the right purposes. Modifying the shuttle flight software to take the human presence out of the equation would not only require a substantial amount of time, but would also technically be classified as treason.

Wilson preferred not to engage in treason if he could avoid it. And so here he was, on the shuttle, about to do something stupid.

On the shuttle display, Wilson called up the heat map he'd created, and a timer. The heat map registered each of the suspect missile silos; the timer counted down until the scheduled arrival of the Utche, now less than ten minutes away. From the mission data given to Ambassador Abumwe, Wilson had a rough idea of where the Utche planned to skip into Danavar space. He plotted the shuttle in another direction entirely and opened up the throttle to put sufficient distance between himself and the *Clarke,* counting the kilometers until he reached what he estimated to be a good, safe distance.

Now for the tricky part, Wilson thought, and tapped his instrument panel to start broadcasting a signal on the Utche's communication bands.

"Come out, come out, wherever you are," Wilson said to the missiles.

The missiles did not hear Wilson. They heard the shuttle's signal instead and erupted from their silos, one, two, three, four, five. Wilson saw them twice, first on the shuttle's monitor and second through the *Clarke*'s sensor data, ported into his BrainPal.

"Five missiles on you, locked and tracking," Wilson heard Schmidt say, through the instrument panel.

"Come on, let's play," Wilson said, and pushed the shuttle as fast as it would go. It was not as fast as the missiles could go, but that wasn't the point. The point was twofold. First, to get the missiles as far away from where the Utche would be as possible. Second, to get the missiles spaced so that the explosion from the first missile on the shuttle would destroy all the other missiles, moving too quickly to avoid being damaged.

To manage that, Wilson had broadcast his signal from a point as close to equidistant to all five silos as could be managed and still be a safe distance from the *Clarke*. If everything worked out correctly, the missile impacts would be within a second of each other.

Wilson looked at the missile tracks. So far, so good. He had roughly a minute before the first impact. More than enough time.

Wilson unstrapped himself from the pilot seat, picked up the oxygen container, secured it on his unitard combat belt and fastened the mask over his mouth and nose. He ordered his combat unitard to close over his face, sealing the mask in. He picked up the black box and pinged its charge status; it was at 80 percent, which Wilson guessed would have to be good enough. He disconnected it from the external battery and then walked to the shuttle door, carrying the black box in one hand and the battery in the other. He positioned himself at what he hoped was the right spot, took a very deep breath and chucked the battery at the door release button. It hit square on and the door slid open.

Explosive decompression sucked Wilson out the door a fraction of a second earlier than he expected. He missed braining himself on the still-opening door by about a millimeter.

Wilson tumbled away from the shuttle on the vector the decompressing air had placed him but kept pace with the shuttle in terms of its forward motion, a testament to fundamental Newtonian physics. This was going to be bad news in roughly forty seconds, when the first missile hit the shuttle; even without an atmosphere to create a shock wave that would turn his innards to jelly, Wilson could still be fried and punctured by shrapnel.

He looked down at the *Polk*'s black box, tightly gripped close to his abdomen, and sent it a signal that informed it that it had been ejected from a spaceship. Then, despite the fact that his visual feed was now being handled by his BrainPal, he closed his eyes to fight the vertigo of the stars wheeling haphazardly around him. The BrainPal, interpreting this correctly, cut off the outside feed and provided Wilson with a tactical display instead. Wilson waited.

Do your thing, baby, he thought to the black box.

The black box got the signal. Wilson felt a snap as the black box's inertial field factored his mass into its calculus and tightened around him. On the tactical display coming from his BrainPal, Wilson saw the representation of the shuttle pull away from him with increasing speed, and saw the missiles flash by his position, their velocity increasing toward the shuttle even as his was decreasing. Within a few seconds, he had slowed sufficiently that he was no longer in immediate danger of the shuttle impact.

In all, his little plan had worked out reasonably well so far.

Let's still not ever do this again, Wilson said to himself.

Agreed, himself said back.

"First impact in ten seconds," Wilson heard Schmidt say, via his BrainPal. Wilson had his BrainPal present him with a stabilized, enhanced visual of outside space and watched as the now invisible missiles bore down on the hapless, also invisible shuttle.

There was a series of short, sharp light bursts, like tiny firecrackers going off two streets away.

"Impact," Schmidt said. Wilson smiled.

"Shit," Schmidt said. Wilson stopped smiling and snapped up his BrainPal tactical display.

The shuttle and four of the missiles had been destroyed. One missile had survived and was casting about for a target.

On the periphery of the tactical display, a new object appeared. It was the *Kaligm*. The Utche had arrived.

Send that message to the Utche NOW, Wilson subvocalized to Schmidt, and the BrainPal transmuted it to a reasonable facsimile of Wilson's own voice.

"Captain Coloma refuses," Schmidt said a second later.

What? Wilson sent. *Tell her it's an order. Invoke my security clearance. Do it now.*

"She says to shut up, you're distracting her," Schmidt said.

Distracting her from what? Wilson sent.

The *Clarke* started broadcasting a warning to the Utche, warning them of the missile attack, telling them to be silent and to leave Danavar space.

On the Utche's broadcast bands.

The last missile locked on and thrust itself toward the *Clarke*.

Oh, God, Wilson thought, and his BrainPal sent the thought to Schmidt.

"Thirty seconds to impact," Schmidt said.

"Twenty seconds . . ."

"Ten . . .

"This is it, Harry."

Silence.

X.

Wilson estimated he had fifteen minutes of air left when the Utche shuttle sidled up to his position and opened an outside airlock for him. On the inside, a space-suited Utche guided him in, closed the airlock and, when the air cycle had finished, opened the inner seal to the shuttle. Wilson unsealed his head, took off the oxygen mask, inhaled and then suppressed his gag reflex. Utche did not smell particularly wonderful to humans. He looked up and saw several Utche looking at him curiously.

"Hi," he said, to no one of them in particular.

"Are you well?" one of them asked, in a voice that sounded as if it were being spoken while inhaling.

"I'm fine," Wilson said. "How is the *Clarke*?"

"You are asking of your ship," said another, in a similar inward-breathing voice.

"Yes," Wilson said.

"It is most damaged," said the first one.

"Are there dead?" Wilson asked. "Are there injured?"

"You are a soldier," the second one said. "May you understand our language? It would be easier to say there."

Wilson nodded and booted up the Utche translation routine he'd received with the *Clarke*'s new orders. "Speak your own language," he said. "I will respond in mine."

"I am Ambassador Suel," the second one said. As the ambassador spoke, a second voice superimposed and spoke in English. "We don't yet know the extent of the damage to your ship or the casualties because we only just now reestablished communication, and that through an emergency transmitter on the *Clarke*. When we reestablished contact we intended to offer assistance and to bring your crew onto our ship. But Ambassador Abumwe insisted that we must first retrieve you before we came to the *Clarke*. She was most insistent."

"As I was about to run out of oxygen, I appreciate her insistence," Wilson said.

"I am Sub-Ambassador Dorb," said the first Utche. "Would you tell us how you came to be floating out here in space without a ship around you?"

"I had a ship," Wilson said. "It was eaten by a school of missiles."

"I am afraid I don't understand what you mean by that," Dorb said, after a glance to his (her? its?) boss.

"I will be happy to explain," Wilson said. "I would be even happier to explain on the way to the *Clarke*."

Abumwe, Coloma and Schmidt, as well as the majority of the *Clarke*'s diplomatic mission, were on hand when the Utche shuttle door irised open and Ambassadors Suel and Dorb exited, with Wilson directly behind.

"Ambassador Suel," Abumwe said, and a device attached to a lanyard translated for her. She bowed. "I am Ambassador Ode Abumwe. I apologize for the lack of live translator."

"Ambassador Abumwe," Suel said in his own language, and returned the bow. "No apology is needed. Your Lieutenant Wilson has very quickly briefed us on how it is you have come to be here in place of Ambassador Bair, and what you and the crew of the *Clarke* have done on our behalf. We will of course have to confirm the data for ourselves, but in the meantime I wish to convey our gratitude."

"Your gratitude is appreciated but not required," Abumwe said. "We have done only what was necessary. As to the data"—Abumwe nodded to Schmidt, who came forward and presented a data card to Dorb—"on that data card you will find both the black box recordings of the *Polk* and all the data recorded by us since we arrived in Danavar space. We wish to be open and direct with you and leave no doubt of our intentions or deeds during these negotiations."

Wilson blinked at this; black box data and the *Clarke* data records were almost certainly classified materials. Abumwe was taking a hell of a risk offering them up to the Utche prior to a signed treaty. He glanced at Abumwe, whose expression was unreadable; whatever else she was, she was in full diplomatic mode now.

"Thank you, Ambassador," Suel said. "But I wonder if we should not suspend these negotiations for the time being. Your ship is damaged and you undoubtedly have casualties among your crew. Your focus should be on your own people. We would of course stand ready to assist."

Captain Coloma stepped forward and saluted Suel. "Captain Sophia Coloma," she said. "Welcome to the *Clarke*, Ambassador."

"Thank you, Captain," the ambassador said.

"Ambassador, the *Clarke* is damaged and will require repair, but her life support and energy systems are stable," Coloma said. "We had a brief time to model and prepare for the missile strike and because of it were able to sustain the strike with minimal casualties and no deaths. While we will welcome your assistance, particularly with our communications systems, at this point we are in no immediate danger. Please do not let us be a hindrance to your negotiations."

"That is good to hear," Suel said. "Even so—"

"Ambassador, if I may," Abumwe said. "The crew of the *Clarke* risked everything, including their own lives, so that you and your crew might be safe and that we might secure this treaty. This man on my staff"—Abumwe nodded toward Wilson—"let four missiles chase him down and escaped death by throwing himself out of a shuttle and into the cold vacuum of space. It would be disrespectful of us to allow their efforts to be repaid with a *postponement* of our work."

Suel and Dorb looked over to Wilson, as if to get his thought on the matter. Wilson glanced over to Abumwe, who was expressionless.

"Well, I sure as hell don't want to have to come back here again," he said, to Suel and Dorb.

Suel and Dorb stared at him for a moment, and then made a sound that Wilson's BrainPal translated as [laughter].

Twenty minutes later, the Utche shuttle left the *Clarke* with Abumwe and her diplomatic team aboard. From the shuttle bay control room, Coloma, Wilson and Schmidt watched it depart.

"Thank Christ that's over," Coloma said, as it cleared the bay. She pivoted to return to the bridge, without looking at Wilson or Schmidt.

"The ship's not really secure, is it," Wilson said, to her back.

"Of course it's not," she said, turning back. "The only true thing I said was that we had no deaths, although it's probably more accurate to say that we don't have any deaths *yet*. As for the rest of it, our life support and energy systems are hanging by a thread, most of the other systems are dead or failing, and it will be a miracle if the *Clarke* ever moves from this spot under her own power. And to top it all off, some idiot destroyed our shuttle."

"Sorry about that," Wilson said.

"Hmmm," Coloma said. She started to turn again.

"It was a very great thing, to risk your ship for the Utche," Wilson said. "I didn't ask you to do that. That came from you, Captain Coloma. It's a victory, if you ask me. Ma'am."

Coloma paused for a second and then walked off, with no response.

"I don't think she likes me much," Wilson said, to Schmidt.

"Your charm is best described as idiosyncratic," Schmidt said.

"So why do *you* like me?" Wilson said.

"I don't think I've actually ever admitted to liking you," Schmidt said.

"Now that you mention it, I think you may be right," Wilson said.

"You're not boring," Schmidt said.

"Which is what you like most about me," Wilson said.

"No, boring is good," Schmidt said, and waved his hand around the shuttle bay. "This is the shit that's going to kill me."

XI.

Colonel Abel Rigney and Colonel Liz Egan sat in a hole-in-the-wall commissary at Phoenix Station, eating cheeseburgers.

"These are fantastic cheeseburgers," Rigney said.

"They're even better when you have a genetically-engineered body that never gets fat," Egan said. She took another bite of her burger.

"True," Rigney said. "Maybe I'll have another."

"Do," Egan said. "Test your metabolism."

"So, you read the report," Rigney said to Egan between his own bites.

"All I do is read reports," Egan said. "Read reports and scare midlevel bureaucrats. Which report are we talking about?"

"The one on the final round of negotiations with the Utche," Rigney said. "With the *Clarke,* and Ambassador Abumwe and Lieutenant Wilson."

"I did," Egan said.

"What's the final disposition of the *Clarke*?" Rigney asked.

"What did you find out about those missile fragments?" Egan asked.

"I asked you first," Rigney said.

"And I'm not in the second grade, so that tactic doesn't work with me," Egan said, and took another bite.

"We took a chunk of missile your dockworkers fished out of the *Clarke* and found a part number on it. The missile tracks back to a frigate called the *Brainerd*. This particular missile was reported launched and destroyed in a live-fire training exercise eighteen months ago. All the data I've seen confirms the official story," Rigney said.

"So we have ghost missiles being used by mystery ships to undermine secret diplomatic negotiations," Egan said.

"That's about the size of it," Rigney said. He set down his burger.

"Secretary Galeano isn't going to be very pleased that one of our own missiles was used to severely damage one of her department's ships," Egan said.

"That's all right," Rigney said. "My bosses aren't very pleased that a mole in the Department of State told whoever was using our own missiles against your ship where that ship was going to be and with whom it was negotiating."

"You have evidence of that?" Egan asked.

"No," Rigney said. "But we have pretty good evidence that the Utche sprung no leaks. The process of elimination applies from there."

"I'd like to see that evidence about the Utche," Egan said.

"I'd like to show it to you," Rigney said. "But you have a mole problem."

Egan looked at Rigney narrowly. "You better smile when you say that, Abel," she said.

"To be clear," Rigney said, "I would—and *have*, you'll recall from our combat days—trust you with my life. It's not you I'm worried about. It's everyone else in your department. Someone with a high enough security clearance to know about the Utche talks is engaging in treason, Liz. Selling us out to our enemies. Which enemies, we don't know. But our *friends* don't blow up one of our ships and try to go after a second."

Egan said nothing to this, choosing to stab a fry into ketchup instead.

"Which brings us back to the *Clarke*," Rigney said. "How is the ship?"

"We're trying to decide which will cost less, a complete rehaul or scrapping it and building a new ship," Egan said. "If we scrap it, at the very least we recoup the salvage value."

"That bad," Rigney said.

"The CDF makes excellent ship-to-ship missiles," Egan said. "Why do you ask?"

"For a B-team, Abumwe and her team were pretty impressive, don't you think?" Rigney said.

"They did all right," Egan said.

"Really," Rigney said, and held up a hand to start ticking off points on his fingers. "Wilson and Schmidt develop a new protocol for locating powerless CDF black boxes and retrieve data revealing what happened to the *Polk*. Then Wilson takes multiple spacewalks clad only in a CDF combat unitard and discovers a plan to destroy the Utche diplomatic mission with our missiles. He destroys four of those missiles and then Captain Coloma sacrifices her own ship to make sure the last missile doesn't hit the Utche. Coloma then flat-out lies to the Utche about the state of her ship to make sure Abumwe has a shot at the negotiations, and Abumwe basically strong-arms the Utche—the *Utche*—into completing their negotiations. Which they *do*, with only a day's preparation."

"They did all right," Egan said again.

"What more would you *like* them to do?" Rigney asked. "Walk on water?"

"Where is this going, Abel?" Egan asked.

"You said the most notable negotiation these folks did before this was another situation where they were forced to think on their feet and improvise," Rigney said. "Has it occurred to you that the reason Abumwe and her people are on your B-list is not because they're not good at what they do, but because you're not putting them in the right situations?"

"We didn't know these negotiations were going to be the 'right' situation," Egan said.

"No, but now you know what *are* the right situations for them," Rigney said. "High-risk, high-reward situations where the path to success isn't laid out but has to be cut by machete through a jungle filled with poison toads."

"The poison toads are a nice touch," Egan said, reaching for another french fry.

"You see what I'm getting at," Rigney said.

"I do," Egan said. "But I'm not entirely sure I'm going to be able to convince the secretary that a bunch of B-listers is who she wants for high-risk, high-reward missions."

"Not all of them," Rigney said. "Just the ones where the usual diplomatic bullshit won't work."

"Why do you care?" Egan said. "You seem awfully passionate about a bunch of people you had no idea existed just a week ago."

"You say it yourself every time you scare your State Department middle managers," Rigney said. "We're running out of time. We don't have the Earth anymore, and we need more friends than we've got if we're going to survive. Part of that can be something like the *Clarke* crew already is—a fire team we parachute in when nothing else is working."

"And when they fail?" Egan said.

"Then they fail in a situation where failure is an expected outcome," Rigney said. "But if they succeed, then we're much better off."

"If we appoint them to be this 'fire team,' as you say, then we're already raising expectations for whatever they do," Egan said.

"There's a simple solution for that," Rigney said. "Don't tell them they're a fire team."

"How awfully cruel," Egan said.

Rigney shrugged. "Abumwe and her people are already aware that they're not at the grown-ups' table," he said. "Why do you think she browbeat the Utche into negotiations? She knows an opportunity when she sees it. She wants those opportunities, and she and her team are going to beat their brains in to get them."

"And destroy their ships to get them, apparently," Egan said. "This fire team idea of yours could get expensive, fast."

"What's the plan for the *Clarke*'s crew?" Rigney asked.

"It hasn't been decided," Egan said. "We might put Abumwe and her diplomatic team on a different ship. Coloma's going to have to face an inquiry about intentionally putting her ship in the path of a missile. She's going to get cleared, but it's still a process. Wilson's on loan from CDF Research and Development. Presumably at some point they're going to want him back."

"Do you think you could put any decisions on the *Clarke*'s crew on hold for a few weeks?" Rigney asked.

"You seem awfully excited about these people," Egan said. "But even if I did put them in career limbo for your own amusement, there's no guarantee the secretary would sign off on your 'fire team' concept."

"Would it help if the CDF had a list of fires it would prefer to be put out through diplomacy than gunfire?" Rigney asked.

"Ah," Egan said. "*Now* we're getting to it. And I can already tell you how that idea's going to go over. When I first joined the secretary's team as CDF liaison, it took her six weeks to have a conversation with me longer than three words, all monosyllables. If I come to her with a list of requests from the CDF and a handpicked team, she'll communicate to me with grunts."

"All the more reason to use this team," Rigney said. "It's full of nobodies. She'll think she's screwing us. Tell her about the request and then suggest these people. It'll work brilliantly."

"Would you like me to ask her not to throw you in the briar patch while I'm at it?" Egan asked.

"Just this one request for now," Rigney said.

Egan was quiet for a few moments as she picked at her fries. Rigney finished his burger and waited.

"I'll take her temperature on it," Egan said, finally. "But if I were you, I wouldn't get my hopes up."

"I never get my hopes up," Rigney said. "It's how I've lived this long."

"And in the meantime I'll keep the *Clarke* crew from being reassigned elsewhere," Egan said.

"Thank you," Rigney said.

"You owe me," Egan said.

"Of course I do," Rigney said.

"Now I have to go," Egan said, pushing up from the table. "More children to scare."

"You have fun with that," Rigney said.

"You know I do," Egan said. She turned to go.

"Hey, Liz," Rigney said. "That estimate you give the

kids, the one about humans having thirty years before we're extinct. How much exaggeration is in that?"

"Do you want the truth?" Egan asked.

"Yes," Rigney said.

"Almost none at all," Egan said. "If anything, it's optimistic."

She left. Rigney stared at the remains of their meal.

"Well, hell," he said. "If we're doomed, maybe I will have that second cheeseburger after all."

Walk the Plank

[Transcript Begins]

CHENZIRA EL-MASRI: —okay, I'm not really interested in who you have in the medical bay, Aurel. Right now I'm focused on finding those damn cargo containers. If we don't track those down, it's not going to be a very happy next few months around here.

AUREL SPURLEA: If I didn't think the two of them were related, I wouldn't be bothering you, Chen. Are you recording this, Magda?

MAGDA GANAS: Just started the recorder.

SPURLEA: Chen, the guy in the sick bay isn't from around here.

EL-MASRI: What do you mean, "not from around here"? We're a wildcat colony. It's not like there's anywhere else to be from around here.

SPURLEA: He says he's from the *Erie Morningstar*.

EL-MASRI: That doesn't make any sense. The *Erie Morningstar* isn't supposed to be landing anyone. It's supposed to be sending down the containers on autopilot. The whole point of doing it this way is to take humans out of it.

GANAS: We know that, Chen. We were there when the cargo schedules were drawn up, too. That's why you need to see this guy. No matter what else, he's not one of us. He's come from *somewhere*. And since the *Erie Morningstar* was supposed to deliver two days ago, and he's here today, it's not a bad guess that he's telling the truth when he says he's from there.

EL-MASRI: So you think he came down on one of the containers.

GANAS: It seems likely.

EL-MASRI: That wouldn't have been a fun ride.

SPURLEA: Here we are. Chen, a couple of things real quick. One, he's messed up physically and we have him on pain relievers.

EL-MASRI: I thought I gave orders—

SPURLEA: Before you bitch at me, we've watered them down as much as we can and still have them have any effect. But believe me, this guy needs *something*. Two, he's got the Rot in his leg.

EL-MASRI: How bad?

SPURLEA: Real bad. I cleaned it out best I can, but it's a pretty good chance it's in the bloodstream by now, and you know what that means. But he's not from around here and *he* doesn't know what that means, and I don't see much point in telling him at this point. My goal is to keep him coherent long enough for you to talk to him and then keep him from too much pain while we figure out what to do with him after that.

EL-MASRI: Christ, Aurel. If he's got the Rot, I think you know what to do with him.

SPURLEA: I'm still waiting for the blood work to come back. If it's not set in there, we can take the leg and save him.

EL-MASRI: And then do what with him? Look around, Aurel. It's not like we can support anyone *else* here, much less a recovering amputee who can't do any work.

GANAS: Maybe you should talk to him first before deciding to leave him out for the packs.

EL-MASRI: I'm not unsympathetic to his situation,

Magda. But my job is to think about the whole colony.

GANAS: What the whole colony needs right now is for
you to hear this guy's story. Then you'll have a better
idea what to think.

EL-MASRI: What's this guy's name?

SPURLEA: Malik Damanis.

EL-MASRI: Malik. Fine.

[Door opens, stops.]

EL-MASRI (quietly): Lovely.

SPURLEA: There's a reason we call it the Rot.

EL-MASRI: Yeah.

[Door opens all the way.]

EL-MASRI: Malik . . . Hey, Malik.

MALIK DAMANIS: Yes. Sorry, I was dozing.

EL-MASRI: That's fine.

DAMANIS: Is Doctor Spurlea here? I think the pain is
coming back.

SPURLEA: I'm here. I'll give you another shot, Malik, but
it's going to have to wait for a few minutes. I need you
to be all here for your conversation with our colony
leader.

DAMANIS: That's you?

EL-MASRI: That's me. My name is Chenzira El-Masri.

DAMANIS: Malik Damanis. Uh, I guess you knew that.

EL-MASRI: I did. Malik, Aurel and Magda here tell me
that you say you're from the *Erie Morningstar*.

DAMANIS: I am.

EL-MASRI: What do you do there?

DAMANIS: I'm an ordinary deckhand. I mostly work
loading and unloading cargo.

EL-MASRI: You look pretty young. This your first ship?

DAMANIS: I'm nineteen standard, sir. No, I was on another ship before this, the *Shining Star*. I've been doing this since I turned twenty in Erie years, which is about sixteen years standard. This is my first tour on the *Morningstar,* though. Or was.

EL-MASRI: Was, you say.

DAMANIS: Yes, sir. She's gone, sir.

EL-MASRI: Gone as in left? She's gone off to her next destination.

DAMANIS: No. Gone as in gone, sir. She was taken. And I think everyone else who was on her might be dead now.

EL-MASRI: Malik, I think you need to explain this to me a little better. Was the ship all right when you skipped into our system?

DAMANIS: As far as I know. The ship stays on Erie time, and it was the middle of the night when we skipped. Captain Gahzini prefers to do it that way so that when we move cargo, we do it in the morning when we're fresh. Or that's what he tells us. Since the cargo we had for you was already packed when it came on board, it didn't really matter. The captain does what the captain does. So we arrived in the middle of the night for us.

EL-MASRI: Were you working then?

DAMANIS: No, sir, I was asleep in the crew quarters, along with most of the rest of the crew. We had a night's watch on at the time. The first thing I knew about anything going on was the captain sounding a general alert. It blasted on and everyone fell out of their bunks. We didn't think anything of it at the time.

EL-MASRI: You didn't think anything of a general alert? Doesn't that usually mean you're in an emergency?

DAMANIS: It does, but Captain Gahzini runs a lot of drills, sir. He says that just because we're a merchant ship doesn't mean we shouldn't have discipline. So every three or four skips he'll run a drill, and since the captain likes to skip in the middle of the night, that means we get woken up by a lot of general alerts.

EL-MASRI: All right.

DAMANIS: So we fall out of bunks, get dressed and then wait for the announcement about what the drill is this time. Is it a micrometeor puncture, or is it a systems failure of some sort, or what is it. Then finally Chief Officer Khosa comes on the public address system and says, "We are being boarded." And we all look at each other, because this is a new one; we haven't ever practiced something like this. We have no idea what to do. Doctor, my leg is really hurting.

SPURLEA: I know, Malik. I'll give you something as soon as you're done talking.

DAMANIS: Can I get something in the meantime? Anything?

GANAS: I can give him some ibuprofen.

SPURLEA: We're running low on that, Magda.

GANAS: I'll take it out of my own stash.

SPURLEA: All right.

GANAS: Malik, I'm going to go get you that ibuprofen. It will be just a minute.

DAMANIS: Thank you, Doctor Ganas.

EL-MASRI: You said you never drilled for being boarded. But there have always been pirates.

DAMANIS: We've drilled for being pursued by pirates. For that, most of the crew locks down while defensive teams prep countermeasures and the cargo crew preps to jettison the cargo. We work in space. Pirates can't swing over on ropes and take a ship. They run you down and threaten you to get you to hand over your cargo. Only then do they board the ship, take the cargo and go. That's why the last resort is throwing out the cargo. If you don't have it anymore, they have no reason to keep pursuing you.

EL-MASRI: So these weren't pirates.

DAMANIS: We didn't know what they were. At first we didn't know that there *was* anyone. We still thought it was a drill. Chief Khosa tells us we're being boarded and we have about two or three seconds to wonder what that means, and then he comes back on the PA and says, "This is not a drill." That's when we knew something was really up. But we didn't know what to think. We weren't drilled on this. We stood around looking at each other. Then Bosun Zarrani came into the quarters, told us we were being boarded and that we were to stay in quarters until they heard from him or the captain sounded an "all clear." Then he picked seven of us to follow him. I was one of the ones he picked.

EL-MASRI: Why did he pick you?

DAMANIS: Me or all of us?

EL-MASRI: Both.

DAMANIS: He picked all of us to be a security detail. He picked me, I think, because I was where he could see me. I didn't know he wanted me to be part of a security detail until he took us into his office, opened up a footlocker and started handing out shock sticks.

SPURLEA: Shock sticks? Why didn't you have firearms?

DAMANIS: It's a spaceship. Guns with bullets aren't a good idea on any ship that works in vacuum. And the only reason to have weapons on the ship at all is to deal with someone who's gotten into a fight or is drunk and out of control. And for that, a shock stick is what you want. You zap someone, they go down, you shove them in the brig until they sober up and calm down. So we have shock sticks. Zarrani handed them out to us. There were six of them and eight of us, so I and Tariq Murwani didn't have any. Bosun Zarrani said that we got to be scouts and told us to turn our PDAs to a general channel so that everyone would know where the enemy was. That didn't make much sense to me. I figured that we knew where they would come in.

EL-MASRI: Through the airlocks.

DAMANIS: Yes, sir. They'd open them up from the outside and then get through that way. I think Zarrani and Captain Gahzini were thinking the same thing because Zarrani took two of the crew with the shock sticks with him to the port maintenance airlock while the other three went to the starboard maintenance airlocks. But we were wrong.

EL-MASRI: How did they get in?

DAMANIS: They cut through the hull forward and aft and dropped in maybe a dozen soldiers in each spot. I saw the aft breach and the soldiers dropping in and yelled into my PDA about it and then ran, because the soldiers were carrying assault rifles.

SPURLEA: I thought you didn't want projectile weapons on a spaceship.

DAMANIS: We don't, sir. The soldiers did. Their job was to take over the ship. And maybe they thought that since they were cutting a couple of holes through the hull anyway, what's a few bullet holes here and there, right?

GANAS: Here we go. Three tablets.

DAMANIS: Thank you.

GANAS: Let me get you some water.

DAMANIS: It's too late. I already swallowed them. How long will it take for it to start working?

GANAS: Those were extra-strength, so not long at all.

DAMANIS: That's good. My leg hurts a lot. I think it's getting worse.

SPURLEA: Let me look.

DAMANIS: *Ahhhhh—*

SPURLEA: Sorry about that.

DAMANIS: It's okay, Doctor. But it's like I told you. It hurts a lot.

SPURLEA: I'll see what I can do about cleaning it out again after we're done talking here.

DAMANIS: I'll definitely need some real painkillers for that. The last time you did it I thought I was going to hit the roof.

SPURLEA: I'll be as careful as I can.

DAMANIS: I know you're doing your best, Doctor Spurlea.

EL-MASRI: You say these were soldiers. Were they Colonial Defense Forces?

DAMANIS: I don't think so. They weren't wearing CDF uniforms. These were bulkier and black, and there were helmets covering their heads. We couldn't see their faces or much of anything else. I suppose that makes sense, since they were coming in from space.

GANAS: If they were cutting through the hull, wouldn't bulkheads close off to contain the breach?

DAMANIS: I think they're supposed to, but the automatic systems are sensitive to pressure loss. These guys were coming through without any air going out behind them. I think they must have made a temporary airlock on the outside hull before they cut through.

EL-MASRI: Your captain still could have thrown up the bulkheads to keep them contained.

DAMANIS: The forward breach was right above the bridge deck. The very first thing they did, as far as I can tell, was to take the bridge and Captain Gahzini. Once they had the bridge, they had control of the ship. I was told by one of the bridge crew that when they came through, they ordered the captain to give them his command codes. He refused and they shot Chief Khosa in the gut. He was lying screaming on the deck and they told the captain they would gut shoot every person on the bridge unless he gave over the codes. Once the captain did that, they shot Khosa through the head to put him out of his misery, and then they had the ship.

EL-MASRI: What happened then?

DAMANIS: The soliders went through the ship and collected the crew at gunpoint and took them to the cargo bay. I and the others on the security detail were trying to avoid the soldiers as long as we could, but eventually they found us all. I got caught near the mess hall. I stepped out into a corridor and there was a soldier on either side of me, rifles pointed at my chest and head. I tried going back where I was, but when I turned there was another soldier behind me, rifle up. I put up my hands and that was it. I was taken to the cargo bay like everyone else.

EL-MASRI: And through all of this none of the soldiers told you what they wanted.

DAMANIS: No, sir. When I was taken to the cargo deck, I saw all the other crew members on the deck, kneeling, hands behind their head. The only one standing was Bosun Zarrani, who was quoting Colonial Union merchant maritime law to one of the soldiers. The soldier seemed to ignore him for a little while, then drew a sidearm. He shot the bosun in the face, and then Zarrani was dead. And that was it for anyone asking questions.

SPURLEA: So the entire crew was there.

DAMANIS: Everyone but the captain and a helmsman named Qalat. And Khosa, but he was dead already.

EL-MASRI: So you were all in the cargo bay. How did *you* get from there to here, Malik?

DAMANIS: The *Erie Morningstar* had four autopilot container carriers. Two of them were full of the supplies for your colony. The other two were empty. The soldiers opened up those two and ordered us in, half into one, half into the other.

EL-MASRI: And you just went in?

DAMANIS: A couple of us resisted. They shot them in the head. They didn't waste any time talking to us or bargaining with us. As far as I can tell, except for the ones on the bridge getting the command codes from the captain, they didn't talk at all. There was no point in it, and they didn't have to talk to get us to do what they wanted.

EL-MASRI: After you were all in, what happened next?

DAMANIS: They sealed us into the cargo containers. Everything went pitch-black and people started screaming, and then a couple of us turned our PDAs on so their screens would give light. That seemed to calm people a bit. After that we could hear the sounds of people moving and talking—the soldiers would apparently talk to each other, not to us—but I couldn't hear anything clear enough to make out what they were saying or doing. And then there was another sound. It was the sound of the cargo bay's purge cycle. That's when people started screaming again. It meant the cargo bay door was being opened and we were being thrown out.

GANAS: They were tossing the crew over the side.

DAMANIS: Yes, ma'am. Although one of the crew members in my container suggested something else. Once the container started moving and it was clear it was thrown off the ship, someone in the container started screaming, "We're walking the plank! We're walking the plank! We're walking the plank!" He kept doing this for a minute or two before I heard a thump and he shut up. I think someone punched him to make him quiet.

EL-MASRI: The cargo containers aren't designed for live transport.

DAMANIS: No, sir. They are airtight and they're insulated, so the cargo inside won't freeze in space or heat up excessively on reentry. But there's also no artificial gravity or anywhere to secure yourself. The closest thing to that are the pallet restraints at the bottom of the container. We use them to strap down the cargo pallets, but they don't do much good if you're not a pallet. I still grabbed one and tied it to my arm, as close as I could to the restraint anchor so at least *I* wouldn't go floating off. I thought it might help when we hit the atmosphere.

EL-MASRI: Did it?

DAMANIS: A little. We hit the atmosphere and everything began to shake and move. I held on to my pallet strap, but even then I was being whipped back and forth as the strap rotated around its anchor. I'd be slammed to the floor of the container, whip around in an arc and be slammed down again on the other side. I curled into a ball as much as I could and put my arms around my head to protect it, but it wasn't enough; I lost consciousness a couple of times in there. If I hadn't wrapped the strap around my arm, I would have been flung up into the container with the others.

GANAS: What happened to the others?

DAMANIS: People began to be slammed into walls and the floor and into each other, harder and faster as we dropped. A couple of times people hit me, but I was down near the floor, so most of the time they were hitting each other or the walls. They were screaming as they were flying about, and every once in a while you would hear a snap and then someone's screaming would either get louder or it would stop. After one really hard bump, a woman hit the floor next to me headfirst and I could hear her neck go. *She* stopped screaming. There were at least fifty of us in the container. I'd guess about ten or fifteen people died during reentry, and maybe that many others broke their arms or legs.

SPURLEA: It was a good thing you held on to that strap.

DAMANIS: [laughs] Look at my leg now, Doc. Tell me again how lucky I am.

GANAS: Is the ibuprofen helping now?

DAMANIS: A little. May I have some water now, please?

GANAS: Yes, of course.

EL-MASRI: Once you made it through the first part of the atmosphere, did things settle?

DAMANIS: Some. The autopilot kicked in and stabilized us, but then the parachutes deployed and everyone who was still floating was jammed to the floor of the container. That was more broken bones, but then at least everyone was on the floor of the container, because gravity had finally taken hold. Then there was a crashing sound, and everyone was thrown around. We were going through the trees, or whatever you have here for trees. Then there was a final crash, the container fell on its side, the doors flew open, and we were finally on the ground.

GANAS: Your water.

DAMANIS: Thank you.

SPURLEA: What was your physical condition at that point, Malik?

DAMANIS: I was hurt pretty badly. I'm pretty sure I had a concussion. But I could walk and I didn't have any broken bones. I unwrapped myself from the pallet strap and I headed for the door, and as I got outside some of the crew who had gotten out before me were standing in a small clearing, looking up and pointing, so I looked up where they were looking.

EL-MASRI: What were they pointing at?

DAMANIS: It was the other cargo container. It was tumbling and falling. The autopilot must have gotten damaged or something, because it wasn't stabilizing itself and its parachutes didn't deploy. We watched it tumble for twenty, thirty seconds, and then the trees got in the way and we couldn't see it anymore. But then a few seconds later we heard the sound of trees breaking and a huge crash. The container had hit the ground at close to full speed. If anyone had still been alive in that container before it hit, they didn't survive after. At least I don't see how they could.

EL-MASRI: Did you see any other containers falling?

DAMANIS: I stopped looking after that.

EL-MASRI: Malik, will you excuse me for a moment?

DAMANIS: Yes, sir. Does this mean we're done talking now? Can I get that shot now?

EL-MASRI: Hold on a minute, Malik. I'll be back to ask you some more questions.

DAMANIS: My leg is really hurting, sir.

EL-MASRI: It won't be long. Aurel, Magda?

[Door opens, closes.]

EL-MASRI: Why did you bring that recorder out here?

GANAS: Malik isn't going to say anything unless you're there.

EL-MASRI: Is it turned off right now?

GANAS: Yes.

EL-MASRI: Where did Malik come from? What direction, I mean?

SPURLEA: The couple who found him said they saw him come out of the forest to the east of the colony.

EL-MASRI: Do we have any people looking for the containers in that direction?

SPURLEA: Magda?

GANAS: We sent out five teams, and they all headed in different directions, so at least one of them is headed in an easterly direction.

EL-MASRI: Recall the other teams and have them go east as well. There's a chance our supplies are in that direction.

SPURLEA: You think pirates are going to eject cargo, Chen?

EL-MASRI: I think whoever took over the *Erie Morningstar* was interested in the ship, not the cargo. That's why they kept the captain and the helmsman and made everyone else walk the plank. It's entirely possible they tossed out the cargo with the crew. If they did, then we need to find it. We need those supplies.

GANAS: What about the survivors?

EL-MASRI: What survivors?

GANAS: Malik said that at least some of the crew in his container survived the landing. Do you want our people to go looking for them, too?

EL-MASRI: I think our first priority is looking for those supplies, Magda.

GANAS: That's pretty harsh, Chen. These people literally fall out of the sky and crash-land here, and you're not in the least concerned about them.

EL-MASRI: Look. I'm not going to apologize for the fact that when push comes to shove, I'm going to put the people of this colony before everyone else. This is why you all hired me as your colony leader, remember? You wanted someone with frontier experience, who was familiar with the tough decisions you have to make on the bleeding edge of human civilization. This is one of those decisions, Magda. Do we prioritize finding supplies for our people, who are healthy but won't be *very soon* if we don't get the soil treatments and seed stock and emergency rations that were in the cargo shipment the *Erie Morningstar* had in her, or do we prioritize a bunch of people we don't know, the majority of whom it would seem are injured or dying, who would be nothing but a drain on our almost nonexistent resources? I'm the colony leader. I have to make a choice, and I choose *us*. Now, maybe you find that inhumane, but at the moment, ask me if I give a shit. This soil here kills everything we plant in it. Almost everything that grows or lives here we can't eat or is trying to kill us or both. We're down to the last three weeks of stores, and that's if we stretch. I have two hundred fifty people relying on me to save their lives. That's my job. I'm doing it by telling our people to look for those cargo containers first. End of story.

SPURLEA: At the very least, you should ask him to try to describe where he landed so that we can narrow down where we're searching. Wherever it was, he was able to walk to here from there in only a slightly better condition than he's in right now. That means it's not too far away. The more we know, the better we can find the cargo containers, if they exist.

EL-MASRI: You ask him.

SPURLEA: If I ask him, all he's going to do is keep asking for painkillers. That was the deal: He talks to you, and when he's done I'll give him something. So you need to do it.

EL-MASRI: How long until you know about his blood work? Whether he's got the Rot all through his system.

SPURLEA: I checked on my PDA while you were talking to him. The cultures are still growing. I'll know for sure in the next thirty minutes or so.

EL-MASRI: Fine. Magda, please let the search teams know to focus east, and that we'll hopefully give them more detailed information on where to look soon. Tell Drew Talford to send it wideband. It'll be faster than you trying to raise every party one at a time.

GANAS: What do we do if one of the search teams happens to find the *Erie Morningstar* survivors?

EL-MASRI: Note where they are, but steer clear of them for now. *If* we find the cargo containers with our supplies, we can go back and deal with them. But for now, let them be. We have other priorities.

GANAS: Here, Aurel. Make sure to record everything Malik says.

SPURLEA: Will do.

EL-MASRI: All right, let's get back in there.

[Door opens, closes.]

DAMANIS: I thought you had forgotten about me.

EL-MASRI: We wouldn't do that, Malik.

DAMANIS: That's good to hear. I'm sorry to take up so much of your time. You must be busy as colony leader.

EL-MASRI: Well, talking to you has been helpful, and you can be a little more helpful to me still, Malik.

DAMANIS: How can I do that?

EL-MASRI: I need you to tell me everything you can about where you landed and how you got here from there. That will help us find where you landed, and might help us find the rest of your crew.

DAMANIS: I'll tell you, but I don't think you'll find the rest of my crew. I think they're all dead.

EL-MASRI: You said that at least a few of your crewmates were alive when you landed. You've survived so far. So it stands to reason some of them might have as well.

DAMANIS: Unh.

EL-MASRI: Why are you shaking your head?

SPURLEA: Malik, did something else happen to your crew before you came here?

DAMANIS: Yes.

EL-MASRI: Tell us about it. It could be useful to us.

DAMANIS: After we landed, those of us who were mostly uninjured started helping those who were worse off. There were about ten of us at that point. We went back into the container so we could see who was living and who was dead. The dead we moved to one side of the container. The living we moved out of the container so we could see how badly they were injured. About half had broken bones but were still conscious or still able to move around. The rest were either unconscious or not able to move because they were too injured or in too much pain. We went back into the container and took the clothes off the dead to make slings and braces, and to make bandages where people were bleeding or had open breaks.

SPURLEA: So, ten relatively uninjured, about ten or fifteen somewhat injured and the same number severely injured. The rest dead.

DAMANIS: Yes. May I have some more water?

SPURLEA: Of course.

DAMANIS: When we were done with that, those of us who were still uninjured got together to discuss what to do next. Some of us wanted to find your colony. We knew it was down here because that's why we were over your planet in the first place, and we knew you couldn't be too far away. But none of our PDAs survived the fall and we couldn't signal you, or use them to keep track of whoever wandered off. Most of us wanted to build a better camp and get ourselves squared away, find some water and some food before we did anything else. I said we should move the dead out of the container and the living back in, so they would at least have shelter. One guy, Nadeem Davi, started talking about how we should consider the possibility of using the dead for food. We argued about that so long that we didn't notice what had happened to the forest.

EL-MASRI: What had happened?

DAMANIS: It had gone dead silent. Like it does when there's a predator around, right? Everything that could get eaten just shuts up and hides. We finally noticed it when we all stopped talking. It was dead silent except for our injured. And then—

SPURLEA: And then a pack of animals was on you.

DAMANIS: You *know* about these things?

EL-MASRI: We just call it "the pack." We don't call them anything else because we've never caught one by it-self. You don't see them, or you see dozens of them. There's nothing in between.

DAMANIS: I didn't know that. I saw them coming out of the woods and they reminded me of the stories my grandmother told me of hyenas in Africa. There were just so many of them. One or two for every one of us.

EL-MASRI: We lost fourteen people to the pack early on before we learned not to wander too far into the woods alone. We go out in groups of four or five and always go armed. They seem to have gotten good at recognizing rifles. We don't see them as much as we used to.

DAMANIS: They made up for it with us. They went for the injured ones first, went right for their necks and open wounds. There was nothing we could do for them. Some of the less injured tried to run or crawl, but the pack went for their injuries, too. Like they knew that was going to cause us the most pain and drag us down so they could have us. Then at least a couple dozen got into a smaller pack and headed to-ward those of us who were still uninjured. Some of us tried to run, and didn't notice that there was another small pack flanking us. Nadeem was one of those; he went down fast and six of them were on him before any of us could do anything. Then the rest of them came right at us.

SPURLEA: How did you manage to escape?

DAMANIS: I didn't at first. One of the pack things bit

into my calf and took a chunk of it. I managed to kick it off and then ran as fast as I could in the other direction. By that time the rest of the crew was down and I guess the pack decided there was more than enough where they were. They didn't need to follow me. I just kept running until my leg gave out on me.

EL-MASRI: Do you remember which direction you mostly ran? North? South?

DAMANIS: I don't know. Mostly south? I remember the sun being to my right when I could see it, and I think it was morning here when we landed. So, south?

EL-MASRI: What happened then?

DAMANIS: I rested, but not too long, because my leg was already beginning to hurt, and I didn't want it to stiffen up on me. I kept heading south, and after a while, maybe ten minutes, I came to a stream. I remembered reading somewhere once that if you ever get lost in the woods that you should find a stream and then walk downstream, because sooner or later you'd find civilization that way. So after I drank some water and washed out my wound, I just started walking downstream. I walked and then I would rest for a couple of minutes and then I would start walking again. Eventually I came out of the woods and saw your colony. I saw a couple of people in a field.

SPURLEA: That would be the Yangs. They found him out in what was supposed to be their sorghum field.

EL-MASRI: Go on, Malik.

DAMANIS: I tried yelling to them and waving my hands, but I didn't know if they could hear me or not. Then I passed out, and when I woke up I was here, and Doctor Spurlea was trying to fix my leg. That woke me up.

EL-MASRI: I don't doubt that.

DAMANIS: And that's everything, sir. That's everything I know.

EL-MASRI: All right. Thank you, Malik.

DAMANIS: You're welcome, sir. Can I have my painkillers now? I'm really going to start crying soon.

SPURLEA: Absolutely, Malik. Give me one minute to talk
to Chen here, and I'll come right back and hook you
up.

[Door opens, closes.]

EL-MASRI: Well, at least now we know how he got the
Rot. That pack bite would do it.

SPURLEA: And if it didn't, washing the wound in the
stream water did.

EL-MASRI: You can't blame him for not knowing that
the stream is packed with the Rot's bacteria.

SPURLEA: Believe me, I don't. His blood work just pinged,
by the way.

EL-MASRI: Bad news?

SPURLEA: Don't make it sound like you *care,* Chen.

EL-MASRI: Just tell me.

SPURLEA: He's got it in his blood. He's got about twenty-
four hours before the septicemia blows him up from
the inside.

EL-MASRI: We don't have enough painkillers for you to
let him ride out that whole time, Aurel. That's how
we got into this situation with the painkillers in the
first place.

SPURLEA: I know.

EL-MASRI: You're going to take care of this, then.

SPURLEA: When I go back in I'll give him enough to get
him to sleep. I'll take care of it from there.

EL-MASRI: I'm sorry I have to be like this to you about
it.

SPURLEA: I understand, Chen. I do. I'm just certain that
when I die and meet Hippocrates, he's going to be
sorely disappointed in me.

EL-MASRI: He's going to die anyway, and painfully. You wouldn't be doing him any favors.

SPURLEA: I'm going to change the subject by saying, Look, here comes Magda.

GANAS: The easterly team found the containers with the crew from the *Erie Morningstar*.

EL-MASRI: What's the report?

GANAS: Everyone's dead. Death at impact at one site. Death by the pack, it looks like, at the other. They're less than a klick apart, with the death-by-impact site being the most northerly one. The team took pictures, so if you want to have nightmares tonight, you can look.

EL-MASRI: No other containers?

GANAS: If they're there, they haven't found them yet.

EL-MASRI: Have them keep looking. Give all the other search teams the coordinates and fan out from there.

GANAS: How is Malik?

SPURLEA: The Rot's in his blood.

GANAS: Jesus.

SPURLEA: Just another perfect day here in New Seattle.

EL-MASRI: Look at it this way. It's unlikely to get much worse.

GANAS: Don't jinx it.

EL-MASRI: Thank you, Aurel, Magda. I'll let you know when or if we find those supplies.

SPURLEA: Thank you, Chen.

GANAS: There goes a right bastard.

SPURLEA: We knew what he was when we hired him.

GANAS: I know, but it's painful to be reminded of it so frequently.

SPURLEA: Without him we might be dead already.

GANAS: Which is also painful to be reminded of so frequently.

SPURLEA: Come on. We have to give Malik his painkillers.

GANAS: Did Chen tell you to finish him off after you did?

SPURLEA: He did.

GANAS: Will you?

SPURLEA: I don't know.

GANAS: You're a good and decent man, Aurel. You really, truly are. How you ended up on a wildcat colony is beyond me.

SPURLEA: You're one to talk, Magda. Let's go in.

GANAS: All right.

SPURLEA: And turn that off. Whatever I do, I don't want a record of it anywhere but on my conscience.

[Transcript Ends]

We Only Need the Heads

Hart Schmidt went to Ambassador Abumwe's temporary office on Phoenix Station when she pinged him, but she wasn't there. Schmidt knew that the ambassador not being in her office wasn't a good enough excuse for him not to be in her presence when commanded, so he did a hasty PDA search on his boss. Three minutes later, he walked up to her in an observation lounge.

"Ambassador," he said.

"Mr. Schmidt," the ambassador said, not turning to him. Schmidt followed her gaze out the wall-sized window of the observation deck, to the heavily damaged ship hovering at a slight distance from the station itself.

"The *Clarke*," Schmidt said.

"Very good, Schmidt," Abumwe said, in a tone that informed him that, as with so many of the things he said to her in his role as a functionary on her diplomatic team, he was not telling her anything she didn't already know.

Schmidt made an involuntary, nervous throat clearing in response. "I saw Neva Balla earlier today," he said, naming the *Clarke*'s executive officer. "She tells me that it's not looking good for the *Clarke*. The damage it took on our last mission is pretty extensive. Fixing it will be nearly as expensive as building a new ship. She thinks it's likely they'll simply scrap it."

"And do what with the crew?" Abumwe said.

"She didn't say," Schmidt said. "She said the crew is

being kept together, at least for the moment. There's a chance the Colonial Union may just take a new ship and assign the *Clarke*'s crew to it. They might even name it the *Clarke,* if they're going to scrap this one." Schmidt motioned in the direction of the ship.

"Hmmmm," Abumwe said, and then lapsed back into silence, staring at the *Clarke*.

Schmidt spent a few more uncomfortable minutes before clearing his throat again. "You pinged me, Ambassador?" he said, reminding her he was there.

"You say the *Clarke* crew hasn't been reassigned," Abumwe said, as if their earlier conversation hadn't had an extended pause in it.

"Not yet," Schmidt said.

"And yet, *my* team has," Abumwe said, finally looking over at Schmidt. "Most of it, anyway. The Department of State assures me that the reassignments are only temporary—they need my people to fill in holes on other missions—but in the meantime I'm left with two people on my team. They left me Hillary Drolet, and they left me you. I know why they left me Hillary. She's my assistant. I don't know why they chose to take every *other* member of my team, assign them some presumably important task, and leave *you* doing nothing at all."

"I don't have any good answer to that, ma'am," was the only thing that Schmidt could say that wouldn't have immediately put his entire diplomatic career in jeopardy.

"Hmmmm," Abumwe said again, and turned back to the *Clarke*.

Schmidt assumed this was his cue to depart and began stepping back out of the observation deck, perchance to avail himself of a stiff drink at the nearest commissary, when Abumwe spoke again.

"Do you have your PDA with you?" she asked him.

"Yes, ma'am," Schmidt said.

"Check it now," Abumwe said. "We have new orders."

Schmidt drew out the PDA from his jacket pocket, swiped it on and read the new orders flashing in his mail queue. "We're being attached to the Bula negotiations," he said, reading the orders.

"Apparently so," Abumwe said. "Deputy Ambassador Zala ruptured her appendix and has to withdraw. Normally protocol would have her assistant step up and continue negotiations, but Zala's plank of the negotiations hasn't formally started, and for protocol reasons it's important for the Colonial Union to have someone of sufficient rank head this portion of the process. So here we are."

"What part of the negotiations are we taking over?" Schmidt asked.

"There's a reason I'm having you *read* the orders, Schmidt," Abumwe said. Her tone had returned. She turned to face him again.

"Sorry, ma'am," Schmidt said, hastily, and gestured at his PDA. "I'm not there yet."

Abumwe grimaced but kept whatever comment about Schmidt that was running through her head to herself. "Trade and tourism access to Bula worlds," she said instead. "How many ships, how large the ships, how many humans on the ground on Bulati and its colony worlds at one time, and so on."

"We've done that before," Schmidt said. "That shouldn't be a problem."

"There's a wrinkle that's not in your orders," Abumwe said. Schmidt looked up from his PDA. "There's a Bula colony world named Wantji. It was one of the last ones the Bula claimed before the Conclave told the unaffiliated races they could no longer colonize. They haven't put any of their people on it yet because they don't know how the Conclave would react to that."

"What about it?" Schmidt asked.

"Three days ago, the CDF received a skip drone from Wantji with an emergency distress message in it," Abumwe said.

Why would the Bula on an officially uninhabited planet send the Colonial Defense Forces a distress message? Schmidt almost asked, but didn't. He realized it was exactly the sort of question that would make the ambassador think he was even more stupid than she already believed he was. Instead he attempted to figure out the question on his own.

After a few seconds, it came to him. "A wildcat colony," he said.

"Yes," Abumwe said. "A wildcat colony that the Bula don't appear to know anything about at the moment."

"We're not telling them it's there?" Schmidt asked.

"Not yet," Abumwe said. "The CDF is sending a ship first."

"We're sending a *warship* into Bula territory to check on a human colony that's not supposed to be there?" Schmidt said, slightly incredulously. "Ambassador, this is a very bad idea—"

"Of course it's a bad idea!" Abumwe snapped. "Stop informing me of obvious things, Schmidt."

"Sorry," Schmidt said.

"Our job in the negotiations is twofold," Abumwe said. "We negotiate the trade and tourism rights. We also negotiate them *slowly enough* that the *Tubingen* is able to get to Wantji and pluck that wildcat colony—or what's left of it—from the planet."

"Without telling the Bula," Schmidt said. He kept the skepticism from his voice as politely as possible.

"The thinking is that if the Bula aren't aware of it now, there is no point in making them aware," Abumwe said. "And if they become aware, then the wildcatters will have been removed before they present a genuine diplomatic issue."

"As long as they overlook a CDF ship having done time over their planet," Schmidt said.

"The thinking is that the *Tubingen* will be long gone before the Bula know they're there," Abumwe said.

Schmidt refrained from saying, *It's still a bad idea,* and chose something else instead. "You said it's the *Tubingen* that's heading to this colony planet," he said.

"Yes," Abumwe said. "What about it?"

Schmidt accessed his PDA and searched through his message queue. "Harry Wilson was attached to the *Tubingen* a few days ago," he said, and turned his PDA to the ambassador to show her the message Wilson had sent him. "Its CDF platoon lost their systems guy on Brindle. Harry was stepping in for their current mission. Which would be this one, wouldn't it."

"Yet another team member of mine farmed out," Abumwe said. "What is your point?"

"My point is that it could be useful for us to have someone on the ground on this," Schmidt said. "You know we're getting dealt a bad hand here, ma'am. At the very least Harry can tell us how bad of a hand it actually is."

"Asking your CDF friend for information on an active military mission is a fine way to get yourself shot, Schmidt," Abumwe said.

"I suppose it would be," Schmidt said.

Abumwe was silent at this for a moment. "I don't think you should risk being caught doing something like that," she said, eventually.

"I understand you entirely, ma'am," Schmidt said. He turned to go.

"Schmidt," Abumwe said.

"Yes, ma'am," Schmidt said.

"You understand that earlier I was implying that they left you with me because you were largely useless," Abumwe said.

"I got that, yes," Schmidt said, after a second.

"I'm sure you did," Abumwe said. "Now. Prove me wrong." She returned her gaze to the *Clarke*.

Oh boy, Harry, Schmidt thought as he walked away. *I hope you're having an easier time of things than I am right now.*

The shuttle from the *Tubingen* hit the atmosphere of the planet like a rock punching into an earthen dam, throwing off heat and rattling the platoon of Colonial Defense Forces soldiers inside as if they were plastic balls in a child's popper.

"This is nice," Lieutenant Harry Wilson said, to no one in particular, then directed his attention to his fellow lieutenant Heather Lee, the platoon commander. "It's funny how something like air can feel so bumpy."

Lee shrugged. "We have restraints," she said. "And this isn't a social call."

"I know," Wilson said. The shuttle rattled again. "But this has always been my least favorite part of a mission. Aside from, you know. The shooting and killing and being shot and possibly eaten by aliens."

Lee did not look impressed with Wilson. "Been a while since you've dropped, Lieutenant?"

Wilson nodded. "Did my combat time and then transferred into research and technical advising for the diplomatic corps. Don't have to do many drops for that. And the ones I do come down nice and easy."

"Consider this a refresher course," Lee said. The shuttle rattled again. Something creaked worryingly.

"Space," Wilson said, and sank back into his restraints. "It's *fantastic*."

"It *is* fantastic, sir," said the soldier next to Lee. Wilson automatically had his BrainPal query the man's identity; instantly, text floated over the soldier's head to let Wilson know he was speaking to Private Albert Jefferson.

Wilson glanced over to Lee, the platoon leader, who caught the glance and gave another, most infinitesimal of shrugs, as if to say, *He's new*.

"I was attempting sarcasm, Private," Wilson said.

"I know that, sir," Jefferson said. "But I'm being serious. Space is fantastic. All of this. It is awesome."

"Well, except for the cold and vacuum and the unbearable silent death of it," Wilson said.

"Death?" Jefferson said, and smiled. "Begging the lieutenant's pardon, but death was back home on Earth. Do you know what I was doing three months ago, sir?"

"I'm guessing being old," Wilson said.

"I was hooked up to a dialysis machine, praying I would make it to my seventy-fifth birthday," Jefferson said. "I'd already gotten one transplant, and they didn't want to give me another because they knew I was going to leave anyway. Cheaper to hook me up. I barely made it. But I got to seventy-five, signed up and a week later, boom. New body, new life, new career. Space is awesome."

The shuttle hit an air pocket of some sort, tumbling the transport before the pilot could right the ship again. "There's the minor problem that you might have to kill things," Wilson said, to Jefferson. "Or get killed. Or fall out of the sky. You're a soldier now. These are the occupational hazards."

"Fair trade," Jefferson said.

"Is it," Wilson said. "First mission?"

"Yes, sir," Jefferson said.

"I'll be interested to know if your answer to that is the same a year from now," Wilson said.

Jefferson grinned. "You strike me as a 'glass half-empty' kind of guy, sir," he said.

"I'm a 'the glass is half-empty and filled with poison' kind of guy, actually," Wilson said.

"Yes, sir," Jefferson said.

Lee nodded suddenly, not at Wilson or Jefferson, but at the message she was getting from her BrainPal. "Drop-off in two," she said. "Fire teams." The soldiers formed up into groups of four. "Wilson. You're with me." Wilson nodded.

"You know, I was one of the last people off, sir," Jefferson said to Wilson a minute later, as the shuttle zeroed in on its landing site.

"Off of what?" Wilson said. He was distracted; he was going over the mission specs on his BrainPal.

"Off of Earth," Jefferson said. "The day I went up the Nairobi beanstalk, that guy brought that alien fleet into Earth orbit. Scared the hell out of all of us. We thought we were under attack. Then the fleet started transmitting all sorts of things about the Colonial Union."

"You mean, like the fact it had been socially engineering the Earth for centuries to keep it a farm for colonists and soldiers," Wilson said.

Jefferson snorted quietly. "That's a little paranoid, don't you think, sir? I think this fellow—"

"John Perry," Wilson said.

"—has some explaining to do about how he managed to head up an alien fleet in the first place. Anyway, my transport ship was one of the last out of Earth dock. There were one or two more, but after that I'm told the Earth stopped sending us soldiers and colonists. They want to renegotiate their relationship to the Colonial Union, is how I've heard it."

"Doesn't seem unreasonable, all things considered," said Wilson.

The shuttle landed with a muted thump and settled into the earth.

"All I know, sir, is I'm glad this Perry guy waited until I was gone," Jefferson said. "Otherwise I'd still be old and missing my kidneys and probably near death. Whatever's out here is better than what I had there."

The shuttle door cracked open and the outside air rushed in, hot and sticky and rich with the scent of death and decomposition. From the platoon came a few audible groans and the sound of at least one person gagging. Then the platoon began its disembarkment by fire teams.

Wilson looked over at Jefferson, whose face had registered the full effect of the smell coming off the planet. "I hope you're right," Wilson said. "But from the smell of it, we're probably near death here, too."

They stepped out of the shuttle and onto a new world.

The Bula sub-ambassador looked not unlike a lemur, as all Bula did, and carried the jeweled amulet that signified her station in the diplomatic corps. She had an unpronounceable name, which all things considered was not unusual, but insisted that Abumwe and her staff call her "Sub-Ambassador Ting." "It is close enough for government work," she said, through a translator device on her lanyard as she shook Abumwe's hand.

"Then welcome, Sub-Ambassador Ting," Abumwe said.

"Thank you, Ambassador Abumwe," Ting said, and motioned for her, Drolet and Schmidt to sit across from her and her two staff at the conference room table. "We are delighted that someone such as yourself was available for these negotiations on such short notice. It is a shame about Katerina Zala. Please send her my regards."

"I shall," Abumwe said. She sat.

"What is this 'appendix' she ruptured?" Ting asked, sitting herself.

"It's a vestigial organ attached to the larger digestive system," Abumwe said. "Sometimes it gets inflamed. A rupture can cause sepsis and death if not treated."

"It sounds horrible," Ting said.

"It was caught early enough that Deputy Ambassador

Zala was in no real danger," Abumwe said. "She will be fine in a few days."

"That's good to hear," Ting said. "Interesting how such a small part can threaten the health of an entire system."

"I suppose it is," Abumwe said.

Ting sat there for a moment, companionably silent, and then with a start grabbed the PDA her assistant had laid before her. "Well, let us begin, shall we. We don't want our diplomatic system grinding to a halt because of *us*."

The hand-tooled sign at the edge of the colony read, "New Seattle." As far as Wilson could see, it was the only thing in the colony that hadn't burned.

"Teams, report in," Lee said. There were no teams other than her own near her; her voice was being carried by BrainPal. Wilson opened up the general channel in his own head.

"Team one here," said Blaine Givens, the team leader. "I've got nothing but burned huts and dead bodies."

"Team two here," said Muhamad Ahmed. "I've got the same."

"Team three," said Janet Mulray. "More of the same. Whatever happened here isn't happening now." The three other teams reported the same.

"Anybody finding survivors?" Lee asked. Responses came in: None so far. "Keep looking," she said.

"I need to get to the colony HQ," Wilson said. "That's why I'm here."

Lee nodded and moved her team forward.

"I thought we weren't colonizing anymore," Jefferson said to Wilson as they moved into the colony. "The aliens told us they'd vaporize any planet we colonized."

"Not 'the aliens,'" Wilson said. "The Conclave. There's a difference."

"What's the difference?" Jefferson asked.

"There are about six hundred different alien races we deal with," Wilson said. "Maybe two-thirds of them are in the Conclave. The rest of them are like us, unaffiliated." He routed around a dead colonist who lay, charred, in the path.

"And what does that mean, sir?" Jefferson asked, routing around the same body but letting his eyes linger on it.

"It means they're like us," Wilson said. "If they colonize, the Conclave will blast the crap out of them, too."

"But this is a colony," Jefferson said, turning his eyes back to Wilson. "Our colony."

"It's a wildcat colony," Wilson said. "It's not sanctioned by the Colonial Union. And this is someone else's planet anyway."

"The Conclave's?" Jefferson asked.

Wilson shook his head. "No, the Bula. Another group of aliens entirely." He motioned at the burned-out huts and sheds around them. "When these guys headed here, they were on their own. No support from the CU. And no defense, either."

"So not our colony," Jefferson said.

"No," Wilson said.

"Will the aliens see it that way, sir?" Jefferson asked. "Either group, I mean."

"Since we'd be screwed either way if they didn't, let's hope so," Wilson said. He looked up and saw that he and Jefferson had gotten off the pace of Lee. "Come on, Jefferson." He jogged to catch up with the platoon leader.

Two minutes later, Wilson and Lee's squad were in front of a partially collapsed Quonset hut. "I think this is it," Lee said, to Wilson. "The HQ, I mean."

"How do you figure?" Wilson said.

"Largest building inside the colony proper," Lee said. "Have to have some place for town meetings."

"I can't argue with that logic," Wilson said, and looked at the hut, concerned about its stability. He looked over at Lee and her squad.

"After you, Lieutenant," Lee said. Wilson sighed and pried open the door to the hut.

Inside the hut were two bodies and a whole lot of mess.

"Looks like something's been at them," Lee said, tapping one with a foot. Wilson saw Jefferson, looking at the body, turn a sicklier shade of green than he already was.

"How long have they been dead, do you think?" Wilson asked.

Lee shrugged. "Between the time they sent the distress call and we got here? Couldn't be less than a week."

"Since when do wildcat colonies report back?" Wilson asked.

"I just go where they tell me, Lieutenant," Lee said. She motioned to Jefferson and pointed at one of the bodies. "Check that body for an ID chip. Colonists sometimes put them in so they can keep track of each other."

"You want me to go through the body?" Jefferson asked, clearly horrified.

"Ping it," Lee said, impatiently. "Use your BrainPal. If there's a chip, it'll respond."

Wilson turned away from Lee and Jefferson's truly compelling discussion and headed farther into the hut. The bodies had been in an open area that he suspected, true to Lee's hunch, was used for colony gatherings. Farther in were a set of what used to be cubicles and a small enclosed room.

The cubicles were a shattered mess; the room, from the outside, at least, looked intact. Wilson was hoping the colony's computing and communications hardware were in there.

The room door was locked. Wilson jiggled the door

handle a couple of times to be sure, then looked at the other side of the door. He pulled out his multipurpose tool, formed it into a crowbar and pulled the pins out of the door hinges. He set the door aside and looked into the room.

Every piece of equipment had been hammered into oblivion.

"Crap," Wilson said to himself. He went into the room anyway to see if anything was salvageable.

"Find anything?" Lee asked a few minutes later, appearing by the door.

"If someone likes puzzles, they could have fun with this," Wilson said. He stood up and gestured to the remains of the equipment.

"So nothing you can use," Lee said.

"No," Wilson said. He bent down and grabbed a piece of debris and held it out for Lee to take. "That's supposed to be the memory core. It's been hammered out of usability. I'll take it back and try to get something out of it anyway, but I wouldn't be holding out hope."

"Maybe some of the colonists' computers and handhelds will have something," Lee said. "I'll have my people collect them."

"That would be nice," Wilson said. "Although if everything tied through this central server, it's possible everything got wiped before this got broken up."

"It wasn't just destroyed in the fighting," Lee said.

Wilson shook his head and motioned to the wreckage. "Locked room. No other damage to this part of the hut. And it looked to me like the damage here was methodical. Whoever did it didn't want what was stored on it to get captured."

"But you said the door was locked," Lee said. "Whoever ran over this place didn't stop to check the computer."

"Yeah," Wilson said, and then looked over at Lee. "What about you? Get anything off the bodies?"

"Yeah, once Jefferson figured out what he was doing," Lee said. "Martina and Vasily Ivanovich. In the absence of any other evidence to the contrary, I've nominated them as the two who ran the computers here. I'm having the teams check the other bodies for ID chips, too."

"Anything else but their names?" Wilson asked.

"The usual biometric data," Lee said. "I pinged the *Tub* to see if there was anything in its databases, but there wasn't anything. I wasn't expecting there to be, unless they happened to be ex-CDF."

"Just two more idiots on a spectacularly ill-advised colonization attempt," Wilson said.

"With about a hundred and fifty other idiots," Lee said.

"And thus the Colonial Union is infinitesimally smarter," Wilson said. Lee snorted.

In the distance came the sound of someone retching. Lee craned back to look. "Oh, look, it's Jefferson," she said. "He's popped."

Wilson got up to look. "That took a little bit longer than I expected," he said.

"He's been driving us all a little crazy with the gung ho thing," Lee said.

"He's new," Wilson said.

"Hopefully it wears off," Lee said, "before the rest of us kill him."

Wilson smiled at this and then threaded back through the mess to Jefferson.

"Sorry, sir," he said. He was kneeling by the body of the late Vasily Ivanovich, a puddle of sick off to his side. His other two fire team members had found some other place to be.

"You're hanging out near two partially decomposed, partially eaten bodies," Wilson said. "Being sick is a perfectly rational response."

"If you say so," Jefferson said.

"I do say so," Wilson said. "My first mission, I almost wet myself. Throwing up is fine."

"Thank you, sir," Jefferson said.

Wilson patted Jefferson on the back and glanced over at Vasily Ivanovich. The man was a mess, bloated and with a significant amount of his abdomen chewed away by scavengers. From his vantage point, Wilson could see into the gnawed-on remains of Ivanovich's digestive system.

Inside of which something glinted.

Wilson frowned. "What is that?" he said.

"What is what, sir?" Jefferson asked.

Wilson ignored him and looked closer and then, after a minute, thrust his glove into what remained of Ivanovich's stomach.

Jefferson gagged but didn't have anything else to throw up, so instead he stared openly at the small, glittery thing in Wilson's gore-coated hand. Wilson delicately picked out the thing with his other hand and held it up in the light.

"What is that?" Jefferson asked.

"It's a data card," Wilson said.

"What was it doing in his stomach?" Jefferson asked.

"I have no idea," Wilson said, and then turned his head. "Lee!" he shouted.

"What?" Lee shouted back from the other side of the hut.

"Have your people look for a functioning PDA and bring it to me immediately," he said. "One that takes data cards."

Shortly thereafter, Wilson had jammed the data card

into a handheld and connected his BrainPal to the computer.

"Why would he swallow a data card?" Lee asked, as she watched Wilson.

"He wanted to keep the data out of enemy hands," Wilson said. He was simultaneously going through the file hierarchy on the data card.

"That's why he destroyed the computer and communications equipment," Lee said.

"I'd have more answers for you if you let me actually concentrate on what I'm doing," Wilson said. Lee shut up, slightly annoyed. Wilson ignored this, closed his eyes and focused on his data.

Several minutes later, Wilson opened his eyes and looked at Ivanovich with something that approached wonder.

Lee noticed. "What?" she said. "What is it?"

Wilson looked up at Lee blankly, and then back to Ivanovich, and then at the body of Martina Ivanovich.

"Wilson," Lee said.

"I think we better take back these bodies," Wilson said.

"Why?" Lee asked, looking at the corpses.

"I'm not sure I can tell you," Wilson said. "I don't think you have the clearance."

Lee looked back at Wilson, annoyed.

"It's not about you," Wilson assured her. "I'm pretty confident I don't have the clearance either."

Lee, not precisely satisfied, looked back at the Ivanoviches. "So you want us to haul these up to the *Tub*."

"You don't have to bring all of them," Wilson said.

"Come again?" Lee said.

"You don't have to bring their entire bodies," Wilson said. "Their heads will do just fine."

"You feel it, too, don't you," Abumwe said to Schmidt, during a break in negotiations. The two were in the conference room hallway, drinking the tea Schmidt had gotten them.

"Feel what, ma'am?" Schmidt said.

Abumwe sighed. "Schmidt, if you don't want me to keep believing that you are entirely useless to me, then you have to actually *be* useful to me," she said.

Schmidt nodded. "All right," he said. "There's something not right about Sub-Ambassador Ting."

"That's right," Abumwe said. "Now tell me what that something not right is."

"I don't know," Schmidt said. He saw Abumwe get a look on her face and held up his hand peremptorily. This surprised Abumwe into silence. "Sorry," Schmidt said, hastily. "I say I don't know because I'm not sure what the cause of it is. But I know what the result is. She's being too easy on us in the negotiations. We're getting too many of the things we want from her. We're getting something close to a rubber stamp."

"Yes," Abumwe said. "I'd like to know why."

"Maybe she's just a bad negotiator," Schmidt said.

"The Bula pulled out these parts of the negotiations specifically for more detailed attention," Abumwe said. "This suggests they are not trivial to the Bula. The Bula also aren't known for being pushovers in negotiations. I don't think they'd put a poor negotiator in charge of this part of the process."

"Do we know anything about Ting?" Schmidt asked.

"Nothing Hillary could find," Abumwe said. "The Colonial Union files on diplomatic missions focus on the primary diplomats, not the secondary ones. I have her looking for more, but I don't expect to find too much. In the meantime, what are your suggestions?"

Schmidt took a small moment to internally register surprise that Abumwe was indeed asking for options from him, and then said, "Keep doing what we're doing. We *are* getting what we want from her. The thing we have to worry about at this point is getting them too soon, and getting done before the *Tubingen* finishes her mission."

"I can come up with some reason to suspend negotiations until tomorrow," Abumwe said. "I can ask for some more time to research some particular point. That won't be difficult to do."

"All right," Schmidt said.

"On the subject of the *Tubingen,* any news from your friend?" Abumwe asked.

"I sent him an encrypted note on the next skip drone to the ship," Schmidt said.

"You shouldn't trust our encryption," Abumwe said.

"I don't," Schmidt assured her. "But I think it would have been suspicious for me to send him an unencrypted note, considering the mission. The note itself is innocuous blather, which contains a line that says, 'It was like that time on Phoenix Station.'"

"What does that mean?" Abumwe said.

"Basically it means 'Tell me if something interesting is going on,'" Schmidt said. "He'll understand it."

"Do you want to explain to me how it is the two of you have your own little secret code?" Abumwe said. "Did you make it up together when you were six?"

"Uh," Schmidt said, uncomfortable. "It just sort of came about."

"Really," Abumwe said.

"Harry would see you pissed at me during some negotiation or another and came up with it as a way to let me know he was interested in knowing the details later," Schmidt said, quickly. He looked away as he said it.

"Are you actually that scared of me, Schmidt?" Abumwe said, after a second.

"I wouldn't say 'scared,'" Schmidt said. "I would say I have a healthy respect for your working methods."

"Yes, well," Abumwe said. "For the moment, at least, your terrified obsequiousness is not going to be useful to me. So stop it."

"I'll try," Schmidt said.

"And let me know if you hear from your friend," Abumwe said. "I don't know what Sub-Ambassador Ting is up to, either. It's making me uncomfortable. But I have a worry that somehow that wildcat colony on Wantji is involved. If it is, I want to know how before anyone else."

"You want me to do what?" asked Doctor Tomek. They had taken the entire bodies of the Ivanoviches after all, and both of them were now spread out on examination tables. Doctor Tomek was too much of a professional to register displeasure at the sight and smell of the decayed bodies, but she was not notably pleased with Lieutenant Wilson for bringing them into her medical bay unannounced.

"Scan their brains," Wilson said. "I'm looking for something."

"What are you looking for?" Tomek asked.

"I'll tell you if I find it," Wilson said.

"Sorry, I don't work that way," Tomek said. She glanced over to Lieutenant Lee, who had remained after her soldiers had hauled the Ivanoviches into the medical bay. "Who is this guy?" she asked, pointing at Wilson.

"He's temporarily replacing Mitchusson," Lee said. "We're borrowing him from a diplomatic mission. And there's something else about him."

"What?" Tomek asked.

Lee motioned with her head to Wilson, who took that as his cue.

"I've got top-level security clearance that allows me to order anyone on the ship to do what I want them to do," Wilson said, to Tomek. "It's left over from my last mission. They didn't get around to revoking it from me."

"I've already complained to Captain Augustyn about it," Lee said. "He agrees it's a crock of shit but also that there's nothing we can do about it right now. He'll send a complaint with the next skip drone. Until then, you've got to do what he tells you."

"It's still my medical bay," Tomek said.

"Which is why I'm asking *you* to do the scan," Wilson said, and nodded at the body scanner tucked into a cubbyhole in the back of the medical bay. "I've serviced those, and have trained on them. I could do the scan myself. But you'd do it better. I'm not trying to shut you out, Doctor. But if what I'm looking for isn't actually there, then it's best for everyone if my paranoid delusions are kept to myself."

"And if it is there?" Tomek asked.

"Then things begin to get really complicated," Wilson said. "So let's hope we don't find it."

Tomek glanced back over to Lee, who shrugged. Wilson caught the substance of the shrug. *Humor this idiot,* it said. *We'll be rid of him soon enough.* Well, that worked for him.

Tomek walked over to the cubbyhole and retrieved the scanner and the reflection plate, then came back to the examining table that held Vasily Ivanovich. She donned gloves, gently lifted Ivanovich's head and set the plate behind it.

"Where's the visual going?" Wilson asked. Tomek motioned with her head to the display above the examination table; Wilson turned it on. "Ready when you are," he said. Tomek positioned the scanner, activated it and after a couple of seconds looked up at the display.

"What the hell?" she asked, after a moment.

"Lovely," Wilson said, looking at the display. "And by 'lovely,' I mean 'Oh, crap.'"

"What is it?" Lee asked, coming over to get a better look at the thing Wilson and Tomek were looking at.

"I'll give you a hint," Wilson said. "We've all got one in our head."

"That's a *BrainPal*?" Lee asked, pointing at the screen.

"Got it in one," Wilson said, and leaned in toward the display. "Looks like a little different design than the version I worked on when I was in CDF Research and Development. But it can't be anything else."

"This guy is a civilian," Tomek said. "What the hell is he doing with a BrainPal?"

"Two possible explanations," Wilson said. "One, it's not a BrainPal, and we're looking at a really coincidentally-arranged tumor. Two, our friend Vasily Ivanovich isn't really a civilian. One of these is more likely than the other."

Tomek glanced over at Martina Ivanovich. "What about her?" she asked.

"I suspect they're a matching set," Wilson said. "Shall we find out?"

They were indeed a matching set.

"You know what this means," Tomek said, after she shut off the scanner.

Wilson nodded. "I told you this would get complicated."

Lee looked over at the two of them. "I'm not following."

"We've got BrainPals in the heads of two apparent civilians," Wilson said. "Which means they're probably not civilians. Which suggests this wildcat colony might not be the freelance colonization effort that it's been advertised as being. And now we know why all the computers and records were destroyed by the colonists."

"Except for the data chip you found in this guy," Lee said, pointing to Vasily Ivanovich.

"I don't think he swallowed it to *save* it," Wilson said. "I think he swallowed it because they were being overrun and he didn't have time to destroy it any other way."

"What was on the chip?" Tomek said.

"A bunch of daily status reports," Wilson said. Lee frowned at this, clearly not seeing how that would matter. "It's not what data were on the chip that was important," Wilson continued. "It was the fact that data were saved in a memory structure that's proprietary to Brain-Pals. The fact it exists implies someone was using a Brain-Pal. The fact the BrainPal exists implies this is more than just a wildcat colony."

"We need to tell Captain Augustyn about this," Lee said.

"He's the captain," Tomek said. "He probably already knows."

"If he already knew, he probably wouldn't have let me order you to examine these two," Wilson said. "No matter what my security level. No, I think this is going to be as much of a surprise to him as it is to us."

"So we tell him," Lee said. "We tell him, right?"

"Yes," Wilson said. "He'll send a skip drone detailing what we've found. And I expect that immediately thereafter we'll get new orders, telling us that it's no longer just an extraction job."

"What will it be now?" Lee asked.

"A cover-up," Tomek said, and Wilson nodded. "Destroy any evidence this was anything *but* a wildcat colony."

"We're supposed to be destroying all the evidence anyway," Lee said.

"Not just down *there*," Wilson said. He pointed to the Ivanoviches. "I mean turning these two—and their

BrainPals—into a fine powder. Not to mention obliterating any information on what we just found out, and that data card we found. And if these two really were still active in the CDF, I suspect they'll be posthumously demoted for not blowing their own heads off with a shotgun."

Lee went to speak with Captain Augustyn; Tomek stored the bodies. Wilson wandered toward the officers mess to get a cup of coffee. As he did so, he pinged his BrainPal's message queue and found there was a message there from Hart Schmidt. Wilson smiled and prepared for a delightful dose of Schmidt's special brand of wan neuroticism. He stopped smiling when Hart noted he'd been assigned to be Ambassador Abumwe's right-hand man for the Bula negotiations and that Sub-Ambassador Ting's personality was like that one time on Phoenix Station he and Wilson had met up with that other Bula.

"Shit," Wilson said. There's no way that Hart put *that* phrasing in *that* sentence coincidentally.

Wilson thought about it for several minutes before muttering, "Fuck it," composing a note and encrypting it. Then with his BrainPal he took an image of his coffee, created a steganographic picture with it and the encoded note, addressed it to Hart and sent it off to the data queue for transmission on the next skip drone, which given the bombshell Lee was dropping into Captain Augustyn's lap at the moment would probably go out almost instantly.

Wilson wasn't under the impression that his sleight-of-hand encoding of the message into the image of the coffee would stay unnoticed forever. What he was hoping for was that it would stay encrypted long enough that Hart could do whatever he needed with the information before it got found out.

"Hopefully that won't take too long," Wilson said, to his coffee. His coffee was mute on the subject. Wilson slurped some of it and then called up the data he'd transferred from Vasily Ivanovich's data card into his BrainPal. They were indeed entirely pedestrian reports on colony life, but Wilson had already found something important in there. He didn't want to miss anything else. He suspected he didn't have all that much time left to go through the data before he was ordered to delete all of it.

Schmidt didn't know what strings Ambassador Abumwe had to pull to get her way, but she pulled them. Across the table from her and Schmidt were Anissa Rodabaugh, chief of the mission for the Bula negotiations, Colonel Liz Egan, the liaison between the Colonial Defense Forces and the Department of State, and Colonel Abel Rigney, whose exact position was not known to Hart but whose presence here was nevertheless slightly unsettling. The three of them eyed Abumwe coolly; she returned the favor. No one was paying attention to Schmidt, and he was fine with that.

"We're here," Egan said, to Abumwe. "You have five minutes before you and Ambassador Rodabaugh have to get back to it. So tell us why you so urgently needed to see us all."

"You haven't been entirely forthcoming with me about this wildcat colony on Wantji," Abumwe said. Schmidt noted the clipped tone that Abumwe's voice took on when she was especially irritated; he wondered if it was noticeable to anyone else at the table.

"In what way?" Egan asked.

"In that it's not a wildcat colony at all, it's an under-the-radar Colonial Defense Forces outpost," Abumwe said.

This received about ten seconds of silence, with Rod-abaugh, Egan and Rigney studiously not looking at one another. "I'm not entirely sure why you think that is," Egan said.

"Are we going to waste the next five minutes with this sort of bullshit, Colonel?" Abumwe said. "Or are we actually going to talk about how this is going to affect our negotiations?"

"It's not going to affect the negotiations at all—," Rodabaugh said.

"Really," Abumwe said, cutting her off. Schmidt noted the chagrin on Rodabaugh's face at this, but she and Abumwe were technically of the same diplomatic rank, so there was little she could do about it. "Because, Anissa, I have a Bula sub-ambassador I've been talking to for the last day who I am almost entirely certain knows more about this so-called colony than I do. I think as a result I'm being led down a very short pier. I think when I get pushed off, the entire negotiation is going to go down with me. If I fail at a negotiation because of my own fail-ures, I accept that. If I fail because I'm being screwed by my own side, that I will not accept."

Colonel Rigney, who had been silent to this point, turned to Schmidt. "Your friend Harry Wilson's on the *Tubingen*," he said, to Schmidt. "I just checked through my BrainPal. He's the one who's feeding you informa-tion."

Schmidt opened his mouth, but Abumwe reached out to touch Schmidt on the shoulder. This as much as any-thing else shocked Schmidt into silence; he couldn't re-member another time Abumwe had physically touched him before. "If Hart or Harry Wilson have done any-thing, it's been on my orders," she said.

"You ordered him and Wilson to essentially spy on a Colonial Defense Forces mission," Rigney said.

"I reminded them of their obligation to help me achieve our goals as diplomats," Abumwe said.

"By spying on the Colonial Defense Forces mission," Rigney repeated.

"I appreciate the attempt to run out the clock by distracting me into a side discussion, Colonel Rigney, but let's not," Abumwe said. "I repeat: We have a military mission on a Bula world. I'm almost certain the Bula we are negotiating with are aware of it."

"What's your proof of that?" Rodabaugh asked.

"Nothing hard," Abumwe said. "But I know when people aren't negotiating in good faith."

"That's it?" Rodabaugh said. "You have a *feeling*? You're dealing with an alien species, for Christ's sake. Their whole psychology is entirely different."

"And that doesn't matter at all, because in fact we have an illegal military outpost on this alien species' planet," Abumwe said. "If I am wrong, then we lose nothing. If I am right, however, then we risk the failure of the entire process."

"What do you want from us, Ambassador?" Egan asked Abumwe.

"I want to know what's really going on," Abumwe said. "It's bad enough that I went into negotiations having to deal with the possibility that the Bula would discover we snuck a military ship into their territory to remove an attacked wildcat colony, but at least I could spin that if I had to. There is no way to spin a CDF ship coming to the aid of a covert military installation."

"It wasn't a covert military operation," Rigney said, leaning forward.

This got Egan's attention. "Are you really going to do this, Abel?" she asked, turning to Rigney.

"She already knows more than she should, Liz," Rigney said. "I don't think a little context is going to matter at this point." He turned back to Abumwe. "It really is a wildcat colony," he said.

"A wildcat colony with CDF soldiers in it," Abumwe said. The skepticism in her voice was impossible to miss.

"Yes," Rigney said. "Since the Conclave has restricted us and other unaffiliated species from colonizing, we've been dropping a few CDF members into wildcat colonies. The rest of the colonists don't know. We modify their bodies to look and act like natural human bodies, but keep their BrainPals in. They record data and send it along occasionally. We recruit CDF members with a background in technical work so they usually end up being in control of their colonies' communications systems."

"To what end?" Abumwe asked.

"We want to see how the Conclave responds to wildcat colonies," Rigney said. "Whether it sees them as a threat, whether they respond to them the same way as an official colony, and whether ultimately wildcat colonies—or colonies that give the appearance of being wildcat colonies—are a way we can keep expanding our presence without having a conflict with the Conclave."

"And you thought colonizing a planet already claimed by another species was a smart thing to do," Abumwe said.

Rigney spread his hands. "We don't pick the planets," he said. "We just put our people into the colony undercover."

"How many of your people were on Wantji?" Abumwe asked.

"We typically put in a couple of people," Rigney said. "Most wildcat colonies are small. We'll put in one for every fifty colonists or so." He turned to Schmidt. "How many did your friend Wilson wash up?"

Schmidt glanced over at Abumwe, who nodded. "Two, sir," he said.

"That sounds about right," Rigney said. He settled back in his chair.

"What do we do about this?" Abumwe asked.

"And by 'we,' you mean 'you,' " Rigney said.

"Yes," Abumwe said.

"We don't do anything," Egan said. "The Bula haven't brought it up to us."

"We're not going to be the ones to bring it up to them," Rodabaugh said. "If they do ask about the wildcat colony, then we tell them that as soon as we found out about it, we moved to remove them—so quickly that we didn't ask permission first, so sorry. We'll be out of there before then."

"And if they find out about the CDF members among them?" Abumwe asked.

Rigney pointed at Schmidt. "We have them," he said. "We have them both. More specifically, we have their heads, where their BrainPals are."

Abumwe gawked at the three of them. "You're joking, right?" she said. "The Bula are not that stupid."

"No one said they are stupid," Rigney said. "But all our intelligence suggests that the Bula don't know the wildcat colony was there, and they weren't the ones who attacked it. We're going to proceed with the negotiations as they are."

"And if they ask me directly about it? Contrary to all expectation they might," Abumwe said.

"Then you don't know anything about it," Rodabaugh said.

"To be clear, you're asking me to lie to the Bula," Abumwe said, to Rodabaugh.

"Yes," Rodabaugh said.

"You understand I think this is a bad idea," Abumwe said.

Rodabaugh looked annoyed with Abumwe, but it was Egan who answered. "The directive for this is coming from over all of our heads, Ambassador," she said. "And none of us have the luxury of arguing with it."

"Right," Abumwe said. She got up and walked out of the room without uttering another word.

From their side of the table, Rodabaugh, Egan and Rigney looked over at Schmidt.

"Thanks for coming," he said, tried to smile, and failed.

Harry Wilson entered the bridge of the *Tubingen;* a surprised Captain Jack Augustyn looked up, along with his executive officer and other bridge crew. He gave them a couple of seconds for their BrainPals to register and label him. Then he said, "I think we're in trouble."

Wilson saw Captain Augustyn have an internal debate whether to jump on him for his unconventional entrance and then make a choice, in the space of half a second. "Explain," he said.

"We have a couple of CDF corpses in the meat locker right now," Wilson said.

"Yes," Augustyn said. "So what?"

"I think there should be another one in there," Wilson said.

"Excuse me?" Augustyn said.

"We have two dead CDF," Wilson said. "I think there was another one in the colony. I've been going through Vasily Ivanovich's data. It's where I found the data stored in a BrainPal-readable format. But some of the documents aren't originally Vasily's. Some of them are from Martina Ivanovich, who forwarded them to Vasily using a BrainPal-to-BrainPal protocol. And some of them are from a guy named Drew Talford. Who also sent them BrainPal to BrainPal."

"We have our people on the planet now, identifying the dead," Augustyn said. "They'll find him."

"They *have* found him," Wilson said. "I wouldn't be bothering you with this if I hadn't already checked."

"If they found him, then what's the problem?" asked Selena Yuan, the *Tubingen*'s executive officer.

"They didn't find *all* of him," Wilson said. "He's missing his head."

"I would imagine a lot of the colonists are missing limbs and body parts," Augustyn said. "They were attacked. And it's been a week since the attack, so scavengers have been at them."

"Lots of them are missing body parts," Wilson agreed, and then sent Augustyn and Yuan an image through his BrainPal. "None of the rest of them are missing a body part that's been cleanly separated from the rest of their body."

There was a moment while Augustyn and Yuan examined the picture. "No one's found the head," Augustyn asked, after a minute.

"No," Wilson said. "I've been having them look intensively for a couple of hours. There are bodies missing heads, but the heads are usually found not too far away, or the separation is ragged. This guy's head isn't near the body. It isn't anywhere."

"Some animal could have run off with it," Yuan suggested.

"It's possible," Wilson said. "On the other hand, when the head of a CDF soldier has been cut cleanly from his body and his head is nowhere to be found, I'd suggest it's not prudent to assume some animal is making a snack of it."

"You assume it's been taken by whoever attacked the colony," Augustyn said.

"Yes," Wilson said. "And while I'm at it, I think that whoever told us that the Bula didn't know the colony was here guessed really badly wrong. I think not only did the Bula know it was here, I'd be guessing they're the ones who made the raid. If they didn't know it was here, I'm willing to bet whoever attacked it took that head to the Bula, because evidence of a CDF presence on one of their planets is worth more than a little bit of cash."

"But they couldn't have known about the CDF presence here," Yuan said. "*We* didn't."

"At this point, I don't think it matters if they did *before*," Wilson said. "I think it matters that they do *now*. And if they do now—"

"Then they know we're here now," Augustyn said.

"Right," Wilson said. "In which case it's not the colony that's the CU's biggest diplomatic problem at the moment. It's us."

Augustyn was already ignoring Wilson to focus on contacting his ground forces to get them off the planet.

They'd gotten only about half of them up before six Bula warships skipped above Wantji and trained their weapons, already hot, on the *Tubingen*.

Abumwe's negotiations with Sub-Ambassador Ting were winding down when Schmidt heard a pleasant ping from the sub-ambassador's PDA. Ting excused herself for a moment, picked up the device, appeared to read a note there and performed the Bula equivalent of a smile.

"Good news?" Abumwe asked.

"It might be," Ting said, and set the PDA down. She turned to her assistant, leaned over and spoke quietly into his closest ear. The assistant got up and walked out of the room.

"I apologize, but there are things I will need to conclude our negotiations, and I don't have them with me at the moment," Ting said. "I hope you don't mind waiting a moment while my assistant retrieves them."

"Not at all," Abumwe said.

"Thank you," Ting said. "I think you and I have established a good rapport, Ambassador Abumwe. I wish every negotiating partner I've had could be as pleasant and easy to work with."

"Thank you," Abumwe said. "We have enough issues to deal with without adding unnecessary conflict to the negotiations."

"I agree entirely," Ting said. The door behind her opened and her assistant returned, carrying a medium-sized case, which he set on the table. "And I believe that this common belief will aid us both now."

"What is that?" Abumwe asked, motioning to the case.

"Ambassador, you remember yesterday, when we were talking about Ambassador Zala's appendix," Ting said, ignoring Abumwe's question.

"Yes, of course," Abumwe said.

"I noted to you how it was strange such a small part of a system could threaten the entire health of the whole," Ting said.

"Yes," Abumwe said, looking at the case.

"Then you will understand when I say that what you tell me now, here in our little side room, away from the larger negotiation between the Colonial Union and the Bula, will have an immediate impact on the health of the whole process," Ting said. "I asked for the right to do this, on the grounds that the specifics of our negotiation—the physical visitation of our people between our planets—lent itself to this particular task. All I had to do was wait until we had all the information we needed."

Abumwe smiled. "I'm afraid I'm not entirely following you, Sub-Ambassador Ting."

"I'm very sure that's not true, Ambassador Abumwe," Ting said. "Please tell me what you know about the Colonial Defense Forces presence on Wantji."

"I beg your pardon?" Abumwe said.

"Please tell me what you know about the Colonial Defense Forces presence on Wantji," Ting said.

Schmidt glanced over at his boss and wondered if the tension that he could see in her neck and in her posture would be at all noticeable to an alien not entirely familiar with human physiological cues. "I'm not a member of the Colonial Defense Forces, so I'm not sure that I would be qualified to answer a question about its presence on *any* world," Abumwe said. "But I know people in the CDF who would be better able to answer your question."

"Ambassador, that was a delightfully artful evasion," Ting said. "I couldn't have done it better, were I in your position. But I am afraid I really must insist that you give me a direct answer this time. Please tell me what you know about the Colonial Defense Forces presence on Wantji."

"I can't tell you anything about it," Abumwe said, opening her hands in a *I would help you if I could* gesture.

"'Can't' is a strategically ambiguous word to use here," Ting said. "Can't because you don't know? Or can't because you've been ordered not to say? Perhaps the fault here is mine, Ambassador. I have been too imprecise in what I've been asking. Let me try again. This is a question that you may answer with a 'yes' or a 'no.' Indeed, I must insist that it is answered with a 'yes' or a 'no.' Ambassador Abumwe, are you personally aware that there was a Colonial Defense Forces presence on Wantji?"

"Sub-Ambassador Ting—," Abumwe began.

"Ambassador Abumwe," Ting said, pleasantly but forcefully, "if I do not receive a 'yes' or 'no' answer to my question, I am afraid I will have to suspend our negotiations. If I suspend my negotiations, then my superiors will suspend theirs. The entire process will fail because you have not been able to offer a simple response to a direct question. I believe I am being perfectly clear about this. So, a final time: Are you personally aware that there was a Colonial Defense Forces presence on Wantji?"

"No," Abumwe said. "I am not aware of that."

Ting smiled a Bula smile and opened her hands in a very humanlike gesture, as if saying, *There, see?* "That's all I needed, Ambassador," she said. "A simple answer to a direct question. Thank you. I do apologize for adding this conflict to our negotiations, and especially sorry to do it to you. As I said, I believe we've had excellent rapport up to now."

Schmidt saw the tension drain out of Abumwe's neck and shoulders. "Thank you for your apology, but it's not necessary. I would just like to finish up our work."

"Oh, we have," Ting said, and stood. Abumwe and Schmidt hastily stood with her. "We finished the moment you lied to me."

"When I lied to you," Abumwe said.

"Yes, just now," Ting said. "Bear in mind, Ambassador Abumwe, I am almost entirely certain that you were ordered to lie to me by your superiors. I have negotiated with enough humans to know what someone being ordered to lie looks like. Nevertheless, you *did* just lie to me, and that was the test, to see whether you would or not. You did."

"Sub-Ambassador Ting, I assure you that whatever you believe I know, my actions should not have an effect on the larger negotiations—," Abumwe said.

Ting held up her hand. "I promise you, Ambassador Abumwe, that your people and mine are not done negotiating," she said. "What we are negotiating, however, has changed substantially." She motioned toward the case. "And now, at last, we come to this."

"What is in the case?" Abumwe asked.

"A gift," Ting said. "Of sorts. It's more accurate to say we're returning something that used to belong to the Colonial Defense Forces. It's actually two objects, one inside the other. We considered removing the second from the first, but then we realized that you—humans, not you personally—could argue the first didn't come from the second. So we felt it best to leave it in place."

"You're being vague," Abumwe said.

"Yes," Ting said. "Perhaps I don't want to ruin the surprise. You may open it if you like."

"I think it might be better if I didn't," Abumwe said.

"Your choice," Ting said. "However, I would appreciate it if you convey to your superiors a message I have from my superiors."

"What is it?" Abumwe asked.

"Tell them that after they've opened that case, when we reconvene, the subject of negotiations will be remuneration for the Colonial Union's illegal Colonial Defense Forces presence in our territory," Ting said. "Not only for the illegal settlement on Wantji, but also the warship we've currently in our custody. The *Tubingen*, I believe it is called."

"You've attacked the *Tubingen*?" Schmidt said, and immediately regretted the lapse.

"No," Ting said, turning to Schmidt, amused. "But we're not letting it go anywhere, either. Its crew will be returned to you eventually. Our new round of negotiations, I believe, will set the price for the return of the ship itself." She turned back to Abumwe. "You may tell your superiors that as well, Ambassador Abumwe."

Abumwe nodded.

Ting smiled and gathered up her PDA. "And so farewell, Ambassador Abumwe, Mr. Schmidt. Perhaps your next set of negotiations will fare better for you." She left the room, followed by her assistant. The case was left on the table.

Abumwe and Schmidt looked at it. Neither made a move to open it.

A Voice in the Wilderness

Albert Birnbaum, the "Voice in the Wilderness" and once the fourth most popular audio talk show host in the United States, told his car to ring his producer. "Are the numbers in?" he asked when she answered, not bothering to introduce himself, because, well. Aside from the caller ID, she would know who he was the second he opened his mouth.

"The numbers are in," Louisa Smart said, to Birnbaum. He imagined her at her desk, headset on, mostly because he almost never saw her in any other context.

"How are they?" Birnbaum asked. "Are they good? Are they better than last month? Tell me they are better than last month."

"Are you sitting down?" Smart asked.

"I'm *driving,* Louisa," Birnbaum said. "Of *course* I'm sitting down."

"You're not supposed to be driving yourself," Smart reminded him. "You've had your manual driving license pulled. If you get pulled over and they check your car's trip monitor and see you have the autodrive off, you're going to get it."

"You're my producer, Louisa," Birnbaum said. "Not my mom. Now quit stalling and give me the numbers."

Smart sighed. "You're down twelve percent from last month," she said.

"What? *Bullshit,* Louisa," Birnbaum said.

"Al, why the hell would I lie to you?" Smart asked. "You think I *like* listening to you panic?"

"That's gotta be bullshit," Birnbaum continued, ignoring Smart's comment. "There's no possible way we can lose one listener in eight in a single goddamn month."

"I don't make up the numbers, Al," Smart said. "I just tell you what they are."

Birnbaum said nothing for a few seconds. Then he started hitting his dashboard, making him swerve on the road. "Shit!" he said. "Shit shit fuck shit shit shittity shit!"

"Sometimes it's amazing to me that you talk for a living," Smart said.

"I'm off the clock," Birnbaum said. "I'm allowed to be inarticulate on my own time."

"These numbers mean that you're down by a third for the year," Smart said. "You're going to miss your ad guarantees. Again. That means we're going to have to do another set of make-goods. Again."

"I know how it works, Louisa," Birnbaum said.

"It means we're going to finish the quarter in the red," Smart said. "That's two quarters out of the last three we're down. You know what *that* means."

"It doesn't mean anything other than we make sure we're in the black next quarter," Birnbaum said.

"Wrong again," Strong said. "It means that Walter puts you on his watch list. And when Walter puts you on the watch list, you're one step away from cancellation. Then that 'Voice in the Wilderness' bit of yours won't just be a clever affectation. You really will be out in the cold."

"Walter's not going to cancel me," Birnbaum said. "I'm his favorite talk show host."

"You remember Bob Arrohead? The guy you replaced? He was Walter's favorite, too," Smart said. "And then he had three bad quarters in a row and he was out on his ass. Walter didn't build a multibillion media empire by being sentimental about his favorites. He'd cancel his grandmother if she had three red quarters in a row."

"I could make it alone if I had to," Birnbaum said. "Run a lean, mean operation on my own. It's totally possible."

"That's what Bob Arrohead does now," Smart said. "You should ask him how that's working out for him. If you can find him. If you can find anyone who knows how to find him."

"Yes, but he doesn't have *you*," Birnbaum said. He was not above base flattery.

And Smart was not above throwing it back in his face. "And if you get canceled and leave SilverDelta, neither will you," she said. "My contract is with the company, not with you, Al. But thank you so much for the attempted head pat. Where are you, anyway?"

"I'm heading to Ben's soccer match," Birnbaum said.

"Your kid's soccer match doesn't start until four thirty, Al," Smart said. "You need to lie better to someone who has your calendar up on her screen. You're going off to meet the groupie you met at the Broadcasters Association meeting, aren't you?"

"I don't know who you're talking about," Birnbaum said.

Smart sighed, and then Birnbaum heard her count to five, quietly. "You know what? You're right. I'm not your mother," she said. "You want to bang some groupie, *again*, fine with me. Just bear in mind that Walter is not going to be as free with the hush money when you're two quarters in the red as he was when you were his top earner. And remember that you have no prenup, and Judith, unlike your second wife, is *not* stupid, but *you* might be, which is how she maneuvered you into not having a prenup. I hope the validation of your middle-aged ego and three minutes of exercise is worth it."

"I treasure these calls, Louisa," Birnbaum said. "Especially your subtle digs at my sexual technique."

"Spend less time banging groupies and more time on your show, Al," Smart said. "You're not fading because your politics have suddenly gotten unpopular. You're fading because you're getting lazy and bored. You get lazy and bored in this business, and guess what? You're out of the business. And then the groupies dry up."

"Thanks for *that* image," Birnbaum said.

"I'm not kidding, Al," Smart said. "You got a quarter to turn it around. You know it and so do I. You better get to work." She disconnected.

They caught up to him as he was heading out of the lobby of the hotel. "Mr. Birnbaum," the young man said to him.

Birnbaum held up his hand and tried to keep walking. "Can't sign autographs now," he said. "I'm going to be late for my kid's soccer match."

"I'm not here for an autograph," the young man said to him. "I'm here with a business proposition."

"You can direct those to my manager," Birnbaum said, yelling back to the young man as he blew past. "That's what I pay Chad to do: field business propositions."

"Down twelve percent this month, Mr. Birnbaum?" the young man called out to him as he headed into the revolving door.

Birnbaum took the entire circuit of the revolving door and came back to the young man. "Excuse me?" he said.

"I said, 'Down twelve percent?'" the young man said.

"How do you know about my numbers?" Birnbaum said. "That's proprietary information."

"A talk show host who spends as much time as you do linking to leaked documents and video shouldn't need to ask a question like that," the young man said. "How I know your numbers isn't really the important thing here, Mr. Birnbaum. The important thing here is how I can help you get those numbers up."

"I'm sorry, I have no idea who you are," Birnbaum said. "As a corollary to that, I have no idea why I should care about or listen to you."

"My name is Michael Washington," the young man said. "On my own, I am no one you should particularly care about. The people who I represent, you might want to listen to."

"And who are they?" Birnbaum said.

"A group who knows the advantage of a mutually beneficial relationship," Washington said.

Birnbaum smiled. "That's it? Are you serious? A shadowy, mysterious group? Look, Michael, I may get traction on conspiracy theories from time to time—they're fun and the listeners love 'em. It doesn't mean I think they actually exist."

"They're neither shadowy nor mysterious," Washington said. "They simply prefer to remain anonymous at this point."

"How nice for them," Birnbaum said. "When they're serious about whatever thing it is they want, and they have *names,* they can talk to Chad. Otherwise you're wasting my time and theirs."

Washington offered Birnbaum his card. "I understand entirely, Mr. Birnbaum, and apologize for taking up your time. However, once you have your meeting with Walter tomorrow, if you change your mind, here's how you can reach me."

Birnbaum didn't take the card. "I don't have a meeting scheduled with Walter tomorrow," he said.

"Just because you don't have it scheduled doesn't mean you're not going to have it," Washington said. He waggled the card slightly.

Birnbaum left without taking it and without looking back at Washington.

He was late for Ben's soccer match. Ben's team lost.

Birnbaum wrapped up his morning show and was texting his new toy about the possibility of another hotel get-together when he looked up from his PDA and saw Walter Kring, all six feet ten inches of him, standing right in front of him.

"Walter," Birnbaum said, trying not to lose composure at the sight of his boss.

Kring nodded toward Birnbaum's PDA. "Sending a message to Judith?" he asked.

"Pretty much," Birnbaum said.

"Good," Kring said. "She's a great lady, Al. Smartest thing you ever did was marry her. You'd be an idiot to mess with that. You can tell her I said so."

"I'll do that," Birnbaum said. "What brings you down here to the salt mines today, Walter?" SilverDelta's recording studios were on the first two floors of the company's Washington, D.C., building; Walter's offices took up the whole of the fourteenth floor and had a lift to the roof for his helicopter, which he used daily to commute from Annapolis. The CEO of SilverDelta rarely dropped below the tenth floor on any given day.

"I'm firing someone," Kring said.

"Pardon?" Birnbaum's mouth puckered up as if he'd sucked on a block of alum.

"Alice Valenta," Kring said. "We just got the numbers in for the quarter. She's been down too long and she's not coming back up. Time to move on. And you know how I feel about these things, Al. Firing people isn't something you farm out. You should be able to shoot your own dog, you should be able to fire your own people. It's respectful."

"I agree entirely," Birnbaum said.

"I know you do," Kring said. "It's Leadership 101."

Birnbaum swallowed and nodded, suddenly having nothing to say.

"I'm just glad you haven't made me come down here on your behalf, Al," Kring said, leaning over him in a way that he probably couldn't help, being two meters tall, but which made Birnbaum impressively aware just how much he was the beta dog in this particular situation. It took actual force of will not to avert his eyes. "You wouldn't do that to me, would you?" Kring said.

"Of course not, Walter," Birnbaum said. He actually turned on his performance voice to say it, because if he used his normal voice, it would have cracked.

Kring straightened up and clasped Birnbaum on the shoulder. "That's what I like to hear. We should do lunch sometime. It's been far too long."

"I'd like that," Birnbaum lied.

"Fine," Kring said. "I'll have Jason set it up. Sometime next week, probably."

"Great," Birnbaum said.

"Now, you'll have to excuse me, Al," Kring said. "Not every meeting I'm having today is going to be as nice as the one we're having." Birnbaum nodded his assent and Kring wandered off without another word, down the hall to Studio Eight, soon to be Alice Valenta's former work space.

Birnbaum waited until Kring was out of sight and simultaneously exhaled and shuddered. He reached into his pants pocket, ostensibly to retrieve his vehicle fob but in reality to check if he had spotted himself.

Birnbaum's PDA vibrated, alerting him to an incoming text. It read, *When do you want to meet?* Birnbaum started writing back that under further consideration, another hotel meet-up wouldn't work this week, when he realized the text hadn't come from his new toy. He backtracked the text.

Who is this? he wrote, and sent.

It's Michael Washington, was the reply.

How do you know this PDA? Birnbaum sent. It was his private PDA; he was under the impression that the only people who knew the number were Judith, Ben, Louisa Smart and the new toy.

The same way I knew which hotel you were at with that woman who is not your wife, said the response. *You should focus less on that and more on how to save your job, Mr. Birnbaum. Do you want to meet?*

He did.

They met at Bonner's, which was the sort of wood-paneled bar that people making entertainment shows used when politicians had meetings with shadowy figures.

"Before we do or say anything else, I need to know how you know so much about me," Birnbaum said as Washington sat in his booth, not even bothering with the pleasantries. "You know both my personal and professional business in a way no one else in the world knows or should know."

"Louisa Smart knows," Washington said, mildly.

"So you're getting the information from her?" Birnbaum said. "You're paying my producer to spy on me? Is that it?"

"No, Mr. Birnbaum," Washington said. "After ten years you should know your producer better than that."

"Then how are you doing it? Are you with the government? Our government? Someone else's?" Birnbaum unconsciously slipped into his paranoid rhetoric mode, which brought him much fame in earlier years. "How extensive is the surveillance web on me? Are you monitoring people other than me? How high up does this go? Because I swear to you, I will follow up on this, as far up as it goes. At the risk to *my own life and freedom.*"

"Do you really believe there is a government conspiracy against you, Mr. Birmbaum?" Washington said.

"You tell *me*," Birnbaum said.

Washington held out his PDA. "Your PDA," he said.

"What about my PDA?" Birnbaum said.

"Give it to me for a moment, please," Washington said.

"You bugged my PDA?" Birnbaum exclaimed. "You're tapped into the network at the root!"

"Your PDA, please," Washington said, still extending his hand. Birnbaum gave it to him, with some trepidation. Washington took it, made a few wiping motions, pressed the screen and then handed it back to Birnbaum. He looked at it, confused.

"You're showing me the *Voice in the Wilderness* 'gram," he said.

"Yes," Washington said. "The free 'gram you give out so people can listen to your show and then send text or voice comments, along with location tags so you know where the comments are from, geographically, when you read or play them on air. Which means your 'gram has the ability to send and receive audio and also track your movements. And because you had it built cheaply by flat-rate coders who make their money banging out 'grams like yours fast and sloppy, it's incredibly easy to hack into."

"Wait," Birnbaum said. "You used *my own* 'gram against me?"

"Yes," Washington said. "You get what you pay for with coders, Mr. Birnbaum."

"What about Walter?" Birnbaum said. "You said I would have a meeting with him and I did. How did you know that?"

"The monthly numbers were in," Washington said. "The quarter was ending. There were show hosts who have been lagging. Kring is famous for firing people face-to-face. So I made a guess. Work the odds, Mr. Birnbaum, on the chance you might see Walter Kring today. And since I put the suggestion into your head that you'd have a meeting, any encounter you might have would qualify. After that, it just took monitoring your PDA to catch you after the 'meeting' took place."

Birnbaum put his PDA away, a certain look on his face.

Washington caught it. "You're disappointed, aren't you," he said. "That I'm *not* from the government. That there's not a global conspiracy following you."

"Don't be stupid," Birnbaum said. "I already told you that I don't personally go in for that stuff." His expression was unchanged.

"I do apologize," Washington said. "I'm sorry I'm not more nefarious or well connected into the murky corners of national and global politics."

"Then who are you?" Birnbaum said.

"As I've told you before, I represent a group who wants to offer you a solution to your current set of problems," Washington said.

Birnbaum almost asked, *Who are your clients, really?* but was distracted by what Washington said. "And what exactly is my problem?"

"Namely, that you're shedding listeners at an accelerating rate on your way to becoming a has-been in the national political conversation," Washington said.

Birnbaum thought about arguing that assertion but realized that would not actually get him any answers, so he let it go. "And how do your friends propose to fix that?" he asked instead.

"By suggesting a topic for you to consider," Washington said.

"Is this a bribe?" Birnbaum asked. "A payment for espousing a certain view? Because I don't do that." He had in fact done it, once or twice or ten or more times, in deals that were in point of fact often negotiated at Bonner's. Birnbaum squared it with his morals by figuring they were usually things he was likely to say anyway, so what he was doing was merely illegal, not unethical. However, one always led with being nonbribable. It gave those attempting to bribe a sense of accomplishment.

"There is no money to be exchanged," Washington said.

Birnbaum made that face again. Washington laughed. "Mr. Birnbaum, you have more than enough money. For now, at least. What my clients are offering is something much more valuable: the ability to not only climb back up to the position of fame and personal power that you held not too long ago, but to exceed it. You were the number four audio talker in the land once, although not for very long. My clients are offering you a chance to go to number one and stay there, for as long as you want to be there."

"And how are they going to manage that?" Birnbaum wanted to know.

"Mr. Birnbaum, I assume, given your profession, you know who William Randolph Hearst was," Washington said.

"He was a newspaper publisher," Birnbaum said. That was the extent of his knowledge; Birnbaum's knowledge of American history was solid regarding the founding and the last fifty years, and everything else was a bit of a blank.

"Yes," Washington said. "A newspaper publisher. In the late 1800s the United States and Spain were warming up for a war over Cuba, and Hearst sent an illustrator to Cuba to make pictures of the event. When the illustrator got there, he sent a telegram to Hearst saying that as far as he could see, there was no war coming and that he was going home. Hearst sent back that he should stay and said, 'You furnish the pictures, and I will furnish the war.' And he did."

Birnbaum looked at Washington blankly.

"Mr. Birnbaum, my clients need someone to furnish the pictures, as it were," Washington said. "Someone to start a discussion. Once the discussion starts, my clients can take care of the rest. But it has to start and it has to start somewhere other than with my clients."

"I furnish the pictures and they will furnish the war," Birnbaum said. "What's the war, here?"

"Not a real war," Washington said. "And indeed, what you'd be saying could prevent a real war."

Birnbaum thought about this. "No money, though," he said.

Washington smiled. "No," he said. "Just audience, fame and power. Money often follows those, however."

"And you can guarantee the first three," Birnbaum said.

"Furnish the pictures, Mr. Birnbaum," Washington said, "and the war comes. Pretty damn quickly, too, I would add."

Birnbaum's opportunity to furnish the pictures came the very next day.

"Can we talk about world government?" Jason from Canoga Park was saying to Birnbaum. Jason from Canoga Park was one of Birnbaum's most reliable listeners in that sooner or later everything came back to world government, the fear of world government and how whatever topic was the subject of discussion would eventually lead to world government. You could set your world government clock by Jason from Canoga Park.

"I love talking about world government, Jason, you know that," Birnbaum said, more or less on automatic. "How is it coming this time?"

"Well, it's obvious, isn't it?" Jason said. "Right now the big discussion is whether or not we should resume diplomatic relations with the Colonial Union. Note the 'we' there, Al. It's not 'we' as in 'we the United States,' is it? No, it's not. It's 'we' as in 'we the people of Earth.' Which just means 'we the world government of Earth, which is being constituted in secret, right under your nose.' Every day we talk about relations with the Colonial Union, every day we discuss whether to send diplomats to the Colonial Union, is a day the tentacles of the world government constrict further on the throat of individual freedom, Al."

"It's a compelling point, Jason," Birnbaum said, using the phrase that in his mind meant *You are completely full of shit, but arguing with you would be pointless, so I am going to change the subject on you,* "and you bring up a topic which has been on my mind a lot recently, which is the Colonial Union. Have you been following the official narrative on the CU, Jason?"

"As it relates to world government?" Jason asked.

"Sure," Birnbaum said, "and every other topic, too. The official narrative, the one the government is fronting and all the other governments fell in line behind, is that for—what? two hundred years?—the Colonial Union has been holding back the people of Earth. It's been keeping us from leaving the planet except under its own terms, using us to farm soldiers and colonists, and keeping us down by not sharing its technology and understanding of our place in the universe. And you know what, Jason? Despite everything this particular administration in Washington has been wrong about over the last six years, and there's been a *lot,* that's fair. Those are fair points to make.

"But they're also the *wrong* points to make. They are the *myopic* points to make. They are—should we say it? dare we say it? let's go ahead and say it—they are the *politically advantageous* points for this administration to make. Look at the facts. What's the U.S. economic growth been for the last three or four years? Come on, people, it's been in the Dumpster. You know this. I know this. Everyone knows this. And why has it been in the Dumpster? Because of the economic policies of this administration, hundreds of millions of decent Americans, the ones that wake up every morning and go to work and do what they're supposed to do, do what we ask them to do—people like you and me, Jason—well . . . we're hurting, aren't we? We are. Every day of the year.

"Now we come to the point where our beloved leader, the resident in the White House, can no longer hide under the canard of a so-called global economic downturn, and has to face the music with the American people about his policies. And then, like a miracle from the skies, here comes John Perry and that Conclave fleet, telling us that the Colonial Union, *not* the president, *not* the administration's policies, *not* the so-called global recession, is the root of our woes. How *convenient* for our beloved leader, don't you think, Jason?"

By this time, Louisa Smart was tapping on the glass from the control room. Birnbaum looked over. *What the hell?* Smart mouthed silently. Birnbaum held up his hands placatingly, to say, *Don't worry, I've got this.*

"I'm not sure what this has to do with the world government," Jason said, doubtfully.

"Well, it's got *everything* to do with the world government, doesn't it, Jason?" Birnbaum said. "For the last several months we're not talking about anything *but* the Colonial Union, and what we should do concerning the Colonial Union, and what we should do about the Colonial Union, and whether it can be trusted. Every day we talk about the Colonial Union is a day that we don't talk about our own needs, our own problems, and the faults of our own government—and the current administration. I say it's time to change the discussion. I say it's time to change the official narrative. I say it's time to get to the truth, rather than the spin.

"And here's the truth. I'm going to give it to you now. And it's not going to be popular because it's going to run maybe a little counter to what the official narrative is, and we know how protective the administration and its little enablers in the media are about the official narrative, don't we? But here's the truth, and just, you know, try it on for size and see how you like the fit.

"The Colonial Union? It's the best thing that ever happened to the planet Earth. Hands down, no contest, no silver or bronze. Yes, it kept the Earth in its own protective bubble. But have you seen the reports? In our local neighborhood of space, there are, what? Six hundred intelligent alien species, almost all of whom have attacked humans in some way, including John Perry's hallowed Conclave, which would have wiped out a whole planetary colony if the Colonial Union hadn't stopped them? If you think they would wipe out a colony, what makes you think any of them would spare the Earth if they thought we were important?

"And you say, Well, fine, the Colonial Union kept us *safe,* but it also kept space from us Earthlings unless we became soldiers or colonists. But think about what that means—it means every person who went into space from Earth filled a role designed to protect humanity out there in the stars, or to build humanity's place in the stars. You know that I take no backseat to anyone in my praise and honor of those who serve this nation in uniform. Why should I do any less for those who serve in a uniform that protects all of humankind, including those of us here on Earth? Our people—*Earthlings,* ladies and gentlemen—are the ones the Colonial Union turns to when it comes time to keep us *all* alive. The official narrative calls it *slavery.* I call it *duty.* When I turn seventy-five, do I want to sit here on Earth in a rocking chair, napping my days away until I kick off? Hell, no! Paint me green and put me in space! This administration isn't *protecting* me from the Colonial Union by keeping me or anyone else from joining the Colonial Defense Forces. It's *threatening the survival of all of us* by starving the one organization designed to keep all of us safe!

"And I know there are still some of you out there clinging to the official narrative, saying to me, Well, it kept us down technologically and socially, didn't it? I ask you, did it? Did it really? Or did it make it so that we, out of all humans anywhere, are the ones totally technologically self-sufficient? We don't have the advantage of seeing how other alien races do things. If we want something, we have to build it ourselves. We have a knowledge base no other species can hope to match because they spend all their time poaching technology from everyone else! And far from controlling us, the Colonial Union left us here on Earth alone to pursue our own political and national destinies. Jason, do you think that if the Colonial Union hadn't had our backs all this time, that we could have avoided a world government? That people wouldn't have been screaming for a world government in the face of almost certain alien race subjugation?"

"Uh—," Jason began.

"You know they would have," Birnbaum continued. "And maybe some people want the same government here that they have in Beijing and New Delhi and Cairo and Paris, but I don't. Are we so naïve as to believe the world government that we have would be like the one right here in America? Hell, this administration has been busy enough trying to trade in our rights to make us more like everyone else!

"So I say, throw out the official narrative, people. Get with the truth. The truth is, the Colonial Union hasn't been keeping us down. It's been keeping us free. The longer we delude ourselves into thinking otherwise, the closer we are to doom as a species. And maybe I don't have all the answers—I'm just a guy talking on a show, after all—but I do know that at the end of the day, humanity needs to fight to stay alive in the universe. I want to stand with the fighters. Where do you stand, people? That's the question I want to talk about when we come back from the commercial break. Jason from Canoga Park, thanks for calling in."

"I have one more point—"

Birnbaum closed the circuit and shut Jason down, then threw to Louisa Smart for the commercials.

"Okay, seriously, what the hell was *that*?" Smart said, over the headset. "Since when do you have a bug in your ass about the Colonial Union?"

"You said you wanted me to spend more time thinking about how to turn the show around," Birnbaum said.

"You think championing the group that's been pissing on Earth for two hundred years is a winning strategy for that?" Smart said. "I question your judgment, more than I usually do."

"Trust me, Louisa," Birnbaum said. "This is going to work."

"You don't actually believe what you just spouted, do you?" Smart said.

"If it gets the numbers up, I believe every goddamned word of it," Birnbaum said. "And for the sake of your job, Louisa, so should you."

"I have a job whether you're here or not," Smart reminded him. "So I think I'll keep my own opinion out of the 'sale' rack, if it's all the same to you." She looked down at her monitor and made a face.

"What is it?" Birnbaum asked.

"It looks like you pinked *somebody*," Smart said. "I've got a caller here from Foggy Bottom. It's not every day we have someone from the State Department calling in, that's for sure."

"Are we sure it's from the State Department?" Birnbaum asked.

"I'm checking the name right now," Smart said. "Yup. It's a deputy undersecretary for space affairs. Small fry in the grand scheme of things."

"Doesn't matter," Birnbaum said. "Get him on when we come back. I'm going to light him up."

"Her," Smart said.

"Whatever," Birnbaum said, and girded himself for battle.

Having furnished the pictures, Birnbaum fully expected Washington's clients to furnish a war. What he wasn't expecting was a blitzkrieg.

Birnbaum's show numbers for the day were actually about 1 percent below average; fewer than a million people heard his rant live, streamed to the listening implement of their choice. Within ten minutes of the rant, however, the archived version of the rant started picking up listeners. Relatively slowly at first, the archived version's numbers began to climb as more political sites linked in. Within two hours, the archived version reached another million people. Within three, it was two million. Within four, four million. The show archive's hits grew at a roughly geometric rate for several hours afterward. Overnight there were seven million downloads of the *Voice in the Wilderness* PDA 'gram. By the next day's show—a show devoted entirely to the subject of the Colonial Union, as were the next several shows—the live audience was 5.2 million. By the end of the week, it was twenty million live streams per show.

Like a crack in an overburdened dam, Birnbaum's pro–Colonial Union rant created a rapid collapse in a polite silence from various political quarters, followed by a

swamping flood of agreement with Birnbaum's vituper-
ation for the current administration position of holding
the Colonial Union at arm's length. Birnbaum had occupied a sweet spot in the media discourse—not so in-
fluential that he was unable to promote a potentially
unpopular (and possibly crazy) theory, but not so ob-
scure that he could be dismissed outright as a kook. Too
many Washington insiders, politicians and journalists
knew him too well for that.

The administration, wholly unprepared for the tsunami
of opposing views on this particular topic, flubbed its immediate response to Birnbaum and his followers, beginning with the unfortunately clueless deputy undersecretary
for space affairs who had called in to Birnbaum's show,
who was so thoroughly dismantled by Birnbaum that
three days later she tendered her resignation and headed
to her home state of Montana, where she would eventually become a high school history teacher.

At least she was well out of it. The government's response was so poorly done that for several days its hapless
handling of the event threatened to eclipse the discussion
of the Colonial Union itself.

Threatened but did not eclipse, in part because Birnbaum, who knew a good break when he saw one, simply
wouldn't let it. From his newly elevated vantage point,
Birnbaum dispensed opinion, gathered useful tidbits of
information from insiders who, two weeks before,
wouldn't have given him the time of day, and set the daily
agenda for discussion on the topic of the Colonial Union.

Others attempted to seize the issue from him, of course.
Rival talk show hosts, stunned by his sudden ascendancy,
claimed the Colonial Union topic for their own but could
not match his head start; even the (formerly) more influ-
ential show hosts looked like also-rans on the subject.
Eventually, all but the most oblivious of them ceded
supremacy on the topic to him and focused on other

subjects. Politicians would try to change the subject; Birnbaum would either get them on the show to serve his purposes or harangue them when they wouldn't set foot into his studio.

Either way the subject was his, and he milked it for all it was worth, carefully tweaking his message for states- manlike effect. No, of course the Colonial Union should not be excused for keeping us in the dark, he would say, but we have to understand the context in which that decision was made. No, we should never be subjugated to the Colonial Union or be just another colony in their union, he'd say other times, but there were distinct ad- vantages in an alliance of equal partners. Of course we should consider the Conclave's positions and see what advantages talking to it holds for us, he'd say still other times, but should we also forget we are human? To whom, at the end of the day, do we truly owe our allegiance, if not our own species?

Every now and again, Louisa Smart would ask him if he truly believed the things he was saying to his new, widely expanded audience. Birnbaum would refer her to his original answer to the question. Eventually Smart stopped asking.

The new monthlies came in. Live audience of the show was up 2,500 percent. Archived show up a similar num- ber. Forty million downloads of the PDA 'gram. Birn- baum called his agent and told her to renegotiate his latest contract with SilverDelta. She did, despite the fact it had been negotiated less than two years earlier. Walter Kring might have been a six-foot-ten-inch alpha male right through to his bones, but he was strangely terrified of Monica Blaustein, persistent Jewish grandmother from New York, five feet tall in her flats. He could also read a ratings sheet and knew a gold mine when he saw it.

Birnbaum's life became the show and sleeping. His thing on the side, miffed at the inattention, dropped him.

His relationship with Judith, his third wife, the smart one, the one who had maneuvered him out of the pre-nup, became commensurately better in nearly all respects. His son Ben's soccer team actually won a soccer game. Birnbaum didn't feel he could really take credit for that last one.

"This isn't going to last," Smart pointed out to him two months into the ride.

"What is it with you?" Birnbaum asked her. "You're a downer."

"It's called being a realist, Al," she said. "I'm delighted that everything's coming up roses for you at the moment. But you're a single-issue show right now. And no matter what, the fact is this issue is going to get solved one way or another in the not-all-that-distant future. And then where will you be? You will be last month's fad. I know you have a shiny new contract and all, but Kring will still cut your ass if you have three bad quarters in a row. And now, for better or worse, you have much, much further to fall."

"I like that you think I don't know that," Birnbaum said. "Fortunately for the both of us, I am taking steps to deal with that."

"Do tell," Smart said.

"The Rally," Birnbaum said, making sure the capital "R" was evident in his voice.

"Ah, the rally," Smart said, omitting the capital. "This is the rally on the Mall in support of the Colonial Union, which you have planned for two weeks from now."

"Yes, that one," Birnbaum said.

"You'll note that the subject of the rally is the Colonial Union," Smart said. "Which is to say, that single issue that you're not branching out from."

"It's not what the Rally is about," Birnbaum said. "It's who is going to be there with me. I've got both the Senate majority leader and House minority leader up there on the stage with me. I've been cultivating my relationships with them for the last six weeks, Louisa. They've been feeding me all sorts of information, because we have midterms coming up. They want the House back and I'm going to be the one to get it for them. So after the Rally, we begin the shift away from the Colonial Union and back to matters closer to home. We'll ride the Colonial Union thing as long as we can, of course. But this way, when that horse rides into the sunset I'm still in a position to influence the political course of the nation."

"As long as you don't mind being a political party's cabana boy," Smart said.

"I prefer 'unofficial agenda setter' myself," Birnbaum said. "And if I deliver this election, then I think I'll be able to call myself something else. It's all upside."

"Is this the part where I stand at your side as you roll into Rome in triumph, whispering 'Remember thou art mortal' into your ear?" Smart asked.

"I don't entirely get the reference," Birnbaum said. His world history knowledge was marginally worse than his United States history knowledge.

Smart rolled her eyes. "Of course not," she said. "Remember it anyway, Al. It might come in handy one day."

Birnbaum made a note to remember it but forgot because he was busy with his show, the Rally and everything that would follow after it. It came back to him briefly on the day of the Rally, when, after stirring fifteen-minute speeches from the House minority leader and the Senate majority leader, Birnbaum ascended the podium and stood at the lectern on the stage of the Rally, looking out at a sea of seventy thousand faces (fewer than the one hundred thousand faces they had been hoping for, but more than enough, and anyway they'd round up because it was all estimates in any event). The faces, mostly male, mostly middle-aged, looked up at him with admiration and fervor and the knowledge that they were part of something bigger, something that he, Albert Birnbaum, had started.

Remember thou art mortal, Birnbaum heard Louisa Smart say in his head. He smiled at it; Louisa wasn't at the Rally because of a wedding. He'd rib her about it later. Birnbaum brought up his notes on the lectern monitor and opened his mouth to speak and then was deeply confused when he was facedown on the podium, gasping like a fish and feeling sticky from the blood spurting out of what remained of his shoulder. His ears registered a crack, as if distant thunder were finally catching up with lightning, then he heard screams and the sound of seventy thousand panicked people trying to run, and then blacked out.

Birnbaum looked up and saw Michael Washington looking down at him.

"How did you get in here?" Birnbaum asked, after he had taken a couple of minutes to remember who he was (Albert Birnbaum), where he was (Washington Sacred Heart Catholic Hospital), what time it was (2:47 a.m.) and why he was there (he'd been shot).

Washington pointed with a gloved hand to the badge on his chest, and Birnbaum realized Washington was in a police uniform. "That's not real," Birnbaum protested.

"Actually it is," Washington said. "I usually work plain clothes, but this was useful for the moment."

"I thought you were some sort of *facilitator,*" Birnbaum said. "You have *clients.*"

"I am and I do," Washington said. "Some cops tend bar on the side. This is what I do."

"You're joking," Birnbaum said.

"That's entirely possible," Washington said.

"Why are you here now?" Birnbaum asked.

"Because we have unfinished business," Washington said.

"I don't know what you're talking about," Birnbaum said. "You asked me to pimp a pro–Colonial Union story. I did that."

"And you did a fine job with it," Washington said. "Although at the end things were beginning to flag. You had fewer people at your rally than you had anticipated."

"We had a hundred thousand," Birnbaum said, weakly.

"No," Washington said. "But I appreciate you making the effort there."

Birnbaum's mind began to wander, but he focused on Washington again. "So what unfinished business do we have?" he asked.

"You dying," Washington said. "You were supposed to have been assassinated at the rally, but our marksman didn't make the shot. He blamed it on a gust of wind between him and the target. So it fell to me."

Birnbaum was confused. "Why do you want me dead? I did what you asked."

"And again, you did a fine job," Washington said. "But now the discussion needs to be brought to another level. Making you a martyr to the cause will do that. Nothing like a public assassination to embed the topic into the national consciousness."

"I don't understand," Birnbaum said, increasingly confused.

"I know," Washington said. "But you never understood, Mr. Birnbaum. You didn't want to understand all that much, I think. You never even really cared who I worked for. All you were interested in was what I was dangling in front of you. You never took your eyes off that."

"Who *do* you work for?" Birnbaum croaked.

"I work for the Colonial Union, of course," Washington said. "They needed some way to change the conversation. Or, alternately, I work for Russians and the Brazilians, who are upset that the United States is taking the lead in the international discussions about the Colonial Union and wanted to disrupt its momentum. No, I work for the political party not in the White House, who was looking to change the election calculus. Actually, all of those were lies: I work for a cabal who wants to form a world government."

Birnbaum bulged his eyes at him, disbelieving.

"The time to have demanded an answer was before you took the job, Mr. Birnbaum," Washington said. "Now you'll never know." He held up a syringe. "You woke up because I injected you with this. It's shutting down your nervous system as we speak. It's intentionally obvious. We want it to be clear you were assassinated. There are enough clues planted in various places for a merry chase. You'll be even more famous now. And with that fame will come influence. Not that *you* will be able to use it, of course. But others will, and that will be enough. Fame, power and an audience, Mr. Birnbaum. It's what you were promised. It's what you were given."

Birnbaum said nothing to this; he'd died midmonologue. Washington smiled, planted the syringe in Birnbaum's bed and walked out of the room.

"They have the assassin on video," Jason from Canoga Park said, to Louisa Smart, who had taken over the show, temporarily, for the memorial broadcast. "They have him on video injecting him and talking to him before he died. That was when it happened. When he revealed the plot of the world government."

"We can't know that," Smart said, and for the millionth time wondered how Birnbaum managed to talk to his listeners without wanting to crawl down the stream to strangle them. "The video is low resolution and has no audio. We'll never know what they had to say to each other."

"What else could it be?" Jason said. "Who else could have managed it?"

"It's a compelling point, Jason," Smart said, preparing to switch over to the next caller and whatever *their* cockamamie theory would be.

"I'm going to miss Al," Jason said, before she could unplug him. "He called himself the Voice in the Wilderness. But if he was, we were all in the wilderness with him. Who will be that voice now? Who will call to us? And what will they say?"

Smart had no good answer to that. She just went to the next caller instead.

EPISODE FIVE

"So, Captain Coloma," Department of State Deputy Undersecretary Jamie Maciejewski said. "It's not every starship captain who intentionally maneuvers her ship into the path of a speeding missile."

Captain Sophia Coloma set her jaw and tried very hard not to crack her own molars while doing so. There were a number of ways she expected this final inquiry into her actions in the Danavar system to go. This being the opening statement was not one of them.

In Coloma's head a full list of responses, most not in the least appropriate for the furtherance of her career, scrolled past. After several seconds, she found one she could use. "You have my full report on the matter, sir," she said.

"Yes, of course," Maciejewski said, and then indicated with a hand State Department Fleet Commander Lance Brode and CDF liaison Elizabeth Egan, who with Maciejewski constituted the final inquiry panel. "We have your full report. We also have the reports of your XO, Commander Balla, of Ambassador Abumwe, and of Harry Wilson, the Colonial Defense Forces adjunct on the *Clarke* at the time of the incident."

"We also have the report of Shipmaster Gollock," Brode said. "Outlining the damage the *Clarke* took from the missile. I'll have you know she was quite impressed with you. She tells me that the fact that you managed to get the *Clarke* back to Phoenix Station at all is a minor miracle; by all rights the ship should have cracked in half from material stresses during the ship's acceleration to skip distance."

"She also says that the damage to the *Clarke* is extensive enough that repairs will take longer to make than it would take for us to just build an entire new Robertson-class diplomatic ship," Maciejewski said. "It would possibly be more expensive to boot."

"And then there is the matter of the lives you put at risk," Egan said. "The lives of your crew. The lives of the diplomatic mission to the Utche. More than three hundred people, all told."

"I minimized the risk as much as possible," Coloma said. *In the roughly thirty seconds I had to make a plan,* she thought but did not say.

"Yes," Egan said. "I read your report. And there were no deaths from your actions. There were, however, casualties, several serious and life-threatening."

What do you want from me? Coloma felt like barking at the inquiry panel. The *Clarke* wasn't supposed to have been in the Danavar system to begin with; the diplomatic team on it was chosen at the last minute to replace a diplomatic mission to the Utche that had gone missing and was presumed dead. When the *Clarke* arrived they discovered traps had been set for the Utche, using stolen Colonial Union missiles that would make it look as if the humans had attacked their alien counterparts. Harry Wilson—Coloma had to keep in check some choice opinions just thinking the name—took out all but one of the missiles by using the *Clarke*'s shuttle as a decoy, destroying the shuttle and nearly killing himself in the process. Then the Utche arrived and Coloma had no choice other than to draw the final missile to the *Clarke,* rather than have it home in on the Utche ship, strike it and start a war the Colonial Union couldn't afford at the moment.

What do you want from me? Coloma asked again in her mind. She wouldn't ask the question; she couldn't afford to give the inquiry panel that sort of opening. She had no doubt they would tell her, and that it would be something other than what she had done.

So instead she said, "Yes, there were casualties."

"They might have been avoided," Egan said.

"Yes," Coloma said. "I could have avoided them entirely by allowing the missile—a Colonial Union Melierax Series Seven—to hit the Utche ship, which would have been unprepared and unready for the attack. That strike would have likely crippled the ship, if it did not destroy it outright, and would have caused substantial casualties, including potentially scores of deaths. That seemed the less advisable course of action."

"No one disputes your actions spared the Utche ship considerable damage, and the Colonial Union an uncomfortable diplomatic incident," Maciejewski said.

"But there still is the matter of the ship," Brode said.

"I'm well aware of the matter of the *Clarke*," Coloma said. "It's my ship."

"Not anymore," Brode said.

"Pardon?" Coloma said. She dug her fingernails into her palms to keep herself from leaping across the room to grab Brode by the collar.

"You've been relieved of your command of the *Clarke*," Brode said. "The determination has been made to scrap the ship. Command has been transferred to the port crew that will disassemble it. This is all standard practice for scrapped ships, Captain. It's not a reflection on your service."

"Yes, sir," Coloma said, and doubted that. "What is my next command? And what is the disposition of my staff and crew?"

"In part, that's what this inquiry is about, Captain Coloma," Egan said, and glanced over at Brode, coolly.

"It's regrettable that you had to learn about the disposition of your ship in this way, in this forum. But now that you do know, you should know what we're going to decide is not what we think about what you did, but where we think you should go next. Do you understand the difference here?"

"With apologies, ma'am, I'm not entirely sure I do," Coloma said. Her entire body was coated in a cold sweat that accompanied the realization that she was now a captain without a ship, which meant in a very real sense she was no longer a captain at all. Her body wanted to shiver, to shake off the clamminess she felt. She didn't dare.

"Then understand that the best thing you can do now is to help us understand your thinking at every step in your actions," Egan said. "We have your report. We know what you did. We want a better idea of the why."

"You know the why," Coloma said before she could stop, and almost immediately regretted it. "I did it to stop a war."

"We all agree you stopped a war," Maciejewski said. "We have to decide whether how you did it justifies giving you another command."

"I understand," Coloma said. She would not admit any defeat into her voice.

"Very good," Maciejewski said. "Then let's begin at the decision to let the missile hit your ship. Let's take it second by second, shall we."

The *Clarke*, like other large ships, did not dock with Phoenix Station directly. It was positioned a small distance away, in the section of station devoted to repair. Coloma stood at the edge of the repair transport bay, watching crews load into the work shuttles that would take them to the *Clarke*, to strip the ship of anything and everything valuable or salvageable before cutting down the hull itself into manageable plates to be recycled into something else entirely—another ship, structural elements for a space station, weapons or perhaps foil to wrap leftovers in. Coloma smiled wryly at the idea of a leftover bit of steak being wrapped in the skin of the *Clarke,* and then she stopped smiling.

She had to admit that in the last couple of weeks she'd gotten very good at making herself depressed.

In her peripheral vision, Coloma saw someone walking up to her. She knew without turning that it was Neva Balla, her executive officer. Balla had a hitch in her gait, an artifact, so Balla claimed, of an equestrian injury in her youth. The practical result of it was that there was no doubt of her identity when she came up on you. Balla could be wearing a bag on her head and Coloma would know it was her.

"Having one last look at the *Clarke*?" Balla asked Coloma as she walked up.

"No," Coloma said; Balla looked at her quizzically. "She's no longer the *Clarke.* When they decommissioned her, they took her name. Now she's just CUDS-RC-1181. For whatever time it takes to render her down to parts, anyway."

"What happens to the name?" Balla asked.

"They put it back into the rotation," Coloma said. "Some other ship will have it eventually. That is, if they don't decide to retire it for being too ignominious."

Balla nodded, but then motioned to the ship. "*Clarke* or not, she was still your ship."

"Yes," Coloma said. "Yes, she was."

The two stood there silently for a moment, watching the shuttles angle toward what used to be their ship.

"So what did you find out?" Coloma asked Balla after a moment.

"We're still on hold," Balla said. "All of us. You, me, the senior staff of the *Clarke.* Some of the crew have been reassigned to fill holes in other ship rosters, but almost no officers and none of those above the rank of lieutenant junior grade."

Coloma nodded. The reassignment of her crew would normally come through her, but technically speaking they were no longer her crew and she no longer their captain. Balla had friends in the Department of State's higher reaches, or more accurately, she had friends who were assistants and aides to the department's higher reaches. It worked out the same, informationwise. "Do we have any idea why no one important's been reassigned?"

"They're still doing their investigation of the Danavar incident," Balla said.

"Yes, but in our crew that only involves you and me and Marcos Basquez," Coloma said, naming the *Clarke*'s chief engineer. "And Marcos isn't being investigated like the two of us are."

"It's still easier to have us around," Balla said. "But there's another wrinkle to it as well."

"What's that?" Coloma asked.

"The *Clarke*'s diplomatic team hasn't been formally reassigned, either," Balla said. "Some of them have been added on to existing missions or negotiations in a temporary capacity, but none of them has been made permanent."

"Who did you hear this from?" Coloma asked.

"Hart Schmidt," Balla said. "He and Ambassador Abumwe were attached to the Bula negotiations last week."

Coloma winced at this. The Bula negotiations had gone poorly, in part because the Colonial Defense Forces had established a clandestine base on an underdeveloped Bula colony world and had gotten caught red-handed trying to evacuate it; that was the rumor, in any event. Abumwe and Schmidt having anything to do with that would not look good for them.

"So we're all in limbo," Coloma said.

"It looks like," Balla said. "At least you're not being singled out, ma'am."

Coloma laughed at this. "Not singled out, but being punished, that's for sure."

"I don't know why we would be punished," Balla said. "We were dropped into a diplomatic process at the last minute, discovered a trap, and kept the trap from snapping shut. All without a single death. And the negotiations with the Utche were successfully completed on top of that. They give people medals for less."

Coloma motioned to what used to be the *Clarke*. "Maybe they were just very attached to the ship."

Balla smiled. "It seems unlikely," she said.

"Why not?" Coloma said. "I was."

"You did the right thing, Captain," Balla said, becoming serious. "I said so to the investigators. So did Ambassador Abumwe and Lieutenant Wilson. If they don't see that, to hell with them."

"Thank you, Neva," Coloma said. "It's good of you to say that. Remember it when they assign us to a tow barge."

"There are worse assignments," Balla said.

Coloma was about to respond when her PDA pinged. She swiped to her message queue and read the mail there. Then she shut down the screen, put the PDA away and returned her gaze to what used to be the *Clarke*.

Balla watched her captain for a moment. "You're killing me over here," she finally said.

"Remember when you said that there are worse assignments than a tow barge?" Coloma said, to her XO.

"Considering it's the second to last thing I said, yes," Balla said. "Why?"

"Because we may have just gotten one of those assignments," Coloma said.

"The ship was the *Porchester*," Colonel Abel Rigney said. "At least for its first thirty years of service, when it was a Hampshire-class corvette in the CDF. Then it was transferred to the Department of State and renamed the *Ballantine*, after an old secretary of the department. That was another twenty years of service as a courier and supply ship. It was decommissioned last year."

Coloma stood on the bridge with Rigney and Balla and looked over the quiet banks of monitors. The atmosphere on the ship was thin and cold, befitting a ship that no longer had a crew or a purpose. "Any immediate reason for the decommissioning?" she asked.

"Other than age? No," Rigney said. "She ran fine. *Runs* fine, as you'll discover when you put her through her paces. She's just old. There are a lot of klicks on this ship, and eventually being on her began to look like a hardship assignment."

"Hmmm," Coloma said.

"But it's all a matter of perspective, isn't it," Rigney said, quickly, moving past the implied but unintentional insult he'd just offered Coloma. "If you're new to space travel, and don't have your own fleet of ships, then what you and I see as old and past its prime will look shiny and new. The folks from Earth who we are proposing to sell this ship to are going to look at this baby as their first step into the wider universe. It's right about their speed."

"So that's my job," Coloma said. "Take a hand-me-down and convince the rubes they're getting something that's top of the line."

"I wouldn't put it like that, Captain," Rigney said. "We're not trying to deceive the folks from Earth. They know we're not offering them the latest technology. But they also know they're not trained and ready to handle our latest ships. The only real spacefaring tech they've had to this point are shuttlecraft working around the space station over their planet. We've handled everything else up to now."

"So we're giving them a ship with training wheels on it," Coloma said.

"We prefer to think of it as that we're offering them a classic piece of technology to learn on and build from," Rigney said. "You know the Earth folks aren't happy with the Colonial Union right now."

Coloma nodded; that was common knowledge. And she couldn't blame them. If she were from Earth and discovered that the Colonial Union had been using the entire planet as a farm for soldiers and colonists, she'd be pissed at it, too.

"What you probably don't know is that the Earth folks aren't just talking to us," Rigney said. "The Conclave has been very aggressively courting them, too. It would be very bad for the Colonial Union if Earth decided to join the Conclave, and not just because we'd be fresh out of colonists and CDF. This ship is one of the ways we're hoping to get back on their good side."

"Then why are you selling it to them, sir?" Balla asked. "Why not just give it to them?"

"We're already gifting the Earth folks lots of other technology," Rigney said. "We don't want to start looking like we're offering reparations. And anyway, the governments of Earth are suspicious of us. They're worried that we're offering up Trojan horses to them. If we make them pay for this ship, they're more likely to trust us. Don't ask me about the psychology here. I'm just telling you what they tell me. We're still giving it to them at a sharply reduced price, and mostly in barter. I think we're selling it mostly for field corn."

"We're selling it to the Earth folks as a way to get our foot in the door," Coloma said.

Rigney rolled his hand toward Coloma. "Precisely," he said. "And so we come to you and your crew. It's perfectly reasonable that you would see a temporary assignment to a decommissioned ship as punishment for what happened at Danavar. But in fact, Captain Coloma, Commander Balla, what we're asking you to do is a task that's of great importance to the Colonial Union. Your job is to highlight the ship, to make the Earth people feel that it's going to be of benefit to them, answer all their questions and give them a positive experience with the Colonial Union. If you pull it off, you'll be doing the Colonial Union a service. A very significant service. One that means you'll be able to write your own ticket afterward."

"I have your word on that, Colonel?" Coloma asked.

"No," Rigney said. "But that's my point. Sell this ship and you won't need my word."

"Understood," Coloma said.

"Good," Rigney said. "Now. Tour the ship, check out the systems, tell me what you need, and you'll get it. But do it quickly. You have two weeks from today before the Earth delegation arrives to see what this ship can do. Be ready for them. Be ready for us."

"Here's the problem," Marcos Basquez said, pointing to a series of tubes in the engine room of the ship. He was yelling over the din of his crew banging away at updates and repairs.

"I see tubes, Marcos," Coloma said.

"You see power conduits," Basquez said.

"And?" Coloma said.

"We have two types of engines on a spaceship," Basquez said. "We got the conventional engines, which push us through normal space, and we got the skip drive, which punches holes in space-time. Both of them are powered from the same source, okay? These days, because we know what we're doing, we can seat the engines and the skip drive in the same place. Fifty years ago, when this pile of shit was put together, we had to separate the two." He pointed to the power conduits. "These are the conduits that send power to the skip drive from the engine."

"All right," Coloma said. "So what?"

"So they're degraded and need to be replaced," Basquez said.

"So replace them," Coloma said.

Basquez shook his head. "If it were that easy, I wouldn't be telling you about it. This engine design is half a century old. This ship was the last of its kind in service. There isn't another ship out there with this engine design. They haven't made replacement stock for this engine design in more than a decade."

"You can't replace the conduits because the replacement conduits don't exist," Coloma said.

"Right," Basquez said.

"Power conduits are still being made," Coloma said. "We had them all over the *Clarke*."

"Right, but they're not rated for this sort of power output," Basquez said. "Trying to use the current standard conduit here would be like stuffing a Great Dane into a Chihuahua sweater."

Coloma had to stop for a moment to take in the visual Basquez just offered. Then she said, "Would these conduits last through our mission? We're only skipping to the Rus system and back."

"There's two ways of answering that," Basquez said. "The first one is to say that these conduits *probably* won't overload and rupture, or destroy this section of the ship, or rupture the hull, or kill everyone on board, including those important Earth visitors. The second one is that if you decide not to replace them, I hope you don't mind if I do my work remotely, like from Phoenix Station."

"What do you suggest?" Coloma asked.

"How much time do we have before we have to be under way?" Basquez asked.

"Twelve days," Coloma said.

"We have two options," Basquez said. "We comb through CDF and civilian shipyards looking for this size of conduit and hope they're not as degraded as these are, or we commission some made from scratch from the shipyards, based on this specification, and hope they arrive in time."

"Do both," Coloma said.

"Belt and suspenders, very wise," said Basquez. "This is the part where you send a note to that Rigney guy telling him to yell at people to get those parts here on time, right? I want a couple of days with them to make sure they have the capacity we'll need."

"I'll do it on my way to my next meeting," Coloma said.

"This is why I like working with you, Captain," Basquez said, and then turned his attention to one of his engineers, who evidently needed yelling at.

Rigney promised to get the conduit specialists at the CDF shipyards on Phoenix Station on the job and told Coloma to have Basquez send the specs to him directly. Coloma smiled as she disconnected from her talk with Rigney. Civilian captains and ships were almost always prioritized below Colonial Defense Forces ships when it came time to allot materials and expertise; it was nice to be at the front of the line for once.

Coloma's next meeting, in one of the ship's tiny conference rooms, was with Lieutenant Harry Wilson.

"Captain," Wilson said as she approached him. He saluted.

"Why do you do that?" Coloma asked him. She sat down at the conference room table.

"Ma'am?" Wilson said, lowering his arm.

"Why do you salute me?" Coloma asked. "You're

Colonial Defense Forces and I am not. You're not required to salute civilian captains."

"You still outrank me," Wilson said.

"That's not what you told me at Danavar, when you flashed your security clearance at me and ordered me to give you my shuttle," Coloma said. "Which you then destroyed."

"Sorry about that, ma'am," Wilson said. "It was necessary at the time."

"You still have that security clearance?" Coloma asked.

"I do," Wilson said. "I think they forgot they gave it to me. I'm pretty harmless with it. I use it mostly to check box scores for baseball games back on Earth."

"I understand you've just returned from being a hostage," Coloma said.

"Yes, ma'am," Wilson said. "An unfortunate incident with the Bula. We ended up with six of their ships planning to blow us out of the sky. Ambassador Abumwe was part of the diplomatic team that got us released. They're still ironing out the details of the ransom, I believe. Letting us go early was a sign of good faith. They have other things to hold over us."

"You certainly find yourself in the middle of a number of interesting incidents," Coloma said.

"I wouldn't mind not having that talent," Wilson said.

"I have a job for you," Coloma said. "I'm prepping this ship to display and then sell to a group of representatives from Earth. I need someone to be their guide and liaison while they are here on the ship. I want you to do it."

"Seems to me you have an entire diplomatic corps you can call on to do that job," Wilson said. "I'm a CDF tech specialist."

"You're from Earth," Coloma said. "All the diplomats I could use are from the Colonial Union. My job is to make these people comfortable with the ship and with us. I think it would be useful to have someone here who speaks their language."

"I might not speak their language," Wilson said. "There are a couple hundred of them in service on Earth."

"It's an expression," Coloma said, testily, and pulled out her PDA. "I meant someone who has a shared history with them and who can cogently describe the advantages of the Colonial Union to them. Your technical background will come in handy because that means you can explain details of the ship to them, which no normal diplomat could do. Also, the files I have on these representatives say that they are all from either the United States or Canada. I think you will be able to speak their language just fine." She played her fingers across the PDA. "There. I've sent you their information."

"Thank you," Wilson said. "If you want me, I'm happy to serve in this role for you. I'm just surprised you want me. I was pretty sure I was on your shit list, Captain."

"You were," Coloma said. "You are. But help me with this and you'll get off of it."

"Yes, ma'am," Wilson said.

"Good. Then we're done here," Coloma said. "You're dismissed."

"Of course," Wilson said, and then saluted Coloma again.

"I already told you that wasn't necessary," Coloma said to Wilson.

"You put your ship in the path of a missile meant to kill members of an alien race, and kept the Colonial Union from having to fight a fight we'd have lost," Wilson said. "That deserves a salute, ma'am."

Coloma returned the salute. Wilson left.

Basquez got his conduits a day before departure and was not in the least happy about it. "We've barely got time to install them, much less test them," Basquez said, through the PDA. "And I haven't had time to update the engineering systems down here. We're still working off of fifty-year-old stations. You need to ask your Rigney for a delay."

"I already did and he already said no," Coloma said. She was in the shuttle bay's control room with Balla and Wilson, waiting for the arrival of the Earth diplomats. "They've got these people on a tight schedule."

"His precious schedule will be disrupted if we blow the hell up," Basquez said.

"Is that really going to be a problem?" Coloma said.

There was a pause on the other end of the PDA. "No," Basquez admitted. "I did a preliminary test of their throughput when I unpacked them. They should hold up."

"It will take us three days to get to skip distance," Coloma said. "That should be more than enough time to do your tests."

"It would be better to do the tests here in the dock," Basquez said.

"I'm not disagreeing with you, Marcos," Coloma said. "But it's not up to us."

"Right," Basquez said. "I'll have these bastards installed in about six hours, and I'll run a few more tests off the engineering stations. If I can, I'll update the stations with new software tomorrow. It might give us more accurate readings."

"Fine," Coloma said. "Let me know." She ended the discussion.

"Problems?" Balla asked her.

"Other than Basquez being paranoid, no," Coloma said.

"It's not a bad thing for an engineer to be paranoid," Balla said.

"I prefer them that way," Coloma said. "Just not when I'm busy with other things."

"The shuttle is twenty klicks out and slowing," Wilson said. "I'm going to purge atmosphere and open the doors."

"Do it," Coloma said. Wilson nodded and communicated directly with the shuttle bay systems with the Brain-Pal computer in his head. There was a chugging sound as the bay reclaimers sucked in the air and stored it for rerelease. When the bay was sufficiently airless, Wilson cracked up the bay doors. The shuttle hovered silently outside.

"Here come the Earthlings," Wilson said.

The shuttle landed. Wilson closed the doors and reintroduced the atmosphere; when it was back, the three of them filed out to wait for the shuttle door to open and disgorge its passengers.

To Coloma's eye they did not seem especially impressive: three men and two women, all middle-aged and homogeneous in appearance and attitude. She introduced herself, Balla and Wilson; the leader of the Earth contingent introduced himself as Marlon Tiege and likewise announced his team, fumbling over the names of two of them. "Sorry," he said. "We've had a long journey."

"Of course," Coloma said. "Lieutenant Wilson will be your liaison while you are here; he'll be more than happy to show you your quarters. We're on standard universal time on this ship, and we're scheduled to depart from Phoenix Station at 0530 tomorrow morning; until then, please rest and relax. If you need anything, Wilson will make it happen."

"I am at your service," Wilson said, and then smiled. "My files tell me you're from Chicago, Mr. Tiege."

"That's right," Tiege said.

"Cubs or White Sox?" Wilson asked.

"You have to ask?" Tiege said. "Cubs."

"Then I feel honor-bound to inform you I'm a Cards

fan," Wilson said. "I hope that won't cause a diplomatic incident."

Tiege smiled. "I think in this one case I'll be willing to let it pass."

"We're talking baseball," Wilson said to Coloma, noting her look, which was positioned between puzzlement and irritation. "It's a popular team sport in the United States. His favorite team and my favorite team are in the same division, which means they are rivals and frequently play against each other."

"Ah," Coloma said.

"They don't have baseball up here?" Tiege asked Wilson.

"Mostly not," Wilson said. "Colonists are from different parts of the world. The closest most colonies come is cricket."

"That's crazy talk," Tiege said.

"Tell me about it," Wilson said, and then motioned with his hand, leading the Earth mission from the shuttle bay while Tiege nattered on about the Cubs.

"What just happened?" Coloma asked Balla, after a minute.

"You said you wanted someone who would speak their language," Balla reminded her.

"I expected to be able to speak their language a little," Coloma said.

"Better learn more about baby bears," suggested Balla.

The first day of the trip consisted of Wilson giving the visitors a tour of the ship. Coloma wasn't thrilled when the contingent from Earth showed up on her bridge, but the entire point of the trip was to sell them on the ship, so she did her best impression of a polite, engaged captain who had nothing better to do than answer inane questions about her ship. While she was doing this, she would occasionally glance over at Wilson, who seemed preoccupied.

"What is it?" Coloma asked him, when Balla had led the Earth contingent over to the life support and energy management displays.

"What is what?" Wilson said.

"Something is bothering you," Coloma said.

"It's nothing," Wilson said. Then, "I'll tell you about it later, ma'am."

Coloma considered pressing him on the subject, but then Tiege and his cohort returned to Wilson, who took them elsewhere. Coloma made a note to follow up with Wilson and then got lost in the day-to-day management of the ship.

It was as Rigney had advertised to her: old but serviceable. Its systems ran well, with the occasional bump occasioned by the fact that she and every other crew member had to learn archaic systems. Some of the systems, like those in the engine room, had never been updated because the systems they were tied to had never been updated, either. Other systems were revamped when the ship made the transition from military to civilian use, and others—like the weapons systems—were removed almost entirely. Regardless, none of the systems were newer than fifteen years old, a period of time two years longer than Coloma herself had been in the Department of State's fleet service. Fortunately, neither the CDF nor the Department of State was the sort of organization to radically change the interface of its command systems. Even engineering's fifty-year-old consoles were simple enough to navigate through once you made a few concessions to antiquity.

It's not a bad ship, Coloma said to herself. The people of Earth weren't getting something new, but they weren't getting a lemon, either. She'd hesitate to go so far as to call it a classic, however.

Sometime later, Coloma's PDA pinged; it was Basquez. "I think we may have a problem," he said.

"What kind of problem?" Coloma asked.

"The sort where I think you might want to come down and have me explain it to you in person," Basquez said.

"I tried updating the engineering software on the consoles, but that didn't work because the consoles are fifty years old and the hardware can't keep up with the new software," Basquez said, handing his PDA to Coloma. "So I went in the opposite direction. I took the software from the consoles, ported it into my PDA and created a virtual environment to run it. Then I updated it inside that environment to boost its sensitivity. And that's where I saw this." He pointed to a section of the PDA, which was displaying a picture of what looked like a glowing tube.

Coloma squinted. "Saw what?" she asked. "What am I looking at?"

"You're looking at the energy flow through a section of the conduit we just installed," Basquez said. "And this"—he pointed again at a section of the PDA, tapping it for emphasis—"is a kink in the flow."

"What does that mean?" Coloma said.

"Right now it doesn't mean anything," Basquez said. "We're only passing ten percent of capacity through the conduit to prep and test the skip drive. It's a disruption of maybe one ten-thousandth of the total flow. Small enough that if I hadn't updated the software, I would have missed it. The thing is, there's a reason we keep power flows as smooth as possible—disruptions introduce chaos, and chaos can mean ruptures. If we push more capacity through the conduit, there's no guarantee that the disruption won't scale at a geometric or logarithmic rate, and then—"

"And then we would have a rupture and then we'd be screwed," Coloma said.

"It's a very small risk, but you're the one the Colonial Union is telling to make this thing go off without a hitch," Basquez said. "So this is a hitch. A potential hitch."

"What do you want to do about it?" Coloma said.

"I want to take down that chunk of tube and run some scanners through it," Basquez said. "Find out what's causing the problem. If it's an imperfection in the physical conduit or the sheathing inside, that's something we can fix here. If it's something else . . . well, I have no clue what else it could be except a physical imperfection, but if it's something else, we should figure out what it is and what we can do about it."

"Does this set us back on our itinerary?" Coloma asked.

"It might, but it shouldn't," Basquez said. "I'm about 99.99 percent sure it's something we can deal with here. My people will need about ninety minutes to take down that section, another sixty to scan it the way it should be scanned, about ten minutes to buff out any imperfections we find, and another ninety minutes to reinstall the section and run some tests. If everything checks out, we can push more power through on schedule. You won't miss your skip."

"Then stop talking to me about it and do it," Coloma said.

"Yes, ma'am," Basquez said. "I'll let you know when everything's cleaned up."

"Good," Coloma said. She turned away from Basquez and saw Wilson walking up to her. "You've lost your flock," she said to him.

"I didn't lose them, I parked them in the officers lounge to watch a video," he said. "Then I went to the bridge to find you, and Balla said you were here."

"What is it?" Coloma said.

"It's our Earthlings," Wilson said. "I'm pretty sure they're not actually from Earth. Not recently, anyway."

"You're basing your suspicions on a baseball team?" Neva Balla asked, disbelievingly. Coloma had her report to the conference room she and Wilson were in and had Wilson repeat what he had said to her.

"It's not just any baseball team, it's the *Cubs,*" Wilson said, and then held out his hands in a helpless sort of gesture. "Listen, you have to understand something. In all of the history of professional sports, the Cubs are the ultimate symbol of complete failure. The championship of baseball is something called the World Series, and it's been so long since the Cubs have won it that no one who is alive could remember the last time they won it. It's so long that no one alive knew anyone who was alive when they won it. We're talking *centuries* of abject failure here."

"So what?" Balla said.

"So the Cubs won the World Series two years ago," Wilson said. He nodded to Coloma. "I made a joke to Captain Coloma here that I've been using that security clearance I have to check baseball box scores. Well, it's not a lie, I do. I like having that connection back home. Yesterday when Tiege mentioned being a Cubs fan, I sent in a request for the Cubs' season stats going back to when I left Earth. As a Cards fan, I wanted to rub his face in his team's continued failure. But then I found out the Cubs had broken their streak."

Balla looked at Wilson blankly.

"Two years ago the Cubs won a hundred and one games," Wilson continued. "That's the most games they've won in over a century. They only lost a single game in their entire playoff run, and swept the Cards—my team—in their divisional series. In game four of the World Series, some kid named Jorge Alamazar pitched the first perfect game in a World Series since the twenti-eth century."

Balla looked over to her captain. "This isn't my sport," she said. "I don't know what any of this means."

"It means," Wilson said, "that there's no possible way a Cubs fan who has been on Earth anytime in the last two years would fail to tell any baseball fan that the Cubs won the Series. And when I identified myself as a Cards fan, Tiege's first reaction should have been to rub the Cubbies' victory in my face. It's simply impossible."

"Maybe he's not that big of a fan," Balla said.

"If he's from Chicago, it's not something he would miss," Wilson said. "And we talked enough about base-ball last night that I'm pretty confident he's not just a casual viewer of the sport. But I grant you could be right, and he's either not enough of a fan or too polite to mention the Cubs ending a centuries-long drought. So I checked."

"How did you do that?" Balla asked.

"I talked about the Cubs being the ultimate symbol of professional sports futility," Wilson said. "I needled Tiege about it for about ten full minutes. He took it and admit-ted it was true. He doesn't know the Cubs won the Se-ries. He doesn't know because the Colonial Union is still enforcing a news blackout from the Earth. He doesn't know because either he's a colonist bred and born or is former Colonial Defense Forces who retired and colonized."

"What about the other people on his team?" Balla asked.

"I talked to them all and casually dropped questions about life on Earth," Wilson said. "They're all very nice people, just like Tiege is, but if any of them know any-thing about Earth anytime since about a decade ago, it got past me. None of them seemed to be able to name things that anyone from the United States or Canada should know, like names of sitting presidents or prime ministers, popular music or entertainment figures, or anything about big stories of the last year. A hurricane hit South Carolina last year and flattened most of Charleston. One of the women, Kelle Laflin, says she's from Charleston but seems completely oblivious that the hurricane happened."

"Then what's going on?" Balla said.

"We're asking the same question," Coloma said. "We have a team from Earth here to buy this ship from the Colonial Union. But if they're not from Earth, where are they from? And what do they intend with the ship?"

Balla turned to Wilson. "You shouldn't have left them alone," she said.

"I have a crew member watching the door," Wilson said. "They'll let me know if one or more of them try to slip away. I'm also tracking their PDAs, which so far, at least, they don't seem to separate themselves from. So far none of them show the slightest inclination to sneak off."

"What we're trying to decide now is what Colonel Rigney knows about this," Coloma said. "He's the one we've been dealing with for this mission. It seems impossible to me he's not behind this charade."

"Don't be too sure," Wilson said. "The Colonial Defense Forces have a long history of inborn sneakiness. It's one of the things that got us in trouble with the Earth in the first place. It's entirely possible someone above Rigney is pulling a fast one on him, too."

"But it still doesn't make any sense," Balla said. "No matter who has dropped fake Earth diplomats here, we're still not going to be selling this ship to anyone on Earth. This charade doesn't add up."

"There's something we're not getting," Wilson said. "We might not have all the information we need."

"Tell me where we can get more information," Coloma said. "I'm open to suggestion."

Coloma's PDA pinged. It was Basquez. "We have a problem," he said.

"Is this another 'I think we have a potential energy flow' kind of problem?" Coloma asked.

"No, this is a 'Holy shit, we're all definitely going to die a horrible death in the cold endless dark of space' kind of problem," Basquez said.

"We'll be right down," Coloma said.

"Well, this *is* interesting," Wilson said, looking at the pinprick-sized object at the end of his finger. He, Coloma, Balla and Basquez were in engineering, beside a chunk of conduit and a brace of instruments Basquez used to examine the conduit. Basquez had shooed away the rest of his crew, who were now hovering some distance away, trying to listen in.

"It's a bomb, isn't it," Basquez said.

"Yeah, I think it is," Wilson said.

"What sort of damage could a bomb that size do?" Coloma said. "I can barely even see it."

"If there's antimatter inside, it could do quite a lot," Wilson said. "You don't need a lot of that stuff to make a big mess."

Coloma peered at the tiny thing again. "If it was antimatter, it would have annihilated itself already."

"Not necessarily," Wilson said, still gazing at the pinprick. "When I was working at CDF Research and Development, there was a team working on pellet shot–sized antimatter containment units. You generate a suspending energy field and wrap it in a compound that acts like a battery and powers the energy field inside. When the power runs out, the energy field collapses and the antimatter connects with the wrapping. Kablam."

"They got it to work?" Basquez asked.

"When I was there? No," Wilson said, glancing over to Basquez. "But they were some very clever kids. And we were decoding some of the latest technology we'd stolen from the Consu, who are at least a couple millennia ahead of us in these things. And I was there a couple of years ago." His gaze went back to the pinprick. "So they could have had time to perfect this little baby, sure."

"You couldn't take down the whole ship with that," Balla said. "Antimatter or not."

Wilson opened his mouth, but Basquez got there first. "You wouldn't need to," he said. "All you have to do is rupture the conduit and the energy inside would take it from there. Hell, you wouldn't even need to rupture it. If this tore up the inside of the conduit enough, the disruption of the energy flow would be all you need to make it burst apart."

"And that has the added advantage of making it look like an explosion based on material failure rather than an actual bombing," Wilson said.

"Yeah," Basquez said. "If the black box survived, it would only show the rupture, not the bomb going off."

"Time this thing so it goes off right before a skip, when you're feeding energy to the skip drive," Wilson said. "No one would be the wiser."

"Rigney said we needed to keep to a schedule," Basquez said, to Coloma.

"Wait, you don't think *we* planted this bomb, do you?" Balla asked.

Coloma, Wilson and Basquez were silent.

"That doesn't make any sense," Balla said, forcefully. "It makes no sense at all for the Colonial Union to blow up its own ship."

"It doesn't make sense for the Colonial Union to put fake Earthlings on the ship, either," Wilson pointed out. "And yet here they are."

"Wait, what?" Basquez said. "Those diplomats aren't from Earth? What the hell?"

"Later, Marcos," Coloma said. Basquez lapsed into silence, glowering at this latest twist of events. Coloma turned to Wilson. "I am open to suggestions, Lieutenant."

"I have no answers to give you," Wilson said. "I don't think any of us have any answers at this point. So I would suggest we try finding alternate means of acquiring answers."

Coloma thought about this for a moment. Then she said, "I know how we can do that."

"Everything's ready," Coloma said, to Wilson, via her PDA. Her words were being ported into his BrainPal so he'd be the only one to hear them. Wilson, on the floor of the shuttle bay with the fake Earthlings, glanced over to the shuttle bay control room and gave her a very brief nod. Then he turned his attention to the Earthlings.

"We've already seen the shuttle bay, you know, Harry," Marlon Tiege said to Wilson. "Twice, now."

"I'm about to show it to you in a whole new way, Marlon, I promise," Wilson said.

"Sounds exciting," Tiege said, smiling.

"Just you *wait*," Wilson said. "But first, a question for you."

"Shoot," Tiege said.

"You know by now that I enjoy giving you shit about the Cubs," Wilson said.

"They would kick you out of the Cards fan club if you didn't," Tiege said.

"Yes, they would," Wilson said. "I'm wondering what you would ever do if the Cubbies actually ever took the Series."

"You mean, before or after my heart attack?" Tiege said. "I would probably kiss every woman I saw. And most of the men, too."

"The Cubs won the Series two years ago, Marlon," Wilson said.

"What?" Tiege said.

"Swept the Yankees in four. Final game of the Series, the Cubs hurler pitched a perfect game. Cubs won a hundred and one games on the way to the playoffs. The Cubbies are world champions, Marlon. Just thought you should know."

Coloma watched Marlon Tiege's face and noted that the man's physiognomy was not well suited to showing two emotions at once: utter joy at the news about the Cubs and complete dismay that he'd been caught in a lie. She couldn't say, however, that she was not enjoying the spectacle of the man's face trying to contain both at the same time.

"Where are you from, Marlon?" Wilson asked.

"I'm from Chicago," Tiege said, regaining his composure.

"Where are you from most recently?" Wilson asked.

"Harry, come on," Tiege said. "This is crazy."

Wilson ignored him and turned to one of the women, Kelle Laflin. "Last year a hurricane smacked straight into Charleston," he said, and watched her go pale. "You must remember."

She nodded mutely.

"Great," Wilson said. "What was the name they gave the hurricane?"

Coloma noted that Laflin's face was already primed for dismay.

Wilson turned back to Tiege. "Here's the deal, Marlon." He pointed over to the control room. Tiege followed the vector of the point to see Captain Coloma sitting there, behind a console. "When I give the captain the signal, she's going to start pumping air out of this shuttle bay. It'll take a minute for that cycle to happen. Now, don't worry about me, I'm Colonial Defense Forces, which means that I can hold my breath for a good ten minutes if I have to, and I also have my combat uniform on under my clothes at the moment. So I'll be fine. You and your friends, however, will likely die quite painfully as your lungs collapse and vomit blood into the vacuum."

"You can't do that," Tiege said. "We're a diplomatic mission."

"Yes, but from whom?" Wilson said. "Because you're not from Earth, Marlon."

"Are you sure about that?" Tiege said. "Because if you're wrong, think about what will happen when the Earth finds out you've killed us."

"Yes, well," Wilson said, and fished out a small plastic case that contained the pinprick bomb in it, resting on a ball of cotton. "You would have been dead anyway after this bomb went off, and we along with you. This way, the rest of us still get to live. Last chance, Marlon."

"Harry, I can't—," Tiege began, and Wilson held up his hand.

"Have it your way," he said, and nodded to Coloma. She started the purge cycle. The shuttle bay was filled with the sound of air being sucked into reservoirs.

"Wait!" Tiege said. Wilson motioned to Coloma with their agreed-upon signal and sent a "stop" message to her PDA via his BrainPal. Coloma aborted the purge cycle and waited.

Marlon Tiege stood there for a moment, sweating. Then he cracked a rueful smile and turned to Wilson.

"I'm from Chicago, and these days I live on Erie. I'm going to tell you everything I know about this mission and you have my word on that," he said, to Wilson. "But you have to tell me one thing first, Harry."

"What is it?" Wilson asked.

"That you weren't just fucking with me about the Cubs," Tiege said.

"You want explanations," Colonel Abel Rigney said to Coloma from behind his desk at Phoenix Station. In a chair in front of the desk, Colonel Liz Egan sat, watching Coloma.

"What I want is to walk you out of an airlock," Coloma said, to Rigney. She glanced over to Egan in her chair. "And possibly walk you out after him." She returned her gaze to Rigney. "But for now, an explanation will do."

Rigney smiled slightly at this. "You remember Danavar, of course," he said. "A CDF frigate named the *Polk* destroyed, the Utche ship targeted and your own ship mortally wounded."

"Yes," Coloma said.

"And you know about the recent incident with the Bula," Egan said. "A human wildcat colony on one of their worlds was attacked, and it was discovered that three modified, undercover CDF members were among them. When we tried to retrieve what was left of the colony, the Bula surrounded the ship and we had to ransom it and its crew back from them."

"I knew about some of that from Wilson and Ambassador Abumwe's people," Coloma said.

"I'm sure you did," Rigney said. "Our problem is that we suspect whoever ambushed the *Polk* and your ship at Danavar got information about the *Polk*'s mission from us. Same with that wildcat colony in Bula territory."

"Got the information from the CDF?" Coloma asked.

"Or from the Department of State," Egan said. "Or both."

"You have a spy," Coloma said.

"Spies, more likely," Egan said. "Both of those missions are a lot of ground to cover for one person."

"We needed a way to pinpoint where the leak was coming from, and how much they knew. So we decided to go fishing," Rigney said. "We had a decommissioned spacecraft, and after your actions with the *Clarke*, we had a spacecraft crew without a ship. It seemed like an opportune time to cast out a line and see what we came up with."

"What you came up with was a bomb that would have destroyed my ship and killed everyone on it, including your fake Earth mission," Coloma said.

"Yes," Egan said. "And look what we discovered. We discovered that whoever tried to sabotage you has access to confidential Colonial Defense Forces research. We discovered whoever it was has the ability to access communications through Colonial Defense Forces channels. We discovered they have access to CDF shipyards and fabrication sites. We have a wealth of information that we can sift through to narrow down the person or persons selling us out, and to stop it from happening again. To stop anyone else from dying."

"A fine sentiment," Coloma said. "It glosses over the part where I and my crew and your people all die."

"It was a risk we had to take," Rigney said. "We couldn't tell you because we didn't know where the leaks were coming from. We didn't tell *our* people, either. They're all retired CDF and people who occasionally do work for us when someone being green would be overly conspicuous. They know there's a chance of death involved."

"We didn't," Coloma said.

"We needed to know if someone was going to try to sabotage that mission," Rigney said. "Now we know and now we know more than we ever have before about how these people work. I won't apologize for the actions we took, Captain. I can say I regret that the actions were necessary. And I can say that I'm very glad you didn't die."

Coloma stewed on this for a moment. "What happens now?" she asked, finally.

"What do you mean?" Egan asked.

"I have no command," Coloma said. "I have no ship.

I and my crew are in limbo." She motioned at Egan. "I don't know what your final inquiry has decided about my future." She looked back at Rigney. "You told me that if I completed this mission successfully, I could write my own ticket. I can't tell if this was a successful mission, or even if it was, whether your promise is any more true than anything else you've said to me."

Rigney and Egan looked at each other; Egan nodded. "From our point of view, Captain Coloma, it was a successful mission," Rigney said.

"As for the final inquiry, it's been decided that your actions at Danavar were consistent with the best traditions of command and of diplomacy," Egan said. "You've been awarded a commendation, which has already been placed in your file. Congratulations."

"Thank you," Coloma said, a little numbly.

"As for your ship," Rigney said. "It seems to me you have one. It's a little old, and being stationed on it has been seen as a hardship post. But on the other hand, a hardship posting is better than no posting at all."

"Your crew is already used to the ship by now," Egan said. "And we do need another diplomatic ship in the fleet. Ambassador Abumwe and her staff have a list of assignments and no way to get to them. If you want the ship, it's yours. If you don't want the ship, it's still yours. Congratulations."

"Thank you," Coloma said again, this time completely numbly.

"You're welcome," Egan said. "And you're dismissed, Captain."

"Yes, ma'am," Coloma said.

"And, Captain Coloma," Rigney said.

"Yes, sir," Coloma said.

"Give her a good name." He turned back to Egan, and the two of them fell into a conversation. Coloma walked herself out of the door.

Balla and Wilson were waiting for her outside Rigney's office. "Well?" Balla said.

"I've gotten a commendation," Coloma said. "I've been given a ship. The crew stays together. Abumwe's team is back on board."

"Which ship are we getting?" Wilson asked.

"The one we've been on," Coloma said.

"*That* old hunk of junk," Wilson said.

"Watch it, Lieutenant," Coloma said. "That's my ship. And she has a name. She's the *Clarke*."

The Back Channel

"General, let us return to the matter of humans," Unli Hado said.

From her seat on the podium behind General Tarsem Gau, leader of the Conclave, Hafte Sorvalh sighed as quietly as possible. When the Conclave was formalized and the Grand Assembly was created, with representatives from every member of the Conclave crafting the laws and traditions of the newly-emerging political entity comprising more than four hundred separate races, General Gau promised that every Sur—every forty standard days—he and those who followed him as executive would stand in the well of the assembly and answer questions from the representatives. It was his way of assuring the Conclave members that the leadership could always be held accountable.

Hafte Sorvalh told him at the time that as his trusted advisor, she thought it would be a way for the grasping, ambitious members of the assembly to grandstand and otherwise in all senses be a waste of his time. General Gau had thanked her for her candor in this as in all other things and then went ahead and did it anyway.

Sorvalh had come to believe this was why, at these question-and-answer sessions, he always had her sit behind him. That way, he would not have to see the *I told you so* expression on her face. She had one of those now, listening to the tiresome Hado, from Elpri, pester Gau yet again about the humans.

"Return to the matter, Representative Hado?" Gau said, lightly. "It seems from these sessions that you never leave the matter alone." This received various sounds of amusement from the seated representatives, but Sorvalh marked faces and expressions in the crowd that held no levity in them. Hado was a pest and held a minority view, but it was not to say the minority he was part of was entirely insignificant.

Standing at his bench assignment, Hado moved his face into what Sorvalh knew was a configuration expressing displeasure. "You jest, General," he said.

"I do not jest, Representative Hado," Gau said, equally lightly. "I am merely well aware of your concern for this particular race."

"If you are well aware of it, then perhaps you can tell me—tell the assembly—what plans you have to contain them," Hado said.

"Which 'them'?" Gau said. "You are aware, Representative, that the human race is currently divided into two camps—the Colonial Union and the Earth. The Earth is not a threat to us in any way. It has no ships and no way into space other than what the Colonial Union, from which it is now estranged, allows it. The Colonial Union relied on Earth for soldiers and colonists. Now that supply has been cut off. The Colonial Union knows that what soldiers and colonists it now loses, it cannot replace. This makes it cautious and conservative in its expenditures of both. Indeed, it has been said to me that the Colonial Union is now actually attempting diplomacy on a regular basis!" This received more sounds of amusement. "If the humans are actually attempting to get along with other races, my dear representative, it is an indication of just how cautious they are at this point."

"You believe, General, that because they play at diplomacy that they are no longer a threat," Hado said.

"Not at all," Gau said. "I believe that because they cannot threaten as they have, they now attempt diplomacy."

"The distinction between the two escapes me, General," Hado said.

"I am well aware of that fact, Representative Hado," Gau said. "Nevertheless, the distinction exists. Moreover, the main portion of the Colonial Union's attention at the moment is in a rapprochement with Earth. Since you ask what I plan to do to contain the humans, I will note to you what you should already know, which is that since the Conclave trade fleet carrying Major John Perry appeared over Earth, we have maintained an active diplomatic presence on Earth. We have envoys in five of their major national capitals, and we have made the governments and people of Earth aware that should they choose not to reconcile with the Colonial Union, there is always the option of the Earth joining the Conclave."

This caused a stir among the assembly, and not without reason. The Colonial Union had destroyed the Conclave war fleet over Roanoke Colony, a fleet comprising a ship from each member race of the union. There was not a member race in the Conclave that had not suffered a wound from the humans, or that was not aware how perilously close the Conclave came to collapse in the immediate aftermath of that particular fiasco.

Representative Hado seemed especially incensed. "You would allow into the Conclave the same race who tried to destroy it," he said.

Gau did not answer the question directly. Instead he turned and addressed another representative. "Representative Plora," he said. "Would you please stand."

Representative Plora, an Owspa, shambled up on its spindly legs.

"If memory serves, Representative Hado, in the not-too-distant past, the Elpri and the Owspa shed a significant amount of their blood and treasure trying to eradicate each other from space and history," Gau said. "How many millions of each of your citizens died because of the hatred between your races? And yet both of you are here in this august assembly, peaceable, as your worlds are now peaceable."

"We attacked each other, not the Conclave," Hado said.

"I believe the principle still applies," Gau said, with a tone that suggested he had a hard time believing Hado attempted to make that argument. "And in any event, it was the Colonial Union which attacked the Conclave, not the Earth. To blame the Earth, or the humans who live on it, for the actions of the Colonial Union is to misapprehend how the Earth itself has been used by it. And, to your point, Representative, the longer we may through diplomacy keep Earth from allying itself with the Colonial Union—or joining the Colonial Union outright—the longer we keep the humans from doing any sort of mischief at our door. Is that not what you are asking for?"

Sorvalh watched Hado fidget. It wasn't at all what he was asking for, of course. What he wanted was the Conclave to expunge the human race from every crevice it clung to. But it looked for the moment as if Gau had walked him into a corner. Which, Sorvalh supposed, was one of the reasons he had these ridiculous question-and-answer sessions in the first place. He was very good at walking his opponents into corners.

"What about the disappearing ships?" came another voice, and everyone, including Sorvalh, turned toward Representative Plora, who had remained standing after it had been called on. Plora, suddenly aware that it was the focus of attention, shrank back but did not sit. "There have been reports of more than a dozen ships that have disappeared from systems where Conclave territory borders human territory. Is that not the work of the humans?"

"And if it is, why have we not responded to it?" Hado said, now out of his corner.

General Gau glanced back to Sorvalh at this point. She resisted giving him her *I told you so* expression.

"Yes, we have lost several ships in the last few Sur," General Gau said. "They have largely been merchant ships. These are systems where piracy is not entirely unknown, however. Before we leap to the assumption that humans are behind this, we should explore the more likely explanation that raiders—ostensibly citizens of the Conclave—are the cause."

"How can we know for sure?" Hado said. "Have you made it a priority to know, General? Or are you willing to underestimate the humans for a second time?"

This quieted the assembly. Gau had taken responsibility for the debacle at Roanoke and had never pretended other than that he was responsible. But only a fool would press him on the subject, and it appeared that Unli Hado was that fool.

"It is always a priority for our government to find those of our citizens who are lost to us," Gau said. "We will find them and we will find whoever is behind their disappearance—whoever they are. What we will *not* do, Representative Hado, is use the disappearances of these ships to launch into a fight with a people who have shown how committed they are to trying to destroy us when they feel they are cornered and have no choice left but to fight. You ask me whether I am willing to underestimate the humans. I assure you that I am not. What I am wondering, Representative, is why *you* seem so determined to do so."

Sorvalh visited General Gau later in his personal office. It was cramped, even if one was not a Lalan, who were a tall species, and Hafte Sorvalh was tall for her species.

"It's all right," Gau said, from his desk, as she ducked through the door. "You can say it."

"Say what?" Sorvalh asked.

"Every time you crouch through the door of this office, you come in, you straighten up, and you look around," Gau said. "Every time you get an expression on your face that looks like you have bitten into something slightly unpleasant. So go ahead and say it: My office is cramped."

"I would say it is cozy," Sorvalh said.

Gau laughed in his fashion. "Of course you would," he said.

"It's been commented on by others how small this office is, considering your position," Sorvalh said.

"I have the large public office for meetings, and to impress people when I have to, of course," Gau said. "I'm not blind to the power of impressive spaces. But I've spent most of my life on starships, even after I began to build the Conclave. You get used to not a lot of space. I'm more comfortable here. And no one can say that I give more to myself than to the representatives of any of our member races. And that, too, has its advantages."

"I see your point," Sorvalh said.

"Good," Gau said, and then motioned to the chair that he clearly had brought in for her, because it matched her physiology. "Please, sit."

Sorvalh sat and waited. Gau attempted to wait her out, but waiting out a Lalan is a bad bet on a good day. "All right, say the *other* thing you're thinking," Gau said.

"Unli Hado," Sorvalh said.

"One of the graspingly ambitious types that you warned me about," Gau said.

"He's not going to go away," Sorvalh said. "Nor is he entirely without allies."

"Very few," Gau said.

"But growing," Sorvalh said. "You have me with you for these sessions to count heads. I count heads. There are more of them each session who are either in his orbit or drifting toward him. You won't have to worry about him this time, or the next, or possibly for several sessions down the line. But if this goes on, in time you will have a faction on your hands, and that faction will be agitating for the eradication of the humans. All of them."

"One of the reasons we formed the Conclave was to rid ourselves of the idea that an entire people could or should be eradicated," Gau said.

"I am aware of that," Sorvalh said. "It was one of the reasons why my people gave you and the Conclave their allegiance. I am also aware that ideals are hard to practice, especially when they are new. And I am also aware that there's not a species in the Conclave who doesn't find the humans ... well ... *vexing* is likely the most polite word for it."

"They are that," Gau said.

"Do you really believe that they would be that hard to kill?" Sorvalh asked.

Gau presented an unusual face to Sorvalh. "An unusual and surprising question, coming from you of all people," he said.

"I don't wish them dead, personally," Sorvalh said. "At least, not actively. Nor would the Lalan government support a policy of extinction. But you suggested to Hado they would be a formidable opponent. I am curious if you believe it."

"Are the humans able to stand against us ship to ship, soldier to soldier? No, of course not," Gau said. "Even our defeat at Roanoke, with over four hundred ships destroyed, was not a material blow to our strength. It was one ship out of dozens or hundreds that each of our members had in their own fleets."

"So you don't believe it," Sorvalh said.

"That's not what I said," Gau said. "I said they can't stand against us ship to ship. But if the humans go to war with us, it won't be ship to ship. How many human ships went against us at Roanoke? None. And yet we were defeated—and the blow was immense. The Conclave almost fell, Hafte, not because our material strength had been compromised, but because our psychological strength had. Those ships were not what the humans were aiming for. Our unity was. The humans almost shattered us."

"And you believe they could do it again," Sorvalh said.

"If we pressed them? Why wouldn't they?" Gau said. "Throwing the Conclave nations back into war with each other is an optimum result for the humans. It would keep all of us occupied while they rebuild their strength and position. The real question is not whether the humans—the Colonial Union—could attack and possibly destroy the Conclave, if pressed. The real question is why they haven't tried to do it since Roanoke."

"As you say, they have been busy trying to bring the Earth back into the fold," Sorvalh said.

"Let us hope it takes them a long time," Gau said.

"Or perhaps they have started making war on the Conclave," Sorvalh suggested.

"You're talking about the missing ships," Gau said.

"I am," Sorvalh said. "As tiresome as Representative Hado may be, the disappearance of so many ships near human space is not to be dismissed out of hand."

"I don't dismiss it," Gau said. "The representative-major for the fleet has our investigators scouring the scenes and the nearby populated worlds for information. We have nothing so far."

"Ships rarely disappear so comprehensively," Sorvalh said. "If there's no trace, that in itself says something."

"What it doesn't say is who is responsible, however," Gau said, and then raised a hand as Sorvalh moved to comment. "It's not to say we don't have our intelligence net within the Colonial Union working overtime trying to find connections between the humans and the disappearances. We do. However, if we find it, we will deal with it discreetly, and without the sort of open warfare that Hado and his friends in the assembly so want us to have."

"Your desire for subtlety will frustrate them," Sorvalh said.

"I am fine with them being frustrated," Gau said. "It's a small price to pay for keeping the Conclave intact. However, it is not the discussion of the disappearing ships that is the reason I asked you here, Hafte."

"I am at your service, General," Sorvalh said.

Gau picked up a manuscript sheet on his desk and handed it to her.

She gave him a curious look as she took it. "A hard copy," she said. Her assignments from him were usually offered on her computer.

"It's not a copy," Gau said. "That sheet you have is the only place in the entire Conclave where that information is recorded."

"What is it?" she asked.

"It's a list of new human colonies," Gau said.

Sorvalh looked at Gau, genuinely shocked. The Conclave had forbidden any unaffiliated races from colonizing new planets. If they tried, the new colonies would be displaced, or destroyed if the colonists would not leave. "They can't truly be that stupid," she said.

"They are not," Gau said. "Or at least, officially, the Colonial Union is not." He pointed at the sheet. "These are what the humans call 'wildcat colonies.' It means that they are not sanctioned or supported by the Colonial Union. Most of these sorts of colonies are dead in a year."

"So nothing we could call out the Colonial Union for," Sorvalh said.

"No," Gau said. "Except for this: We have rumors that the Bula found humans attempting a wildcat colony on one of their worlds, and that at least a few of the colonists were Colonial Defense Forces members. The Colonial Union attempted to extract the colony and were discovered doing so by the Bula. It had to part with a substantial ransom to retrieve its citizens and buy the Bula's silence."

"These wildcat colonies aren't actually unofficial at all, then," Sorvalh said. "And we're back to the question of whether they are truly that stupid."

"It's a fine question, but one that is tangential to my real concern," Gau said.

Sorvalh waggled the sheet in her hand. "You're worried that Hado and his friends will find out about these."

"Precisely," Gau said, and pointed at the sheet again. "That's the only written-out list, and it's written out only once to avoid it slipping out easily into the universe. But I am not stupid, nor do I believe my intelligence gatherers talk only to me. Hado and his compatriots will find out. And if they find out and if these colonies really do have Colonial Defense Forces members within them, then we have no choice but to remove the colony. If the colony won't be moved, we'll have to destroy it."

"And if we destroy it, we'll be at war with the Colonial Union," Sorvalh said.

"Or something close enough to it," Gau said. "The humans know they are in a bad position, Hafte. They are dangerous animals on the best of days. Poking at them right now is going to go poorly for everyone involved. I want this problem solved privately before it becomes a public problem."

Sorvalh smiled. "I imagine this is where I come in."

"I've opened up a back channel to the Colonial Union," Gau said.

"And how did you do that?" Sorvalh asked.

"Me to our envoy in Washington, D.C.," Gau said. "Him to John Perry. John Perry to a friend of his in the CDF Special Forces. And so on up the chain of command, and back down again."

Sorvalh gave a motion of assent. "And my job is to meet with the back channel."

"Yes," Gau said. "In this case it will be someone of lower rank than you—apologies for that, the humans are twitchy." Sorvalh offered up a hand expression signaling acceptance and lack of concern. "It's a Colonel Abel Rigney. He's not of especially high rank, but he is very well placed to get things done."

"You want me to show him this list and let him know we know about the CDF soldiers," Sorvalh said.

"What I want you to do is scare him," Gau said. "In your own special way."

"Why, General," Sorvalh said, and gave the appearance once more of being shocked. "I have no idea what you mean."

General Gau smiled at this.

"Well, he was certainly a tall fellow, wasn't he?" Sorvalh said, looking up at the statue in the Lincoln Memorial.

"Tall for a human, yes," Colonel Rigney said. "And especially tall for his time. Abraham Lincoln was president of the United States well before humans made it out into the universe. Not everyone had good nutrition then. People tended to be shorter. So he would have stood out. Among your people, Councillor Sorvalh, he'd be considered something of a runt."

"Ah," Sorvalh said. "Well, we are generally considered tall for most intelligent races we know of. But surely there might be some humans as tall as a Lalan."

"We have basketball players," Rigney said. "They are very tall for humans. The tallest of them might be as tall as the shortest of you."

"Interesting," Sorvalh said, and kept looking at Lincoln.

"Is there someplace you would like to go to talk, Councillor?" Rigney asked, after allowing Sorvalh her moment of contemplation.

Sorvalh turned to the human and smiled at him. "I do apologize, Colonel. I realize you are indulging me by meeting me here at a tourist attraction."

"Not at all," Rigney said. "In fact, I'm glad you did. Before I left Earth I lived in this area. You're giving me an excuse to visit old haunts."

"How wonderful," Sorvalh said. "Have you seen any of your family and friends while you're here?"

Rigney shook his head. "My wife passed on before I left Earth, and we never had children," he said. "My friends would all be in their eighties or nineties now, which is old for humans, so they're mostly dead, and I don't think the ones that are living would be too pleased to see me bounding in, looking like I'm twenty-three years old."

"I can see how that might be a problem," Sorvalh said.

Rigney pointed at Lincoln. "He looks the same as when I left."

"I would hope so!" Sorvalh said. "Colonel, would you mind walking as we talk? I walked down the Mall before I got here and I passed someone selling something called 'churros.' I should like to experiment with human cuisine, I think."

"Oh, churros," Rigney said. "Good choice. By all means, Councillor."

They walked down the stairs of the Lincoln Monument and toward the Mall, Sorvalh walking slowly so as to keep Rigney from having to jog to keep up. Sorvalh noticed other humans looking curiously at her; aliens on Earth were still a rarity, but not so rare now in Washington, D.C., that the people there would not attempt nonchalance. They stared equally at the green human next to her, she noted.

"Thank you for meeting me," Sorvalh said to Rigney.

"I was delighted to," Rigney said. "You gave me an excuse to visit Earth again. That's a rare thing for a CDF member."

"It's convenient how the Earth has become a neutral ground to both of our governments," Sorvalh said.

Rigney winced at this. "Yes, well," he said. "Officially I am not allowed to be pleased by that particular development."

"I understand entirely," Sorvalh said. "Now then, Colonel. To business." She reached into the folds of her gown and produced the manuscript and handed it to Rigney.

He took it and looked at it curiously. "I'm afraid I can't read this," he said, after a moment.

"Come now, Colonel," Sorvalh said. "I know perfectly well that you have one of those computers in your head, just like every other Colonial Defense Forces member. What is the ridiculous name you call them?"

"A BrainPal," Rigney said.

"Yes, that," Sorvalh said. "So I am confident that not only have you already recorded the entire content of that paper into the computer, it has also rendered you a translation."

"All right," Rigney said.

"We aren't going to get anywhere, Colonel, if you are going to insist on fighting me on even the simplest of things," Sorvalh said. "We would not have opened up this back channel if it were not absolutely necessary. Please do me the courtesy of presuming I am not on my first mission of diplomacy."

"My apologies, Councillor," Rigney said, and handed back the document. "I'm in the habit of not revealing everything. Let's just say my automatic reflexes kicked in."

"Very well," Sorvalh said, took the manuscript and then placed it back into the folds of her gown. "Now that you've undoubtedly had time to scan the translation, you can tell me what was written on the document."

"It was a list of uninhabited planets," Rigney said.

"I question that modifier, Colonel," Sorvalh said.

"Officially speaking, I have no idea what you are talking about," Rigney said. "Unofficially, I would be very interested in knowing how you developed that list."

"I am afraid I must keep that a secret," Sorvalh said. "And not just because I was never told. But I assume now we can dispense with the polite fiction that there are not, in fact, ten human colonies where they should not be."

"Those aren't sanctioned colonies," Rigney said. "They're wildcats. We can't stop people from paying spaceship captains to take them to a planet and drop them there without our permission."

"You could, I am certain," Sorvalh said. "But that's not the issue at the moment."

"Does the Conclave blame the Colonial Union for the existence of these wildcat colonies?" Rigney asked.

"We question that they are wildcat colonies at all, Colonel," Sorvalh said. "As wildcat colonies typically do not have Colonial Defense Forces soldiers in their mix of colonists."

Rigney had nothing to say to this. Sorvalh waited a few moments to see if this would change, and then continued. "Colonel Rigney, surely you understand that if we had wanted to vaporize these colonies, we would have done it by now," she said.

"Actually, I don't understand," Rigney said. "Just as I don't understand what the gist of this conversation is."

"The gist, as you say, is that I have a personal message and a bargain for the Colonial Union from General Gau," Sorvalh said. "That is to say, it comes from General Gau in the capacity of his own person, and not General Gau, leader of the Conclave, a federation of four hundred races whose combined might could crush you like a troublesome pest."

Colonel Rigney's face showed a flicker of annoyance at this assessment of the Colonial Union, but he quickly let it go. "I'm ready to hear the message," he said.

"The message is simply that he knows that your 'wildcat' colonies are no such thing and that under different circumstances you would have received notice of this knowledge by having the fleet show up at their doorstep, followed by other reprisals designed to strongly dissuade you from further colonization attempts," Sorvalh said.

"With respect, Councillor," Rigney said, "the last time your fleet showed up at our doorstep, it didn't end well for your fleet."

"That was the second-to-last time," Sorvalh said. "The last time a fleet of ours showed up at your doorstep, you lost the Earth. Beyond that, I think you and I both know that you will not get a chance to repeat your exploits at Roanoke."

"So the general wishes to remind us that normally he'd vaporize these colonies," Rigney said.

"He wishes to remind you of it to make the point that at this time he has no interest in doing that," Sorvalh said.

"And why not?" Rigney asked.

"Because," Sorvalh said.

"Really?" Rigney said, stopping his walk. "'Because' is the reason?"

"The reason is not important," Sorvalh said. "Suffice to say the general doesn't want to have a fight over these colonies at the moment, and it's a good guess that you don't, either. But there are those in the Conclave who would be delighted to have a fight over them. That's something neither you nor the general wants, although almost certainly for different reasons. And while right now the only two people in the Conclave political caste who know of the existence of that list are the general and me, I have no doubt that you know enough about politics to know that secrets don't stay secret long. We have very little time before the content of that list makes its way into the hands of those in the Conclave who would be thrilled to take a torch to your colonies, and to the Colonial Union." Sorvalh started walking again.

After a moment, Rigney followed. "You say we have very little time," he said. "Define 'very little.'"

"You have until the next time General Gau is required to take questions from the Grand Assembly," Sorvalh said. "By that time, the warmongers of the assembly will almost certainly know of the existence of at least some of the colonies, and that CDF soldiers are at them. They will demand the Conclave take action, and the general will have no choice but to do so. That will happen in thirty of our standard days. That would be about thirty-six days on your Colonial Union calendar."

"So much for the message," Rigney said. "What's the bargain?"

"Also simple," Sorvalh said. "Make the colonies disappear and the Conclave won't attack."

"This is easier said than done," Rigney said.

"This is not our concern," Sorvalh said.

"Supposing that there were Colonial Defense Forces soldiers at these colonies," Rigney said, "wouldn't simply removing them be sufficient?"

Sorvalh looked at Rigney as if he were a slow child. Rigney understood enough of the look to put up his hands. "Sorry," he said. "Didn't think it through enough before it came out of my mouth."

"These colonies aren't supposed to exist," Sorvalh said. "We might have been willing to overlook them if they had genuinely been wildcat colonies, at least until they got too large to ignore. But these are known to have CDF soldiers in them. They will never not be targets for the Conclave. They have to be gone before we have to officially take notice of them. You know what the consequences are otherwise, for both of our governments."

Rigney was silent again for a moment. "No bullshit, Councillor?"

Sorvalh didn't know the word "bullshit" but guessed at the context. "No bullshit, Colonel," she said.

"Nine out of ten of those colonies won't be difficult to evacuate," Rigney said. "Their colonists are standard-issue disgruntled Colonial Union citizens, who have vague ideas about freedom from the tyranny of their fellow man or what have you, or simply don't like other people enough to want to have the company of more than about two hundred other of their own kind. Six of these colonies are near starvation anyway and would probably be happy to escape. I would, in their shoes."

"But then there is this other colony," Sorvalh said.

"Yes, then there is this other colony," Rigney said. "Do your people have racists? People who believe they are inherently superior to all other types of intelligent people?"

"We have some," Sorvalh said. "They're generally agreed to be idiots."

"Right," Rigney said. "Well, this other colony is made up almost totally of racists. Not only against other intelligent races—I shudder to think what they would think of *you*—but also against other humans who don't share their same phenotype."

"They sound lovely," Sorvalh said.

"They're assholes," Rigney said. "However, they are also well-armed, well-organized, well-funded assholes, and this particular colony is thriving. They left because they didn't like being part of a mongrel Colonial Union, and they hate us enough that they would probably get off on the idea that by going down in flames, they would consign us to hell as well. Extracting them would be messy."

"Is this actually a problem for the CDF?" Sorvalh asked. "I don't wish to be unpleasantly blunt about this, but the CDF is not known for being an institution that cares deeply about those whom they crush."

"We're not," Rigney said. "And when it comes down to it, we'd get them out, because the alternative would be grim. But in addition to being well armed, well organized and well funded, they're well connected. Their leader is the son of someone high up in the CU government. They're estranged—she's mortified that her son turned out to be a racist shithead—but he's still her son."

"Understood," Sorvalh said.

"As I said, messy," Rigney said.

They had arrived at the churro stand. The churro vendor looked up at Sorvalh, amazed. Rigney ordered for them, and the two of them continued walking after they had received their pastries.

"These are lovely!" Sorvalh exclaimed, after the first bite.

"Glad you think so," Rigney said.

"Colonel Rigney, you're worried that the only way to get these racist, intractable, *asshole* colonists is through bloodshed," Sorvalh said, after she took another bite.

"Yes," Rigney said. "We'll do it to avoid a war, but we'd like a different option."

"Well," Sorvalh said, around her churro, "inasmuch as I am asking you to do this, it would be wrong of me not to offer a possible solution to you."

"I'm listening," Rigney said.

"Understand that what I am going to suggest will be one of those things that never happened," Sorvalh said.

"Since this conversation isn't happening either, this is fine," Rigney said.

"I will also have to ask you to do one other thing for me first," Sorvalh said.

"And what is that?" Rigney asked.

"Buy me another churro," Sorvalh said.

"Take another step, xig, and I'll blow your head off," said the colonist directly in front of Sorvalh. He was pointing a shotgun at her chest.

Sorvalh stopped walking and stood calmly at the frontier of the colony of Deliverance. She had been walking toward it for several minutes, having had her shuttle land at the far reach of a broad meadow on which the colony had situated itself. Her gown swished as she moved, and the necklace she wore featured audio and visual devices feeding back to her ship. She had walked slowly, in order to give the colony enough time to muster a welcoming party, and for another purpose as well. Five heavily armed men stood in front of her now, weapons raised. Two more that she could see lay on colony roofs, zeroed into her position with long-range rifles. Sorvalh assumed there were more she couldn't see, but they didn't concern her at the moment. She would be aware of them soon enough.

"Good morning, gentlemen," she said. She gestured to the markings on their skin. "Those are lovely. Very angular."

"Shut up, xig," said the colonist. "Shut up and turn around and get back in that shuttle of yours and fly off like a good bug."

"My name is Hafte Sorvalh," she said, pleasantly. "It's not 'Xig.'"

"A xig is what you are," said the colonist. "And I don't give a shit what you call yourself. You're leaving."

"Well," Sorvalh said, impressed. "Aren't you *fierce*."

"Fuck you, xig," the colonist said.

"A bit repetitive, however," Sorvalh said.

The colonist raised the shotgun so that it was now pointing at her head. "You'll be going now," he said.

"I won't, actually," Sorvalh said. "And if you or any other member of your merry band tries to shoot me, you'll be dead before you can manage to pull the trigger. You see, my friend, while I was walking toward your compound, my starship orbiting above this location was busy tracking and marking the heat signatures of every living thing in your colony larger than ten of your kilos. You're now all entered into the ship's weapons database, and about a dozen particle weapons are actively tracking twenty or thirty targets each. If any one of you tries to kill me, you will die, horribly, and then everyone else in the colony will follow you as each individual beam cycles through its target list. Every one of you—and your livestock, and your large pets—will be dead in roughly one of your seconds. I will be a mess, because much of what is inside of your head right now will likely get onto me, but I will be alive. And I have a fresh change of clothes in my shuttle."

The colonist and his friends stared at Sorvalh blankly.

"Well, let's get on with it," Sorvalh said. "Either try to kill me or let me do what I came here to do. It's a lovely morning and I would hate to waste it."

"What do you want?" said another colonist.

"I want to talk to your leader," Sorvalh said. "I believe his name is Jaco Smyrt."

"He won't talk to you," said the first colonist.

"Why ever not?" Sorvalh asked.

"Because you're a *xig*," he said, as if it were the most obvious thing in the world.

"That's really unfortunate," Sorvalh said. "Because, you see, if I am not talking to Mr. Smyrt in ten of your minutes, then those particle beams I mentioned to you will cycle through their targets, and you'll all be dead, again. But I suppose if Mr. Smyrt would rather you all be dead, it's all the same to me. You might want to spend those moments with your families, gentlemen."

"I don't believe you," said a third colonist.

"Fair enough," Sorvalh said, and pointed to a small enclosure. "What do you call those animals?"

"Those are goats," said the third colonist.

"And they are adorable," said Sorvalh. "How many can you spare?"

"We can't spare any," said the second colonist.

Sorvalh sighed in exasperation. "How do you expect me to give you a demonstration if you can't spare a single goat?" she said.

"One," said the first colonist.

"You can spare one," Sorvalh said.

"Yes," the first colonist said, and one of the animals exploded before he had even finished saying the word. The rest of the goats, alarmed and covered in gore, bolted toward the farthest reaches of the enclosure.

Four minutes twenty-two seconds later, Jaco Smyrt stood in front of Sorvalh.

"It's a pleasure to meet you," she said, to him. "I see you go in for angular markings as well."

"What do you want, xig?" Smyrt said.

"Again with the 'xig,'" Sorvalh said. "I don't know what it means, but I can tell you don't mean it nicely."

"What do you *want*?" Smyrt said, through gritted teeth.

"It's not what I want, it's what you want," Sorvalh said. "And what you want is to leave this planet."

"What did you just say?" Smyrt asked.

"I believe I was perfectly clear," Sorvalh said. "But allow me to give you additional context. I am a representative of the Conclave. As you may know, we have forbidden further colonization by humans and others. You are, at least to a certain approximation, human. You're not supposed to be here. So I've arranged for you and your entire colony to go. Today."

"The fuck we will," Smyrt said. "I don't answer to the Colonial Union, I don't answer to the Conclave, and I sure as shit don't answer to *you*, xig."

"Of course you don't," Smyrt said. "But allow me to attempt to reason with you anyway. If you leave, then you will live. If you don't leave, then you'll be killed and there will be a state of war between the Conclave and the Colonial Union, which is likely to end very poorly for the Colonial Union. Surely that matters to you."

"I can think of no better way to die than as a martyr for my race and my way of life," Smyrt said. "And if the Colonial Union dies with us, then I will welcome its diluted population as our honor guard into hell."

"A stirring sentiment," Sorvalh said. "I was told you were a believer in racial purity and such things."

"There is only one race, and it is the human race," Smyrt said. "It must be preserved and made pure. But it is better for all of humanity to fall than to remain the denatured thing it is today."

"Marvelous," Sorvalh said. "I must read your literature."

"No xig will ever read our sacred books," Smyrt said.

"It's almost touching how devoted you are to this racial ideal of yours," Sorvalh said.

"I'll die for it," Smyrt said.

"Yes, and so will everyone like you," Sorvalh said. "Because here is the thing. If you don't leave this colony today, you will die—which you are fine with, I understand—but after you're dead, I'll make a study of everyone in this pure colony of yours, to make sure I understand your *essence*. Then the Conclave will go to the Colonial Union and give it an ultimatum: Either every member of *your* pure race of human dies, or every human dies. And, well . . . you know how *mongrels* think, Mr. Smyrt. They have no appreciation for the perfection of purity."

"You can't do that," Smyrt said.

"Of course we *can*," Sorvalh said. "The Conclave outnumbers the Colonial Union in every single possible way. The question is whether we *will* or not. And whether we *will* depends on you, Mr. Smyrt. Leave now, or leave the human race to the mongrels forever. I'll give you ten minutes to think it over."

"That's a disgusting tactic you used," Gau said, as Sorvalh recounted her encounter with the Deliverance colonists.

"Well, of course it was," Sorvalh said. "When you are dealing with disgusting people, you have to speak their language."

"And it worked," Gau said.

"Yes, it did," Sorvalh said. "That ridiculous man was happy to let all of the human race die, but when it was just his tiny phenotypical slice of it, he lost his nerve. And he was convinced that we would have done it, too."

"You assured the other humans we wouldn't, I presume," Gau said.

"Colonel Rigney, whom I was dealing with, did not need the assurance," Sorvalh said. "He understood what I was planning from the start. And as soon as I got that wretched man to agree to leave, he and his team had them in shuttles and off the planet. It was all done by local sundown."

"Then you did well," Gau said.

"I did as you asked," Sorvalh said. "Although I do feel bad about the goat."

"I'd like for you to keep this back channel with Rigney open," Gau said. "If you work well with him, maybe we can keep out of each other's way."

"Your consideration of the humans is going to become a sticking point, General," Sorvalh said. "And although this one meeting went well, I think that sooner or later our two civilizations are going to be back at each other. No back channel is going to change that. The humans are too ambitious. And so are you."

"Then let's work at making it later rather than sooner," Gau said.

"In that case, you'll want this," Sorvalh said, and took the manuscript page from her robes and gave it to General Gau. "Let the information on it—all of it—find its way to Representative Hado. Let him bring it to you in the Grand Assembly. And when he does, announce that you have seen the list, too, and that our forces have been to each of the planets and found no record of human habitation—as they will not, because the Colonial Union was thorough in removing traces. You may then accuse Hado of warmongering and possibly fabricating the document. You will break him there, or at least damage him for long enough that he will cease to be a factor."

Gau took the document. "This is what I mean when I

say you are scary in your own special way, Hafte," he said.

"Why, General," Sorvalh said, "I don't know what you're talking about."

The Dog King

"Don't step on that," Harry Wilson said to Deputy Ambassador Hart Schmidt, as the latter walked up to the shuttle that the former was working on. An array of parts and tools was splayed out on a work blanket; Schmidt was on the edge of it. Wilson himself had his arm shoved deep into an outside compartment of the shuttle. From the inside of the compartment, Schmidt could hear bumping and scraping.

"What are you doing?" Schmidt asked.

"You see tools and parts and my arm shoved inside a small spacecraft, and you really have to ask what I'm doing?" Wilson said.

"I see what you're doing," Schmidt said. "I just question your ability to do it. I know you're the mission's field tech guy, but I didn't know your expertise went to shuttles."

Wilson shrugged as best he could with his arm jammed inside a shuttle. "Captain Coloma needed some help," he said. "This 'new' ship of hers is now the oldest active ship in the fleet, and she's got the rest of the crew going through all its systems with a microscope. She didn't have anyone to go over the shuttle. I didn't have anything else to do, so I volunteered."

Schmidt backed up a step and looked over the shuttle. "I don't recognize this design," he said, after a minute.

"That's probably because you weren't born when this

thing was first put into service," Wilson said. "This shuttle is even older than the *Clarke*. I guess they wanted to make sure we kept the vintage theme going."

"And you know how to fix these things how, exactly?" Schmidt asked.

Wilson tapped his head with his free hand. "It's called a BrainPal, Hart," he said. "When you have a computer in your head, you can become an instant expert on anything."

"Remind me not to step inside that shuttle until someone actually qualified has worked on it," Schmidt said.

"Chicken," Wilson said, and then smiled triumphantly. "Got it," he said, extracting his arm from the shuttle compartment. In his hand was a small blackened object.

Schmidt leaned forward to look. "What is that?"

"If I had to guess, I'd say it's a bird nest," Wilson said. "But considering that Phoenix doesn't actually have native birds per se on it, it's probably a nest for something else."

"It's a bad sign when a shuttle has animal nests in it," Schmidt said.

"That's not the bad sign," Wilson said. "The bad sign is that this is the third nest I found. I think they may have literally hauled this shuttle out of a junkyard to give it to us."

"Lovely," Schmidt said.

"It's never a dull day in the lower reaches of the Colonial Union diplomatic corps," Wilson said. He set down the nest and reached for a towel to wipe the soot and grime from his hand.

"And this brings us to the reason I came down to see you," Schmidt said. "We just got our new mission assigned to us."

"Really," Wilson said. "Does this one involve me being held hostage? Or possibly being blown up in order to find a mole in the Department of State? Because I've already done those."

"I'm the first to acknowledge that the last couple of missions we've had have not ended on what are traditionally considered high notes," Schmidt said. Wilson smirked. "But I think this one may get us back on the winning track. You know of the Icheloe?"

"Never heard of them," Wilson said.

"Nice people," Schmidt said. "Look a little like a bear mated with a tick, but we can't all be beautiful. Their planet has had a civil war that's been flaring up off and on for a couple hundred years, since the king disappeared from his palace and one faction of his people blamed the other faction."

"Was it their fault?" Wilson said.

"They say no," Schmidt said. "But then they *would,* wouldn't they. In any event, the king left no heir, his sacred crown went missing and apparently between those two things no one faction could legitimately claim the throne, thus the two centuries of civil war."

"See, this is why I can't support monarchy as a system of government," Wilson said. He reached down to start reassembling the portion of the shuttle he had taken apart.

"The good news is that everyone's tired of it all and they're all looking for a face-saving way to end the conflict," Schmidt said. "The bad news is that one of the reasons they are trying to end the conflict is that they are thinking of joining the Conclave, and the Conclave won't accept them as members unless there is a single government for the entire planet. And this is where we come in."

"We're going to help them end their civil war in order to join the Conclave?" Wilson asked. "That seems counterintuitive to our own agenda."

"We've volunteered to mediate between the factions,

yes," Schmidt said. "We're hoping that by doing so, we'll generate enough goodwill that the Icheloe will choose an alliance with us, not the Conclave. That in turn will help us build alliances with other races, with an eye toward establishing a counterweight to the Conclave."

"We tried that before," Wilson said, reaching for a spanner. "When that General Gau fellow was putting the Conclave together, the Colonial Union tried to form an alternative. The Counter-Conclave."

Schmidt handed him the spanner. "That wasn't about building actual alliances, though," he said. "That was about disrupting the Conclave so it couldn't form at all."

Wilson smirked at this. "And we wonder why no other intelligent race out there trusts the Colonial Union any further than they can throw us," he said. He went to work with the spanner.

"It's why this negotiation is important," Schmidt said. "The Colonial Union got a lot of credibility with the Danavar negotiations. The fact we put one of our ships in the path of a missile showed a lot of alien races that we were serious about building diplomatic solutions. If we can be seen as good-faith negotiators and mediators with the Icheloe, we're in a much better position going forward."

"Okay," Wilson said. He replaced the outside panel on the shuttle and began sealing it. "You don't have to sell me on the mission, Hart. I'm going regardless. You just need to tell me what I'm supposed to do."

"Well, so you know, Ambassador Abumwe isn't going to be the lead on this mediation," Schmidt said. "The ambassador and the rest of us will be acting in support of Ambassador Philippa Waverly, who has experience with the Icheloe and who is friendly with a Praetor Gunztar, who is acting as a go-between between the factions on the negotiating council."

"Makes sense," Wilson said.

"Ambassador Waverly doesn't travel alone," Schmidt said. "She's a little quirky."

"Okay," Wilson said, slowly. The shuttle compartment was now completely sealed.

"And the important thing to remember here is that there are no small jobs on a diplomatic mission, and that every task is important in its own unique way," Schmidt said.

"Hold on," Wilson said, and then turned around to face Schmidt directly. "Okay, hit me with it," he said. "Because with an introduction like that, whatever idiot thing you're going to have me do has got to be *good.*"

"And of course, Praetor Gunztar, you remember Tuffy," Ambassador Philippa Waverly said, motioning to her Lhasa apso, which stuck out its tongue and lolled it, winningly, at the Icheloe diplomat. Wilson held the leash attached to the dog's collar. He smiled at Praetor Gunztar as well, not that it was noticed.

"Of course I do," Praetor Gunztar exclaimed in a chittering burst duly translated by a device on his lanyard, and leaned toward the dog, which scampered with excitement. "How could I possibly forget your constant companion. I was worried that you were not going to be able to get him past quarantine."

"He had to go through the same decontamination process as the rest of us," Waverly said, nodding toward the rest of the human diplomatic mission, which included Abumwe and her staff. They had all been formally introduced to their Icheloe counterparts, with the exception of Wilson, who was clearly an adjunct to the dog. "He was very unhappy about that, but I knew he wouldn't want to miss seeing you."

Tuffy the Lhasa apso barked at this, as if to confirm

that his excitement at being close to Praetor Gunztar had elevated him to near bladder-voiding levels of joy.

From behind the leash, Wilson glanced over to Schmidt, who was assiduously not looking in his direction. The entire group of them, human and Icheloe alike, were taking part in a formal presentation ceremony at the royal palace, in the same private garden where the long-missing king was last seen before the mysterious disappearance that plunged his planet into a civil war. The two groups had met in a central square surrounded by low planters arrayed in a circular design, which featured flora from all over the planet. In every planter was a spray of fleur du roi, a gorgeously sweet-smelling native flower that by law could be cultivated only by the king himself; everywhere else on the planet it was allowed only to grow wild.

Wilson remembered vaguely that the fleur du roi, like the aspen on earth, was actually a colony plant, and the sprays of flowers were all clones of one another, connected by a vast root system that could extend for kilometers. He knew this because as part of his dog-minding job, he needed to find out which plants in the private garden could tolerate being peed on by Tuffy. He was pretty sure that the fleur du roi would be hardy enough if it came to that, and it almost certainly would. Tuffy was the only dog on the planet. That was a lot of territory to mark.

"Now that we have all been introduced, I believe it is time to move forward with our initial meeting," Praetor Gunztar said, turning his attention away from the Lhasa apso and back again to Ambassador Waverly. "Today I thought we'd take care of merely procedural items, such as confirming the agenda and opening formal statements."

"That would of course be fine," Waverly said.

"Excellent," Gunztar said. "One reason for a short schedule today is that I would like to offer you and your people a special consideration. You may not know that the royal palace sits above one of the most extensive cave systems on the planet, one that ultimately travels almost two kilometers into the planet and meets up with a vast subterranean river. The caves have been used by the palace as a keep, as a place of refuge and even as a catacomb for the royal family. I would like to offer you a tour of these caves, which no one but Icheloe have been in before. It's a token of our appreciation for the Colonial Union's willingness to mediate these possibly contentious negotiations."

"What an honor," Waverly said. "And of course we accept. The caves really descend that far into the planet?"

"Yes, although we will not follow them down that deep," Gunztar said. "They are blocked off for reasons of security. But what you will see is extensive enough. The cave system is so vast that even now it has never been fully explored."

"How fascinating," Waverly said. "If nothing else, it will give us an impetus to get through the day's business as quickly as possible."

"There's that, too," Gunztar said, and everyone had a laugh, in their own species' fashion, at this. Then the entire mass, human and Icheloe, was herded toward the palace, to the suite of rooms reserved for the negotiations themselves.

As they moved, Waverly glanced toward Abumwe, who in turn glanced toward Schmidt, who held back with Wilson. Wilson stood, hand on leash, restraining the little dog, who was becoming anxious at seeing his mistress wander off without him.

"So, today will just be a couple of hours," Schmidt said. "The agenda's already been agreed to by both sides, so all we're doing is going through the motions. All you have to do is keep Tuffy here busy until we break. After today you and Tuffy will be at our embassy for the duration."

"I've got it, Hart," Wilson said. "This isn't exactly rocket science."

"You've got all your stuff?" Schmidt asked.

Wilson pointed to a jacket pocket. "Kibble and treats here," he said. He pointed to a trouser pocket. "Poop bags here. The pee I'm not picking up."

"Fair enough," Schmidt said.

"They know he's going to do his business, right?" Wilson asked. "It's not going to cause a major diplomatic incident if one of the grounds staff here sees li'l Tuffy in a poop squat, right? Because I am not ready to deal with that sort of thing."

"It's one of the reasons you're staying behind here," Schmidt said. "It's a private garden. He's been given approval for taking care of business. We've been asked not to let him do any digging."

"If he does that, I can just pick him up," Wilson said.

"I know I said it before, but sorry about this, Harry," Schmidt said. "Dog sitting isn't in your job description."

"*De nada,*" Wilson said, and then rephrased at the sight of Schmidt's puzzled expression. "It's no big deal, Hart," he said. "It's like working on the shuttle. Someone's got to do it, and everyone else has something more useful to do. Yes, I'm overqualified to watch the dog. That just means you don't have to worry about anything. And that you owe me drinks after this."

"All right," Schmidt said, smiling. "But if something *does* happen, I have my PDA set to accept your call."

"Will you please get out of here now and go be useful to someone," Wilson said. "Before I have Tuffy here mate with your boot."

Tuffy looked up at Schmidt, apparently hopefully. Schmidt left hastily. Tuffy looked over to Wilson.

"You leave *my* boots alone, pal," Wilson said.

———

I have a problem, Wilson sent to Schmidt, roughly an hour later.

What is it? Schmidt sent back, using the texting function of his PDA so as not to interrupt the talks.

It would be best explained in person, Wilson sent.

Is this about the dog? Schmidt sent.

Sort of, Wilson sent.

Sort of? Schmidt sent. *Is the dog okay?*

Well, it's alive, Wilson sent.

Schmidt got up as quickly and quietly as possible and headed to the garden.

"We give you one thing to do," Schmidt said, as he walked up to Wilson. "One thing. Walk the damn dog. You said I didn't have to worry about *anything*."

Wilson held up his hands. "This is not my fault," he said. "I swear to God."

Schmidt looked around. "Where's the dog?"

"He's here," Wilson said. "Kind of."

"What does that even mean?" Schmidt said.

From somewhere came a muffled bark.

Schmidt looked around. "I hear the dog," he said. "But I can't see it."

The bark repeated, followed by several more. Schmidt followed the noise and eventually found himself at the edge of a planter filled with fleur du roi flowers.

Schmidt looked over to Wilson. "All right, I give up. Where is it?"

Another bark. From inside the planter.

From *below the planter*.

Schmidt looked over to Wilson, confused.

"The flowers ate the dog," Wilson said.

"What?" Schmidt said.

"I swear to God," Wilson said. "One second Tuffy was standing in the planter, peeing on the flowers. The next, the soil below him *opened up* and something pulled him under."

"*What* pulled him under?" Schmidt asked.

"How should I know, Hart?" Wilson said, exasperated. "I'm not a botanist. When I went over and looked, there was a *thing* underneath the dirt. The flowers were sprouting up from it. They're part of it."

Schmidt leaned over the planter for a look. The dirt in the planter had been flung about and below it he could see a large, fibrous bulge with a meter-long seam running across its top surface.

Another bark. From *inside* the bulge.

"Holy shit," Schmidt said.

"I know," Wilson said.

"It's like a Venus flytrap or something," Schmidt said.

"Which is not a good thing for the dog," Wilson pointed out.

"What do we do?" Schmidt asked, looking at Wilson.

"I don't know," Wilson said. "That's why I called you in the first place, Hart."

The dog barked again.

"We can't just leave him down there," Schmidt said.

"I agree," Wilson said. "I am open to suggestion."

Schmidt thought about it for a moment and then abruptly took off in the direction of the entrance to the garden. Wilson watched him go, confused.

Schmidt reemerged a couple of minutes later with an Icheloe, dusty and garbed in items that were caked with dirt.

"This is the garden groundskeeper," Schmidt said. "Talk to him."

"You're going to have to translate for me," Wilson said. "My BrainPal can translate what he says for me, but I can't speak in his language."

"Hold on," Schmidt said. He pulled out his PDA and accessed the translation program, then handed it to Wilson. "Just talk. It'll take care of the rest."

"Hi," Wilson said, to the groundskeeper. The PDA chittered out something in the Icheloe language.

"Hello," said the groundskeeper, and then looked over to the planter that had swallowed the dog. "What have you done to my planter?"

"Well, see, that's the thing," Wilson said. "I didn't do anything to the planter. The planter, on the other hand, ate my dog."

"You're talking about that small noisy creature the human ambassador brought with it?" the groundskeeper asked.

"Yes, that's it," Wilson said. "It went into the planter to relieve itself and the next thing I know it's been swallowed whole."

"Well, of course it was," the groundskeeper said. "What did you expect?"

"I didn't expect anything," Wilson said. "No one told me there was a dog-eating plant here in the garden."

The groundskeeper looked at Wilson and then Schmidt. "No one told you about the kingsflower?"

"The only thing I know about it is that it's a colony plant," Wilson said. "That most if it exists under the dirt and that the flowers are the visible part. The thing about it being carnivorous is new to me."

"The flowers are a lure," the groundskeeper said. "In the wild, a woodland creature will be drawn in by the flowers and while it's grazing it will get pulled under."

"Right," Wilson said. "That's what happened to the dog."

"There's a digestion chamber underneath the flowers," the groundskeeper said. "It's big enough that a large-size animal can't climb out. Eventually one of two things happens. Either the creature starves and dies or asphyxiates and dies. Then the plant digests it and the nutrients go to feed the entire colony."

"How long does that take?" Schmidt asked.

"Three or four of our days," the groundskeeper said, and then pointed at the planter. "This particular kingsflower has been in this garden since before the disappeared king. We usually feed it a kharhn once every ten days or so. Tomorrow is a feeding day, so it was getting a little hungry. That's why it ate your creature."

"I wish someone had told me about this earlier," Wilson said.

The groundskeeper gave the Icheloe equivalent of a shrug. "We thought you knew. I was wondering why you were letting your, what do you call it, a dog?" Wilson nodded. "Why you let your *dog* wander through the kingsflowers, but we were informed ahead of time to allow the creature free rein of the garden. So I decided that it was not my problem."

"Even though you knew the dog could get eaten," Wilson said.

"Maybe you *wanted* the dog to get eaten," the groundskeeper said. "It's entirely possible you brought the dog as a treat for the kingsflower as a diplomatic gesture. *I* don't know. All I do is tend to the plants."

"Well, assuming we didn't want the dog to get eaten, how do we get it back?" Wilson asked.

"I have no idea," the groundskeeper said. "No one has ever asked that question before."

Wilson glanced over to Schmidt, who offered up a helpless gesture with his hands.

"Let me put it this way," Wilson said. "Do you have any objection to me *trying* to retrieve the dog?"

"How are you going to do that?" the groundskeeper wanted to know.

"Go in the same way the dog did," Wilson said. "And hopefully come back out the same way."

"Interesting," the groundskeeper said. "I'll go get some rope."

————

"You should probably rub against the flowers a bit," the groundskeeper said, motioning to the fleur du roi. "Your dog was not especially large. The kingsflower is probably still hungry."

Wilson looked doubtfully at the groundskeeper but nudged the flowers with his feet. "It doesn't seem to be doing anything," he said, kicking at the plant.

"Wait for it," said the groundskeeper.

"How long should I—," Wilson began, and then dirt flew and fibrous tentacles wrapped around his legs, constricting.

"Oh, that's not good," Schmidt said.

"Not helping," Wilson said, to Schmidt.

"Sorry," Schmidt said.

"Don't be alarmed when the plant starts cutting off the circulation to your extremities," the groundskeeper said. "It's a perfectly normal part of the process."

"That's easy for you to say," Wilson said. "You're not losing feeling in your legs."

"Remember that the plant wants to eat you," the groundskeeper said. "It's not going to let you get away. Don't fight it. Let yourself be eaten."

"Don't take this the wrong way, but I'm finding your advice to be less than one hundred percent helpful," Wilson said to the groundskeeper. The plant was now beginning to drag him under.

"I'm sorry," the groundskeeper said. "Usually the kharhn we feed to the kingsflower are already dead. I never get to see anything live fed to it. This is exciting for me."

Wilson fought hard not to roll his eyes. "Glad you're enjoying the show," he said. "Will you hand me that rope now, please?"

"What?" the groundskeeper said, then remembered what he had in his hands. "Right. Sorry." He handed one end of the rope to Wilson, who quickly tied it to himself in a mountain climber hold. Schmidt took the other end from the groundskeeper.

"Don't lose your grip," Wilson said. He was now up to his groin in plant. "I don't want to be fully digested."

"You'll be fine," Schmidt said, encouragingly.

"Next time it's your turn," Wilson said.

"I'll pass," Schmidt said.

More tentacles shot up, roping around Wilson's shoulder and head. "Okay, I am officially not liking this anymore," he said.

"Is it painful?" the groundskeeper asked. "I am asking for science."

"Do you mind if we hold the questions until afterward?" Wilson asked. "I'm kind of busy at the moment."

"Yes, sorry," the groundskeeper said. "I'm just excited. Damn it!" The Icheloe started patting his garments. "I should be recording this."

Wilson glanced over to Schmidt, looking as exasperated as he could under the circumstances. Schmidt shrugged. It had been a strange day.

"This is it," Wilson said. Only his head was above the surface now. Between the tentacles constricting and dragging him down and the pulsing, peristaltic motion of the fleur du roi plant sucking him down into the ground, he was reasonably sure he was going to have post-traumatic flashbacks for months.

"Hold your breath!" the groundskeeper said.

"Why?" Wilson wanted to know.

"It couldn't hurt!" the groundskeeper said. Wilson was going to make a sarcastic reply to this but then realized that, in fact, it couldn't hurt. He took a deep breath.

The plant sucked him fully under.

"This is the best day ever," said the groundskeeper to Schmidt.

———

Wilson had a minute or two of suffocating closeness from the plant as the thing pushed him into its digestive sac. Then there was a drop as he fell from the thing's throat into its belly. The fall was broken by a spongy, wet mass at the bottom: the plant's digestive floor.

"Are you in?" Schmidt said, to Wilson, via his Brain-Pal.

"Where else do you think I would be?" Wilson said, out loud. His BrainPal would forward the voice to Schmidt.

"Can you see Tuffy?" Schmidt asked.

"Give me a second," Wilson said. "It's dark down here. I need to give my eyes a moment to adjust."

"Take your time," Schmidt said.

"Thanks," Wilson said, sarcastically.

Thirty seconds later, Wilson's genetically-engineered eyes had adjusted to the very dim light from above to see his environment, a dank, teardop-shaped organic capsule barely large enough to stand in and stretch his arms.

Wilson looked around and then said, "Uh."

"'Uh'?" Schmidt said. "'Uh' is not usually good."

"Ask the groundskeeper how long it takes this thing to digest something," Wilson said.

"The groundskeeper says it usually takes several days," Schmidt said. "Why?"

"We have a problem," Wilson said.

"Is Tuffy dead already?" Schmidt asked, alarm in his voice.

"I don't know," Wilson said. "The damn thing isn't here."

"Where did he go?" Schmidt asked.

"If I knew that, Hart, I wouldn't be saying 'uh,' now, would I?" Wilson said, irritated. "Give me a minute." He peered hard into the dim. After a minute, he got down on his hands and knees and moved toward a small shadow near the base of the capsule. "There's a tear here," Wilson said, after examining the shadow. "Behind the tear it looks like there's a small tunnel or something."

"The groundskeeper says the rock bed below the palace is riddled with fissures and tunnels," Schmidt said, after a brief pause. "It's part of the cave system that's underneath the palace."

"Do the tunnels and fissures go anywhere?" Wilson asked.

"He says 'maybe,'" Schmidt said. "They've never mapped the entire system."

From deep inside the black tunnel, Wilson heard a very small, echoing bark.

"Okay, good news," Wilson said. "The dog's still alive. Bad news: The dog is still alive somewhere down a very small, dark tunnel."

"Can you go down the tunnel?" Schmidt asked.

Wilson looked and then felt around the wall of the capsule. "How does our groundskeeper friend feel about me tearing into the plant wall a little bit?" he asked.

"He says that in the wild these plants have to deal with wild animals kicking and tearing at their insides all the time, so you're not going to hurt it too much," Schmidt said. "Just don't tear it any more than you have to."

"Got it," Wilson said. "Also, Hart, do me a favor and throw me down a light, please."

"The only light I have is on my PDA," Schmidt said.

"Ask the groundskeeper," Wilson said.

Down the tunnel, there was a sudden, surprised yelp.

"Ask him to hurry, please," Wilson said.

A couple minutes later, the mouth of the plant opened and a small object tumbled down into the capsule. Wilson retrieved the light, switched it on, lifted the tear and shone the light down the tunnel, sweeping it around to get an idea of its dimensions. He figured if he crawled, he might barely be able to make his way down the tunnel. The tunnel itself was long enough that the light shone down into darkness.

"I'm going to have to undo the rope," Wilson said. "It's not long enough to go all the way down this tunnel."

"I don't think that's a good idea," Schmidt said.

"Being swallowed by a carnivorous plant isn't a good idea," Wilson said, undoing the rope. "Compared to that, letting go of the rope is nothing."

"What if you get lost down there?" Schmidt asked.

"My BrainPal will let you know where I am, and I'll let you know if I get stuck," Wilson said. "You'll be able to tell by the screaming panic in my voice."

"Okay," Schmidt said. "Also, I don't know if this is information that you need to know right now, but I just got a ping from Ambassador Waverly's assistant. She says the negotiations should wrap up in an hour and then the ambassador will want Tuffy for, and I swear to God this is a quote, 'a little snuggle time.'"

"Wonderful," Wilson said. "Well, at least now we know how much time we have."

"One hour," Schmidt said. "Happy spelunking. Try not to die."

"Right," Wilson said. He knelt at the tear, tore it just enough to shove his body through, put the light between his teeth, got on his hands and knees and started crawling.

The first hundred meters were the easy part; the tunnel was narrow and low, but dry and relatively straight as it descended through the rock. Wilson figured that if he had to guess, he'd venture it was once a lava tube at some point, but at the moment all he really wanted was for the thing not to collapse on him. He wasn't ordinarily claustrophobic, but he'd also never been dozens of meters down a tube in a rock, either. He thought he was allowed a spot of unease.

After a hundred meters or so, the tube became slightly wider and higher but also more jagged and twisting, and the angle of descent became substantially steeper. Wilson hoped that somewhere along the way the tunnel might become wide enough for him to turn around in; he didn't like the idea of having to back out ass first, dragging the dog along with him.

"How is it going?" Schmidt asked him.

"Come down here and find out," Wilson said, around his light. Schmidt demurred.

Every twenty meters or so Wilson would call out to Tuffy, who would bark some times but not others. After close to an hour of crawling, the barks finally began to sound like they were getting closer. After almost exactly an hour, Wilson could hear two things: Schmidt beginning to sweat up on the surface and the scrabbling sounds of a creature moving some distance ahead.

The tunnel suddenly widened and then disappeared into blackness. Wilson carefully approached what was now the lip of the tunnel, took the light out of his mouth and panned it around.

The cave was about ten meters long, four or five meters wide and roughly five meters deep. To the side of the tunnel lip was a pile of scree that formed a steep slope to the floor of the cave; directly in front of the lip, however, was a straight drop. Wilson's light played across the scree and caught glimpses of dusty paw marks; Tuffy had avoided the drop.

Wilson directed the light to the floor cave, calling out to the dog as he did so. The dog didn't bark, but Wilson heard the clitter of nails on the floor. Suddenly Tuffy was in the light cone, eyes reflecting green up at Wilson.

"There you are, you little pain in the ass," Wilson said. The dog was dusty but otherwise seemed unharmed by his little adventure. He had something in his jaws; Wilson peered closely. It looked like a bone of some sort.

Apparently, Tuffy wasn't the first live animal to get sucked down into the fleur du roi after all; something else fell in and escaped down the tunnel behind the tear, just to die in this dead-end cave.

Tuffy got bored of looking into the light and turned to wander off. As he did, Wilson caught a glimpse of something sparkly attached to the dog; he trained his light on the animal as it moved and focused on the sparkly bit. Whatever it was was stuck to Tuffy in some way, encircling one of the dog's shoulders and riding around to his undercarriage.

"What the hell is that?" Wilson said to himself. He was still following Tuffy with the light, which was why he finally saw the skeleton of the creature the dog had taken his chew toy from. The skeleton was roughly a meter and a half long and mostly intact; it was missing what looked like a rib—which was what Tuffy was now chewing on quite contentedly—and its head. Wilson flicked the light slightly and caught the white flash of something round. *Ah,* thought Wilson. *There's the head, then.*

It took him a few seconds to realize that what he was looking at was the skeleton of an Icheloe adult.

It took another few seconds, and Tuffy wandering through the light cone, sparkling as he did so, before Wilson realized which Icheloe's skeleton it was likely to be.

"Oh, shit," Wilson said, out loud.

"Harry?" Schmidt said, suddenly cutting in. "Uh, just so you know, I'm not alone on this end anymore. And we have a bit of a problem here."

"We have a bit of a problem on this end, too, Hart," Wilson said.

"I'm guessing your problem isn't Ambassador Waverly looking for her dog," Schmidt said.

"No," Wilson said. "It's oh so very much larger."

There was an indignant squawk on the other end of

the line; Wilson imagined Schmidt putting his hand over the PDA's microphone to keep Wilson from hearing ambassadorial venting. "Is it Tuffy? Is Tuffy all right?" More squawking. "Is Tuffy, uh, *alive*?"

"Tuffy is fine, Tuffy is alive, Tuffy is perfectly good," Wilson said. "But I've found something down here that's none of those things."

"What do you mean?" Schmidt said.

"Hart," Wilson said, "I'm pretty sure I just found the lost king."

"Do you hear that?" Ambassador Waverly said, pointing out the window of one of the many sitting rooms of the royal palace. The window was open, and in the distance was a rhythmic chittering that reminded Wilson of the cicadas that would fill the midwestern nights with their white noise. These were not cicadas.

"Those are protesters," Waverly said. "Thousands of Icheloe reactionaries who are here to demand a return to royalty." She pointed at Wilson. "*You* did that. More than a year of background work and persuasion and angling to get us a seat at the table—more than a year to line up the dominoes just right for us to position this negotiation as the first step to make a legitimate counter to the Conclave—and you blow it all in *two hours*. Congratulations, Lieutenant Wilson."

"Wilson didn't intend to find the lost king, Philippa," Ambassador Abumwe said, to her counterpart. She was in the room with Wilson and Waverly. Schmidt was there, too, pulled in because he was, as Waverly put it, an "accomplice" to Wilson's shenanigans. Tuffy was also present, gnawing on a toy ball volunteered by the palace staff. Wilson had discreetly separated Tuffy from the royal bones long before they both had exited the cave. The crown remained with the dog; it had somehow attached itself and refused to be removed. All five were awaiting the return of Praetor Gunztar, who had been pulled into emergency consultations.

"It doesn't matter what he *intended* to do," Waverly shot back. "What matters is what he *did* do. And what he did was single-handedly disrupt a long-running diplomatic process. Now the Icheloe are back on the verge of civil war and we are to blame."

"It doesn't have to be as bad as that," Abumwe said. "If nothing else, we've solved the disappearance of the king, which was the cause of the civil war. The war started because one faction blamed the other for kidnapping and killing him. Now we know that never happened."

"And that simply doesn't *matter,*" Waverly said. "You know as well as I that the disappearance of the king was just the polite fiction the factions needed to go after each other with guns and knives. If it hadn't been the king going missing, they would have found some other reason to go at each other's throats. What's important now is that they wanted to end that fight." Waverly pointed again at Wilson. "But now *he's* dragged up that damn king, giving the hard-liners on both sides a new pointless excuse to go after each other."

"We don't know that will be the outcome," Abumwe said. "You had confidence in the process before. At the end of the day, the Icheloe still want their peace."

"But will they still want it with *us*?" Waverly said, looking over. "Now that we've unnecessarily disrupted their peace process and added complications to it? That's the question. I hope you're right, Ode. I really do. But I have my doubts." She turned her gaze back to Wilson. "And do you have any thoughts on this subject, Lieutenant Wilson?"

Wilson glanced over to Abumwe, whose face was neutral, and at Schmidt, who had preemptively gone pale. "I'm sorry I unnecessarily disrupted your process, Ambassador," he said. "I apologize." In his peripheral vision,

Wilson could see Schmidt's eyes widen. Hart clearly wasn't expecting deference from his friend.

"You apologize," Waverly said, walking over to him. "You're sorry. That's all you have to say."

"Yes, I think so, ma'am," Wilson said. "Unless you think there's something else I should add."

"I think your resignation would be in order," Waverly said.

Wilson smiled at this. "The Colonial Defense Forces isn't generally keen on resignations, Ambassador Waverly."

"And that's your final comment on the matter," Waverly said, persisting.

Wilson glanced very briefly at Abumwe and caught her almost imperceptible shrug. "Well, except to say that I know what to do the next time something like this happens," he said.

"And what is that?" Waverly said.

"Let the plant keep the dog," Wilson said.

Praetor Gunztar opened the door to the room before Waverly had a chance to explode at Wilson. She whirled toward Gunztar instead with such sudden ferocity that even the praetor, who was no great reader of human emotion, could not miss it. "Is everything all right?" he asked.

"Of course, Praetor Gunztar," Waverly said, tightly.

"Very good," Gunztar said, barreling through before Waverly could launch into anything further. "I have news. Some of it is good. Some of it is less so."

"All right," Waverly said.

"The good news—the *great* news—is that leaders of both factions agree that no one was responsible for the killing of the king, except for the king himself," Gunztar said. "It was well-known the king was a heavy drinker and that he would often stroll in his private garden at night. The most obvious explanation is that the king was drunk, collapsed into the kingsflower planter, and the plant pulled him under. When he awoke, he tried to escape and followed the tunnel to his death. The garden was part of his private residence and he was a bachelor; no one looked for him until his staff went to wake him in the morning."

"Didn't anyone at the time think to look inside the plant?" Abumwe asked.

"They did, of course," Gunztar said. "But it was not until much later, when more obvious places were searched. And by that time, there was no trace of the king. It seems that he may have wandered down the tunnel by that time and was either dead or too injured by the fall into the cave to call for help. The bones show his spine was shattered in several places, consistent with a fall."

Wilson, who remembered Tuffy chewing on at least a couple of other bones aside from the rib, kept quiet.

"This is good news because one continual sticking point between the factions has been finding some way to finesse the disappearance of the king," Gunztar said. "The question of blame and responsibility are still sore subjects. Or were. Now they no longer are. During our discussions, the head of the pro-king faction provisionally apologized for blaming the agitators for killing the king. The head of the agitator faction provisionally expressed sorrow at the death of the king. As long as it sticks, the job here has become substantially easier."

"Wow," Wilson said. "And here I thought that the disappearance of the king was just a convenient excuse already warring factions were using to go after each other."

"Of course not," Gunztar said, turning toward Wilson and thereby missing the flush that drove itself up Waverly's neck and face. "To be certain, the factions were ready to fight. But our civil war would not have lasted so long, nor have been so bloody, had one side not accused the other of regicide. And so the Icheloe owe you a particular debt of thanks, Lieutenant Wilson, for what you have done for us today."

"If you thank anyone, you should thank Ambassador Waverly, Praetor Gunztar," Wilson said. "Without her, I would never have found your lost king. After all, she is the one who brought Tuffy."

"Yes, of course," Gunztar said, bowing in the Icheloe way to Ambassador Waverly. She, still furious at Wilson and yet also aware of how he had just transferred credit for the praise to her, nodded mutely. "And that, I'm afraid, brings us to our bad news."

"What's the bad news?" Waverly said.

"It's about Tuffy," Gunztar said. "The crown is attached to him."

"Yes," Waverly said. "It's tangled in his hair. We'll get it out. We'll trim his hair down if we have to."

"It's not that simple," Gunztar said. "You can't get it off him because it's tangled in his hair. You can't get it off him because microscopic fibers have come off the crown and physically attached themselves to him, binding the crown to his physical body."

"What?" Waverly said.

"The crown is permanently attached to Tuffy," Gunztar said. "The scans our medical scientists did when he was brought back to the surface show it."

"How could that possibly happen?" Abumwe asked.

"The crown is a very important symbol of the king," Gunztar said. "Once taken up, it was supposed to never be taken off." He pointed to a set of ridges on his own head. "The crown is designed to sit on the head of the king in such a way that it need never be removed. To assure that it never is, it is made with nanobiotic strands on the inside surface, tuned to graft to the genetic signature of the king. The crown is also sensitive to the electrical signals produced by life. It only comes off at death, when all brain and body activity are quiet."

"How did it get attached to Tuffy?" Waverly said. "He obviously has no genetic relation to your king."

"It's a mystery to us as much as you," Gunztar said.

"Hmmmm," Wilson said.

"What is it, Wilson?" Abumwe said.

"How much of this genetic material would need to be present for the crown to register it?" Wilson said.

"You'd have to ask our scientists," Gunztar said. "Why?"

Wilson motioned to Tuffy, who had dozed off. "When I found him, he was chewing on one of the king's bones," he said. "He'd been in and around that skeleton for at least an hour. More than enough time to get some of the king's genetic material all over him. If the crown wasn't programmed well, it might have registered the genetic material, registered electrical signals from Tuffy being alive and decided, 'Well, close enough.'"

"So we give Tuffy a bath, wash off all the king's, uh, dust, and the crown lets go," Schmidt said. "Right?"

Wilson looked over at Gunztar, who offered up a negative gesture. "No. Only death will cause the crown to let go," he said. He turned to Ambassador Waverly. "And the council, I'm afraid, is adamant that the crown must be removed."

Waverly looked blankly at Gunztar for the ten seconds or so it took for what the praetor said to sink in. Wilson glanced over to Schmidt and Abumwe as if to say, *Here it comes.*

"*You want to kill my dog?!*" Waverly exclaimed to Gunztar.

Gunztar immediately threw up his hands. "We don't *want* to kill Tuffy," he said, quickly. "But you must understand, my friend. The crown is an object of truly immense historical, political and social value. It is no exaggeration to say that it is one of the most iconic and significant objects we Icheloe have. It's been missing for generations. Its importance to us is incalculable. And your *dog* is wearing it."

"It's not *his* fault," Waverly said.

"I agree, of course," Gunztar said. "But ultimately that is neither here nor there. The council is unanimous that the crown must not stay on your dog." He pointed out the window, toward the chittering masses gathered in front of the palace. "The reactionaries we have at the gate don't represent our people at large, but there are enough of them to cause trouble. If they were to find out a *pet* wore the crown of the disappeared king, the riots would last for days. And I would be lying to you if I said there weren't those on the council who didn't find the fact Tuffy wears the crown deeply insulting. One of them even began calling him 'the Dog King.' And not in an affectionate way."

"You're saying Tuffy wearing the crown is jeopardizing our diplomatic mission," Abumwe said.

"Not yet," Gunztar said. "The fact that you found the disappeared king far outweighs the issue of the crown, for now. But the longer it takes for it to be returned to us, the more questions the negotiating council will begin to have about it. Make no mistake that eventually it will jeopardize your mission, and your standing. And the standing of the Colonial Union."

"Philippa," Abumwe said, to Waverly.

Waverly said nothing, looked at them all and then went over to Tuffy, who was by this time on his back, paws adorably in the air, snoring lightly. Waverly sat next to her dog, picked him up, waking him in the process, and began sobbing into his little back. The dog craned his head back and heroically tried to lick the head of his owner, hitting only air instead.

"Oh, come *on*," Wilson said, after roughly thirty seconds of awkward silence from everyone in the room except Ambassador Waverly, who continued sobbing. "I feel like I'm twelve and being made to reread the last couple chapters of *Old Yeller*."

"Lieutenant Wilson, it might be advisable to let Ambassador Waverly have her moment with Tuffy," Praetor Gunztar said. "It is hard to say good-bye to a friend."

"So we're all agreed that we're going to have to kill the dog," Wilson said.

"Wilson," Abumwe said, sharply.

Wilson held up his hand. "I'm not asking just to be an asshole," he assured Abumwe. "I'm asking because if we're all agreed that's what has to happen, then no one will look at me like I'm nuts for offering a completely insane potential solution."

"What solution?" Abumwe asked.

Wilson walked over and stood by Waverly and Tuffy. Tuffy lolled his tongue out at Wilson; Waverly looked up at him with deeply suspicious eyes.

"Badly-designed technology got us into this problem," Wilson said, looking down at Tuffy and Waverly. "Maybe better-designed technology can get us out of it."

"Here you go," Schmidt said, handing Wilson the small wand with a plunger button on top and then motioning with his head to two nervous-looking Icheloe technicians. "Press the button, everything goes down. Press the button again, hopefully everything comes back up again."

"Got it," Wilson said. He watched as another Icheloe technician brought in Tuffy and placed him on a stainless steel table, a small work towel placed in the middle to keep the dog's feet from getting too cold.

"The technicians also wanted me to tell you thank

you for being willing to be the one to press the button," Schmidt said.

"Of course," Wilson said. "Ambassador Waverly already hates my guts. And if this doesn't work, then better it's someone on our side than one of the Icheloe."

"Their thinking exactly," Schmidt said.

"How is Ambassador Waverly, anyway?" Wilson asked. He hadn't seen her for several hours.

"Abumwe is with her now," Schmidt said. "I think the plan is to keep feeding her alcohol."

"It's not a bad plan," Wilson said.

Schmidt looked at his friend. "How do you feel?"

"I feel fine, Hart," Wilson said. "I'd like to get this over with, however."

"Can I get you some juice or anything?" Schmidt asked.

"What you can do is help that technician with Tuffy," Wilson said, nodding to the Icheloe tech holding the squirming dog. "He looks like he's about to lose it." Schmidt hurried over and took the dog from the tech, then settled it down on the table. The tech backed away quickly, obviously relieved to be rid of her burden. The other two techs also quietly excused themselves.

"You want me to go?" Schmidt asked, petting Tuffy to keep the dog still.

"No, I need you to help me," Wilson said. "You might want to move your hands, though."

"Oh, right," Schmidt said, and moved a step away from the dog.

Tuffy moved to go after Schimdt, but Wilson said, "Tuffy!" and snapped his fingers at the same time, drawing the little dog's attention to himself.

"Good dog," Wilson said, to Tuffy, who gave him a happy doggie smile and wagged his fluffy little tail.

Wilson accessed his BrainPal and got the feed on the two small monitors the dog had on his body, one at the top of his head and the other on his chest, close to his heart. The two monitors showed Tuffy's brain and heart electrical activity. There was something else on his body as well, at the back of his neck, close to where his spinal cord met his brain. Wilson didn't have a monitor for it.

"Tuffy! Sit!" Wilson said.

The dog sat, winningly obliging.

"Good boy!" Wilson said. "Play dead!" He pressed the plunger button in his hand.

Tuffy's brain and heart monitors flatlined instantly. The Lhasa apso gave a tiny squeak and collapsed stiffly, like a stuffed animal blown over by a wind gust.

"'Play dead'?" Schmidt said, ten seconds later, after examining the dog. "That's just *cruel*."

"If this doesn't work, I'll have bigger problems than a tasteless joke," Wilson said. "Now, shut up for a couple of minutes, Hart. You're making me nervous."

"Sorry," Schmidt said. Wilson nodded and walked over to the dog on the table.

Tuffy was dead.

Wilson poked the body with a finger. No response at all.

"Any time," Wilson said. The Icheloe had assured him that their biological systems were similar enough to those of Earth vertebrates that Wilson was willing to risk his little experiment. Nevertheless, he wanted the crown to realize its wearer was dead sooner than later.

A minute passed. Two.

"Harry?" Schmidt asked.

"Quiet," Wilson said, staring at the crown, still nestled on the dog's body.

Another two minutes passed. Three.

"What do we do if this doesn't work?" Schmidt asked.

"Are you asking if there's a plan B?" Wilson asked.

"Yeah," Schmidt said.

"Sorry, no," Wilson said.

"Why are you telling me this now?" Schmidt asked.

"Why didn't you ask earlier?" Wilson asked.

Another minute.

"*There*," Wilson said, pointing.

"What?" Schmidt said.

"The crown moved," Wilson said.

"I didn't see anything," Schmidt said.

"You remember that part where my genetically-engineered eyes are about ten times better than yours, right, Hart?" Wilson said.

"Oh, that," Schmidt said.

"Remove the crown, please," Wilson said.

Schmidt reached over to the dog and gently removed the crown from the body. It came off easily.

"Got it," Schmidt said.

"Thank you," Wilson said. "Stand back now." Schmidt backed away from the table.

"Okay, Tuffy," Wilson said, looked at the dog and raised his wand. "Time to learn a new trick."

He plunged the button down a second time.

The dog twitched, peed himself and scrambled up from the table, barking furiously.

"Wow, he's pissed," Schmidt said, smiling.

"True in more than one way, and a totally appropriate response," Wilson said, smiling himself.

The Icheloe flooded back into the room, one of them carrying a bag full of red fluid: Tuffy's actual blood.

"Wait," Wilson said, and realized the Icheloe had no idea what he was saying. He made himself clear through gestures and then turned to Schmidt. "Tell one of them to go get Ambassador Waverly, please," he said. "I want her to see that her dog is fine before we transfuse the poor thing again."

Schmidt nodded and spoke to the Icheloe through his PDA. One of them departed in a hurry.

One of the other Icheloe pointed to the dog and looked

at Wilson. "How is it that you could give this animal your blood?" Wilson's BrainPal translated the Icheloe's chitter as saying. "You're not even the same species."

Wilson reached over and borrowed Schmidt's PDA. "It's called SmartBlood," he said, setting the PDA in front of him. "It's completely non-organic, so the dog's body wouldn't reject it. It also has several times the oxygen-carrying capacity, so we could stop the body's processes for a longer period of time and still have the tissues survive." Wilson reached over and picked up the still-damp dog, who had stopped barking by this time. "And that's what we did. Replaced this little guy's blood with my blood, then stopped this little guy's heart and brain long enough for the crown to think he's dead. Then started him up again."

"It seems risky," the Icheloe said.

"It *was* risky," Wilson said. "But the alternative was worse."

"You mean us breaking off our diplomatic relationship with you," said the other Icheloe.

"Well, I was actually thinking of a dead dog," Wilson said. "But yes, that, too."

Ambassador Waverly appeared in the doorway, Abumwe and Praetor Gunztar behind her. Tuffy saw his mistress and barked happily. Wilson set the dog on the floor; Tuffy's nails skittered adorably across the floor surface as he raced over to Waverly.

Everyone dissolved into a puddle of *awwwww*.

"This is just about the perfect ending, isn't it?" Schmidt said to Wilson, quietly.

"Just about," Wilson agreed.

"And I suppose we are to make a pact never to speak of this again," Schmidt said.

"I think that's the wisest course, yes," Wilson said.

"I concur," Schmidt said. "Furthermore, I suggest that we now commence to get drunk."

"Agreed," Wilson said. "I seem to recall you promising me a drink at the end of all this."

"Do you want us to pour back in that pint of Smart-Blood you gave to Tuffy before we do?" Schmidt said.

"You know, I think I'll be fine without it," Wilson said.

They watched as Waverly and Tuffy wandered off together, followed by some very concerned Icheloe, carrying Tuffy's bag of blood.

The Sound of Rebellion

Heather Lee heard the whisper of the slap's approach before she felt it, a strike designed to bring her back into consciousness. With the hit, she took a sharp intake of breath and tried to get her bearings.

She quickly became aware of three things. One, she was nude underneath a rough blanket that draped her body as she sat in a chair of some sort.

Two, she was restrained, with her wrists, ankles, neck and waist strapped down to the chair.

Three, she was blind, with something tightly binding and covering her head and face.

None of these were positive developments, in Lee's opinion.

"You're awake," said a voice, weirdly modulated. It jumped around in pitch and timbre.

This interested Lee. "What's going on with your voice?" she asked.

There was a brief pause before the response. "That's not the first question we got from your two compatriots," the voice said. "They were more concerned with where they were and why they were being held."

"I'm sorry," Lee said. "I wasn't aware there was a protocol."

This got a chuckle. "My voice is being modulated because we know you have one of those computers in your head," the voice said. "And we know that if you're not recording me already, you will be at some point in time, and that you could use that to record and identify me. I would prefer that not to happen. For the same reason we've blindfolded you, so you cannot record any visual things that would give us away. And of course we've also restrained you so that you stay put for now. We've taken your combat uniform because we know it provides you with strength and defense advantages, and we don't want you to have that. I do apologize for that."

"Do you," Lee said, as dryly as she could in the circumstance.

"Yes," the voice said. "Although you have no reason to believe me at the moment, you should understand that we have no interest in abusing you, either physically or sexually. Removing your combat uniform was a defensive procedure, nothing more."

"I'd believe you more if you hadn't slapped me awake," Lee said.

"You were surprisingly resistant to waking up," the voice said. "How do you feel?"

"I have a headache," Lee said. "My muscles are sore. I am dying of thirst. I have to pee. I am restrained. I'm blind. How are you?"

"Better than you, I will admit," the voice said. "Six, water."

What? Lee thought, and then there was something at her lips, a hard plastic nipple. Liquid came out of it; Lee drank it. It was water, so far as she could tell.

"Thank you," she said, after a minute. "Why did you say 'six'?"

"The person in the room with you is called Six," the voice said. "The number has no significance; it's randomly selected. We change them for every mission."

"What number are you?" Lee asked.

"This time I am Two," the voice said.

"And you're not in the room with me," Lee said.

"I am close by," Two said. "But I have no interest in

having my own voice leak in so you can isolate it. So I listen and watch, and Six takes care of everything else."

"I still need to pee," Lee said.

"Six," Two said. Lee could hear Six move, and then suddenly a portion of the hard bottom of her chair disappeared. "Go ahead," Two said.

"You're kidding," Lee said.

"I'm afraid not," Two said. "Again, apologies. But you can't honestly expect me to unbind you. Even naked and blind, a Colonial Defense Forces soldier is a formidable opponent. There is a pan underneath your chair that will catch your waste. Six will then deal with it."

"I feel as if I should apologize to Six," Lee said. "Especially because eventually I will have to do something else than pee."

"This is not Six's first time doing this," Two said. "We're all professionals here."

"How reassuring," Lee said. Then she made an inward shrug and relieved herself. After she was finished, there was a scrape as a pan was removed and another scraping sound as the bottom of her chair was replaced. There were steps, followed by a door opening and then closing.

"Your compatriots told me that you are Lieutenant Heather Lee, of the Colonial Defense Forces ship *Tubingen*," Two said.

"That's right," Lee said.

"Well, then, Lieutenant Lee, let me tell you how this is going to work," Two said. "You have been captured and you are my prisoner. I am going to ask you questions and you are going to answer them truthfully, as fully and completely as you can. If you do so, then when we are done I will have you released, obviously very far away from where we are now, but released all the same. If you do not do so, or if I catch you in a lie even once, I will kill you. I will not torture you, or abuse you, or have you raped or violated or any such nonsense. I will simply have a shotgun put to your head, in order to kill you, and to destroy that computer in your skull. It's old-fashioned but very effective. I regret to say that one of your compatriots, a Private Jefferson, already tested me on this score and learned to his misfortune that I am not joking. The lesson does him no good at this point, I'm afraid. But I hope his example might be useful to you."

Lee said nothing to this, thinking about Jefferson, who was always too enthusiastic for his own good.

The door opened; presumably Six was coming back into the room. "Six will now feed you and bathe you if you wish and will then leave. I have other matters to attend to for the next few hours. In that time, if you wish, you may consider what I've just told you. Do what we ask, and no harm will come to you. Do anything other than what we ask, and you will be dead. It's a binary choice. I hope you will choose wisely."

Left to herself, Lee reviewed her situation.

First: She knew who she was. Heather Lee, originally of Robeson County, North Carolina. Mother Sarah Oxendine, father Joseph Lee, sister Allie, brothers Joseph Jr. and Richard. In her past life a musician: a guitarist or cellist, depending on the gig. Joined up with the CDF six years previous, stationed with the *Tubingen* for the last two years six months. All this was important. If you were fuzzy on who you were, there were going to be other critical gaps in your knowledge base and you wouldn't know what they were.

Second: She knew where she was, in a general sense, and why she was there. She was on the planet of Zhong Guo. She and her company on the *Tubingen* were dispatched to quell a separatist rebellion in the provincial capital city of Zhoushan. The rebels had taken the local administration headquarters and broadcast media, securing hostages as they did so, and started airing screeds declaring Zhong Guo independent of the Colonial Union and seeking a new union with Earth, the "native and true home of humanity," as they put it. The local police had moved in to clear them out and were surprised when the rebels had more and better firepower than they did; the rebels killed two dozen police and took several more hostage, adding to their store of human shields.

The success of the rebels sparked a series of "Earth Rule" protests in other cities and towns including Liuzhau, Karhgar and Chifeng, the latter of which experienced severe property damage as rioters marched through the central business district, burning shops and buildings in an apparently indiscriminate fashion. By this time, the administration in the planetary capital of New Harbin had had enough and requested CDF intervention.

Lee and her platoon did a standard drop from high altitude at night with cloaking on; they were inside the administration and broadcast buildings before the rebels knew they had even landed on the roof. The fight was brief and lopsided; the rebels had only a few good fighters with them, the ones they had put out in front when the local police had gone at them. The rest of the rebels were recruited from the ranks of the young and excitable and had rather more enthusiasm than skill. The genuinely skilled rebel fighters engaged the CDF and were quickly subdued or killed, being no match for trained Colonial soldiers with superior physical and tactical skills; the rest surrendered without too much resistance.

Two rebel vehicles outside the administration offices opened fire at the building and were turned into glowing piles of slag by the *Tubingen,* which had targeted them from orbit. The hostages, kept in a basement-level wing filled with conference rooms, were dirty and tired but generally unharmed. The entire event took less than thirty minutes, with no casualties on the CDF side.

Their work done, the CDF soldiers asked for and received shore leave in Zhoushan, where they were welcomed enthusiastically, or so it seemed, by the locals, although that might have also been because the Colonial Union was known to pick up the tab for Colonial Defense Forces on shore leave, encouraging the soldiers to spend foolishly and the local shops and vendors to charge exorbitantly. If there were any rebel sympathizers among the burghers of Zhoushan, they kept their mouths shut and took the CDF's money.

The last thing Lee remembered prior to waking up in the room she was in now, she, Jefferson and Private Kiana Hughes were having dinner in a *hofbräuhaus* (Zhong Guo, despite its Chinese naming conventions, had mostly middle and southern Europeans, an irony that Lee, with Chinese ancestry on her father's side, found somewhat amusing). She recalled the three of them getting more than a little drunk, which in retrospect should have been a warning, since thanks to CDF soldiers' genetically-engineered physiology, it was almost impossible for them to actually get smashed. At the time, however, it just seemed like a pleasant buzz. She remembered piling out of the *hofbräuhaus* very late local time, wandering toward the hotel at which they had been booked and then nothing else until now.

Lee ruefully revised her assessment of the state of enthusiasm of the locals for the CDF's work. Clearly, not *everyone* was pleased.

Her memory checked out, and Lee turned her attention to where she might be now. Her BrainPal's internal chronometer told her that she had been out for roughly six hours. Given that expanse of time, it was possible that she, the apparently late Jefferson and (she rather strongly suspected) Hughes were now on the other side of the planet from Zhoushan. She doubted that, however. It would have taken at least some time for Two and Six to have gotten her naked and strapped to a chair and otherwise prepped for what they were planning to do to her. Two also mentioned that he (she? Lee decided to go with "he" in her brain for now) had already had enough time to talk to Jefferson and Hughes and to kill Jefferson when he had not cooperated. For these reasons, Lee suspected she was still somewhere in Zhoushan.

She also suspected, since she was still in fact in the hands of Two and Six and not already rescued by her platoon, that wherever she was had shielding that kept her BrainPal from transmitting her whereabouts. She tested this by trying to make a connection to Hughes and then to several other people in the platoon: nothing. She tried pinging the *Tubingen:* also nothing. Either this room specifically had a signal blocker or she was somewhere that was designed with (or had among its capabilities) the ability to block signals. If it was the latter, that would bring down the number of possible buildings it could be in Zhoushan.

Lee thought again, more deeply, about her situation and realized she was sitting on a clue. She was in a restraint chair of some sort—moreover, a restraint chair designed for someone to sit in for an extended period of time, given that the seat of the chair had a sliding trapdoor to allow waste through. Lee did not fancy herself a connoisseur of restraint systems, but as she was now in her ninth decade of life, she had seen a thing or two. In her experience, restraint chairs showed up in three places: hospitals, prisons and particularly specialized brothels.

Of the three, Lee dismissed the idea of a brothel first. It was possible, but brothels were a place of business and not particularly secure. People lived in them and worked in them, and there were (if the brothel was at all successful) all sorts of new and different clientele coming in and going out at all times of the day. Brothels would ensure some privacy, but probably not so much that a shotgun blast wouldn't be noticed, not to mention a corpse or two being dragged out of the premises.

In a hospital a corpse would not be a problem, but the shotgun blasts probably would be. An abandoned hospital might solve that issue, but hospitals also generally were not signal-proof—too much medical information was shuttled about electronically to make it a feasible idea.

So, a prison or jail seemed to be the mostly likely location: chairs, signal-blocking structure and easy disposal of dead bodies, as the prison would likely have its own morgue. It also meant that whoever was holding her and Hughes also had the ability to discreetly bring people in and out of a prison setting: someone in the local police, or at least the local government.

Lee had been given a map of Zhoushan as part of the briefing for the mission; she called it up on her BrainPal and then winced slightly as the computer in her head activated the visual cortex. Not actually seeing for several hours made even the illusion of light slightly painful. She let her brain acclimate to the visuals and then started scanning through.

As far as she could see (an expression that at the moment held some irony), there were two buildings in Zhoushan she was likely to be in: the municipal jail, which was in downtown Zhoushan and less than a kilometer away from the *hofbräuhaus* from which they were nabbed, and the province prison, which was ten klicks out from the Zhoushan city center. Lee had no detailed maps of either building—they had those only for the administration and broadcast buildings—but either way, she was comforted by at least the idea that she knew where she might be. It could come in handy.

She now turned her attention to her own situation, which she continued to deem not especially positive. The nakedness did not bother her on a personal level, as she'd never been particularly self-conscious about her body, but it did bother her that she was unarmored. Two had been correct that the CDF uniform gave its wearer certain protections and advantages, although its strengths in that regard were more passive than active. The uniform didn't make Lee stronger; it just made her tougher. Without it she would be more vulnerable to physical assault, which she suspected likely to happen despite assurances. Not to mention being vulnerable to shotgun blasts.

Speaking of which, she was also unarmed as well as unarmored. This was a problem, but one she spent little time concerning herself with. There was no point wishing for her weapons when she didn't have them.

The part where she was bound was also of concern to her. As discreetly as she could, she flexed against the binds. They felt soft, slick and supple rather than hard and unyielding, which told her that they were of some sort of woven substance rather than straight-up metal cuffs. She strained against the left arm restraint to see if there was any give to it, but there was none. The other restraints were the same. She had all the genetically-engineered superstrength of a CDF soldier, but no leverage to apply it with. If the binds had even the slightest tear in them, she could work against that, but as far as she could tell, the binds were in excellent condition.

Finally, Lee took stock of her assets, which at the moment consisted of her brain and not much else: She had no eyes, no physical strength and no way to communicate to anyone except possibly to Two, which did her no good, and Six, which likewise did not give her much to go on. And as much as Lee thought she had a reasonably good brain, all things concerned, there was only so much it could do, trapped as it was in her head.

"Well, shit," she said aloud, listening to the sound of her voice travel around the room. The room was large enough and had walls made of a substance that made it acoustically bouncy, probably bare rock or concrete.

Hello, her brain said.

She spent the next half hour alone in her head, occasionally humming to herself. If Two was watching, it might confuse him a bit.

Eventually, the door to the room opened and Six (Lee presumed) came back in.

"Lieutenant Lee," said the voice of Two, "are you ready to begin?"

"I am ready to talk your ears off," Lee said.

For the next two hours, Lee spoke at length about any subject that Two wished to know about, which included current CDF troop strength and disposition, CDF and Colonial Union messaging about the break from Earth, what the two organizations were doing to compensate for the loss of human resources from Earth, the state of rebellions of various colonies, both in Lee's direct experience and from hearsay from other soldiers and Colonial Union staff and the details of Lee's particular mission on Zhong Guo.

Lee answered with facts when she could, informed guesses and estimates when she couldn't and wild supposition when she had to, making sure Two understood which was which and why, so there would be no margin for misunderstanding between the two of them.

"You are certainly being forthcoming," Two said at one point.

"I don't want a shotgun to the face," Lee said.

"I mean that you are offering rather more than your surviving compatriot," Two said.

"I'm the lieutenant," Lee said. "It's my job to know more than the soldiers under me. If I'm offering you more than Private Hughes, it's because I know more, not because she's holding out on you."

"Indeed," Two said. "That's good news for Private Hughes, then."

Lee smiled, knowing now that Hughes was the other soldier held and that for now, at least, she was still alive. "What else do you need to know?" she asked.

"At the moment, nothing," Two said. "But I will be back with more questions later. In the meantime, Six will tend to your needs. Thank you, Lieutenant Lee, for your cooperation."

"Delighted," Lee said. And with that, she assumed, Two had wandered away from his microphone to do whatever it is that he did, presumably talk to fellow conspirators (of which Lee assumed there were at least five).

She heard Six moving about in the room. "Do you mind if I talk?" Lee asked. "I know you can't answer. But I have to admit this entire incident is making me nervous." She bagan talking, primarily about her childhood, while Six fed her and gave her water and then tended to her bodily needs. After twenty minutes, Six went away and Lee shut up.

It was the room's acoustics that had given her the idea. Lee had spent years as a performing and recording musician, and part of her job was to make sure the room, whatever room she was in, wouldn't defeat her instrument or her band. She'd played enough basements with stone and concrete walls to know just how much the sound bouncing off the walls would mess with the performance and also what sorts of materials made what sort of sonic response. She could close her eyes, strike a note in a room and tell you, roughly, how large the room was, what materials the room was made of and whether there were objects in the room bouncing sound off of them. She wasn't, alas, good enough at it to be able to make an entire map of a room that way.

But her BrainPal was.

For two and a half hours Lee had talked, almost

constantly, moving her head as much as she could, risking a neck chafe from her restraining strap. As she talked, her BrainPal took the data from her voice (and from Two's) and used it to paint a picture of the room, marking every surface that sound reflected off of, polling the delay between the ears to locate the surface in the room and adding each additional piece of data to give a complete audio portrait of the room, of Six and of everything within earshot.

What Lee had learned:

One, that Two was (or, more accurately, was speaking to her through) a PDA set up on a table a meter and a half away, directly in front of her. This was the same table on which Six kept the bottles from which she fed Lee soup and water.

Two, Six was a woman, about 165 centimeters tall and weighing about fifty-five kilos. When Lee was talking directly into her face, she got a reasonably good "look" at Six; she guessed Six was roughly forty to fifty years of age, presuming she was not ever in the CDF.

Three, to the side of the chair was another table, less than a meter away, on which sat a shotgun and various surgical, cutting and shearing implements. Which confirmed for Lee that Two was full of shit about the torture assurances, and that she wasn't likely to get out of the room alive—nor was Hughes going to get out of hers.

What Lee suspected: Six would return at some point, Two would declare regretfully that they would have to go over answers again, this time with some added incentive in the form of pain, and then at the end of it she would be fed the shotgun while Two and his friends reviewed any discrepancies in her stories and the stories they got from Hughes. Which meant Lee had an indeterminate but short amount of time to escape the chair, rescue Hughes and escape from wherever they were.

She had no idea how she was going to do that.

"Come on," she said to herself, and thumped the back of her head against the headrest as much as she could with the restraint on her neck. It wasn't a whole lot, but it was enough to clack her jaw, driving her left incisors into the edge of her tongue. There was a small nip of pain and then the odd, not-at-all-coppery taste of Smart-Blood, oozing out from the wound.

Lee grimaced. She could never get used to the taste of SmartBlood. It was the stuff the CDF used to replace human blood in its soldiers for its superior oxygen-handling capabilities; the nanobiotic machines could hold several times more oxygen than red blood cells could. It meant that a CDF soldier could survive without taking a breath far longer than a normal human could. It also meant that SmartBlood could become so superoxygenated that a favorite party trick of CDF soldiers was forcing the nanobots in the SmartBlood, which could be programmed via BrainPal, to incinerate themselves in a flash. It was a surprisingly excellent way to get rid of bloodsucking insects: Let them feed off your flesh and then, as they fly away, ignite the SmartBlood in their bodies.

If only Six were a vampire, Lee thought. *I'd show her.* She spat the SmartBlood that had accumulated in her mouth and did a poor job of it, spattering it onto her right wrist and the restraint over it.

Hello, her brain said again.

As it did so, the door opened. Lee opened up a visual window of the room and started tracking the new sounds and their reflections on them. In a few seconds, Six came into view, positioning herself between the chair Lee was restrained in and the table holding the shotgun and surgical implements. Lee "watched" Six almost disappear as she stopped moving and her sounds ceased except for her breathing and then became silhouetted again when Two spoke from the PDA.

"I'm afraid I have some very bad news, Lieutenant

Lee," Two said. "I took the information you gave me back to my colleagues, and as impressed as they were with your willingness to share, that same willingness has made them suspicious. They believe a CDF soldier would never willingly volunteer the information you have, or as much information as you have. They suspect that while you are telling some of the truth, you may not be telling all of the truth."

"I told you everything I know," Lee said, putting an edge of panic in her voice.

"I know you have," Two said. "And I for one believe you. It's why you're still alive, Lieutenant. But my colleagues are skeptical. I asked them what it would take to relieve them of their skepticism. They suggested we go through the questions again, but this time with a certain added . . . urgency."

"I don't like the sound of that," Lee said.

"I do apologize," Two said. "I told you that we would not torture you. At the time, I thought it was the truth. I regret it is no longer the case."

Lee said nothing to this. She knew by all outward indications it would look as if she were trying to keep from crying.

"Six is a medical practitioner of some note," Two said. "I can promise you that you will be inflicted with only as much pain as is necessary and not a single bit more. Six, you may begin."

Lee opened her mouth just slightly to offer what she hoped would sound like a frightened, keening wail.

Six reached over to the table, picked up a scalpel and moved it toward Lee's right ring finger, slipping the very edge of it underneath the fingernail.

Lee, who had bit her tongue quite severely for several seconds, spat a gout of SmartBlood at Six, covering her arm and the hand wielding the scalpel. In the reflection of the spitting noise she saw Six's chin move sharply, as if she had moved her head to look at Lee quizzically.

"You're going to make some noise now, Six," Lee said, and ordered all the SmartBlood she'd spit out to ignite as furiously as it could.

Six became a bright spot of noise as she jerked back, wailing, arm and hand incinerating. She wheeled in reverse, colliding with the desk that held Two's PDA. It dislodged from its position and fell forward, leaving Two in the dark about what came next.

Lee wailed as well as the bit of SmartBlood that had landed on her wrist burned like hell against her skin. Then she gritted her teeth and as hard as she could started yanking against her right wrist restraint, currently being weakened by the SmartBlood burning into its fibers.

One yank, two yanks, three yanks . . . four. There was a ripping sound, and Lee's right arm was free. Without bothering to put out her wrist or uncover her eyes, she reached over to the table and grabbed the shears and as quickly as possible started cutting her other restraints: left wrist, neck, waist and ankles.

It was when she got to her ankles that Six exclaimed through her pain; Lee guessed that Six had finally figured out what Lee was up to and scrambled toward the table with the shotgun on it. Lee cut through the final restraint and leaped for the table, too late; Six had the shotgun.

Lee yelled, grabbed the scalpel Six had dropped and pushed up, getting inside the radius of the shotgun and driving the scalpel up Six's abdomen. Six made a surprised gasping sound at the sharp, slicing pain, dropped the shotgun and slid to the ground.

Lee finally removed her blindfold, turned off the audio map and blinked down at Six, who was looking at her with something akin to wonder. She was, Lee noted, a bloody mess.

"How did you do that?" Six whispered between panting breaths of agony.

"I have good ears," Lee said.

Six had nothing to say to that or anything else.

Lee grabbed the shotgun, checked the load and then moved quickly to position herself by the door. Less than twenty seconds later, the door burst open and a man came through, sidearm at the ready. Lee dropped him with a shot in the abdomen and then pivoted to get a second man in the doorway square in the chest. She dropped the spent shotgun, picked up the sidearm, checked the clip and went through the door.

There was a hallway with another doorway five meters down. Lee grabbed the second dead man, dragged him down the hallway with her, kicked open the door and hurled the corpse through. She waited until the second shotgun report and then shot the man still holding the shotgun. He went down. Lee resighted and aimed at the PDA sitting on a table, blowing it to pieces. She went into the room and looked at the chair to find Hughes, naked, restrained and understandably anxious.

"Private Hughes," she said. "How are you?"

"Ready to get the *fuck* out of this chair, Lieutenant," Hughes said.

Lee reached over to the table that held surgical instruments and then cut through Hughes's bonds. Hughes pulled the blindfold over her head and looked at her naked lieutenant, blinking.

"This was not what I was expecting the first thing I would see to be," Hughes said, to Lee.

"Knock it off," Lee said, and pointed toward the corpse of the man she'd flung through the door. "Check him for a sidearm and let's get out of here."

"Yes, ma'am," Hughes said, and moved to the corpse.

"What did this one call himself?" Lee said, pointing to the man who held the shotgun.

"One," Hughes said. "But he never called himself it. I didn't even know he was a he until right now. Someone calling himself Two called him that." She found the sidearm, checked its load.

"Right," Lee said. "I killed three more, including that one and one called Six. So that's four dead and at least two still alive."

"Are we going to wait around to meet them?" Hughes asked. "Because I'd prefer not."

"We agree," Lee said. "Come on." They went to the door; Hughes took point. The two of them made their way back down the hall, toward the direction Lee had come from. Another door lay five meters past the door of her room; they opened it and found it empty except for a chair and a spray of gray matter and fluid on the bar floor.

"Jefferson," Lee said. Hughes nodded, unhappy, and they continued onward.

A final door stood near a stairwell. The two banged through and found a small office with a PDA on a desk and very little else.

"This was Two's room," Lee said.

"Where did the son of a bitch get to?" Hughes asked

"I think I scared him off when I set a friend of his on fire," Lee said. She picked up the PDA. "Watch the door," she said to Hughes.

On the PDA were a series of video files of Lee, Hughes and Jefferson as well as other documents Lee didn't bother with. She swiped past all of them to look for the PDA's file system for a specific program. "Here it is," she said, and pressed the button that appeared on the screen.

Lee's BrainPal suddenly came alive with a long queue of increasingly urgent messages from her sergeant, her captain and the *Tubingen* itself.

Hughes, who apparently received a similar queue of urgent messages, smiled. "Nice to know we were missed."

"Make sure they know where we are," Lee said. "And

make sure that if I tell them to, they'll flatten this place into the ground."

"You got it, ma'am," Hughes said.

The two of them moved out of the office and went up the stairs, Lee taking the PDA with her and tucking it under an arm. The stairs emptied out into another short corridor that looked like a wing of a hotel. The two soldiers stalked through it carefully, turned a dogleg and were confronted by a closed door. Lee nodded to Hughes, who opened it and pushed through.

They came through the side of a lobby filled with lumpy-looking older people in ordinary clothing and very attractive younger people wearing almost nothing at all.

"Where the hell are we?" Hughes said.

Lee laughed. "Holy shit," she said. "It *was* a brothel!"

The lobby quieted as the brothel workers and their potential clients got a look at Lee and Hughes.

"*What?*" Hughes said, finally, not dropping her weapon. "You all act like you've never seen a naked woman before."

"I don't think I can tell this story again any differently than I've already told it the last three times, ma'am," Lee said, to Colonel Liz Egan. Egan, as she understood it, was some sort of liaison for the State Department, which had taken considerable interest in her abduction and escape.

"I just need to know if there's any additional detail you can give me regarding this Two person," Egan said.

"No, ma'am," Lee said. "I never saw him or heard him except as a heavily treated voice over that PDA. You have all the files I made, and you have all the files on the PDA I took. There really is nothing else I can tell you about him."

"Her," Egan said.

"Beg pardon, ma'am?" Lee said.

"Her," Egan said. "We're pretty sure Two was Elyssia Gorham, the manager of the Lotus Flower, that brothel you found yourselves in. The office you found the PDA in was hers, and she would be able to keep anyone out of the basement level you were in. The rooms the three of you were held in were private function rooms for clients who either liked rougher pleasures or wanted special event rooms which would be built up and torn down quickly. That also explains the signal blockers. The sort of people who would rent those rooms would want to be assured of their privacy. In all it made it a perfect place to stash the three of you."

"Do we know who drugged us in the first place?" Lee asked.

"We tracked it down to the bartender at the *hofbräuhaus*," Egan said. "He said he was offered a month's salary to drop the drugs in your drink. He needed the money, apparently. It's a good thing he has it, since now he's been fired."

"I didn't think we could be drugged," Lee said. "That's supposed to be one of the benefits of SmartBlood."

"You can't be drugged with anything biological," Egan said. "Whatever you were drugged with was designed with SmartBlood in mind. It's something we'll be needing to look out for in the future. It's already been noted to CDF Research and Development."

"Good," Lee said.

"On the subject of SmartBlood, that was some good thinking on your part to incapacitate your captor," Egan said. "The idea to map your surroundings with sound is also clear thinking. You've been recommended for commendation for both actions. No promotion, sorry."

"Thank you, but I'm not really concerned about a commendation or a promotion," Lee said. "I want to know more about the people who killed Jefferson. When they were interrogating me, they were asking me a lot of questions about what I knew about separatist movements and groups wanting to align their colonies with the Earth instead of the Colonial Union. I don't know anything about that, but it got one of my people killed. I want to know more."

"There's nothing really to say," Egan said. "These are strange times for the Colonial Union. We're busy trying to bring the Earth back into the fold, and in the meantime our colonies are trying to deal with events as best as they can. There's no organized separatist movement, and the Earth isn't actively trying to recruit any colonies. As far as we can tell, these all are the works of isolated groups. The one here on Zhong Guo was just a bit more organized."

"Ah," Lee said. She knew when she was being lied to, but she also knew when not to say anything about it.

Egan stood, Lee rising to follow her. "In any event, Lieutenant, it's nothing I want you to worry about right now. Your commendation comes with two weeks of shore leave at your leisure. May I suggest you take it someplace other than Zhong Guo. And that you stay out of *hofbräuhauses* for the time being."

"Yes, ma'am," Lee said. "Good advice." She saluted and watched Egan walk away. Then she closed her eyes and listened to the sound of the ship around her.

The Observers

"Lieutenant Wilson," Ambassador Ode Abumwe said. "Come in. Sit down, please."

Harry Wilson entered Abumwe's stateroom on the new *Clarke*, which was even smaller and less comfortable than it had been on their previous spaceship. "This is cozy," he said, as he sat.

"If by 'cozy' you mean 'almost insultingly cramped,' then yes, that's exactly what it is," Abumwe said. "If you actually meant 'cozy,' then you should have better standards of personal comfort."

"I did in fact mean the first of those," Wilson assured her.

"Yes, well," Abumwe said. "When you have your spaceship shot out from under you and your replacement starship is half a century old and put together with baling wire and gum, you make do with what you have." She motioned to her walls. "Captain Coloma tells me that this is actually one of the more spacious personal quarters on the ship. Larger than hers, even. I don't know if that's true."

"I have an officer's berth," Wilson said. "I think it's about a third of the size of this stateroom. I can turn around in it, but I can't extend both of my arms out in opposite directions. Hart's is even smaller and he's got a roommate. They're either going to kill each other or start sleeping together simply as a defensive maneuver."

"It's a good thing Mr. Schmidt is using his vacation time, then," Abumwe said.

"It is," Wilson agreed. "He told me he planned to spend it in a hotel room, by himself for a change."

"The romance of the diplomatic life, Lieutenant Wilson," Abumwe said.

"We are living the dream, ma'am," Wilson said.

Abumwe stared at Wilson for a moment, as if she were slightly disbelieving the two of them had actually just made a commiserating joke together. Wilson wouldn't have blamed her if she was. The two of them had not really gotten along for nearly all the time he had been assigned to her mission group. She was acerbic and forbidding; he was sarcastic and aggravating; and both of them were aware that in the larger scheme of things they were hanging on to the bottom rung of the diplomatic ladder. But the last several weeks had been odd times for everyone. If the two of them still weren't what you could call friendly, at the very least they realized that circumstances had put them both on the same side, against most of the rest of the universe.

"Tell me, Wilson, do you remember the time when you reminded me we had something in common?" Abumwe asked the lieutenant.

Wilson frowned, trying to remember. "Sure," he said, after a minute. "We're both from Earth."

Abumwe nodded. "Right," she said. "You lived there for seventy-five years before joining the Colonial Defense Forces. I emigrated when I was a child."

"I seem to recall you not being particularly pleased that I reminded you of the connection," Wilson said.

Abumwe shrugged. "You made the connection right as the Earth and the Colonial Union had their falling-out," she said. "I thought you were making some sort of implication."

"I wasn't trying to recruit you, I swear," Wilson said, risking a little levity.

"I wasn't under the impression you were," Abumwe said. "I simply thought you were making a joke in terrible taste."

"Ah," Wilson said. "Got it."

"But as it turns out, this shared connection has landed us an unusual assignment," Abumwe said. She picked up her PDA, activated it and pressed at the screen. An instant later, Wilson's BrainPal pinged and a note popped up in his field of vision; Abumwe had sent him a file.

Wilson unpacked and quickly scanned the file, closing his eyes to focus. After a minute, he smiled. "The Earthlings are coming," he said.

"That's right," Abumwe said. "The Colonial Union is worried that the Earth still has a lack of confidence in the transparency of our dealings with it. It's worried that the Earth will eventually decide to go it alone, or even worse, start negotiations with the Conclave to join its ranks. So as a gesture of goodwill, it's going to allow a party of observers unimpeded access to one of its current set of diplomatic negotiations. They've selected our upcoming trade talks with the Burfinor. I am told that the secretary herself believes that my personal connection with the Earth—and the connection of my staff, meaning *you*—will have a meaningful positive impact on the relationship between the Colonial Union and the Earth."

"And you believe that line?" Wilson said, opening his eyes.

"Of course not," Abumwe said. "We were picked because our negotiations with the Burfinor are inconsequential. It looks good because we're trading for the Burfinor's biomedical technology, which will be impressive if you've never seen something like it before, and the Earth people haven't. But it's not something that's particularly sensitive. So it doesn't matter if the Earth people watch what we do. The bit about you and me having a history with Earth is just show."

"Do we know if these people are *actually* from Earth?" Wilson asked. "Captain Coloma and I had a run-in with fake Earthlings not too long ago. The CDF was passing off former soldiers as representatives from Earth in order to find a spy. We've gotten played before, ma'am. We need to know whether we're being played again, and if so, what for."

Abumwe smiled, which was a rare enough thing that Wilson took special note of it. "You and I had the same thought on this, which is why I ran this past some of my own people at Phoenix Station," she said. "Everything I can see about these people checks out. But then again I don't have the same familiarity with Earth that you do, so there might be something I'm missing. You have the entire file on all five members of the observer mission. Go through it and let me know if something stands out for you."

"Got it," Wilson said. "Might as well let my personal history actually work for us."

"Yes," Abumwe said. "And another thing, Wilson. You left Earth only a decade ago. You're still close enough to how people from Earth think and do things that you can give us insight into their state of mind regarding the Colonial Union and their relationship to us."

"Well, that depends," Wilson said. "I'm from the United States. If the observers are from elsewhere, I'm not going to be any more useful than anyone else."

"One of them is, I think," Abumwe said. "It's in the files. Go ahead and see. If there is, then make friends with that one."

"All right," Wilson said. "This is the part where I officially note to you that I am supposed to be doing other work for you on this mission, specifically examining the equipment the Burfinor are giving us."

"Of course," Abumwe said, slightly irritated. "Do your actual job, and do this. In fact, combine the two and invite one of the observers to help you run your tests. We will score additional transparency points for that. All the while you'll be learning things from them."

"Spying on them," Wilson said.

"I prefer the term 'observing,'" Abumwe said. "After all, they will be observing *us*. There's no reason not to return the favor."

The humans from Earth constituted a carefully selected group, the members chosen to represent the entire planet, not only a single continent or political group or interest. From Europe, there was Franz Meyer, an economist and author. South America yielded Luiza Carvalho, a lawyer and diplomat. From Africa, Thierry Bourkou, an engineer. North America offered Danielle Lowen, a doctor. Asia presented Liu Cong, a diplomat who was the head of the observer mission.

Ambassador Abumwe welcomed them warmly to the *Clarke,* introduced Captain Coloma and Executive Officer Neva Balla and made introductions of her own staff. Wilson was introduced last of all, as the liaison between the observer mission and Abumwe. "Whatever you want or whatever questions you have, Wilson is here for you," Abumwe said.

Wilson nodded and shook hands with Liu and, as agreed to by Abumwe, addressed him in standard Chinese. "Welcome to our ship, and I look forward to assisting you however I may," he said, to the diplomat.

Liu smiled, glanced over to Abumwe and then turned his attention back to Wilson. "Thank you, Lieutenant," he said. "I was not made aware that you spoke anything other than English."

Wilson waited for his BrainPal to translate and then thought up a response; his BrainPal translated it and gave him the pronunciation, which he then attempted. "I don't," he said. "The computer in my head is able to translate what you say and offers me a response in the same language. So you may talk to me in whatever language you like. However, I ask that you let me respond in English, because I am sure I am mangling your language right now."

Liu laughed. "Indeed you are," he said, in unaccented English. "Your pronunciation is terrible. But I appreciate the effort. Can you do the same trick for my colleagues?"

Wilson could and did, conversing briefly in Brazilian Portuguese, Arabic and German before bringing his attention to Lowen.

"I don't believe I need to do the translation trick with you," he said to her.

"*Répétez, s'il vous plaît?*" Lowen said.

"Uh," Wilson said, and scrambled to respond in French.

"No, no, I'm just messing with you," Lowen said, quickly. "I'm from Colorado."

"We've known each other thirty seconds and already I can tell you're difficult, Ms. Lowen," Wilson said, testing.

"I prefer to think of it as challenging, Lieutenant Wilson," Lowen said. "I assumed you'd be able to handle it."

"I don't mind," Wilson assured her.

"You sound midwesterny to me," Lowen said. "Maybe Ohio?"

"Indiana," Wilson said.

"Did you hear about the Cubs?" Lowen said.

Wilson smiled. "I heard something about that, yes."

"They finally won a World Series and the world did not end," Lowen said. "All those prophecies, shot to hell."

"Disappointing, really," Wilson said.

"Not to me," Lowen said. "The Earth is where I keep all my stuff."

"You and Lieutenant Wilson seem to get along, Doctor Lowen," Liu said, watching the exchange between the two.

"We seem to speak each other's language, yes," Lowen said.

"Perhaps you wouldn't mind being our point person with the lieutenant," Liu said. "It would be easier to route all our requests for him through a single person."

"If you like, Ambassador Liu," Lowen said, and turned back to Wilson. "That work for you, Lieutenant?"

"Will you submit all your requests in French?" Wilson asked.

"If you really have a hankering to experience my genuinely atrocious high school French any more than you already have, then, sure," Lowen said.

"Then we have a deal," Wilson said.

"Merveilleux," Lowen said.

Wilson glanced over to Abumwe, whose expression was caught between amusement and annoyance. *Well, you wanted me to make friends with the American,* Wilson thought.

The negotiations with the Burfinor did not go well.

"We regret to inform you that our minister in charge of trade has said that the initial conditions for our negotiation are, in her mind, too unfavorable toward us," said Blblllblblb Doodoodo, whose first name was most accurately pronounced by humans by rapidly moving their finger back and forth on their lips and then crooning the second half.

"That is indeed regrettable," Abumwe said. Wilson, who was in the back of the conference room, ready to give a report that he now suspected he would not give, could see the set in Abumwe's jaw that signaled her irritation at this unexpected speed bump, but he did not imagine it was noticeable to anyone who hadn't been with her for some time. At the very least, none of the observers from Earth seemed to notice. They seemed far more engaged in Doodoodo. Wilson reminded himself that the Earthlings were still new to spending time in the company of alien species; the Burfinor might be the first intelligent non-humans that any of them had ever seen in person. "Could you give us some further context to explain this change in opinion?" Abumwe asked.

"There is no doubt that the Colonial Union will benefit from the biomedical scanners we have offered to you," Doodoodo said.

"Wilson?" Abumwe said, not looking at him.

"I've run the preliminary diagnostics on the machine we were given for review," Wilson said. "It performed as advertised, at least for the time I had to work with it, which means it has an order of magnitude higher diagnostic ability than our own bioscanners. I'd want to spend more time with it, and I haven't gotten to the other items we're negotiating for. But in a general sense, the scanners do what they say, say what they do."

"Precisely," said Doodoodo. "These are of immense value to your colonies."

"And so are our spaceships to yours," Abumwe pointed out. The Colonial Union was hoping to sell five recently-retired frigates to the Burfinor in exchange for several hundred of the scanners.

"But there is a fundamental mismatch in the technologies, is there not?" Doodoodo said. "The technology we are offering you is state of the biomedical art; what you are offering us is a generation or more behind your latest ships."

"The technology is robust," Abumwe insisted. "I would remind you that we arrived here in a ship that is several generations older than the ships we are offering you. It's still spaceworthy and in fine repair."

"Yes, of course," Doodoodo said. "We're well aware how the *Clarke* is intended to be an advertisement for selling us these discounted goods. Nevertheless, the minister feels that the imbalance is too great. We seek a renegotiation."

"These are initial terms that your minister originally sought out," Abumwe said. "To make these changes now is highly unusual."

Doodoodo tugged at the base of his eyestalks, gently. "I believe the minister is of the opinion that circumstances have changed." One of Doodoodo's eyes, possibly unconsciously, swiveled to take in the Earthling observers.

Abumwe did not fail to catch the implication but could do nothing about it in the moment. Instead she pressed forward, hoping to have Doodoodo go back to his boss with a request to reconsider her change in the negotiations. Doodoodo was exceedingly pleasant and sympathetic to his human counterpart but promised nothing.

During all this, Liu and his Earth counterparts said nothing and gave no indication of whatever they might be thinking. Wilson tried to catch Lowen's eye for an indication of her thoughts, but she kept her focus forward, at Doodoodo.

Negotiations for the day ended shortly thereafter, and the humans, frustrated, rode the shuttle back to the *Clarke* in silence, and dispersed from the shuttle bay equally quiet. Wilson watched Abumwe stalk off, followed by her assistant. The other members of Abumwe's staff on the shuttle milled about uncertainly for a moment before heading out themselves. In a corner of the bay, the Earth contingent huddled together for a moment, talking; at one point, Lowen popped her head up and looked in

Wilson's direction. Wilson tried not to read anything into it.

Eventually, the Earth cluster broke up and Liu and Lowen walked directly toward Wilson.

"Greetings, Earthlings," Wilson said.

Liu looked politely puzzled; Lowen smiled. "How long have you been waiting to use that?" she asked.

"For at least a dozen years," Wilson said.

"Was it everything you wanted it to be?" Lowen asked.

"It really was," Wilson said.

"It was an interesting trade session you had today," Liu said, diplomatically.

"That's one way of putting it, yes," Wilson said.

"So what happened back there?" Lowen said.

"You mean, why did a routine trade agreement fly off the rails, embarrassing the Colonial Union in front of the observers whom it wanted to impress with its diplomatic acumen?" Wilson said. He noted Liu's expression to his summation of the day's events, discreet though it was.

"Yes, that would be the event to which I was referring," Lowen said.

"The answer is implicit in the question," Wilson said. "You were there. The Burfinor know something of the Colonial Union's predicament with Earth. I suppose they figured that we would be motivated to make a deal of any sort in order not to embarrass ourselves in front of you."

"It didn't work," Lowen said.

"Yes, well," Wilson said. "The Burfinor don't know Ambassador Abumwe very well. She's persistent, and she doesn't like surprises."

"What will happen now?" Liu asked.

"I expect that Ambassador Abumwe will go back tomorrow, inform Doodoodo that any new terms are entirely unacceptable and as politely as possible threaten to walk out of the negotiations," Wilson said. "At which point our Burfinor friend is likely to walk back the request for new terms, because while it would be nice for the Colonial Union to get our hands on some sweet new biomedical scanners, the Burfinor have a low-grade border war simmering with the Eroj and are running low on ships. So they need this trade agreement more than we do, and if it fails, they lose more."

"Interesting," Liu said again.

"We didn't want you to be bored," Wilson said.

"You also didn't want us to see a diplomatic negotiation where the Colonial Union would be at an actual disadvantage," Lowen said, looking directly at Wilson.

"And you're surprised by this?" Wilson asked, looking at both Liu and Lowen equally.

"No," Liu said. "Although I'll admit to being mildly surprised that you admit it."

Wilson shrugged. "I'm a glorified tech support, not a trained diplomat," he said. "I'm allowed to say obvious things."

"Your boss might not be happy with you saying 'obvious things' to us," Lowen noted.

Liu opened his mouth before Wilson did. "On the contrary, I think Ambassador Abumwe knew exactly what she was doing when she assigned Lieutenant Wilson as our liaison," he said.

"She's the opposite of stupid," Wilson agreed.

"So I am learning," Liu said, and then yawned. "I'm sorry," he said. "Space travel is still new to me and I've discovered that it wears me out. I believe I will get some rest."

"How are you finding your quarters?" Wilson asked.

"They're cozy," Liu said.

"What a diplomatic way of putting that," Wilson said.

Liu laughed. "Yes, well. That's *my* job," he said. He excused himself and exited.

"Nice fellow," Wilson said, as he left.

"An excellent fellow," Lowen said. "One of the best diplomats in the world, and one of the nicest people you'd want to meet. He even gave up his private berth for Franz to use and roomed with Thierry. Franz got a bit claustrophobic. Said he'd seen prison cells that were larger."

"It's probably true," Wilson said.

"The irony is that the person who is going to suffer most for it is Thierry," Lowen said. "Liu is brilliant and wonderful, but he also snores like a freight train. Thierry's got to suffer through that now. Don't be surprised if for the next few days you see him look very, very tired."

"You could prescribe him something to get to sleep," Wilson said. "You're a doctor, after all."

"I don't think my scripting privileges extend past Neptune," Lowen said. "And anyway, Franz travels with a white noise generator to help him get to sleep. He's already given it to Thierry for the duration. He should be fine. *Should* be."

"Good," Wilson said. "And you? How are your quarters?"

"They suck," Lowen said. "And Luiza already claimed the bottom bunk."

"It's a hard life you lead," Wilson said.

"If people only knew," Lowen said. "Speaking of which, who do I have to kill to get a drink around here?"

"Fortunately, no one," Wilson said. "There's an officers lounge three decks down. It offers a regrettable selection of terrible light beers and inferior spirits."

"I can fix that," Lowen said. "I travel with a bottle of eighteen-year-old Laphroaig in my case."

"That's not necessarily healthy," Wilson said.

"Relax," Lowen said. "If I were genuinely an alcoholic, I'd take along something much cheaper. I brought it on the off chance I might have to butter up one of you folks and pretend to be friendly and such."

"Thank God you didn't have to do *that,*" Wilson said.

"Before we arrived, I thought I might ask Ambassador Abumwe if she'd like a drink," Lowen said. "But I don't really get the sense she's the sort to appreciate a good buttering up."

"I think you've accurately assessed the ambassador," Wilson said.

"You, on the other hand," Lowen said, pointing at Wilson.

"I am all about the buttering, Dr. Lowen," Wilson assured her.

"Wonderful," Lowen said. "First stop, the crawl space you folks laughingly call officers berths on this ship. Second stop, officers lounge. Hopefully, it is larger."

The officers lounge was larger, but not by much.

"Does the Colonial Union have something against personal space?" Lowen asked, hoisting the Laphroaig onto the very small table. The officers lounge was empty, except for Lowen, Wilson and the Laphroaig.

"It's an old ship," Wilson explained while selecting a pair of cups from the lounge's cupboard. "In the old days, people were smaller and appreciated a good snuggle."

"I am suspicious of the veracity of your statement," Lowen said.

"That's probably wise," Wilson said. He came over to the table and set down the cups. They made a *click* as they connected with the table.

Lowen, puzzled, reached for one of the cups. "Magnetic," she said, lifting the cup.

"Yes," Wilson said. "The artificial gravity doesn't frequently cut out, but when it does it's nice not to have cups floating about randomly."

"What about the stuff in the cups?" Lowen asked. "What happens to that?"

"It gets slurped frantically," Wilson said, picking up his own cup and waggling it in front of Lowen. Lowen eyed Wilson sardonically, opened the Laphroaig, tipped in a finger and a half and gave herself an equal amount. "To artificial gravity," she said, in a toast.

"To artificial gravity," Wilson said.

They drank.

Drink two, some minutes later:

"So, is it easy?" Lowen said.

"Is what easy?" Wilson asked.

Lowen waved at Wilson's body. "Being green."

"I can't believe you just went there," Wilson said.

"I know," Lowen said. "Jim Henson and several generations of his descendants are now rolling in their graves, many dozens of light-years away."

"It *is* a funny joke," Wilson said. "Or at least was, the first six hundred times I heard it."

"It's a serious question, though!" Lowen said. "I'm asking from a place of medical curiosity, you know. I want to know if all those so-called improvements they give you Colonial Defense Forces soldiers are actually all that."

"Well, start with this," Wilson said. "How old do I look to you?"

Lowen looked. "I don't know, maybe twenty-two? Twenty-five, tops? You being green messes with my age sense. A lot younger than me, and I'm thirty-five. But you're not younger than me, are you?"

"I'm ninety," Wilson said.

"Get out," Lowen said.

"More or less," Wilson said. "You're out here long enough and you eventually lose track unless you check. It's because as long as you're CDF, you don't actually age."

"How is that even possible?" Lowen said. "Entropy still works out here, right? Physics hasn't totally broken down?"

Wilson extended an arm. "You're engaging in the pathetic fallacy," he said. "Just because I look like a human being doesn't mean I am. This body has more genetic material that's not strictly human than it does material that is human. And it heavily integrates machines as well. My blood is actually a bunch of nanobots in a fluid. I am and every other CDF soldier is a genetically-modified cyborg."

"But you're still *you*, right?" Lowen asked. "You're still the same *person* you were when you left Earth. Still the same consciousness."

"That's a question of some contention among us soldiers," Wilson said, setting his arm back down. "When you transfer over to the new body, the machine that does the transfer makes it at least seem like for an instant you're in two bodies at once. It *feels* like you as a person make the transfer. But I think it's equally possible that what happens is that memories are transferred over to a brain specially prepared for them, it wakes up, and there's just enough cross talk between the two separate brains to give the *illusion* of a transfer before the old one shuts down."

"In which case, you're actually dead," Lowen said. "The *real* you. And this you is a fake."

"Right." Wilson took another sip of his drink. "Mind you, the CDF could show you graphs and charts that show that actual consciousness transfer happens. But I think this is one of those things you can't *really* model from the outside. I have to accept the possibility that I could be a fake Harry Wilson."

"And this doesn't bother you," Lowen said.

"In a metaphysical sense, sure," Wilson said. "But in a day-to-day sense, I don't think about it much. On the inside, it sure *feels* like I've been around for ninety years, and ultimately this version of me likes being alive. So."

"Wow, this conversation went places I wasn't expecting it to go," Lowen said.

"If you think that's weird, wait until I tell you that thanks to the mechanics of the skip drive, you're in an entirely different universe and will never see your friends and family again," Wilson said.

"Wait, what?" Lowen said.

Wilson motioned to the Laphroaig bottle. "Better pour yourself another drink," he said.

Drink four, sometime later:

"You know what the Colonial Union's problem is, don't you?" Lowen asked.

"There's just one problem?" Wilson responded.

"It's arrogance!" Lowen said, ignoring Wilson's question. "What sort of government decides that the smart thing to do, the prudent thing to do, the *wise* thing to do, is to keep an entire planet in an arrested state of development, just to use it to farm colonists and soldiers?"

"If you're expecting me to act as defense for the Colonial Union's practices, it's going to be a very short debate," Wilson said.

"And not just any planet," Lowen said, ignoring Wilson again. Wilson smiled; clearly Lowen was self-winding when she was tipsy. "But Earth! I mean, seriously, are you fucking kidding me? The cradle of human life in the universe, the place from which we all spring, our home planet, for crying out loud. And a couple hundred years ago some pricks on Phoenix thought, Hey, screw them. Honestly, what did you *think* was going to happen when we found out how badly you've been messing with us? And for how long?"

"I reiterate my comment that if you're expecting me

to defend the Colonial Union, you're going to be sorely disappointed," Wilson said.

"But you're one of them!" Lowen said. "You know how they think, at least, right? So what were they thinking?"

"I think they were thinking that they would never have to deal with the Earth finding out anything," Wilson said. "And for the sake of accuracy, the Colonial Union *did* do a very fine job of keeping the Earth in the dark for a couple of centuries. If it hadn't tried to kill off a friend of mine, and his entire family, *and* his colony, for the purposes of political expediency, they'd probably still be getting away with it."

"Hold on," Lowen said. "You know John Perry?"

"We left Earth on the same boat," Wilson said. "We were part of the same group of friends. We called ourselves the Old Farts. There were seven of us then. There's three of us now. Me, John and Jesse Gonzales."

"Where is she?" Lowen asked.

"She's on the colony of Erie," Wilson said. "She and I were together for a while, but she eventually wanted to leave the CDF and I didn't. She married a guy on Erie and has twin daughters now. She's happy."

"But all the rest are dead," Lowen said.

"They told us when we joined that three-quarters of us would be dead in ten years," Wilson said. He was lost in thought for a moment, then looked up at Lowen and smiled. "So strictly on a percentage basis, the Old Farts beat the odds." He drank.

"I'm sorry to bring up memories," Lowen said, after a minute.

"We're talking and drinking, Doctor Lowen," Wilson said. "Memories will surface just as a matter of course."

"You can call me Danielle, you know," Lowen said. "Or Dani. Either is fine. I figure if we've drunk this much Scotch together, we should be on a first-name basis."

"I can't argue with that," Wilson said. "Then call me Harry."

"Hello, Harry."

"Hello, Dani."

They clinked their cups together.

"They're renaming my high school after your friend," Lowen said. "It was Hickenlooper High. Now it's going to be Perry High."

"There is no higher honor to be bestowed," Wilson said.

"I'm actually kind of annoyed by it," Lowen said. "I get mail now saying, 'Greetings, Perry Graduates,' and I'm all, 'What? I didn't go there.'"

"If I know John at all, he'd be mildly embarrassed to have your high school's name changed out from under you," Wilson said.

"Well, to be fair, the man *did* free my entire planet from the Colonial Union's systematic and centuries-long campaign of repression and social engineering," Lowen said. "So I guess I shouldn't begrudge him the high school."

"Possibly not," Wilson agreed.

"But that just brings us back around to the original question: What the hell was the Colonial Union thinking?" Lowen asked.

"Do you want a serious answer?" Wilson asked.

"Sure, if it's not too complicated," Lowen said. "I'm a little drunk."

"I'll use small words," Wilson promised. "I would be willing to bet that in the beginning the Colonial Union justified it by thinking that they were both protecting the Earth by taking the focus off it and onto the Colonial Union worlds, and then also helping humanity in general by using the Earth to help our colonies grow as quickly as they could with new immigrants and soldiers."

"So that's at first," Lowen said. "What about later?"

"Later? Habit," Wilson said.

Lowen blinked. "'Habit'? That's it? That's all you got?"

Wilson shrugged. "I didn't say it was a *good* answer," he said. "Just a serious one."

"It's a good thing I'm a diplomat," Lowen said. "Or I would tell you what I *really* thought of that."

"I can guess," Wilson said.

"And what do *you* think, Harry?" Lowen asked. "Do you think that Earth and the Colonial Union should have an alliance? After everything that's happened?"

"I'm not sure I'm the best-qualified person out there to answer that," Wilson said.

"Oh, come on," Lowen said, and waved at the officers lounge, whose population was still limited to the two of them and the Laphroaig. "It's just you and me."

"I think that it's a scary universe out there," Wilson said. "With not a lot of humans in it."

"But what about the Conclave?" Lowen asked. "Four hundred alien races not actively killing each other. Doesn't that make it a little less scary?"

"For those four hundred races? Sure," Wilson said. "As long as it lasts. For everyone else? Still scary."

"You're cheerful," Lowen said.

"I prefer 'realist,' " Wilson said.

Six drinks, even later:

"Are you green everywhere?" Lowen asked.

"Excuse me?" Wilson said.

"I am asking purely on scientific grounds," Lowen said.

"Thanks," Wilson said, dryly. "That makes it so much better."

"I mean, unless you prefer unscientific reasons for me asking," Lowen said.

"Why, Dr. Lowen . . ." Wilson feigned shock. "I am not that kind of boy."

"Once again, I am skeptical," Lowen said.

"Tell you what," Wilson said. "Ask me that question sometime when you haven't just consumed a substantial portion of a bottle of fine single-malt Scotch whiskey in a single sitting. If you're moved to do so, you might get a different answer from me."

"Fine," Lowen said sourly, and then looked over at Wilson somewhat as an owl would. "You're not drunk," she said.

"No," Wilson said.

"You drank as much as me, and I'm drunk as a skunk," she said. "Even accounting for body mass, you should be plastered, too."

"Benefit of the new body," Wilson said. "A much higher alcohol tolerance. It's more complicated than that, but it's late and you're drunk, so maybe we'll save it for tomorrow. Speaking of which, it's time to get you into your crawl space, if you want to be at the negotiations tomorrow without a hangover." He stood up and offered his hand to Lowen.

She took it, wobbling only slightly. "Whoa," she said. "Someone did something to the artificial gravity."

"Yes," Wilson said. "That's it exactly. Come on." He navigated her through the corridors and up the decks to the berths Captain Coloma had assigned to the observers.

"Almost there," Wilson said to Lowen.

"About time," Lowen said. "I think you took the scenic route. The scenic route that spins a bit."

"Maybe I'll bring you some water," Wilson said. "And some crackers."

"This is an excellent idea," Lowen said, and then jumped a little at the noise of the door of one of the berths flying open and slamming against the bulkhead.

Wilson looked toward the noise and saw Thierry Bourkou, looking frantic. "Is everything all right, Mr. Bourkou?" he asked.

Bourkou turned to Wilson, saw Lowen on his arm and rushed toward them. "Dani, Dani, come quick," he said. "It's Cong."

"What's Cong?" Lowen asked, less tired and slurred than moments before. Wilson could see the panic on her colleague's face, and his alarmed tone was pushing the drunkenness down. "What is it?"

"He's not breathing," Bourkou said. "He's blue and he's not breathing." He grabbed Lowen's hand and pulled her down the corridor toward his berth. "He's not breathing and I think he might be dead."

"He was fine when he lay down," Bourkou said. "He and I have both been feeling tired, so we both took naps at the same time. Then he started snoring, so I turned on the white noise machine. Then I fell asleep. When I woke up I told him I was going to get him some tea and asked him if he wanted any. He didn't respond, so I went to shake him. That's when I saw his lips were blue."

All of the observers were in the *Clarke*'s medical bay, along with Wilson, Abumwe, Captain Coloma and Doctor Inge Stone, the *Clarke*'s chief medical officer. Liu was also there, on a stretcher.

"Did he say anything other than that he was tired?" Stone asked Bourkou. "Did he complain about any other pains or ailments?"

Bourkou shook his head. "I've known Cong for ten years," he said. "He's always been healthy. The worst that's ever happened to him is that he broke his foot when a motorcycle ran over it while he was crossing a street."

"What happened to him?" Franz Meyer asked. After Liu, he was the ranking diplomat among the observers.

"It's hard to say," Stone said. "In small enclosed areas carbon monoxide poisoning often kills people, but that doesn't make sense here. Mr. Liu is not presenting symptoms and Mr. Bourkou here was unaffected, which he wouldn't have been if it were carbon monoxide. In any event there is nothing near those berths which generates or outputs that."

"What about the white noise generator?" Lowen asked. She was alert now, through a combination of caffeine, ibuprofen and nerves. "Is that something that could have done this?"

"Of course not," Meyer said, almost scornfully. "It has no moving parts other than the speakers. It doesn't output anything but white noise."

"What about allergies or sensitivities?" Stone asked.

Meyer shook his head this time. "He was lactose-intolerant, but that wouldn't have done this. And other than that he was not allergic to anything. It's as Thierry said. He's a healthy man. *Was* a healthy man."

"Aren't we overlooking something here?" asked Luiza Carvalho. Everyone looked to her; it was the first time she had spoken since the group gathered in the medical bay.

"Overlooking what?" asked Coloma.

"The possibility this isn't a natural death," Carvalho said. "Cong was a healthy man, with no previous health issues."

"With all due respect, Ms. Carvalho, that's probably further than we need to go for an explanation," Stone said. "It's rather more likely Mr. Liu fell prey to a previously undiagnosed condition. It's not uncommon, especially for people who have been superficially healthy. Their lack of obvious health issues means they don't get in to see a doctor as often as others would. That lets not-so-obvious issues sneak up on them."

"I understand that the simplest explanation is usually

the correct one," Carvalho said. "Of course. But I also know that in my home country of Brazil, assassination by poisoning has made a comeback. Last year a senator from Mato Grosso was killed by arsenic."

"A political assassination?" Abumwe asked.

"No," Carvalho admitted. "He was poisoned by his wife for sleeping with one of his legislative aides."

"To be indelicate, may we assume such a situation is not happening here?" Abumwe asked.

Meyer looked around at his colleagues. "It's safe to say that none of us were sleeping with Cong," he said, to Abumwe. "It's also safe to say that none of us had any professional reason to want him dead, either. With the exception of Thierry, none of us knew him prior to this mission. The mission selection criteria were as much political as anything else. We all represent different political interests at home, so there was no direct competition or professional jealousy."

"Do all of your factions get along?" Wilson asked.

"For the most part," Meyer said, and then pointed at Lowen. "Doctor Lowen represents America's interests here, and the United States, for better or worse, still maintains a somewhat contentious primary position in global politics, especially post-Perry. The other political interests sought to minimize its influence on this mission, which is why Liu Cong was selected to head the mission, over U.S. objections, and why the U.S. representative—apologies here, Dani—is the most junior on the mission. But none of that rose to the level of skullduggery."

"And I was with Lieutenant Wilson here for several hours, in any event," Lowen said. This raised eyebrows, both Meyer's and Abumwe's. "Cong asked me to get to know our Colonial Union liaison better so we could get a better understanding of the lay of the land. So I did." She turned to Wilson. "No offense," she said.

"None taken," Wilson said, amused.

"So it seems like poisoning or assassination is off the table," Stone said.

"Unless it was someone on the Colonial Union side," Carvalho said.

Abumwe, Wilson and Coloma exchanged glances.

This did not go unnoticed. "Okay, what was that?" asked Lowen.

"You mean the sudden, significant glances," Wilson said, before Abumwe or Coloma could say anything.

"Yes, that would be what I'm talking about," said Lowen.

"We've had some recent incidents of sabotage," Abumwe said, shooting an irritated glance at Wilson.

"On this ship?" Meyer asked.

"Not originating on this ship, no," Coloma said. "But affecting the ship."

"And you think this could be another one of these?" Meyer said.

"I doubt that it is," Abumwe said.

"But you can't be one hundred percent sure," Meyer persisted.

"No, we can't," Abumwe said.

"What am I missing here?" Stone asked, to Abumwe and Coloma.

"Later, Inge," Coloma said. Stone closed her mouth, unhappy.

"I think we may have a potential issue here," Meyer said.

"What do you suggest we do about it?" Abumwe asked.

"I think we need an autopsy," Meyer said. "The sooner, the better."

"Doctor Stone can certainly perform one," Coloma said. Meyer shook his head; Coloma frowned. "Is that not acceptable?"

"Not by herself," Meyer said. "With no offense offered to Doctor Stone, this has become a politically sensitive event. If someone from within the Colonial Union has been sabotaging your efforts, then all of the Colonial Union's apparatus becomes suspect. I have no doubt at all that Doctor Stone will do a fine job with the autopsy. I also have no doubt at all that there are politicians back on Earth who would look at a Colonial Union doctor clearing the Colonial Union of the suspicious death of an Earth diplomat and use it for their own agendas, whatever those agendas might be."

"There's a problem, then," Stone said. "Because all of my staff are Colonial Union, too."

Meyer looked over to Lowen, who nodded. "I'll do the autopsy with you," she said, to Stone.

Stone blinked. "Are you a medical doctor?" she asked.

Lowen nodded. "University of Pennsylvania," she said. "Specialized in hematology and nephrology. Practiced my specialty for about three months before I joined the State Department as an advisor."

"Doctor Lowen is eliding the fact that her father is United States Secretary of State Saul Lowen," Meyer said, smiling. "And that she was more or less dragooned into this role at her father's behest. Which is to take nothing away from her own talents."

"Anyway," Lowen said, slightly embarrassed by Meyer's commentary. "I have the degree and I have the experience. Between the two of us we can make sure no one complains about the results of the autopsy."

Stone looked at Coloma, who looked over to Abumwe. Abumwe gave a nod. So did Coloma. "All right," she said. "When do you want to start?"

"I need some sleep," Lowen said. "I think we could all use some sleep. We all have a busy day tomorrow." Stone nodded her assent; the Earth observers excused themselves and headed to their berths.

"What the hell were you thinking?" Coloma asked Wilson after they had gone.

"You mean, about letting them know about the sabotage," Wilson said. Coloma nodded. "Look. They already caught us in the reaction. They knew something was up. We could have either lied poorly and had them distrust us, or we could tell them the truth and gain a little trust. The leader of their mission has died, and we don't know why. We can use all the trust we can get."

"The next time you get the urge to make diplomatic decisions, look to me first," Abumwe said. "You've done it before, so I know you can do it now. This isn't your mission and it's not your call to make about what we tell them and what we don't."

"Yes, Ambassador," Wilson said. "I wasn't intentionally trying to make your job harder."

"Lieutenant, I don't give a damn about your *intentions*," Abumwe said. "I thought you knew that by now."

"I do," Wilson said. "Sorry."

"You're dismissed, Wilson," Abumwe said. "The grown-ups need to talk in private." She turned to Coloma and Stone. Wilson took the hint and left.

Lowen was waiting in the corridor for him.

"You're supposed to be asleep," Wilson said.

"I wanted to apologize to you," Lowen said. "I'm pretty sure what I said in there about spending time with you came out wrong."

"That part where you said that you were spending time with me on Liu's orders," Wilson said.

"Yeah, that," Lowen said.

"Would it make you feel better to know that my boss told me to spend time with you?" Wilson said.

"Not really," Lowen said.

"I won't admit it to you, then," Wilson said. "At least not until you've had time to collect yourself."

"Thanks," Lowen said, wryly.

Wilson reached out and touched Lowen's arm in sympathy. "Okay, seriously," he said. "How are you?"

"Oh, you know," Lowen said. "My boss is dead and he was a really nice man, and tomorrow I have to cut into him to see if someone murdered him. I'm just *great.*"

"Come on," Wilson said, and put his arm around her. "I'll walk you back to your berth."

"Did your boss tell you to do that?" Lowen asked, jokingly.

"No," Wilson said, seriously. "This one's on me."

Abumwe's supreme irritation, first at the disposition of the trade negotiations at the end of the first day, and then at the death of Liu Cong and the possible implication thereof, was evident in the second day of negotiations. Abumwe began by tearing Doodoodo a new one, in as brilliant a show of venomous politeness as Wilson had ever seen in his life. Doodoodo and his fellow negotiators actually began to cringe, in the Burfinor fashion, which Wilson decided was more of a scrotal-like contraction than anything else.

Watching the ambassador do her work, and doing it with something approaching vengeful joy, Wilson realized his long-held wish that Abumwe would actually *relax* from time to time was clearly in error. This was a person who operated best and most efficiently when she was truly and genuinely pissed off; wishing for her to mellow out was like wishing an alpha predator would switch to grains. It was missing the point.

Wilson's BrainPal pinged, internally and unseen by the others in the negotiating parties. It was Lowen. *Can you talk?* the message said.

No, but you can, Wilson sent. *You're coming through my BrainPal. No one else will be bothered.*

Hold on, switching to voice, Lowen sent, and then her

voice came through. "I think we have a big problem," she said.

Define "problem," Wilson sent.

"We've finished the autopsy," Lowen sent. "Physically there was nothing wrong with Cong. Everything looked healthy and as close to perfect as a man his age could be. There are no ruptures or aneurysms, no organ damage or scarring. Nothing. There is no reason he should be dead."

That indicates foul play to you? Wilson sent.

"Yes," Lowen said. "And there's another thing, which is the reason I'm talking to you. I took some of his blood for testing and I'm seeing a lot of anomalies in it. There's a concentration of foreign particles in it that I haven't seen before."

Poison compounds? Wilson asked.

"I don't think so," Lowen said.

Have you shown them to Stone? Wilson asked.

"Not yet," Lowen said. "I thought you actually might be more help for this. Can you receive images?"

Sure, Wilson sent.

"Okay, sending now," Lowen said. A notice of a received image flashed in Wilson's peripheral vision; he pulled it up.

It's blood cells, Wilson sent.

"It's not just blood cells," Lowen said.

Wilson paid closer attention and saw specks amid the cells. He zoomed in. The specks gained in size and detail. Wilson frowned and called up a separate image and compared the two.

They look like SmartBlood nanobots, Wilson finally sent.

"That's what I thought they might be," Lowen said. "And that's bad. Because they're not supposed to be there. Just like Cong isn't supposed to be dead. If you have someone who isn't supposed to be dead and no physical reason that he should have died, and you also have a high concentration of foreign material in his blood, it's not hard deduction that the one has to do with the other."

So you think a Colonial did this, Wilson sent.

"I have no idea who did this," Lowen said. "I just know what it looks like."

Wilson had nothing to say to this.

"I'm going to go tell Stone what I found and then I'll have to tell Franz," Lowen said. "I'm sure Stone will tell Coloma and Abumwe. I think we have about an hour before this all gets bad."

Okay, Wilson sent.

"If you can think of something between now and then that will keep this from going to hell, I wouldn't mind," Lowen said.

I'll see what I can do, Wilson sent.

"Sorry, Harry," Lowen said, and disconnected.

Wilson sat silently for a moment, watching Abumwe and Doodoodo as the two of them danced their verbal diplomatic dance about what was the correct balance of trade between starships and biomedical scanners. Then he sent a priority message to Abumwe's PDA.

Take a ten-minute break, it said. *Trust me.*

Abumwe didn't acknowledge the priority message for a few minutes; she was too busy hammering on Doodoodo. When the Burfinor representative finally managed to get a word in edgewise, she glanced down at her PDA and then glanced over at Wilson with a nearly unnoticeable expression that no one else would register as, *You have got to be fucking kidding me.* Wilson acknowledged this with an equally subtle expression that he hoped would read, *I am so very not fucking kidding you.* Abumwe stared at him for a second longer, then interrupted Doodoodo to ask for a quick recess. Doodoodo, flustered because he thought he was on a roll, agreed. Abumwe motioned to Wilson to join her in the hall.

"You don't seem to be remembering our discussion from last night," Abumwe said.

"Lowen found what looks like SmartBlood nanobots in Liu's blood," Wilson said, ignoring Abumwe's statement. "If Stone hasn't updated you about it yet, you'll get the message soon. And so will Meyer and the rest of the observers."

"And?" Abumwe said. "Not that I don't care, but Liu is dead and these negotiations are not, and you didn't need to interrupt them to give me an update I would be receiving anyway."

"I didn't interrupt you for that," Wilson said. "I interrupted you because I need you to have them give me that scanner test unit back. Immediately."

"Why?" Abumwe said.

"Because I think there's something very fishy about SmartBlood nanobots being found in Liu's bloodstream, and I want to get a much better look at them," Wilson said. "The equipment in the medical bay came standard issue with the *Clarke* when it rolled off the line fifty years ago. We need better tools."

"And you need it now why?" Abumwe said.

"Because when today's negotiations are done, the shit is going to hit the fan," Wilson said. "Ambassador, a diplomat from Earth is dead and it looks like the Colonial Union did it. When Meyer and the rest of the observers get back to the *Clarke*, they're going to send a drone back to Phoenix Station and to the Earth's mission there. They're going to be recalled and we're going to be obliged to take them back immediately. So you're going to fail this negotiation, there's going to be a deeper division between Earth and the Colonial Union and all the blame is going to come back to us. Again."

"Unless you can figure this out between now and then," Abumwe said.

"Yes," Wilson said. "SmartBlood is tech, Ambassador. Tech is what I do. And I already know how to operate these machines because I worked with them while I was evaluating them. But I need one *now*. And you need to get it for me."

"You think this will work?" Abumwe asked.

Wilson held his hands out in a *maybe?* motion. "I know if we don't try this, then we're screwed. If this is a shot in the dark, it's still a shot."

Abumwe took out her PDA and opened a line to Hillary Drolet, her assistant. "Tell Doodoodo I need to see him in the hall. Now." She cut the connection and looked back to Wilson. "Anything else you want? As long as I am taking requests."

"I need to borrow the shuttle to go back to the *Clarke*," Wilson said. "I want both Lowen and Stone to watch me so there's no doubt what I find."

"Fine," Abumwe said.

"I'd also like for you to drag on negotiations today as long as you can," Wilson said.

"I don't think that will be a problem," Abumwe said.

Doodoodo appeared in the hallway, eyestalks waggling apologetically.

"And if at all possible, you might want to get that deal done today," Wilson said, looking at Doodoodo. "Just in case."

"Lieutenant Wilson, I am already far ahead of you on this one," Abumwe said.

"Someone in this room is a killer!" Wilson said.

"Please don't say that when they actually show up," Lowen said.

"That's why I'm saying it now," Wilson said.

Wilson, Lowen and Stone were in the medical bay, awaiting Abumwe, Meyer, Bourkou and Coloma. Coloma was on her way from the bridge; the others were coming from the shuttle that had just docked.

"They're on their way," Lowen said, glancing at her PDA. "Franz tells me they wrapped up the negotiations today, too. Abumwe apparently got an excellent deal for the scanners."

"Good," Wilson said, and patted the scanner he had been using. "Maybe that will mean I can keep mine. This thing is sweet."

Coloma arrived; Abumwe, Meyer and Bourkou followed a minute after.

"Now that we're all here, let's get started," Wilson said. "If you'll check your PDAs, you'll see some images I sent to you." Everyone in the room aside from Wilson, Stone and Lowen reached for their PDAs. "What you're seeing there is a sample of Liu Cong's blood. In it you'll see red and white blood cells, platelets and also something else. That something else looks like SmartBlood nanobots. For those of you from Earth, SmartBlood is the non-organic substance that replaces blood in Colonial Defense Forces soldiers. It has superior oxygen-handling properties and other benefits."

"How did that get into his blood?" Meyer asked.

"That's an interesting question," Wilson said. "Almost as interesting as the other question I have, which is *when* did it get into his blood."

"If this is a Colonial Union product, then it would seem that it would have gotten into his system out here," Bourkou said.

"I would have thought so, too," Wilson said. "But then I got a closer look at the nanobots. Go ahead and look at the second image I sent you."

They turned to look at the second picture, which showed two similar-looking objects, one next to the other.

"The first object is a close-up of what we found in Liu's blood," Wilson said. "The second is a close-up of an actual SmartBlood nanobot, which was taken from me, a couple of hours ago." He held up his thumb to show the pinprick there.

"They look the same to me," Meyer said.

"Yes, and I suspect they're supposed to," Wilson said. "It's not until you look inside of them, in substantial detail, that you notice particular differences. If all we had was the *Clarke*'s equipment, we wouldn't have been able to see the differences. Even with the Colonial Union's top-of-the-line equipment, it would have taken some time. Fortunately, we have some new toys. So go ahead and flip to the next image."

Everyone forwarded to the third image.

"I don't expect any of you to know what you're looking at here, but those with some technical experience with SmartBlood will note two major differences with the internal structure," Wilson said. "The first has to do with how the nanobots handle oxygen sequestration. The second has to do with the radio receiver in the 'bot."

"What do these differences mean?" Abumwe asked.

"With regard to oxygen sequestration, it means the 'bots are able to hold on to substantially more oxygen molecules," Wilson says. "It doesn't do anything with them, though. SmartBlood is designed to facilitate oxygen transfer to body tissue. What's in Liu's blood, however, doesn't do that. It just holds on to the oxygen. It goes, grabs the oxygen in the lungs, and doesn't let go. There's less oxygen for the actual red blood cells to carry, and less for the body tissues to take in."

"This stuff suffocated Cong," Lowen said.

"Right," Wilson said. "As for the receiver, well, Smart-Blood takes direction from its owner's BrainPal via an encrypted channel and reverts by default to its primary role, which is oxygen transport." He pointed to Abumwe's

PDA. "This stuff also communicates by encrypted signal. Its default state is off, however. It's only on the job when it's receiving a signal. Its signal doesn't come from a BrainPal, however."

"Where does it come from?" Meyer asked.

Lowen held up an object. It was Meyer's white noise generator.

"It can't be," Meyer said.

"It *can* be," Wilson said. "And it is, because we checked it. How do you think we can describe what this stuff does? This is why I said the interesting question is *when* this stuff got into Liu's blood. Because this"—Wilson pointed to the white noise generator, which Lowen now set on the table—"strongly suggests that it happened before you folks left Earth."

"How did you find it?" Abumwe asked.

"We walked through Liu's death," Stone said. "We knew when he died, and we knew that these 'bots needed a transmitter, and Mr. Bourkou said that he had been running the white noise generator to drown out Liu's snoring."

"You can't think I did it," Bourkou said.

"You set this thing off in the same room," Wilson said.

"It's not even mine," Bourkou said. "Franz let me borrow it. It's his."

"That's true," Wilson said, turning to Meyer.

Meyer looked shocked. "I didn't kill Cong! And this doesn't make logical sense in any event. Cong was supposed to have a berth to himself. This thing wasn't supposed to have been in the same room."

"A very good point," Wilson said. "Which is why I checked the effective transmitting radius of the generator's 'bot transmitter. It's about twenty meters. Your berth is right next door, and the berths are narrow enough that Liu's bunk is well within the radius, even accounting for signal attenuation through the common bulkhead."

"We'd been traveling for more than a week before we arrived here," Meyer said. "Before this we had individual staterooms, but we were still close enough for this thing to work. I used it every night. Nothing happened to Cong."

"Interestingly, there are two transmitters in the white noise generator," Wilson said. "One of them affects the 'bots. The second affects the first transmitter. It turns it on or off."

"So it wouldn't have done anything until you got here," Lowen said.

"This is crazy," Meyer said. "I don't have a remote control for this thing! Go to my berth! Check for yourself!"

Wilson looked over at Captain Coloma. "I'll have crew go through his berth," she said.

"Have you dumped trash recently?" Wilson said.

"No," Coloma said. "We usually don't dump until we return to Phoenix Station, and when we do, we don't do it in other people's systems. That's rude."

"Then I would suggest we look through the trash," Wilson said. "I can give you the transmitting frequency if it helps." Coloma nodded.

"Why did you do it?" Bourkou asked Meyer.

"I didn't do it!" Meyer yelled. "You are just as likely to have done it as I am, Thierry. You had the generator in your possession. You're the one who convinced Cong to give up his berth for me. I didn't ask him."

"You complained about claustrophia," Bourkou said.

"I joked about claustrophobia, you ass," Meyer said.

"And I wasn't the one who suggested it to him," Bourkou said. "It was Luiza. So don't pin it on me."

A strange expression crossed Meyer's face. Wilson caught it. So did Abumwe. "What it is it?" she asked Meyer.

Meyer looked around at the group, as if debating whether to say something, then sighed. "I've been sleeping with Luiza Carvalho for the last three months," he said. "During the selection process for this mission and then since. It's not a relationship, it's more taking advantage of a mutual opportunity. I didn't think it would matter since neither of us was in a position to select the other for the mission."

"All right," Abumwe said. "So?"

"So Luiza always complained about me sleeping badly," Meyer said, and pointed at the white noise generator. "Two weeks ago, after we knew who was on the mission, she bought me *that*. Said it would help me sleep."

"Luiza was the one who suggested to Meyer that he let me borrow the generator," Bourkou said. "To counteract Cong's snoring."

"Where is Ms. Carvalho?" Stone asked.

"She said she was going to her berth," Abumwe said. "Lieutenant Wilson didn't ask for her to be here, so I didn't ask her to come."

"We should probably have someone get her," Wilson said, but Coloma was already on her PDA, ordering someone to get her.

Coloma's PDA pinged almost immediately thereafter; it was Neva Balla. Coloma put her executive officer on the speaker so everyone in the room could hear. "We have a problem," Balla said. "There's someone in the portside maintenance airlock. It looks like one of the Earth people."

"Send me the image," Coloma said. When she got it, she bounced it to the PDAs of everyone else in the room.

It was Luiza Carvalho.

"What is she doing?" Lowen asked.

"Lock out the airlock," Coloma said.

"It's too late," Balla said. "She's already started the purge cycle."

"She must have been listening in somehow," Abumwe said.

"How the hell did she get in there?" Coloma asked, angry.

"The same way she got Meyer and Bourkou to help her kill Liu," Wilson said.

"But why did she do it?" Meyer said. "Who is she working with? Who is she working for?"

"We're not going to get an answer to that," Wilson said.

"Well, we know one thing, at least," Lowen said.

"What's that?" Wilson asked.

"Whoever's been sabotaging you up here, it looks like they're on the job down there on Earth," Lowen said.

"Almost got away with it, too," Wilson said. "If we didn't have that scanner, it would have looked like the Colonial Union killed him. By the time it was cleared up, it would have been too late to fix it."

No one said anything to that.

In the video feed, Carvalho looked up to where the camera was, as if looking at the group in the medical bay.

She waved.

The air purged out of the airlock. Carvalho exhaled and kept exhaling long enough to stay conscious until the hull lock opened.

She let herself out.

"Dani," Wilson said.

"Yeah, Harry," Lowen said.

"You still have the Laphroaig?" Wilson asked.

"I do," Lowen said.

"Good," Wilson said. "Because right now, I think we all need a drink."

This Must Be the Place

Hart Schmidt took the shuttle from the *Clarke* to Phoenix Station and an interstation tram to the station's main commuter bay, and then he caught one of the ferries that arrived at and departed from Phoenix Station every fifteen minutes. The ferry headed down to the Phoenix Station Terminal at the Phoenix City Hub, which aggregated most of the civilian mass transportation for the oldest and most populous city of the oldest and most populous human interstellar colony planet.

Upon exiting the ferry, Hart walked through spaceport terminal C and boarded the interterminal tram for the PCH main terminal. Three minutes later, Hart exited the tram, went from the platform to the immensely long escalator and emerged in the main terminal. It was one of the largest single buildings humans had ever built, a vast domed structure that housed stores, shops, offices, hotels and even apartments for those who worked at the hub, schools for their children, hospitals and even a jail, although Hart had no personal experience with the last two.

Hart smiled as he came out into the main terminal and stepped onto the terminal floor. In his mind, as always, he imagined the mass of humanity bustling through suddenly grabbing the hands of the people next to them and waltzing in unison. He was pretty sure he'd seen a scene like that in a movie once, either here in the main terminal or in a terminal or station much like it. It never happened, of course. It didn't mean that Hart didn't keep wishing for it.

His first stop was the PCH Campbell Main Terminal Hotel. Hart checked into a one-step-above-standard-sized room, dropped his bag at the foot of the queen-sized bed and then immediately gloried, after months of sharing his broom-closet-sized "officer quarters" on the *Clarke* with another diplomat, in having nearly forty square meters of no one else in his living space.

Hart sighed contentedly and immediately fell into a nap. Three hours later he awoke, took a shower that was indecently hot and indecently long and ordered room service, not neglecting a hot fudge sundae. He tipped the room service delivery person exorbitantly, ate until he felt he would explode, switched the entertainment display to the classic movies channel and watched hundred-year-old stories of early colonial drama and adventure, starring actors long dead, until his eyes snapped shut seemingly of their own accord. He slept dreamlessly, the display on, for close to ten hours.

Late the next morning, Hart checked out of the Campbell, took another interterminal tram to train terminal A and hopped on train 311, with travel to Catahoula, Lafourche, Feliciana and Terrebonne. Schmidt stayed on the train all the way to Terrebonne and then had to run to connect with the Tangipahopa express, which he caught as the doors were closing. At Tangipahopa, he boarded the Iberia local and got off at the third stop, Crowley. A car was waiting for him there. He smiled as he recognized Broussard Kueltzo, the driver.

"Brous!" he said, giving the man a hug. "Happy Harvest."

"Long time, Hart," Brous said. "Happy Harvest to you, too."

"How are you doing?" Hart asked.

"The same as always," he said. "Working for your dad, hauling his ass from place to place. Keeping up the Kueltzo family tradition of being the power behind the Schmidt family throne."

"Come on," Hart said. "We're not *that* helpless."

"It's okay for you to think that," Brous said. "But I have to tell you that one day last month I had to take Mom into the hospital for tests, and your mother was out at one of her organization meetings. Your dad called my mom's PDA, asking how to work the coffee machine. She's getting blood drawn and she's walking him through pressing buttons. Your dad is one of the most powerful people on Phoenix, Hart, but he'd starve in a day if he was left on his own."

"Fair enough," Hart said. "How is your mother?" Magda Kueltzo might or might not actually be the power behind the Schmidt throne, but there was no doubt most of the family was deeply fond of her.

"Much better," Brous said. "In fact, she's busy working the meal you're going to be stuffing down your throat in just a few hours, so we better get you to it." He took Hart's bag and swung it into the car's backseat. The two men hopped into the front; Brous punched in the destination and the car drove itself.

"It's not a very demanding job," Hart ventured as the car pulled itself away from the station.

"That's sort of the point," Brous said. "In my quote unquote spare time, I get to work on the poetry, which incidentally has been doing very well, thanks for asking. That is insofar as poetry does well, which you understand is a highly relative thing and has been for centuries. I am an established poet now, and I make almost nothing for it."

"Sorry about that," Hart said.

Brous shrugged. "It's not so bad. Your dad has been generous in that way of his. You know how he is. Always thumping on about people having to make their own way in the world and the value of an honest day's labor. He'd rather die than fund a grant. But he gives me a ridiculously easy job and pays me well enough that I can work on my words."

"He likes being the patron," Hart said.

"Right," Brous said. "I won the Nova Acadia Poetry medal last year for my book and he was more proud of it than I was. I let him put the medal in his office."

"That's Dad," Hart said.

Brous nodded. "He did the same thing with Lisa," he said, mentioning his sister. "Had her scrub toilets at the house for a year, then paid her enough for it to survive grad school in virology. Went to her doctoral ceremony. Insisted on getting a picture. It's on his desk."

"That's great," Hart said.

"I know you and he have gone a few rounds on things," Brous ventured.

"He's still irritated that I went into the Colonial Union diplomatic service rather than into Phoenix politics," Hart said.

"He'll get over it eventually," Brous suggested.

"How long are you going to keep the job?" Hart asked, changing the subject.

"It's funny you should ask," Brous said, catching the attempt and rolling with it. "The medal helped me get a teaching position at University of Metairie. It was supposed to start at the beginning of the fall, but I asked for them to set it back a semester so I could help your dad through the election season."

"How did it go?" Hart said.

"Oh, man," Brous said. "You haven't been following it at all?"

"I've been in space," Hart said.

"It was brutal," Brous said. "Not for your dad, of course. No one even ran against him here. They're going to have to wheel him out of his office. But the rest of the PHP took a thumping. Lost sixty seats in the regional parliament. Lost ninety-five in the global. The New Greens formed a coalition with the Unionists and put in a new prime minister and heads of department."

"How did that happen?" Hart asked. "I've been away for a while, but not so long that Phoenix should have suddenly gone squishy. I say that as a squishy sort, understand."

"Understood," Brous said. "I voted New Green in the regional myself. Don't tell your dad."

"Deep dark secret," Hart promised.

"The PHP got lazy," Brous said. "They've been in power so long, they forgot they could be voted out. Some bad people in key positions, a couple of stupid scandals, and a charismatic head of the New Green party. Add it all up and people took a chance on someone new. It won't last, I think; the New Greens and the Unionists are already arguing and the PHP will do some housecleaning. But in the meantime your dad is in a foul mood about it. Even more so because he was one of the architects of the global party strategy. The collapse makes him look bad personally, or so he feels."

"Oh, boy," Hart said. "This will make it a cheerful Harvest Day."

"Yeah, he's been moody," Brous said. "Your mother has been keeping him in line, but you're going to have the whole family at home this Harvest, and you know how he gets with the whole clan there. Especially with Brandt rising in the Unionist party."

"The Schmidt boys," Hart said. "Brandt the traitor, Hart the underachiever and Wes . . . well, Wes."

Brous smiled at that. "Don't you forget your sister," he said.

"No one forgets Catherine, Brous," Hart said. "Catherine the Unforgettable."

"They're all already there, you know," Brous said. "At the house. They all got in last night. All of them, all their spouses and children. I'm not going to lie to you, Hart. One of the reasons I came to get you was so I could have a few minutes of quiet."

Hart grinned at this.

Presently the Schmidt family compound came into view, all 120 acres of it, with the main house set on a hill, rising above the orchards, fields and lawns. Home.

"I remember when I was six and Mom came to work here," Brous said. "I remember driving up to this place and thinking there was no way one family could live in that much space."

"Well, after you arrived, it wasn't just one family," Hart said.

"True enough," Brous said. "I'll tell you another story you'll find amusing. When I was in college, I brought my girlfriend to the carriage house and she was amazed we had so much living space there. I was afraid to take her up to the main house after that. I figured she'd stop being impressed with me."

"Was she?" Hart asked.

"No," Brous said. "She became unimpressed with me for other reasons entirely." He switched the car to manual, led it up the rest of the driveway and stopped at the front door. "Here you are, Hart. The entire family is inside, waiting for you."

"What would it cost for you to drive me back?" Hart joked.

"In a couple of days I'll do it for free," Brous said. "Until then, my friend, you're stuck."

"Ah, the prodigal spaceman returns," Brandt Schmidt said. He, like the rest of the Schmidt siblings, lounged on the back patio of the main house, watching the various children and spouses on the front surface of the back lawn. Brandt came up to Hart to give him a hug, followed by Catherine and Wes. Brandt pressed the cocktail he had in his hand into Hart's. "I haven't started on this one yet," he said. "I'll make another."

"Where's Mom and Dad?" Hart asked, sipping the drink. He frowned. It was a gin and tonic, more than a little heavy on the gin.

"Mom's in with Magda, fussing over dinner," Brandt said, going over to the patio bar to mix himself another highball. "She'll be back presently. Dad's in his office, yelling at some functionary of the Phoenix Home Party. That will take a while."

"Ah," Hart said. Best to miss out on that.

"You heard about the latest elections," Brandt said.

"A bit," Hart said.

"Then you'll understand why he's in a bit of a *mood,*" Brandt said.

"It doesn't help that you continue to needle him about it," Catherine said, to Brandt.

"I'm not *needling* him about it," Brandt said. "I'm just not letting him get away with revising recent electoral history."

"That's pretty much the definition of 'needling,'" Wes said, laconically, from his lounge, which was close to fully reclined. His eyes were closed, a tumbler of something brown on the patio itself, by his outstretched hand.

"I recognize I'm telling him things he doesn't want to hear right now," Brandt said.

"Needling," Catherine and Wes said, simultaneously. They were twins and could do that from time to time. Hart smiled.

"Fine, I'm needling him," Brandt said, took a sip of his gin and tonic, frowned and went back to the bar to add a splash more tonic. "But after so many years of listening to him talk about the historical import of each election and the PHP's role in it, I think it's perfectly fine to have a bit of turnabout."

"That's exactly what this Harvest Day needs," Catherine said. "Another perfectly good dinner from Magda growing cold because you and Dad are going at it again at the table."

"Speak for yourself," Wes said. "They never stopped me from eating."

"Well, Wes, you've always had a special talent for tuning out," Catherine said. "It puts the rest of us off our appetite."

"I don't apologize for being the only one of us who has any interest at all in politics," Brandt said.

"No one wants you to apologize," Catherine said. "And you know we all have an interest in politics."

"I don't," Wes said.

"We all have an interest in politics except for Wes," Catherine amended, "who is just happy to coast on the benefits of the family having a good political name. So, by all means, Brandt, discuss politics all you like with Dad. Just wait until we get to the pie before you start going after each other."

"Politics and pie," Wes said. "Mmmmmm." He started fumbling about for his drink, connected with it and brought it to his lips, eyes still closed.

Brandt turned to Hart. "Help me out here," he said.

Hart shook his head. "I wouldn't mind getting through an entire Harvest Day without you and Dad tossing verbal knives at each other," he said. "I'm not here to talk politics. I'm here to spend time with my family."

Brandt rolled his eyes at his younger brother. "Have you *met* our family, Hart?"

"Oh, don't pester Hart about planetside politics," Catherine said. "This is the first time he's spent any time at home in Lord knows how long."

"Last Harvest Day," Hart volunteered.

"You can't genuinely expect him to keep up with the relatively trivial politics of Phoenix when he's grappling with Colonial Union–wide crises," Catherine said to Brandt, and then swiveled her head to Hart. "What was your most recent interstellar diplomatic triumph, Hart?"

"I helped electrocute a dog in order to save a peace negotiation," Hart said.

"What?" Catherine asked, momentarily flummoxed.

Wes cracked open an eye to look at Hart. "Is this like sacrificing a chicken to the gods?" he asked.

"It's more complicated than it sounds," Hart said. "And I would note that the dog survived."

"Well, thank goodness for *that*," Brandt said, and turned to his sister. "I stand corrected, fair Catherine. Hart's clearly got more important things on his mind than mere *politics*."

Before Catherine could retort, Isabel Schmidt descended and embraced her youngest son. "Oh, Hart," she said. She gave him a peck on the cheek. "So good to see you, son. I can't believe it's been another whole year." She stepped back. "You look almost exactly the same."

"He *is* almost exactly the same," Brandt said. "He's not old enough yet to age poorly."

"Oh, Brandt, do shut up," Isabel said, not unkindly. "He's thirty. That's plenty old to start aging badly. You started at twenty-seven."

"Ouch, Mother," Brandt said.

"You brought it up, honey," Isabel said, and then turned her attention back to Hart. "You still enjoying the Colonial Union diplomatic service?" she asked. "Not getting bored with it?"

"It's not boring," Hart admitted.

"You still working with, oh, what's her name," Isabel said. "Ottumwa?"

"Abumwe," Hart said.

"That's the one," Isabel said. "Sorry. You know I'm terrible with names."

"It's all right," Hart said. "And yes, I'm still working with her."

"Is she still an asshole?" Catherine asked. "The last time you were home, the stories you told about her made her sound like a real piece of work."

"What stories do your assistants tell about you?" Brandt asked his sister.

"If they tell stories, they don't stay my assistants," Catherine said.

"She's gotten better," Hart said. "Or at the very least, I think I understand her better."

"That's good to hear," Isabel said.

"Ask him about the dog," Wes drawled from his lounge.

"The dog?" Isabel said, looking over to Wes and then back to Hart. "What about a dog?"

"You know what, I think I'll tell you that one later, Mom," Hart said. "Maybe after dinner."

"Does it end badly for the dog?" Isabel asked.

"End? No," Hart said. "It ends fine for the dog. It *middles* poorly for him, though."

"Diplomacy is awesome," Wes said.

"We thought you were coming in yesterday," Isabel said, changing the subject.

"I got hung up at the hub," Hart said, remembering his hotel room. "It was easier to head out first thing in the morning."

"Well, but you're staying for the week, right?" Isabel said.

"Five days, yes," Hart said. He had another night at the Campbell reserved before he headed back to the *Clarke*. He intended to use it.

"Okay, good," Isabel said. "If you have time, I have someone I'd like you to meet."

"Oh, Mom," Catherine said. "Are you really going to try this again?"

"There's nothing wrong with introducing Hart to some options," Isabel said.

"Does this option have a name?" Hart asked.

"Lizzie Chao," Isabel said.

"This is the same Lizzie Chao who I went to high school with," Hart said.

"I believe so," Isabel said.

"She's married," Hart said.

"She's separated," Isabel said.

"Which means she's married with an option to trade up," Catherine said.

"Mom, I remember Lizzie," Hart said. "She's really not my type."

"She has a brother," Wes said, from his lounge.

"He's not my type, either," Hart said.

"Who *is* your type these days, Hart?" Isabel asked.

"I don't have a type these days," Hart said. "Mom, I work out of a spaceship all year around. I share quarters that are smaller than our kitchen pantry. I spend my days trying to convince aliens we don't want to blow them up anymore. That's an all-day job. Given my circumstances, it would be foolish to attempt any sort of relationship. It wouldn't be fair to the other person, or to me, for that matter."

"Hart, you know I hate sounding like the stereotypical mother," Isabel said. "But you're the only one of my children who isn't in a relationship and having children. Even Wes managed it."

"Thanks, Mom," Wes said, lifting his hand in a lazy wave.

"I don't want you to end up feeling the good things in life are passing you by," Isabel said, to Hart.

"I don't feel that way," Hart said.

"Not now," Isabel said. "But honey, you're thirty and

you're still at deputy level. If it doesn't happen for you in the next year or two, it's not going to happen. And then where are you going to be? I love you and want you to be happy. But it's time you start thinking realistically about these things and whether the CU diplomatic service is really the best use of your talents and your life."

Hart leaned over and gave his mother a peck on the cheek. "I'm going to go up and unpack, and then I'm going to check in on Dad," he said. He swallowed the rest of his drink and walked into the house.

"Subtlety still counts for something, Mom," Hart heard Catherine say as he entered the house. If his mother responded, however, it was lost to Hart.

Hart found his father, Alastair Schmidt, in his home office, situated in his parents' wing of the third floor, which included their bedroom, its master bath suite, attached and separate wardrobes, individual offices, library and drawing room. The children's wing of the house was no less appointed but arranged differently.

Alastair Schmidt was standing behind his desk, listening to one of his political underlings give him a report through a speaker. The underling was no doubt in a Phoenix Home Party cubicle in Phoenix City, trying desperately to get out of the office in order to celebrate Harvest Day with his family but pinned to his desk by the baleful attention of Schmidt, one of the grand old men of the party and of Phoenix global politics generally.

Hart poked his head around the open door and waved to let his father know he was home; his father waved him into the room brusquely and then turned his attention back to his unfortunate apparatchik. "I wasn't asking why the data was difficult to locate, Klaus," he said. "I was asking why we don't seem to have it at all. 'Difficult to locate' and 'not in our possession' are two entirely separate things."

"I understand that, Minister Schmidt," Klaus the apparatchik was saying. "What I'm saying is that we're hampered by the holiday. Most people are out. The requests we filed are in and will be honored, but they have to wait until people get back."

"Well, you're in, aren't you?" Alastair said.

"Yes," Klaus said, and Hart caught the slight edge of misery in his voice at the fact. "But—"

"And the entire government doesn't in fact shut all the way down even on major global holidays," Alastair said, cutting off Klaus before he could offer another objection. "So your job right now is to find the people who are still working today, just like you are, get that data and those projections, and have them on my desk in an encrypted file before I go to bed tonight. And I have to tell you, Klaus, that I tend to go to bed early on Harvest Day. It's all that pie."

"Yes, Minister Schmidt," Klaus said, unhappily.

"Good," Alastair said. "Happy Harvest, Klaus."

"Happ—" Klaus was cut off as Alastair severed the connection.

"His Harvest isn't going to be happy because you're making him work on Harvest Day," Hart observed.

"If he'd gotten me that data yesterday like I asked and like he'd promised, he'd be at home, chewing on a drumstick," Alastair said. "But he didn't, so he's not, and that's on him."

"I noticed he still called you 'minister,' " Hart said.

"Ah, so you know about the election," Alastair said. "Brandt gloating, is he?"

"I heard it from other sources," Hart said.

"Officially, the Green-Union government is extending an olive branch to the PHP by asking me to stay on as minister for trade and transport," Alastair said.

"Unofficially, the point was made to the coalition that they have no one near competent to run the ministry, and that if they are going to screw up any one ministry, the one they don't want to screw up is the one that makes sure food arrives where it's supposed to and that people are able to get to work."

"It's a legitimate point," Hart said.

"Personally, the sooner this Green-Union coalition collapses, the happier I'll be, and I gave some thought to turning it down, just to watch the ensuing train wreck," Alastair said. "But then I realized that there would probably be actual train wrecks, and that's the sort of thing that will get everyone's head on a spike, not just the heads of those in the coalition."

Hart smiled. "That famous Alastair Schmidt compassion," he said.

"Don't you start," Alastair said. "I get enough of that from Brandt. It's not that I don't care. I do. But I'm also still pissed about the election results." He motioned at the chair in front of the desk, offering Hart the seat; Hart took it. Alastair sat in his own seat, regarding his son.

"How is life in the Colonial Union diplomatic corps?" Alastair asked. "I imagine it must be exciting, what with the collapse of relations between the Earth and the Colonial Union."

"We live in interesting times, yes," Hart said.

"And your Ambassador Abumwe seems to be in the thick of things lately," Alastair said. "Dashing between assignments all across known space."

"They have been keeping her busy," Hart said.

"And you've been busy as well?" Alastair asked.

"Mostly," Hart said. "I'm doing a lot of work with Lieutenant Harry Wilson, who is a CDF technician who handles various tasks for us."

"I know," Alastair said. "I have a friend who works

for the Department of State. Keeps me up-to-date on the diplomatic reports from the *Clarke*."

"Is that so," Hart said.

"Not a whole lot of future in electrocuting dogs, Hart," Alastair said.

"*There* we go," Hart said.

"Am I wrong?" Alastair asked.

"Do you actually read the reports you get, Dad?" Hart said. "If you read the report about the dog, then you know what happened was that we ended up saving the peace negotiations and helped secure an alliance for the Colonial Union with a race that had been leaning toward aligning with the Conclave."

"Sure, after you carelessly allowed the dog to be eaten by a carnivorous plant, revealing the death site of a king whose disappearance started the race's civil war, the discovery of which threatened a peace process that by all indications wasn't threatened before," Alastair said. "You don't get credit for putting out fires you set yourself, Hart."

"The official report reads differently than your interpretation, Dad," Hart said.

"Of course it does," Alastair said. "If I were your bosses, I would write it that way, too. But I'm not your boss, and I can read between the lines better than most."

"Are you going somewhere with this, Dad?" Hart said.

"I think it's time you came back to Phoenix," Alastair said. "You gave the Colonial Union your best shot, and they've misused your talent. They stuck you with a diplomatic team that's been catching lost-cause missions for years, and assigned you to a CDF grunt who uses you for menial tasks. You're too accommodating to complain, and maybe you're even having fun, but you're not going anywhere, Hart. And maybe that's fine early in your career, but you're not early in your career anymore. You've dead-ended. It's over."

"Not that I agree with you," Hart said, "but why do you care, Dad? You've always told us that we have to make our own path, and you told us that we would have to sink or swim on our own. You're a veritable raft of tough-love metaphors on the subject. If you think I'm sinking, you should be willing to let me sink."

"Because it's not just about *you*, Hart," Alastair said. He pointed at the speaker through which he had been yelling at Klaus. "I'm seventy-two years old, for Christ's sake. Do you think I want to be spending my time keeping some poor bastard from enjoying his Harvest Day? No, what I want to do is tell the PHP to get along without me and spend more time with those grandkids of mine."

Hart stared at his father blankly. At no point in the past had his father ever evinced more than the most cursory interest in his grandchildren. *Maybe that's because they're not interesting yet*, a part of Hart's brain said, and he could see the point. His father had become more engaged with his own children the older they got. And he could have his softer side; Hart's eyes flickered to the medal case on the wall, holding Brous's Nova Acadia award.

"I can't do that because I don't have the right people following me," Alastair continued. "Brandt's gloating because the Unionists have their share of power, but the thing is the reason it happened is because the PHP hasn't cultivated new talent, and now it's biting us in the ass."

"Wait," Hart said. "Dad, are you wanting me to join the PHP? Because I have to tell you, that's really not going to happen."

"You're missing my point," Alastair said. "The PHP hasn't developed new talent, but neither have the Greens or the Unionists. I'm still on the job because the whole next generation of political talent on Phoenix are, with very few exceptions, complete incompetents." He pointed in the direction of the patio, where the rest of the family was. "Brandt thinks I get annoyed with him because he's in with the Unionists. I get annoyed with him because he's not rising through its leadership fast enough."

"Brandt likes politics," Hart said. "I don't."

"Brandt likes everything *around* politics," Alastair said. "He doesn't give a crap about the politics itself, yet. That will come. It will come to Catherine, too. She's busy building a power base in the charity world, rolling over people and getting them to thank her for it by supporting her works. When she finally transfers over into politics, she's going to make a beeline for prime minister."

"And what about Wes?" Hart asked.

"Wes is Wes," Alastair said. "One in every family. I love him, but I think of him as a sarcastic pet."

"I don't think I would tell Wes that if I were you," Hart said.

"He figured it out a long time ago," Alastair said. "I think he's at peace with it, especially as it requires nothing from him. As I said. One in every family. We can't afford two."

"So you want me to come home," Hart said. "And what do I do then? Just walk into some political role you've picked out for me? Because no one will see the obvious nepotism in that, Dad."

"Give me some credit for subtlety," Alastair said. "Do you really think Brandt is where he is with the Unionists all on his own? No. They saw the value in the Schmidt brand name, as it were, and we came to an arrangement about what they'd get in return for fast-tracking him in the organization."

"I would *definitely* not tell Brandt that if I were you," Hart said.

"Of course not," Alastair said. "But I am telling *you* so that you will understand how these things work."

"It's still nepotism," Hart said.

"I prefer to think of it as advancing people who are a known quantity," Alastair said. "And aren't you a known quantity, Hart? Don't you have skills, honed through your diplomatic career, that would have immediate use at a high level? Would you really want to start near the bottom? You're a little old for that now."

"You've just admitted the Colonial Union diplomatic corps taught me skills," Hart said.

"I never said you didn't have them," Alastair said. "I said they were being wasted. Do you want to use them as they ought to be used? This is the place, Hart. It's time to let the Colonial Union take care of the Colonial Union. Come back to Phoenix, Hart. I need you. We need you."

"Lizzie Chao needs me," Hart said, ruefully.

"Oh, no, stay away from her," Alastair said. "She's bad news. She's been banging my field rep here in Crowley."

"Dad!" Hart said.

"Don't tell your mother," Alastair said. "She thinks Lizzie is a nice girl. And maybe she is nice. Just without very good judgment."

"We wouldn't want that," Hart said.

"You've had enough bad judgment in your life so far, Hart," Alastair said. "Time to start making some better choices."

"Didn't expect to see you again so soon," Brous Kueltzo said. He was leaning up against the car, reading a message on his PDA. Hart had walked down to the carriage house.

"I needed to get away from the family for a bit," Hart said.

"Already, huh?" Brous said.

"Yeah," Hart said.

"And you still have four days to go," Brous said. "I'll pray for you."

"Brous, can I ask you a question?" Hart said.

"Sure," Brous said.

"Did you ever resent us?" Hart asked. "Ever resent me?"

"You mean, for being obscenely rich and entitled and a member of one of the most important families on the entire planet through absolutely no effort of your own and for having everything you ever wanted served up to you on a platter without any idea how hard it was for the rest of us?" Brous said.

"Uh, yes," Hart said, taken slightly aback. "Yes. That."

"There was a period where I did, yeah," Brous said. "I mean, what do you expect? Resentment is about sixty percent of being a teenager. And all of you—you, Catherine, Wes, Brandt—were pretty clueless about the rarefied air you lived in. Down here in the flats, living above the garage? Yeah, there was some resentment there."

"Do you resent us now?" Hart said.

"No," Brous said. "For one thing, bringing that college girlfriend back to the carriage house brought home the point that all things considered, I was doing just fine. I went to the same schools you did, and your family supported and cared for me, my sister and my mom, and not just in some distant noblesse oblige way, but as friends. Hell, Hart. I write *poetry*, you know? I have that because of you guys."

"Okay," Hart said.

"I mean, you all still have your moments of class cluelessness, trust me on this, and you all poke at each other in vaguely obnoxious ways," Brous said. "But I think even if you had no money, Brandt would be a status seeker, Catherine would steamroll everyone, Wes would float along, and you'd do your thing, which is to watch and help. You'd all be you. Everything else is circumstance."

"It's good to know you think so," Hart said.

"I do," Brous said. "Don't get me wrong. If you want to divest yourself of your share of the family trust fund and give to me, I'll take it. I'll let you sleep above the garage when you need to."

"Thanks," Hart said, wryly.

"What brought about this moment of questioning, if you don't mind me asking?" Brous asked.

"Oh, you know," Hart said. "Dad pressuring me to leave the diplomatic corps and join the family business, which is apparently running this entire planet."

"Ah, *that*," Brous said.

"Yes, that," Hart said.

"That's another reason why I don't resent you guys," Brous said. "This whole 'born to rule' shit's gotta get tiring. All I have to do is drive your dad and string words together."

"What if you don't want to rule?" Hart said.

"Don't rule," Brous said. "I'm not sure why you're asking that, though, Hart. You've done a pretty good job of not ruling so far."

"What do you mean?" Hart asked.

"There's four of you," Brous said. "Two of you are primed to go into the family business: Brandt, because he likes the perks, and Catherine, because she's actually good at it. Two of you want nothing to do with it: Wes, who figured out early that one of you gets to be the screwup, so it might as well be him, and you. The screwup slot was already claimed by Wes, so you did the only logical thing left to third sons of a noble family—you went elsewhere to seek your fortune."

"Wow, you've actually thought about this a lot," Hart said.

Brous shrugged. "I'm a writer," he said. "And I've had a lot of time to observe you guys."

"You could have told me all this earlier," Hart said.

"You didn't ask," Brous said.

"Ah," Hart said.

"Also, I could be wrong," Brous said. "I've learned over time I'm full of just about as much shit as anyone."

"No, I don't think you are," Hart said. "Wrong, I mean. I remain neutral about the 'full of shit' part."

"Fair enough," Brous said. "It sounds like you're having a moment of existentialist crisis here, Hart, if you don't mind me saying."

"Maybe I am," Hart said. "I'm trying to decide what I want to be when I grow up. A nice thing to wonder about when you're thirty."

"I don't think it matters what age you are when you figure it out," Brous said. "I think the important thing is to figure it out before someone else tells you what you want to be, and they get it wrong."

"Who's giving the toast this year?" Isabel asked. They were all seated at the table: Alastair and Isabel, Hart, Catherine, Wes and Brandt and their spouses. The children were sequestered away in the next room, on low tables, and were busy throwing peas and rolls at one another while the nannies vainly tried to keep control.

"I'll give the toast," Alastair said.

"You give the toast every year," Isabel said. "And your toasts are boring, dear. Too long and too full of politics."

"It's the family business," Alastair said. "It's a family dinner. What else should we talk about?"

"And besides which, you're still bitter about the election, and I don't want to hear about it tonight," Isabel said. "So no toast from you."

"I'll give the toast," Brandt said.

"Oh, hell, no," Alastair said.

"Alastair," Isabel said, admonishingly.

"You thought *my* toast was going to be long and boring and full of politics," Alastair said. "The gloater in chief here will positively outstrip your expectations of me."

"Dad does have a point," Catherine said.

"Then you say it, dear," Isabel said to her.

"Indeed," Brandt said, clearly a little hurt at having his toast proposal rebuffed. "Regale us with tales of the people you've met and crushed in the last year."

"The hell with this," Wes said, and reached for the mashed potatoes.

"Wes," Isabel said.

"What?" Wes said, spooning out a heap of potatoes. "By the time you figure out who's toasting what, everything will be dry and cold. I have too much respect for Madga's work for that."

"I'll make the toast," Hart said.

"Ho!" Brandt said. "This is a first."

"Quiet, Brandt," Isabel said, and turned her attention to her youngest. "Go ahead, dear."

Hart stood, picked up his glass of wine and looked over the table.

"Every year, whoever makes the toast gets to talk about the events in their life from the last year," Hart said. "Well, I have to say this has been an eventful year. I got spit on by aliens as part of a diplomatic negotiation. My ship was attacked with a missile and almost blew up around me. I got a human head delivered to me by an alien as part of another, entirely different negotiation. And, as you all recently learned, I helped zap a dog into unconsciousness as part of a third negotiation. All the while living day to day in a ship that's the oldest one in service, sleeping in a bunk that's barely wide enough for me, rooming with a guy who is either snoring or passing gas most of the night.

"If you think about it, it's a ridiculous way to live. It really is. And, as has also been pointed out to me recently, it's a way that doesn't seem to hold much of a future for me, assigned as I am to a low-ranking ambassador who has had to fight her way to the sorts of missions that more exalted diplomats would turn down as a waste of their talents and abilities. It does make you wonder why I do it. Why I *have* done it.

"And then I remember why I do it. Because as strange, and exhausting, and enervating, and, yes, even humiliating as it can be, at the end of the day, when everything goes right, it's the most exciting thing I've ever done. Ever. I stand there and I can't believe that I've been part of a group who meets with people who are not human but can still reason, and that we've reasoned together, and through that reason have agreed to live together, without killing each other or demanding more of the other than what each of us needs from the other.

"And it's happening at a time in our history that's never been more critical to humanity. We are out here, all of us, without the sort of protection and growth that Earth has always provided us before. And because of that, every negotiation, every agreement, every action we take—even those of us on the bottom rung of the diplomatic service—makes a difference for the future of humanity. For the future of this planet and every planet like it. For the future of everyone at this table.

"I love all of you. Dad, I love your dedication to Phoenix and your desire to keep it running. Mom, I love that you care for each of us, even when you snipe at us a little. Brandt, I love your ambition and drive. Catherine, I love the fact that one day you will rule us all. Wes, I love that you are the family jester, who keeps us honest. I love you and your wives and husbands and your children. I love Magda and Brous and Lisa, who have lived their lives with us.

"I was told recently by someone that if I wanted to make a difference, that this must be the place. Here, on Phoenix. With love and respect, I disagree. Dad, Brandt and Catherine will take care of Phoenix for us. My job is to take care of the rest of it. That's what I do. That's what I'm going to keep doing. That's where what I do matters.

"So to each of you, my family, a toast. Keep Phoenix safe for me. I'll work on everything else. When I come back for Harvest Day next year, I'll let you know how it's going. That's a promise. Cheers."

Hart drank. Everyone drank but Alastair, who waited until he caught his son's eye. Then he raised his glass a second time and drank.

"That was worth holding off on the potatoes for," Wes said. "Now pass me the gravy, please."

A Problem of Proportion

Captain Sophia Coloma's first thought at registering the missile bearing down on the *Clarke* was, *This again.* Her second was to yell at Helmsman Cabot for evasive action. Cabot responded admirably, slamming the ship into avoidance mode and launching the ship's countermeasures. The *Clarke* groaned at the sudden change of vector; the artificial gravity indulged a moment where it felt as if the field would snap and every unsecured object on the *Clarke* would launch toward the top bulkheads at a couple hundred kilometers an hour.

The gravity held, the ship dove in physical space and the countermeasures dazzled the missile into missing its quarry. It blasted past the *Clarke* and immediately began searching for its target as it did.

"The missile is Acke make," Cabot said, reading the data on his console. "The *Clarke*'s got its transmitter in memory. Unless they've changed it up, we can keep it confused."

"Two more missiles launched and targeting," Executive Officer Neva Balla said. "Impact in sixty-three seconds."

"Same make," Cabot said. "Jamming them now."

"Which ship is shooting at us?" Coloma asked.

"It's the smaller one," Balla said.

"What's the other one doing?" Coloma asked.

"Firing on the first ship," Balla said.

Coloma pulled up a tactical image on her console. The smaller ship, a long needle with a bulbous engine compartment far aft and a smaller bulb forward, remained a mystery to the *Clarke*'s computer. The larger ship, however, resolved to the *Nurimal*, a frigate of Lalan manufacture.

A Conclave warship, in other words.

Damn it, Coloma thought. *We fell right into the trap.*

"These new missiles aren't responding to jamming," Cabot said.

"Evade," Coloma said.

"They're tracking our moves," Cabot said. "They're going to hit."

"That frigate is moving its port beam guns," Coloma said. "They're swinging our way."

The Conclave thought that other ship was us, Coloma thought. *Fired on it, it fired back. When we showed up, it fired on us as a matter of defense.*

Now the *Nurimal* knew who the real enemy was and wasn't wasting any time dealing with it.

So much for diplomacy, Coloma thought. *Next life, I'm getting a ship with guns.*

The *Nurimal* fired its particle beam weapons. Focused, high-energy beams lanced forward and tunneled into their targets.

The missiles heading for the *Clarke* exploded kilometers out from the ship. The first missile, now wandering aimlessly nearly a hundred klicks from the *Clarke,* was vaporized mere seconds thereafter.

"That . . . was not what I was expecting," Balla said.

The *Nurimal* swung its beam weapons around, focusing them on the third ship, lancing that ship's engine pod. The ship's engines shattered, severing from the ship proper. The forward portions of the ship went dark, power lost, and began spinning with the angular momentum gained by the force of the engine compartment eruption.

"Is it dead?" Coloma asked.

"It's not firing at us anymore, at least," said Cabot.

"I'll take that," Coloma said.

"The *Clarke*'s identified the other ship," Balla said.

"It's the *Nurimal*," Coloma said. "I know."

"Not that one, ma'am," Balla said. "The one it just wrecked. It's the *Urse Damay*. It's an Easo corvette that was turned over to Conclave diplomatic service."

"What the hell is it doing firing on us?" Cabot asked.

"And why is the *Nurimal* firing on it?" said Coloma.

"Captain," Orapan Juntasa, the communications and alarm officer, said. "We're being hailed by the *Nurimal*. The person hailing us says they are the captain." Juntasa was silent for a moment, listening. Her eyes got wide.

"What is it?" Coloma asked.

"They say they want to surrender to us," Juntasa said. "To *you*."

Coloma was silent for a minute at this.

"Ma'am?" Juntasa said. "What do I tell the *Nurimal*?"

"Tell them we've received their message and to please wait," Coloma said. She turned to Balla. "Get Ambassador Abumwe up here right now. She's the reason we're here in the first place. And bring Lieutenant Wilson, too. He's actual military. I don't know if I can accept a surrender. I'm pretty sure *he* can."

Hafte Sorvalh was tall, tall even for a Lalan, and as such would have difficulty navigating the short and narrow corridors of the *Clarke*. As a courtesy to her, the negotiations for the surrender of the *Nurimal* were held in the *Clarke* shuttle bay. Sorvalh was accompanied by Puslan Fotew, captain of the *Nurimal*, who did not appear in the least bit pleased to be on the *Clarke*, and Muhtal Worl, Sorvalh's assistant. On the human side were Coloma, Abumwe, Wilson and Hart Schmidt, whom Wilson had requested and Abumwe had acceded to. They were arrayed at a table hastily acquired from the officers mess. Chairs were provided for all; Wilson guessed they might be of slightly less utility for the Lalans, based on their physiology.

"We have an interesting situation before us," Hafte Sorvalh said, to the humans. Her words were translated by a small machine she wore as a brooch. "One of you is the captain of this ship. One of you is the head of this ship's diplomatic mission. One of you"—she nodded at Wilson—"is a member of the Colonial Union's military. To whom shall my captain here surrender?"

Coloma and Abumwe looked over to Wilson, who nodded. "I am Lieutenant Wilson of the Colonial Defense Forces," he said. "Captain Coloma and Ambassador Abumwe are members of the Colonial Union's civil government, as is Mr. Schmidt here." He nodded at his friend. "The *Nurimal* is a Conclave military ship, so we have decided that as a matter of protocol, I would be the person for whom it would be appropriate to surrender."

"Only a lieutenant?" Sorvalh said. Wilson, who was not an expert on Lalan physiology, nevertheless suspected she was wearing an amused expression. "I'm afraid it might be a little embarrassing for my captain to surrender to someone of your rank."

"I sympathize," Wilson said, and then went off script. "And if I may, Ambassador Sorvalh—"

"Councillor Sorvalh would be more accurate, Lieutenant," Sorvalh said.

"If I may, Councillor Sorvalh," Wilson corrected, "I would ask why your captain seeks to surrender at all. The *Nurimal* clearly outmatches the *Clarke* militarily. If you wished it, you could blow us right out of the sky."

"Which is precisely why I ordered Captain Fotew to surrender her vessel to you," Sorvalh said. "To assure you that we pose not the smallest threat to you."

Wilson glanced over to Captain Fotew, rigid and formal. The fact that she was ordered to surrender explained a lot, about both Fotew's attitude at the moment and the relationship between Fotew and Sorvalh. Wilson could not see Captain Coloma accepting an order from Ambassador Abumwe to surrender her ship; there might be blood on the floor after such a request. "You could have made that point much more clear if you had not housed your diplomatic mission to us in a warship," Wilson pointed out.

"Ah, but if we had done that, you would be dead," Sorvalh said.

Fair point, Wilson thought. "The *Urse Damay* is a Conclave ship," he said.

"It was," Sorvalh said. "Technically, I suppose it still may be. Nevertheless, when it attacked your ship—and also the *Nurimal*—it was under the command of neither the Conclave nor its military, nor was it crewed by citizens of the Conclave."

"What proof do you offer for this assertion?" Wilson asked.

"At the moment, none," Sorvalh said. "As I have none to offer. That may come in the future, as these discussions progress. In the meantime, you have my word, whatever that will be worth to you at the moment."

Wilson glanced over to Abumwe, who gave him a small nod. He turned to Captain Fotew. "With all due respect, Captain, I cannot accept your surrender," he said. "The Colonial Union and the Conclave are not in a state of war, and your military actions, as best I can see, were at no point directed toward the *Clarke* specifically nor at the Colonial Union generally. Indeed, your actions and the actions of your crew saved the *Clarke* and the lives of its crew and passengers. So while I reject your surrender, I offer you my thanks."

Fotew stood there a moment, blinking. "Thank you,

Lieutenant," she said, finally. "I accept your thanks and will share it with my crew."

"Very well done," Sorvalh said, to Wilson. She turned to Abumwe. "For a military officer, he's not a bad diplomat."

"He has his moments, Councillor," Abumwe said.

"If I may, what are we doing about the *Urse Damay*?" Coloma said. "It's damaged, but it's not entirely dead. It still represents a threat to both our ships."

Sorvalh nodded to Fotew, who addressed Coloma. "The *Urse Damay* had missile launchers bolted on to it, holding nine missiles," she said. "Three of them were sent at you. Three of them were sent at us. The remaining three have our weapons trained on them. If they were fired, they would be destroyed before they were launched out of their tubes. That is if the *Urse Damy* had enough power to target either of our ships or fire the missiles at all."

"Have you made contact with the ship?" Coloma asked.

"We ordered its surrender and offered to rescue its crew," Fotew said. "We have heard nothing from it since our battle. We have done nothing else pending our surrender to you."

"If Lieutenant Wilson had accepted our surrender, then it would have been you who would have to coordinate the rescue," Sorvalh said.

"If there were someone still alive on that ship, they would have signaled us by now," Fotew said. "Us or you. The *Urse Damay* is dead, Captain."

Coloma quieted, dissatisfied.

"How will you explain this incident?" Abumwe asked Sorvalh.

"How do you mean?" Sorvalh replied.

"I mean each of our governments have agreed that this discussion of ours is not actually taking place,"

Abumwe said. "If even a discussion is not taking place, I would imagine an actual military battle will be hard to explain."

"The military battle will not be hard to handle politically," Sorvalh said. "The surrender, however, would have been difficult to explain away. Another reason for us to be grateful of the politic choices of your Lieutenant Wilson here."

"If you are so grateful, then perhaps you can give us the answer we came here to get," Abumwe said.

"What answer is that?" Sorvalh said.

"Why the Conclave is targeting and attacking Colonial Union ships," Abumwe said.

"How very interesting," Sorvalh said. "Because we have the very same question for you, about our ships."

"There have been sixteen ships gone missing in the last year," Colonel Abel Rigney explained to Abumwe. He and Abumwe were in the office of Colonel Liz Egan, who sat with them at her office's conference table. "Ten of them in the last four months."

"What do you mean by 'gone missing'?" Abumwe asked. "Destroyed?"

"No, just gone," Rigney said. "As in, once they skipped they were never heard from again. No black boxes, no skip drones, no communication of any sort."

"And no debris?" Abumwe asked.

"None that we could find, and no gas clouds of highly vaporized ships, either," Egan said. "Nothing but space."

Abumwe turned her attention back to Rigney. "These were Colonial Defense Forces ships?"

"No," Rigney said. "Or more accurately, not anymore. The ships that have disappeared were all decommissioned former CDF ships, repurposed for civilian uses. Like the *Clarke,* your ship, was formerly a CDF corvette. Once a ship outlives its usefulness to the CDF, we sell them to individual colonies for local government services, or to commercial concerns who specialize in intercolonial shipping."

"The fact that they were nonmilitary is why we originally didn't notice," Egan said. "Civilian and commercial ships sometimes go missing just as a matter of course. A skip is improperly inputted, or they're prey for raiders or pirates, or they're employed to carry a wildcat colony someplace a wildcat colony shouldn't be and they get shot up. The Colonial Union tracks all legal shipping and travel in Colonial space, so we note when a ship is destroyed or goes missing. But we don't necessarily note what kind of ship it is, or in this case *was*."

"It wasn't until some nerd handling ship registrations noted that a specific type of ship was going missing that we paid attention," Rigney said. "And sure enough, he was right. All the ships on this list are decommissioned frigates or corvettes. All of them were decommissioned in the last five years. Most of them disappeared in systems near Conclave territory."

Abumwe frowned. "That doesn't sound like the Conclave's way of doing things," she said. "They won't let us colonize anymore, but beyond that they haven't recently been openly antagonistic towards the Colonial Union. They don't *need* to be."

"We agree," Egan said. "But there are reasons for the Conclave to want to attack the Colonial Union. They are massively larger than we are, but we still nearly managed to destroy them not all that long ago."

Abumwe nodded. She remembered the CDF destruction of the Conclave fleet over Roanoke Colony and how that pushed the entire Colonial Union to the brink of war with the much larger, much angrier alien confederation.

What saved the Colonial Union, ironically enough, had been the fact that the Conclave's leader and founder,

General Tarsem Gau, had managed to quell a rebellion and keep the Conclave intact—a not exactly small irony considering the CDF's goal was to topple Gau.

"Gau certainly has reasons for wanting the Colonial Union out of the picture," Abumwe said. "I'm not sure how making a few decommissioned former warships disappear will accomplish that."

"We're not sure about it ourselves," Rigney said. "The ships are useless as warships now; we've removed all weapons and defense systems. The ships couldn't have been confused with CDF ships still in service. Making them disappear does nothing to reduce our military capability at all."

"There's another possibility," Egan said. "One I think is more likely, personally. And that is that the Conclave isn't behind the disappearances at all. Someone else is, and trying to make it look like it's the Conclave in the hopes of pushing them and us into another conflict."

"All right," Abumwe said. "Explain what this has to do with me."

"We need to establish a back channel to the Conclave about this," Rigney said. "If they are behind it, we need to tell them that we won't tolerate it, in a way that doesn't let our other enemies know where our military resources might become focused. If they aren't behind it, then it's to our mutual benefit to discover who is—again, as quietly as possible."

"You're getting the job because, to be blunt about it, you already know that someone or some group has been trying to sabotage the Colonial Union's dealings with other species and governments," Egan said. "We don't need to read you in, and we know you and your people can keep your mouths shut."

Abumwe gave a wry half smile. "I appreciate your candor," she said.

"You are also good at what you do," Egan said. "To

be clear. But discretion is of particular value in this case."

"I understand," Abumwe said. "How do you want me to approach the task? I don't have any direct contacts with the Conclave, but I know someone who might."

"Your Lieutenant Wilson?" Egan said.

Abumwe nodded. "He knows John Perry personally," she said, naming the former CDF major who took refuge with the Conclave after the events of Roanoke Colony and then took an alien trade fleet to Earth and informed that planet of their lopsided relationship with the Colonial Union. "It's not a connection I'm keen on exploiting, but it's one I can use if necessary."

"It won't be necessary," Rigney said. "We have a direct line to one of General Gau's inner circle. A councillor named Sorvalh."

"How do we know Sorvalh?" Abumwe asked.

"After the unpleasantness with Major Perry showing up over Earth with a Conclave trade fleet, General Gau decided it would be useful to have an official unofficial way for us to talk to his inner circle," Egan said. "To avoid any *unintentional* unpleasantness."

"If we tell her where to show up, she'll be there," Rigney said. "We just need to get you there."

"And make sure that no one else knows you're coming," said Egan.

"We're not attacking any of your ships," Abumwe said, to Sorvalh.

"Curious," Sorvalh said. "Because in the past several of your months, we have had twenty ships up and disappear."

"Conclave military ships?" Abumwe asked.

"No," Sorvalh said. "Mostly merchant ships and a few repurposed ships."

"Go on," Abumwe said.

"There's not much more to say," Sorvalh said. "All of them were lost in territory that borders Colonial Union space. All of them disappeared without evidence. Ships, gone. Crews, gone. Cargo, gone. Too few ships to constitute an action which merited a response. Too many to just chalk up to chance or fate."

"And you've had none of these ships reappear," Abumwe asked.

"There is one," Sorvalh said. "It's the *Urse Damay*."

"You're joking," Wilson said.

"No, Lieutenant Wilson," Sorvalh said, turning to him. "The *Urse Damay* was one of the first on the list to go, and one that gave us the greatest amount of worry. It's a diplomatic ship, or was, and its disappearance was a possible act of war as far as we were concerned. But we didn't pick up any chatter in our usual channels about it, and for something like this, we would."

"Yet you still think we're behind this," Abumwe said.

"If we were certain, then you would have heard from us already, and not through a diplomatic back channel," Sorvalh said. "We have our suspicions, but we also have no interest in starting a war with the Colonial Union over suspicions. Just as, obviously, you have no desire to start a war with us over your suspicions, either."

"The *Urse Damay* being here should convince you that it's not us who took it," Coloma said. "It fired on us."

"It fired on both of our ships," Captain Fotew said. "And on ours first. We arrived here just before you did. It was here when we arrived."

"If we had arrived first, we would have seen it as a Conclave diplomatic ship," Coloma said. "It's obvious that it was meant to lure the *Clarke* and then attack us."

"That's one way of looking at it," Sorvalh said. "Another way is to have your tame, captured Conclave ship fake an attack on an unarmed diplomatic ship and use that as a propaganda tool. It's not as if the Colonial

Union is above sacrificing a ship or a colony to whip up some righteous anger."

Coloma stiffened at this; Abumwe reached over and took her arm to calm and caution her. "You're not actually suggesting this is the case here."

"I am not," Sorvalh agreed. "I am pointing out that we both have more questions than answers at the moment. Our ship went missing. It's shown up here. It's attacked both of our ships. Who was the *intended* target is, at the moment, a trivial question because we both ended up as targets. The question we should be asking is, who is targeting us both? How did they know we would be here? And are they the same people who have caused *your* ships to disappear?"

Wilson turned back to Fotew. "You say that the *Urse Damay* is dead."

"Incapacitated at the very least," Fotew said. "And not a threat in any event."

"Then I have a suggestion," Wilson said.

"Please," Sorvalh said.

"I think it might be time for a joint field trip," Wilson said.

"Don't do anything fancy," Hart Schmidt said to Wilson. The two of them were in the *Clarke* shuttle bay. The *Nurimal*'s shuttle, with its pilot and two Conclave military, was waiting for Wilson to board. "Look around, see what you can find out, get out of there."

"I want to know when it was you became my mother," Wilson said.

"You keep doing crazy things," Schmidt said. "And then you keep roping me into them with you."

"Someone else can monitor me if you want," Wilson said.

"Don't be stupid, Harry," Schmidt said. He checked

Wilson's combat suit a second time. "You've checked your oxygen supply."

"It's being constantly monitored by my BrainPal," Wilson said. "Plus the combat suit is configured for a vacuum environment. Plus I can hold my breath for ten minutes at a time. Please, Hart. You're my friend, but I'm going to have to kill you."

"All right. Sorry," Schmidt said. "I'll be following you from the bridge. Keep your audio and visual circuits open. Coloma and Abumwe will be there, too, if you have any questions for them and vice versa."

"Just who I want in my head," Wilson said.

One of the Conclave soldiers, a Lalan, poked his head out of the shuttle and motioned to Wilson. "That's my ride," he said.

Schmidt peered at the soldier. "Watch out for these guys," he said.

"They're not going to kill me, Hart," Wilson said. "That would look bad."

"One day you're going to be wrong about these things," Schmidt said.

"When I am, hope that I'm very far away from you," Wilson said. Schmidt grinned at this and headed back to the shuttle bay control room.

Wilson entered the shuttle. The pilot and one of the soldiers were Lalan, like Sorvalh and Captain Fotew. The other was a Fflict, a squat, hairy race. It motioned to Wilson to have a seat. He did and stowed his MP-35 beneath his feet.

"We have translation circuits built into our suits," the Fflict said, in its own language, while a translation came through a speaker on its belt. "You can speak your language and we'll get a translation through our audio feed."

"Likewise," Wilson said, and pointed to the speaker.

"You can turn that off if you like. I'll still be able to understand you just fine."

"Good," the Fflict said, and turned off the speaker. "I hate the way that thing makes me sound." It held up a hand and contracted the appendages twice, in a greeting. "I'm Lieutenant Navill Werd." It pointed toward the Lalans. "Pilot Urgrn Howel, Corporal Lesl Carn."

"Lieutenant Harry Wilson," Wilson said.

"Have you been in a vacuum environment before?" Werd asked.

"Once or twice," Wilson said.

"Good," Werd said. "Now, listen. This is a joint mission, but someone has to be in charge, and I'm going to propose that it's me, on account that I'm already supposed to be in charge of these two, and it's my shuttle besides. Any objection?"

Wilson grinned. "No, sir."

"Wrong gender," Werd said. "But your 'ma'am' doesn't exactly work either, so you might as well keep calling me 'sir.' No need to make things complicated."

"Yes, sir," Wilson said.

"Right, let's get this thing moving," Werd said, then turned to nod at his pilot. The pilot zipped up the shuttle and signaled to the *Clarke* that they were ready to depart; the *Clarke* started the purge cycle for the bay. Corporal Carn eased himself into the copilot's seat.

"This is my first time working with a human," Werd said, to Wilson.

"How's it going so far?" Wilson asked.

"Not bad," Werd said. "You're kind of ugly, though."

"I get that a lot," Wilson said.

"I bet you do," Werd said. "I won't hold it against you."

"Thanks," Wilson said.

"But if you smell, I'm pushing you out an airlock," Werd said.

"Got it," Wilson said.

"Glad we've come to this understanding," Werd said.

"The lieutenant is like this with everyone," Corporal Carn said, looking back at Wilson. "It's not just you."

"It's not my fault everyone else is hideous to look at," Werd said. "You can't all be gorgeous like me."

"How do you even get through the day being as gorgeous as you are, sir?" Wilson asked.

"I really don't know," Werd said. "Just by being a beacon of hope and good looks, I suppose."

"You see what I'm saying here," Carn said.

"He's just jealous," Werd said. "And ugly."

"You guys are a hoot," Wilson said. "And here my friend Hart thought you might try to kill me."

"Of course not," Werd said. "We save that for the second mission."

The shuttle backed out of the bay and headed to the *Urse Damay.*

"All right, who wants to tell me the weird thing about this ship?" Werd said, to no one in particular. The lieutenant's voice came in through Wilson's BrainPal; he, Werd and Carn were all in separate parts of the ship.

"The fact there's not a single living thing on it?" Carn said.

"Close, but no," Werd said.

"That's *not* the weird thing?" Carn said. "If that's not the weird thing, Lieutenant, what is?"

"The fact there's no evidence that a single living thing was ever on it," Wilson said.

"The human gets it," Werd said. "This is the strangest damn thing I have ever seen."

The three soldiers had carefully navigated themselves over to the tumbling front end of the *Urse Damay.* The shuttle pilot had matched the spin and rotation of the ship fragment, and the three traversed across by way of a guide line attached to a magnetic harpoon. Once they were over, the shuttle backed off to a less dangerous distance while continuing to match the tumble.

Inside, the tumble was enough to stick Wilson, Werd and Carn to the bulkheads at crazy angles to the ship's internal layout. The three of them had to be careful when they walked; the open communication channel was occasionally punctuated by the very tall Corporal Carn cursing as he bumped into something.

The front end of the *Urse Damay* had been severed from its prime power source, but emergency power was still being drawn from local batteries; emergency lighting flooded the corridors with a dim but serviceable glow. The glow showed no indication that anyone had walked the corridors in the recent past. Wilson pulled open doors to living quarters, conference rooms and what appeared to be a mess hall, judging from the benches and what looked to be food preparation areas.

They were all empty and sterile.

"Is this ship programmed?" asked Carn. "Like a skip drone?"

"I saw the video replay of its battle with the *Nurimal*," Werd said. "The *Urse Damay* was using tactics that suggest more than just programming, at least to me."

"I agree with that," Wilson said. "It sure looked like someone was here."

"Maybe it's remotely controlled," Carn said.

"We've swept the local area," Wilson said. "We didn't find any drones or smaller ships. I'm sure Captain Fotew had the *Nurimal* do the same thing."

"Then how did this ship fight with no one on it?" Carn asked.

"How do we feel about ghosts?" Werd said.

"I prefer my dead to stay dead," Wilson said.

"The human gets it right again," Werd said. "So we keep looking for something living on the ship."

A few minutes later, Carn was on the open channel. He made a noise; after a second, Wilson's BrainPal translated it to "uh."

"What is it?" Werd asked.

"I think I found something," Carn said.

"Is it alive?" Wilson asked.

"Maybe?" Carn said.

"Carn, you're going to have to be more specific than that," Werd said. Even through the translation, Wilson could hear the exasperation.

"I'm on the bridge," Carn said. "There's no one here. But there's a screen that's on."

"All right," Werd said. "So what?"

"So when I passed by the screen, words came up on it," Carn said.

"What did they say?" Wilson asked.

"'Come back,'" Carn said.

"I thought you said there was no one in the room with you," Werd said.

"There's *not*," Carn said. "Hold on, there's something new on the screen now. More words."

"What's it say this time?" Werd asked.

"'Help me,'" Carn said.

"You said you had expertise with technology," Werd said to Wilson, and pointed to the bridge screen, hovering at an off-kilter angle above them. "Make this thing work."

Wilson grimaced and looked at the screen. The words on the screen were in Lalan; a visual overlay from his BrainPal translated the message. There was no keyboard or operating tool that Wilson could see. He reached up and tapped the screen; nothing. "How do you usually work your screens?" Wilson asked Werd. "Does the Conclave have some sort of standard access interface?"

"I lead people and shoot at things," Werd said. "Access interfaces aren't my thing."

"We have a standard data transmission band," Carn said. "Not the voice transmission band, but for other things."

"Hart?" Wilson said.

"Getting that for you now," Schmidt said, in his head.

"Look," Carn said, pointing at the screen. "New words."

You don't need the data band, the words said in Lalan. *I can hear you on the audio band. But I only understand the Lalan. My translation module is damaged.*

"What language do you speak?" Wilson said, and ordered his BrainPal to translate in Lalan.

Easo, the words said.

Wilson queried his BrainPal, which had the language and began to unpack it. "Is that better?" he asked.

Yes, thank you, the words said.

"Who are you?" Wilson asked.

My name is Rayth Ablant.

"Are you the captain of the *Urse Damay*?" Wilson asked.

In a manner of speaking, yes.

"Why did you attack the *Clarke* and *Nurimal*?" Wilson asked.

I had no choice in the matter.

"Where is everyone?" asked Werd, who apparently had Easo as part of his translation database.

You mean, where is my crew.

"Yes," Werd said.

I have none. It's just me.

"Where are you?" Wilson asked.

That's an interesting question, the words said.

"Are you on the ship?" Wilson asked.

I am the ship.

"I heard that correctly, right?" Carn said, after a minute. "I didn't just get a bad translation, did I?"

"We're asking the same question over here," Schimdt

said to Wilson, although he was the only one on the *Urse Damay* who could hear him.

"You *are* the ship," Wilson repeated.

Yes.

"That's not possible," Werd said.

I wish you were right about that.

"Lieutenant Werd is right," Wilson said. "None of us have been able to create truly intelligent machines."

I never said I was a machine.

"This guy is making me irritated," Werd said, to Wilson. "He's speaking in riddles."

"And he can hear you," Wilson said, making a chopping motion: *Werd, shut up.* "Rayth Ablant, you're going to need to explain yourself better for us. I don't think any of us understand what you're saying."

It's easier to show you.

"All right," Wilson said. "Show me."

Look behind you.

Wilson did. Behind him was a line of displays and a large, black cabinet. He turned back to the display.

Open it. Carefully.

Wilson did.

Hello.

"Oh, fuck me," Wilson said.

"He's a brain in a box," Wilson said. "Literally a brain in a box. I opened up the cabinet and there's a container in there with an Easo brain and nervous system laid out and connected to non-organic data fibers. There's some sort of liquid surrounding the brain, which I suspect is keeping it oxygenated and fed. There's an outtake tube that connects to what looks like a filtering mechanism, with another tube coming out the other end. It all gets recycled. It's pretty impressive, as long as you forget that there's an actual sentient being trapped in there."

Wilson sat once more in the *Clarke* shuttle bay with

Abumwe, Sorvalh, Muhtal Worl and Hart Schmidt. Captains Coloma and Fotew had returned to their posts. Abumwe and Coloma had seen Rayth Ablant from Wilson's own point of view through his BrainPal feed, but Sorvalh wanted a report as well. Wilson offered her his BrainPal feed, but she refused, preferring, as she said, "a live recounting."

"Who was this Ablant?" Sorvalh asked. "He had a life before . . . this."

"He was a pilot on the *Urse Damay,* or so he says," Wilson said. "You would be able to check that better than I would, Councillor."

Sorvalh nodded to Worl, who made a note on his tablet computer. "He was part of a crew," Sorvalh said. "The *Urse Damay* had a core crew of fifty and a diplomatic mission party of a dozen. What happened to them?"

"He says he doesn't know," Wilson said. "He says he had been asleep when the *Urse Damay* was first boarded and that he was knocked unconscious during the invasion. When he woke up he was like this. The people who did this to him didn't tell him anything about the rest of his crew."

"And who are they, the people who did this to him?" Sorvalh asked.

"He says he doesn't know that, either," Wilson said. "He says he's never even technically spoken with them. They communicate with him through text. When he came to, they explained to him his job was to learn how to operate and navigate the *Urse Damay* on his own and that when he became proficient enough, he would be given a mission. This was that mission."

"Do you believe he doesn't know who these people are?" Sorvalh asked Wilson.

"Pardon my French, Councillor, but the guy is a fucking disembodied brain," Wilson said. "It's not like he has any powers of observation other than what they gave him. He says they didn't even give him external inputs until after the ship skipped. He was flying blind for the first half of his mission. It's entirely possible he knows nothing about these people but what they tell him, which is almost nothing."

"You trust him," Sorvalh said.

"I *pity* him," Wilson said. "But I also think he's credible. If he was a willing participant in this, they wouldn't need to put his brain in a box to get him to do what they want him to do."

"Tell the councillor what he was told his payment would be for this mission," Abumwe said to Wilson.

"They told him that if he did this mission, they'd put his brain back into his body and send him home," Wilson said. "His payment would be that he gets to be himself again."

Sorvalh was silent about this for a moment, contemplating. Then she shifted her body weight and addressed Abumwe. "I would ask your indulgence for a moment while I say something terribly blunt."

"Be my guest," Abumwe said.

"It's no great secret that the Colonial Union does things like this all the time," Sorvalh said. She motioned at Wilson. "Your lieutenant here is the result of consciousness allegedly being transferred from one body to another genetically-modified one. He has a computer in his brain which connects to it using inorganic connections that are at least functionally similar to what's connected to this poor creature. Your special forces soldiers are even more modified than he is. We know that you have some special forces soldiers who only tangentially resemble human beings. And we know that one penalty option your Colonial Defense Forces has for its malfeasant soldiers is to place their brains in a container for a period of time."

Abumwe nodded and said, "Your point, Councillor."

"My point, Ambassador, is that whoever did this to Rayth Ablant, their mode of operation is closer to that of the Colonial Union than it is to the Conclave," Sorvalh said.

Abumwe nodded at Wilson again. "Tell her Rayth Ablant's orders," she said.

"He says his orders were to destroy any and all ships that presented themselves after he skipped," Wilson said. "There was no discrimination on the part of his masters. They just pointed him at both of us and hoped for the best."

"To what end?" Sorvalh said.

"Does it matter?" Abumwe said. "If we had been destroyed, the Colonial Union would have blamed you for the ambush. If you had been destroyed, the Conclave would have done the same to us. If we had both been destroyed, our two governments might already be at war. It's as you said earlier, Councillor. At this point, the *why* is almost trivial, unless we know the *who*."

"If your Lieutenant Wilson is correct, and this Rayth Ablant has no way of knowing for whom he works, there's no way for us to know the *who*," Sorvalh said. "All we have to go on are methods, and these methods are closer to yours than ours."

"Rayth Ablant doesn't know who he's working for, but he's not all we have," Wilson said.

"Explain," Sorvalh said.

"He's a brain in a box," Wilson repeated. "And the *box* can tell us a lot of things. Like whose technology it's made out of. If there's anything off the shelf about the thing, then that's a lead to follow. Even if everything is custom-made, we can reverse-engineer it and maybe find out what it's closest to. It's better than what we have now, which is nothing."

"What will that require?" Sorvalh asked.

"Well, for one thing, I want to take Rayth Ablant off

the *Urse Damay*," Wilson said. "The sooner the better. We have a ticking clock here."

"I don't understand," Sorvalh said.

"One of the first things Rayth Ablant said to us was 'help me,'" Wilson said. "He said that because his life support is running off the emergency power batteries. He's got about eight hours left before he exhausts the power supply."

"And you want to bring him here," Sorvalh said, indicating the *Clarke*.

Wilson shook his head. "He's on a Conclave ship," he said. "Wherever the box comes from, it's interfaced with a Conclave power network. Your power systems on the *Nurimal* more closely match those of the *Urse Damay* than ours do." Wilson smiled. "And besides, you have the guns."

Sorvalh returned the smile. "That we do, Lieutenant," she said. "But I can't imagine your boss here will be happy with the Conclave taking possession of that technology."

"As long as you allow Lieutenant Wilson to closely examine the technology, I have no real objection," Abumwe said. "Technology is his job. I trust him to learn what he needs to know."

"Your bosses might not be happy with that, Ambassador Abumwe," Sorvalh said.

"This may be true," Abumwe said. "But that's going to be my problem, not yours."

"When can you get started?" Sorvalh asked Wilson.

"As soon as you requisition Werd and Carn to help me again," Wilson said. "The brain box is not too large, fortunately, but the environment in there makes it difficult to move. And the shuttle for transport, obviously."

Sorvalh nodded to her assistant, who reached again for his tablet computer. "Anything else?" she asked.

"I do have one request," Wilson said.

"Name it," Sorvalh said.

"I'd like you to promise me that once you get Rayth Ablant on your ship, that you connect him to your network," Wilson said.

"And your reason for that is?" Sorvalh asked.

"This poor bastard has spent the last God knows how long running starship operation simulations. All his friends are dead and he's been talking to no one except the sons of bitches who put him in that box," Wilson said. "I think he's probably lonely."

Do you mind if I ask you a question, Rayth Ablant said to Wilson. Wilson had opened the data band so that Rayth Ablant could address him directly through his BrainPal rather than through the display. He kept the text interface, however, because it seemed right.

"Go right ahead," Wilson said. He was busy extracting batteries from underneath the deck of the *Urse Damay*'s bridge and was beginning to sweat inside his vacuum-proof combat suit.

I'd like to know why you're trying to help me.

"You asked for help," Wilson said.

I also tried to blow up your ship with you in it.

"That was before you knew me," Wilson said.

I'm sorry about that.

"I'm not going to tell you not to be sorry," Wilson said, "but I can understand wanting to get your body back."

That's not going to happen now.

"Not through the assholes who did this to you, no," Wilson said. "It's not to say it couldn't happen one day."

It doesn't seem likely.

"You're saying that to a guy who is on his second body," Wilson said. "I'm a little more optimistic about your plight than you are." He hauled out a battery and placed it next to the several others he had extracted.

Werd and Carn were elsewhere in the *Urse Damay,* pulling out batteries of their own. They would serve as the power source for Rayth Ablant's brain box until they were all safely on the *Nurimal.* The trip from the *Urse Damay* to the *Nurimal* would be a matter of a couple of minutes, but Wilson was a big believer in overkill when the downside was someone ending up dead.

Thank you for this.

"Thank you for being a terrible shot," Wilson said. He returned to his task.

You know humans have a bad reputation. Among the rest of us.

"I've heard," Wilson said.

That you're deceptive. That you'll go against your contracts and treaties. That you're terrified of all of us and your way of solving that problem is trying to destroy us all.

"But on the bright side, we all have lovely singing voices," Wilson said.

I'm telling you this because I'm not seeing any of this in you.

"Humans are like anyone," Wilson said. "Is every Easo a good person? Before the Conclave, did your government always do the best thing? Does the Conclave always do the best things now?"

I'm sorry. I didn't mean to start a political discussion.

"You didn't," Wilson said. "I'm talking about the nature of sentient beings everywhere. We all have the entire range of possibilities inside of us. Personally, I don't expect much out of other people. But for myself, whenever possible, I try not to be a complete prick."

And that includes rescuing brains in boxes.

"Well, that includes rescuing a person," Wilson said. "Who at the moment happens to be a brain in a box." He hauled out another battery.

Lieutenant Werd came into the bridge, hauling his

own supply of batteries, and set them down next to Wilson's. They jostled in the slight pseudogravity offered by the ship's tumbling. "How many more of these do you think you need?" he asked Wilson. "Dismantling an entire spaceship was not supposed to be in my job description."

Wilson smiled and counted the batteries. "I think we have enough," he said. "The box here is not that securely bolted into the deck, so we should be able to pull it out easily enough. Lifting things is in your job description, right?"

"Yes," Werd said. "But setting things down costs extra."

"Well, then," Wilson said, "what we have to do now is make sure there's no significant interruption in power flow to the box when we disconnect it from the *Urse Damay*'s system and attach it to the batteries." He pointed to the box's external outlets and the cords that snaked from them into the ship's power system. "There's probably a buffer unit in the box itself. I need to see how much energy it stores."

"Whatever you say, Lieutenant Wilson," Werd said. "This time, you're in charge."

"Thank you, Werd," Wilson said, and opened the door to the box, again carefully, to avoid dislodging any part of the contents. "Between you, me and Carn, we're the very model of cooperation that suggests all of our nations may yet live in peace and harmony."

"Sarcasm is not exclusive to humans," Werd said, "but I will admit you do a good job with it."

Wilson said nothing to that. Instead he peered intently into the box.

"What is it?" Werd asked. Wilson motioned with his head that Werd should come closer. Werd did.

Wilson had separated a thick tangle of wires that plugged into the container holding Rayth Ablant's brain and nervous system to get a look at where the power cords entered the box. Where they entered was indeed what looked like a power buffer, to store a minute or so of energy to assist with an orderly system shutdown in case of loss of power.

There was something else attached to the power buffer as well.

"Ah," Werd said. Wilson nodded. "Carn," Werd said, into his communication circuit.

"Yes, Lieutenant," Carn said.

"Lieutenant Wilson and I realized we've forgotten some tools, and we're going to need you to come help us with them," Werd said. "Head back toward the shuttle. We'll meet you there."

"Sir?" Carn said, slightly confused.

"Acknowledge the order, Corporal," Werd said.

"Order acknowledged," Carn said. "On my way."

Is everything all right.

"Everything is fine," Wilson said, to Rayth Ablant. "I just realized some things in your internal structure here are going to be trickier to deal with than others. I need some different tools. We need to go back to the *Nurimal* for them. We'll return momentarily."

Makes sense to me. Don't be gone too long. The ship is already beginning to shut down.

"I'll be back as soon as I can," Wilson said. "It's a promise."

Rayth Ablant said nothing. Wilson and Werd made their way silently to the shuttle rendezvous; they and Carn made their way back to the shuttlecraft without an additional word.

When the shuttlecraft was on its way, Wilson opened a channel to the *Clarke*. "Hart," he said, to Schmidt, "you need to get Abumwe over to *Nurimal*. Be there as soon as possible. We have a wrinkle. A really big damn wrinkle." He cut the connection before Schmidt could respond and turned to Werd. "I need you to get your people to get me a schematic of the *Urse Damay*'s power systems. There are things I need to know. Right now."

"We might not have them," Werd said. "The *Urse Damay*'s not part of the Conclave military fleet."

"Then I need one of your engineers to explain how Conclave power systems work. We can do that, at least, right?"

"I'm on it," Werd said, and opened up a channel to the *Nurimal*.

Carn looked at the two of them, saw their expressions. "What happened?" he asked.

"We're dealing with complete assholes," Wilson said.

"I thought we knew that," Carn said.

"No, this is new," Wilson said. "There's a bomb attached to the power supply on that box. The one Rayth Ablant is in. It looks like it's set to go off if anything happens to the power going into the box. If we move Rayth Ablant, he's going to die."

"If we don't move him, he's going to die," Carn said. "His power supply is running out."

"And now you know why I said we're dealing with complete assholes here," Wilson said. He was silent the rest of the way to the *Nurimal*.

It's just you this time.

"Yes," Wilson said to Rayth Ablant.

That's not a good sign, I think.

"I told you I would be back," Wilson said.

You're not going to lie to me, are you.

"You said you liked that I wasn't like the humans you had heard about," Wilson said. "So, no, I'm not going to lie to you. But you have to know that the truth is going to be hard to hear."

I am a brain in a box. The truth is already hard to hear.

Wilson smiled. "That's a very philosophical way of looking at things."

When you're a brain in a box, philosophy is what you have.

"There's a bomb in your box," Wilson said. "It's attached to the power buffer. As far as I can tell, it has a monitor that tracks power input. The *Urse Damay*'s power system is integrated with its emergency power systems so that when the first goes down, the second is already running and there's no interruption of power to critical systems, including your box. But if we remove your box from the system entirely, the monitor is going to register it, and the bomb will go off."

It would kill me.

"Yes," Wilson said. "Since you asked me not to lie, I'll tell you I suspect the real point of the bomb is to make sure the technology of that box you're in isn't taken and examined. Your death is an incidental result of that."

On second thought, maybe you can lie to me a little.

"Sorry," Wilson said.

Is there any way to remove me from the box?

"Not that I can see," Wilson said. "At least, not in a way that keeps you alive. The box is, if I may say so, an impressive piece of engineering. If I had more time, I could reverse-engineer the thing and tell you how it works. I don't have that time. I could take you out of the box—the part that's actually you—but I couldn't just then take that part and hook it up to a battery. The box is an integrated system. You can't survive without it."

I'm not going to survive long in it, either.

"I can reattach the batteries we've removed from the system," Wilson said. "It can buy us some more time."

Us?

"I'm here," Wilson said. "I can keep working on this. There's probably something I've missed."

If you tinker with the bomb, then there's a chance you'll set it off.

"Yes," Wilson said.

And when the power goes out, the bomb will explode anyway.

"I imagine the bomb will use the energy in the buffer to set itself off, yes," Wilson said.

Do you dismantle bombs on a regular basis? Is this your specialty?

"I do technology research and development. This is up my alley," Wilson said.

I think this is you lying to me a little.

"I think I might be able to save you," Wilson said.

Why do you want to save me?

"You don't deserve to die like this," Wilson said. "As an afterthought. As a brain in a box. As less than fully yourself."

You said yourself this box is an impressive piece of technology. It looks like whoever did this took some effort to make sure it couldn't be taken. I don't want to insult you, but given that you've had only a very little amount of time with this box, do you really think you're going to find some way to outwit it and save me?

"I'm good at what I do," Wilson said.

If you were that good, you wouldn't be here. No offense.

"I'd like to try," Wilson said.

I would like you to try, if it didn't mean you possibly dying. One of us dying seems inevitable at this point. Both of us dying seems avoidable.

"You asked us to help you," Wilson reminded Rayth Ablant.

You did. You tried. And even right now, if you wanted to keep trying, it's clear I couldn't stop you. But when I asked you to help, you helped. Now I am asking you to stop.

"All right," Wilson said, after a moment.

Thank you.

"What else can I do for you?" Wilson asked. "Do you have friends or family that you want us to contact? Do you have messages for anyone I can send for you?"

I have no real family. Most of my friends were on the Urse Damay. *Most of the people I know are already gone. I have no friends left.*

"That's not entirely true," Wilson said.

Are you volunteering yourself?

"I'd be happy if you considered me your friend," Wilson said.

I did try to kill you.

"That was before you knew me," Wilson repeated. "And now that you do, you've made it clear you won't let me die if you can help it. I think that makes up for your earlier indiscretions."

If you are my friend, then I have a request.

"Name it," Wilson said.

You are a soldier. You've killed before.

"It's not a point of pride," Wilson said. "But yes."

I'm going to die because people who don't care about me have used me and then thrown me away. I'd prefer to leave on my own terms.

"You want me to help you," Wilson said.

If you can. I'm not asking you to do it yourself. If this box is as sensitive as you say it is, if I die, the bomb could go off. I don't want you anywhere near when it does. But I think you could find another way.

"I imagine I could," Wilson said. "Or at the very least I could try."

For your trouble, let me offer you this.

There was a data ping on Wilson's BrainPal: an encrypted file, in a format he wasn't familiar with.

When I had completed my mission—when I had killed your ship and the Conclave ship—I was to feed this into

the ship's guidance system. It's coordinates for my re-
turn trip. Maybe you'll find whoever's behind this there.

"Thank you," Wilson said. "That's incredibly helpful."

When you find them, blow them up a little for me.

Wilson grinned. "You got it," he said.

There's not much time before the emergency power is
entirely used up.

"I'll have to leave you," Wilson said. "Which means
that no matter what happens I'm not coming back."

I wouldn't want you here no matter what happens.
You'll stay in contact with me?

"Yes, of course," Wilson said.

Then you should go now. And hurry, because there's
not a lot of time left.

"This isn't going to be a popular sentiment, but he's going to die anyway," said Captain Fotew. "We don't have
to expend the effort."

"Are you suddenly on a budget, Captain?" Wilson
asked. "Can the Conclave no longer afford a missile or a
particle beam?" They were on the bridge of the *Nurimal,*
along with Abumwe and Sorvalh.

"I said it wouldn't be a popular sentiment," Fotew
said. "But someone ought to point it out, at least."

"Rayth Ablant has given us vital information about
the whereabouts of the people directing him," Wilson
said, and pointed toward the bridge's communications
and science station, where the science officer was already
busily attempting to crack the encryption on the orders.
"He's been cooperative with us since our engagement
with his ship."

"It's not as if he had much of a choice in that," Fotew
said.

"Of course he had a choice," Wilson said. "If he hadn't
signaled to Corporal Carn, we wouldn't know he was
there. We wouldn't know that some organization out

there is taking the Conclave's missing ships and turning them into glorified armed drones. We wouldn't know that whoever this group is, they're a threat to both the Conclave and the Colonial Union equally. And we wouldn't know that neither of our governments is engaging in a stealth war with the other."

"We still don't know that last one, Lieutenant Wilson," Sorvalh said. "Because we still don't know the *who*. We still don't know the players in this game."

"Not yet," Wilson said, motioning back to the science station. "But depending how good your code cracker is over there, this may be a temporary problem. And for the moment, at least, our governments are sharing information, since you've gotten that information from me."

"But this is a problem of proportion, isn't it?" Sorvalh said. "Is what we learn from you going to be worth everything we've expended to learn it? Is what we lose by granting Rayth Ablant his death more than we gain by, for example, what remains of his box when the explosion is over? There's still a lot we could learn from the debris."

Wilson looked over to Abumwe pleadingly. "Councillor," Abumwe said, "not too long ago you chose to surrender your vessel to us. Lieutenant Wilson here refused your surrender. You praised him for his thinking then. Consider his thinking now."

"Consider his thinking?" Sorvalh said, to Abumwe. "Or give him a decision on credit, because of a presumed debt to him?"

"I would prefer the first," Abumwe said. "I would take the second, however."

Sorvalh smiled at this, looked over to Wilson and then to Fotew. "Captain?"

"I think it's a waste," Fotew said. "But it's your call to make, Councillor."

"Prepare a missile," Sorvalh said. Captain Fotew

turned to do her bidding; Sorvalh turned her attention back to Wilson. "You used your credit with me, Lieutenant," she said. "Let's hope that in the future you don't have cause to wish you had spent it on something else."

Wilson nodded and opened up a channel to the *Urse Damay*. "Rayth Ablant," he said.

I am here, came back the text.

"I've gotten you what you wanted," Wilson said.

Just in time. I am down to the last 2 percent of my power.

"Missile prepped and ready for launch," Captain Fotew said, to Sorvalh. Sorvalh nodded to Wilson.

"Just tell me when you want it," Wilson said.

Now is good.

Wilson nodded to Fotew. "Fire," she said, to her weapons station.

"On its way," Wilson said.

Thank you for everything, Lieutenant Wilson.

"Glad to," Wilson said.

I'll miss you.

"Likewise," Wilson said.

There was no response.

"We've cracked the order," the science officer said.

"Tell us," Sorvalh said.

The science officer looked at the humans on the bridge and then Captain Fortew. "Ma'am?" she said.

"You have your orders," Fotew said.

"The coordinates for the return flight of the *Urse Damay* are in this system," the science officer said. "They resolve under the surface of the local star. If it came out of skip there, it would have been destroyed instantly."

"Your friend was never going home, Lieutenant Wilson," Sorvalh said.

"Missile has reached the *Urse Damay*," Fotew said, looking at her bridge display. "Direct hit."

"I'd like to think he just got there on his own, Councillor," Wilson said.

He walked off the bridge of the *Nurimal* and headed toward the shuttle bay, alone.

The Gentle Art of Cracking Heads

"This is a very interesting theory you have, about conspiracy," said Gustavo Vinicius, the undersecretary for administration for the Brazilian consulate in New York City.

Danielle Lowen frowned. She was supposed to be having this meeting with the consul general, but when she arrived at the consulate she was shunted to Vinicius instead. The undersecretary was very handsome, very cocksure and, Lowen suspected, not in the least bright. He was very much the sort of person who exuded the entitled air of nepotism, probably the less-than-useful nephew of a Brazilian senator or ambassador, assigned someplace where his personal flaws would be covered by diplomatic immunity.

There was only so much Lowen could stew about the nepotism. Her father, after all, was the United States secretary of state. But the genial, handsome stupidity of this Vinicius fellow was getting on her nerves.

"Are you suggesting that Luiza Carvalho acted alone?" she asked. "That a career politician, with no record whatsoever of criminal or illegal activity, much less any noticeable political affiliations, suddenly took it into her head to murder Liu Cong, another diplomat? In a manner designed to undermine relations between the Earth and the Colonial Union?"

"It is not impossible," Vinicius said. "People see conspiracies because they believe that one person could not do so much damage. Here in the United States, people are still convinced that the men who shot Presidents Kennedy and Stephenson were part of a conspiracy, when all the evidence pointed to single men, working alone."

"In both cases, however, there was evidence presented," Lowen said. "Which is why I am here now. Your government, Mr. Vinicius, asked the State Department to use this discreet back channel in order to deal with this problem, rather than go through your embassy in Washington. We're happy to do that. But not if you're going to give us the runaround."

"I am not giving you a runaround, I promise," Vinicius said.

"Then why am I meeting with you and not Consul Nascimento?" Lowen asked. "This was supposed to be a high-level, confidential meeting. I flew up from Washington yesterday specifically to take this meeting."

"Consul Nascimento has been at the United Nations all day long," Vinicius said. "There were emergency meetings there. She sends her regrets."

"I was at the United Nations before I came here," Lowen said.

"It is a large institution," Vinicius said. "It's entirely possible that you would not have crossed paths."

"I was assured that I would be given information pertaining to Ms. Carvalho's actions," Lowen said.

"I regret I have nothing to give you at this time," Vinicius said. "It's possible that we may have misunderstood each other in our previous communications."

"Really, Mr. Vinicius?" Lowen said. "Our mutual State Departments, who have been in constant contact since your nation brought its first legation to Washington in 1824, are suddenly having communication difficulties?"

"It is not impossible," Vinicius said, for the second time in their conversation. "There are always subtleties which might go misread."

"I am certain things are going misread at the moment, Mr. Vinicius," Lowen said. "I don't know how subtle they are."

"And if I may say so, Ms. Lowen, in the case of this particular issue, there is so much disinformation going on about the event," Vinicius said. "All sorts of different stories about what happened on this ship where the events took place."

"Is that so," Lowen said.

"Yes," Vinicius. "The eyewitness reports aren't especially credible."

Lowen smiled at Vinicius. "Is this your personal opinion, Mr. Vinicius, or the opinion of the Brazilian Ministry of External Relations?"

Vinicius smiled back and supplied a little hand movement, as if to suggest the answer was, *A little of both*.

"So you're saying that I am not a credible eyewitness," Lowen said.

Vinicius's smile vanished. "Excuse me?" he said.

"You're saying I am not a credible eyewitness," Lowen repeated. "Because I was part of that diplomatic mission, Mr. Vinicius. In fact, not only was I there, I also conducted the autopsy that established that Liu Cong's death was murder, and also helped identify how it was the murder was accomplished. When you say that the eyewitness reports are not credible, you're talking about me, specifically and directly. If what you're saying actually reflects the opinion of the Ministry of External Relations, then we have a problem. A very large problem."

"Ms. Lowen, I—," Vinicius began.

"Mr. Vinicius, it's clear we got off on the wrong foot here, because I was assured there would be actual information for me, and because you are clearly an unprepared idiot," Lowen said, standing. Vinicius rushed to stand as well. "So I suggest we start again. Here's how we're going to do that. I am going to go downstairs and across the street to get a cup of coffee and perhaps a bagel. I will take my time enjoying them. Let's say a half hour. When I return, in half an hour, Consul General Nascimento will be here to give me a full and confidential briefing on everything the Brazilian government knows about Luiza Carvalho, which I will then report back to the secretary of state, who, just in case you didn't know, as it's clear you don't know much of anything, is also my father, which if nothing else assures that he will take my call. If, when I return, Consul Nascimento is here and you are nowhere nearby, I might not suggest that you be fired by the end of the day. If, when I return, she is *not* here, and I have to see your smug face again, then I would suggest you take a long lunch break to book your trip back to Brasília, because you're going to be there by this time tomorrow. Are we clear on these details?"

"Uh," Vinicius said.

"Good," Lowen said. "Then I expect to see Consul Nascimento in half an hour." She walked out of Vinicius's office and was at the consulate's elevator before Vinicius could blink.

Across the street at the doughnut shop, Lowen pulled out her PDA and called her father's office, getting James Prescott, his chief of staff. "How did it go?" Prescott asked, without preamble, as he opened up the connection.

"Pretty much exactly as we anticipated," Lowen said. "Nascimento wasn't there and pawned me off on an egregiously stupid underling."

"Let me guess," Prescott said. "A guy named Vinicius."

"Bing," Lowen said.

"He's got a reputation for stupidity," Prescott said. "His mother is the minister of education."

"I *knew* it," Lowen said. "Mommy's boy made a particularly dumb remark, and that allowed me to tell him to produce Nascimento or I would start a major diplomatic incident."

"Ah, the gentle art of cracking heads," Prescott said.

"Subtle wasn't going to work on this guy," Lowen said, and then the windows of the doughnut shop shattered from the pressure wave created by the exploding building across the street.

Lowen and everyone else in the shop ducked and yelled, and then there was the sound of glass and falling debris outside, all over Sixth Avenue. She opened her eyes cautiously and saw that the glass of the doughnut shop windows, while shattered, had stayed in their frames, and that everyone in the doughnut shop, at least, was alive and unharmed.

Prescott was yelling out of the speaker of her PDA; she put the thing back to her ear. "I'm fine, I'm fine," she said. "Everything's fine."

"What just happened?" Prescott asked.

"Something just happened to the building across the street," Lowen said. She weaved her way through the still-crouching patrons of the doughnut shop and went to the door, opening it gently to avoid dislodging the shattered glass. She looked up.

"I think I'm not going to get that meeting with Nascimento," she said, to Prescott.

"Why not?" Prescott said.

"The Brazilian consulate isn't there anymore," Lowen said. She disconnected the PDA, used it to take pictures of the wreckage on and above Sixth Avenue and then, as a doctor, started to tend to the injured on the street.

"Amazonian separatists," Prescott said. He'd caught the shuttle up from Washington an hour after the bombing. "That's who they're blaming it on."

"You have *got* to be kidding me," Lowen said. She and Prescott were in a staff lounge of the State Department's Office of Foreign Missions. She'd already given her statement to the New York Police Department and the FBI and given copies of her pictures to each. Now she was taking a break before she did the whole thing over again with State.

"I didn't expect you to believe it," Prescott said. "I'm just telling you what the Brazilians are saying. They maintain someone from the group called in and took responsibility. I think we're supposed to overlook that the specific group they're pinning it on has never once perpetrated a violent act, much less traveled to another country and planted a bomb in a secure location."

"They're crafty, those Amazonian separatists," Lowen said.

"You have to admit it's overkill, though," Prescott said. "Blowing up their consulate to avoid talking to you."

"I know you're joking, but I'm going to say it anyway, just to hear myself say it: The Brazilians didn't blow up their own consulate," Lowen said. "Whoever our friend Luiza Carvalho was in bed with did it."

"Yes," Prescott said. "It's still overkill. Especially since the Brazilian ambassador is now down at Foggy Bottom giving your father everything they know about Carvalho's life and associations. If their plan was to intimidate the Brazilian government into silence, it's gone spectacularly wrong."

"I'm guessing it wasn't their plan," Lowen said.

"If you have any idea what the plan is, I'll be happy to hear it," Prescott said. "I have to go back down tonight to meet with Lowen senior."

"I have no idea, Jim," Lowen said. "I'm a doctor, not a private investigator."

"Rampant speculation would be fine," Prescott said.

"Maybe distraction?" Lowen said. "If you blow up a Brazilian consulate on American soil, you focus two governments' attention on one thing: the consulate exploding. We're going to be dealing with that for a few months.

Meanwhile, whatever else these people are doing—like what the plan was behind Carvalho's killing Liu Cong—gets put on the back burner."

"We're still getting the information about Carvalho," Prescott said.

"Yes, but what are we going to do about it?" Lowen said. "You're the U.S. government. You have the choice between focusing on a case of a foreign national killing another foreign national on a Colonial Union ship, on which you have no jurisdiction whatsoever and only a tangential concern with, or you can focus your time and energy on whoever just killed thirty-two people on Sixth Avenue in New York City. Which do you choose?"

"They might be the same people," Prescott said.

"They might be," Lowen said. "But my guess is that if they are, they've kept themselves far enough away from events that there's someone else the direct line points to. And you know how that is. If we have an obvious suspect with an obvious motive, that's where we go."

"Like Amazonian separatists," Prescott said, archly.

"Exactly," Lowen said.

"The timing is still a little bit too perfect," Prescott said. "You stepping out and the consulate going up."

"I think *that* was coincidence," Lowen said. "If they were timing it, they would have waited until Nascimento was back in the office."

"Which would have meant you would have died, too," Prescott said.

"Which would have suited their purposes of distraction even more," Lowen said. "Blowing up the daughter of the secretary of state would definitely have drawn the focus of the United States. Another reason to assume the bomb was set in motion a long time ago."

"When I present your theory to the secretary, I'm going to leave that last part out," Prescott said. He pulled out his PDA to take notes. "I'm sure you'll understand why."

"That's perfectly fine," Lowen said.

"Huh," Prescott said, looking at his PDA.

"What?" Lowen asked.

"I'm sending you a news link that was just forwarded to me," Prescott said.

Lowen pulled out her PDA and opened the link; it was a news story on her tending to the injured on Sixth Avenue after the explosion. There was video of her kneeling over a prone woman.

"Oh, come *on*," Lowen said. "She wasn't even hurt. She just freaked out and collapsed when the bomb went off."

"Check your message queue," Prescott said.

Lowen did. There were several dozen media requests for interviews. "Gaaah," she said, throwing her PDA onto the table, away from her. "I've become part of the distraction."

"I take it this means the State Department should say you're unavailable for interviews at this time," Prescott said.

"Or ever," Lowen said. She went to get some coffee to self-medicate for her quickly approaching headache.

Lowen ended up doing six interviews: one for *The New York Times,* one for *The Washington Post,* two morning news shows and two audio programs. In each she smiled and explained that she was just doing her job, which was not strictly true, as she had given up the daily practice of medicine to work for the U.S. State Department, and anyway her specialty had been hematology. But no one called her on it, because the story of the daughter of the secretary of state arriving like a healing angel at the scene of a terrorist act was too feel-good to mess with.

Lowen cringed as her picture was splashed across screens all over the planet for two whole news cycles, the second news cycle prompted when she received a call from the president, who thanked her for her service to the nation. Lowen thanked the president for the call and made a note to yell at her father, who had undoubtedly set up the media op for his boss, who had to contend with midterm elections and could use a spot of positive public relations.

Lowen didn't want to deal with any more interviews or congratulatory calls or messages or even the offer by the Brazilian Ministry of Tourism to come for a visit. What she really wanted was to get her hands on the file concerning Luiza Carvalho. She pestered both Prescott and her father until it showed up, along with a State Department functionary whose job it was to not let the file out of her sight. Lowen gave her a soda and let her sit down with her at the kitchen table while she read.

After a few minutes, she looked over to the State Department courier. "Seriously, this is it?" she said.

"I didn't read the file, ma'am," the courier said.

The file had nothing of note about Luiza Carvalho. She was born in Belo Horizonte; her parents were both physicians; no brothers or sisters. She attended Universidade Federal de Minas Gerais, earning degrees in economics and law before joining the Brazilian diplomatic corps. Postings in Vietnam, the Siberian States, Ecuador and Mexico before being called up to be part of Brazil's United Nations mission, which was where she had been serving for six years before she took on the *Clarke* mission, where she murdered Liu Cong.

Like all Brazilian foreign service workers, Carvalho was questioned annually by her superiors about her associations and activities and also consented to be randomly "examined" (that is, followed and bugged) by the Brazilian intelligence services to make sure she wasn't doing anything untoward. Aside from some questionable sexual liaisons—"questionable" in terms of taste in partners, not in terms of national security—there was nothing out of the usual.

Carvalho had no associations or friends outside of the foreign service community. The only trips she took were Christmastime visits to Belo Horizonte to spend the holidays with her parents. She took almost no time off except for two years prior to her death, when she was hospitalized for a case of viral meningitis; she spent four days in the hospital and then another two weeks at home recovering. And then it was back to work for her.

No pets.

"This woman is *boring*," Lowen said, out loud but to herself. The courier coughed noncommittally.

An hour later the courier had left, file in hand, and Lowen was left with nothing but a feeling of unsatisfied irritation. She thought perhaps a drink might fix that, but a check of her fridge informed her that the only thing in that appliance was the dregs of some iced tea that she couldn't recall making. Lowen grimaced at the fact that she was coming up with a blank concerning when she had made the tea, then grabbed the pitcher and poured it out into the sink. Then she left her Alexandria condo and walked the two blocks to the nearest well-lit suburban chain theme restaurant, sat at its central bar and ordered something large and fruity for no other reason than to counteract the taste of boring that Luiza Carvalho had left in her mouth.

"That's a big drink," someone said to her a few minutes later. She looked up from her drink to see a generically handsome-looking man standing a few feet from her at the bar.

"The irony is that this is the small size," Lowen said. "The large margarita here comes in a glass the size of a hot tub. It's for when you've decided that alcohol poisoning is a way of life."

The blandly handsome man smiled at this and then cocked his head. "You look familiar," he said.

"Tell me you have better pickup lines than that," Lowen said.

"I do," the man said, "but I wasn't trying to pick you up. You just look familiar." He looked at her more closely and then snapped his fingers. "That's it," he said. "You look like that doctor at the Brazilian consulate bombing."

"I get that a lot," Lowen said.

"I'm sure you do," the man said. "But it couldn't be you, could it. You're here in D.C. and the consulate was in New York."

"Sound logic," Lowen said.

"Do you have an identical twin?" the man asked, and then gestured at the bar stool next to Lowen. "Do you mind?"

Lowen shrugged and made a *whatever* hand movement. The man sat. "I don't have an identical twin, no," she said. "No fraternal twin, either. I have one brother. I pray to God we don't look the same."

"Then you could be that woman's professional double," the man said. "You could hire out for parties."

"I don't think she's that famous," Lowen said.

"Hey, she got a call from the president," the man said. "When was the last time that happened to you?"

"You'd be surprised," Lowen said.

"Cuba libre," the man said to the bartender as she came up. He looked over to Lowen. "I'd offer to buy you a drink, but . . ."

"Oh, Lord, no," Lowen said. "I'll have to hire a taxi to get home after this thing, and I only live a couple of blocks away."

"Cuba libre," the man repeated, and then turned his

attention to Lowen again. He extended his hand. "John Berger," he said.

Lowen took it. "Danielle Lowen," she said.

Berger looked momentarily confused and then smiled. "You *are* that doctor from the Brazilian consulate," he said. "And you work for the State Department. Which is how you could be here and have been in New York yesterday. I'm sorry, let me introduce myself again." Berger held out his hand once more. "Hello, I'm a moron."

Lowen laughed and took his hand a second time. "Hello," she said. "Don't feel bad. I wasn't exactly being forthcoming."

"Well, after all the attention you got the last couple of days, I can see why you might want to lay low," Berger said. He motioned to Lowen's drink. "Is that what the tub of margarita is about?"

"What? No," Lowen said, and made a grimace. "Well, maybe. Not exactly."

"The drink is working," Berger said.

"It's not about the attention, although that certainly could have driven me to drink," Lowen said. "It's about something else, related to my job."

"And what is that, if you don't mind me asking?" Berger said.

"What do you do, Mr. Berger?" Lowen asked.

"John," Berger said. His Cuba libre arrived. He smiled his thanks to the bartender and took a drink. Then it was his turn to grimace. "This is not the best Cuba libre I've had," he said.

Lowen flicked the edge of her margarita glass with her finger. "Next time, go with one of these tubs," she said.

"Maybe I will," Berger said, took another drink of his Cuba libre and then set it down. "I'm a salesman," he said. "Pharmaceuticals."

"I remember *you* guys," Lowen said.

"I bet you do," Berger said.

"Now it makes sense," Lowen said. "Easy conversationalist, blandly attractive, not too quirky, looking for the sale."

"You have me pegged," Berger said.

"You're not going to make the sale," Lowen said. "I mean, no offense. But I plan on walking out of here alone tonight."

"Fair enough," Berger said. "Good conversation was my only goal, anyway."

"Was it," Lowen said, and drank some more of her margarita. "All right, John, a question for you. How do you make a boring person a killer?"

Berger was quiet for a moment. "Now I'm suddenly very glad I won't be making that sale," he said.

"I'm serious," Lowen said. "Hypothetically, you have this person. She's a normal person, right? She has normal parents, has a normal childhood, goes to a normal school, gets normal degrees and then goes and has a normal job. And then one day, for no particularly good reason that anyone could see, she goes and murders some guy. And not in a normal way—I mean, not with a gun or a knife or a bat. No, she does it in a complicated way. How does that happen?"

"Is the guy an ex-lover?" Berger asked. "Hypothetically, I mean."

"Hypothetically, no," Lowen said. "Hypothetically, the best way to describe their relationship would be work colleagues, and not particularly close ones at that."

"And she's not a spy, or a secret agent, or leading a double life as a crafty assassin," Berger said.

"She's completely normal, and completely boring," Lowen said. "Doesn't even have pets. Hypothetically."

Berger took a sip from his Cuba libre. "Then I'm going to go with what I know," he said. "Mental derangement caused by addiction to pharmaceuticals."

"There are drugs that can turn you from a boring person into a methodical murderer, as opposed to turning them into someone who kills everything in the house in a rage, including the fish?" Lowen asked. "I don't remember those being touted to me when I was working as a doctor."

"Well, no, there's nothing that will do something that specific," Berger said. "But you know as well as I do that, one, sometimes drug interactions will do funny things—"

"Turn someone into a methodical murderer?" Lowen asked again, incredulously.

"—and two, there are lots of our products out there that will eat your brain if you overuse them, and if they eat your brain, then you'll start doing uncharacteristic things. Like becoming a methodical murderer, maybe."

"A reasonable hypothesis," Lowen said. "But hypothetically this person was not regularly taking either legal or illegal pharmaceuticals. Next."

"All right," Berger said, and gave the appearance of thinking quickly. "A tumor."

"A tumor," Lowen said.

"Sure, a tumor," Berger said. "A brain tumor starts growing, hypothetically, and starts pressing on a part of the brain that processes things like knowing what is socially appropriate behavior. As the thing grows, our boring person starts putting her mind to murder."

"Interesting," Lowen said. She sipped her drink again.

"I've read stories about such things, and not only because my company sells a pharmaceutical treatment for cutting off the blood supply to tumorous masses in the body," Berger said.

"It's good to read for recreation," Lowen said.

"I think so, too," Berger said.

"And as superficially appealing as that suggestion is, this hypothetical person received a clean bill of health before her last assignment," Lowen said. "It was hypothetically a job that required extensive amounts of travel, so a thorough physical examination was part of the job protocol."

"This hypothetical person is getting very specific," Berger said.

"I don't make up the rules," Lowen said.

"Yes, you do," Berger said. "That's why it's a hypothetical."

"One more chance, Mr. Berger, comma, John," Lowen said. "So make it good."

"Wow, on the spot," Berger said. "Okay. Remote control."

"What?" Lowen said. "Seriously, now."

"Hear me out," Berger said. "If you wanted to do someone in, and have no one know, and completely cover your tracks, how would you do it? You would have someone that no one would ever expect do it. But how do you get them to do it? Skilled assassins may be good at looking like normal people, but the best assassins would be people who are normal people. So you find a normal person. And you put a remote control in their brain."

"You've been reading a few too many science fiction thrillers," Lowen said.

"Not a remote control that gives you gross control over a body, with everything herky jerky," Berger said. "No, what you want is something that will lay across the frontal lobes and then subtly and slowly, over the course of time, bend someone towards doing the unspeakable. Do it so the person doesn't even notice their own personality changing, or questions the necessity to kill someone. They just go ahead and plan it and do it, like they're filing taxes or making a report."

"I think people would notice a remote control in someone's head, though," Lowen said. "Not to mention the hypothetical person would remember someone opening up their skull to get inside of it."

"Well, if you were the sort of people who would make this sort of remote control, you wouldn't make it easy to find," Berger said. "And you wouldn't make it obvious when it was inserted. You'd find some way to slip it into their body when they weren't expecting it." He pointed at Lowen's drink. "Nanobots in your drink, maybe. You'd only need a few and then you could program those few to replicate inside the body until you had enough. The only problem you might have is if the body starts trying to fight off the 'bots and then the person gets sick. That would present as, say, a meningitis of some sort."

Lowen stopped sipping her drink and looked at Berger. "What did you just say?" she said.

"Meningitis," Berger said. "It's when there's a swelling of the brain—"

"I know what meningitis is," Lowen said.

"So it looks like meningitis," Berger said. "At least until the people who have inserted the 'bots tweak the 'bots so that they don't cause an immune response. And then after that, they stay in the brain, mostly passive and mostly undetectable, until they're turned on and they perform their slow counterprogramming."

Berger took another sip from his drink. "After that, it's just a matter of timing," he said. "You get the person with the remote control in the right places, let them use their own brains to take advantage of situations, and slip them just enough instruction and motivation that they do what you want them to, more or less when you want them to do it, and they think it's their own idea. Their own quiet, secret idea that they feel no need to tell anyone else about. If they succeed, then the remote control shuts down and gets excreted out of the body over a few days and no one is the wiser, least of all the person who's been remote controlled."

"And if they fail?" Lowen asked, almost whispering.

"Then the person who's being remote controlled finds a way to get rid of themselves, so no one can find out about the remote control in their brain. Not that they know that's why they're doing it, of course. That's the point of the remote control. Either way, you'll never know that the remote control existed. You have no way of knowing. In fact, the only way you would ever know is if, say, someone who knows about these things tells you about them, perhaps because he's sick of this sort of shit and doesn't care about the consequences anymore."

Berger slugged back the remainder of his Cuba libre and set it down on the bar.

"Hypothetically," he said.

"Who are you?" Lowen said again.

"I told you, I'm a pharmaceutical salesman," Berger said. He reached into his back pocket and took out his wallet and grabbed a couple of bills. "I'm a pharmaceutical salesman who was looking for some interesting conversation. I've had that, and I've had my drink, and now, I'm going to go home. That's not what I suggest *you* do, however, Dr. Lowen. At least not tonight." He dropped the bills onto the bar. "There, that should cover us both." He held out his hand again. "Good night, Danielle," he said.

Lowen shook his hand, dumbly, and then watched him walk out of the restaurant.

The bartender came over, took the bills and reached for Berger's glass. "*No,*" Lowen said, forcefully. The bartender looked at her strangely. "Sorry," Lowen said. "Just . . . don't touch that glass, okay? In fact, I want to buy the glass from you. Ring it up for me. And bring me some coffee, please. Black."

The bartender rolled her eyes at Lowen but went away to ring up the glass. Lowen pulled it closer to her by dragging it by the cocktail napkin underneath and then pulled out her PDA. She called James Prescott.

"Hi, Jim," she said. "Don't tell Dad, but I think I just got put in a hell of a lot of trouble. I need you to come get me. You might bring the FBI with you. Tell them to bring an evidence kit. Hurry, please. I don't want to be out in the open any longer than I have to be."

"You have an interesting relationship with trouble recently," Prescott told her some time later, when they were both safely ensconced at Foggy Bottom, in Prescott's office.

"You don't think I *like* this, do you?" Lowen said. She sank lower into Prescott's couch.

"I don't think 'like' has anything to do with it," Prescott said. "It doesn't change the relevance of my statement, though."

"You understand why I got paranoid, right?" Lowen said to Prescott.

"You mean, random man comes in, tells you a story that, as ridiculous as it is, perfectly explains the problem of Luiza Carvalho murdering Liu Cong, pays for your drink and then tells you not to go home?" Prescott said. "No, I have no idea why you feel paranoid in the slightest."

"You have a bunker underneath this building, right?" Lowen said. "I think I want to go there."

"That's the White House," Prescott said. "And relax. You're safe here."

"Right, because I haven't had any buildings filled with diplomats blow up near me anytime recently," Lowen said.

"Don't make *me* paranoid, Danielle," Prescott said.

The door to Prescott's office opened and Prescott's aide poked his head through. "The FBI just sent you a very preliminary report," he said.

"Thank you, Tony," Prescott said, and reached for his PDA. "Bring me some coffee, please."

"Yes, sir," he said. He turned to Lowen. "And for you, Dr. Lowen?"

"I don't need to be any more jittery, thanks," Lowen said. Tony closed the door.

"First things first," Prescott said, reading the preliminary report. "'John Berger,' or at least the one you met, doesn't exist. They cross-referenced the name with the tax database. There are ten John Bergers in the D.C. metropolitan area, but none of them live in Alexandria and none of them have as their occupation pharmaceutical salesman. This fact, I imagine, does not surprise you."

"Not really," Lowen said.

"The DNA we got off the glass is being processed and maybe they'll have something for us later," Prescott said. "They've run the fingerprints through federal and local and have come up with nothing. They're checking the international databases now. They've also taken the bar security tape and used it to do facial recognition scanning. No results there so far, either."

"So I'm not actually paranoid in this case," Lowen said.

"No, you *are* actually paranoid," Prescott said, setting down his PDA. "You're just paranoid with good reason."

"The story he told me is still nuts," Lowen said.

"That it definitely is," Prescott said. "The only real problem with it is that it's not *completely* impossible. Carvalho killed Liu with blood-borne nanobots specifically designed to asphyxiate him. It's not entirely crazy to believe that someone could design 'bots to work on the brain in the way your friend suggested. The Colonial Union's BrainPals trigger parts of their owners' brains. None of this is particularly new in its details. It's how it's being used that's new. Hypothetically."

Lowen shivered. "You know what, don't use that word with me at the moment, please."

"Okay," Prescott said, a little warily. "The real problem we have with all of this is that we don't have any way to verify it. The Colonial Union let Carvalho float out into space. We have a good story, but good stories aren't enough."

"You believe it," Lowen said.

"I believe it's possible," Prescott said. "I believe it's possible enough that I'm going to recommend to your father that we design a protocol for nanobiotic infestations and their eradication if and when we find them. The nice thing about this story is that even if it's completely crazy, if we get a process out of it, then this particular avenue of sabotage gets closed. If it doesn't exist, then it gets closed before it can become a problem."

"Three cheers for paranoia," Lowen said.

"What would really help, of course, is if we could find this friend of yours," Prescott said. "Conspiracy theories involving remote controls in the brain are more believable when you have people who can accurately describe them."

"I don't think you're going to manage that one," Lowen said.

"Never say never," Prescott said. The door opened and Tony came through, bearing coffee. "Your coffee," he said. "Also, the FBI is requesting visual."

"Right," Prescott said, set his coffee down and picked up the PDA again, pausing briefly to also loop on an earpiece. "This is Prescott," he said, looking into the PDA.

Lowen watched him listen to the PDA, glance over to her and then glance back at the PDA. "Got it," he said, after a minute. "I'm going to mute you for a second." He pressed the screen and looked over at Lowen. "They think they found your friend," he said. "At least, based on the screen shot they got from the security camera. They want you to take a look and confirm."

"All right," Lowen said, and reached for the PDA.

"Uh," Prescott said. "He's kind of a mess."

"You mean he's dead," Lowen said.

"Yes," Prescott said. "You don't sound surprised."

"Give it to me," Lowen said.

Prescott handed it over, along with the earpiece. "This is Danielle Lowen," she said, after she slipped on the earpiece and unmuted the PDA. "Show me."

The image on the screen wheeled for a minute and then resolved to a body lying in an otherwise nondescript alley. The head of the body was covered in blood; as the PDA got closer, Lowen could see the deep crease above the right temple. Someone had cracked the head wide open.

For all that, the face was still blandly handsome, with the residue of a small, tight smile.

"That's him," Lowen said. "Of course it's him."

Earth Below, Sky Above,
Parts One and Two

PART ONE
I.

"I'm not going to lie to you, Harry," Hart Schmidt said. "I'm a little concerned that you've taken me to a maintenance airlock."

"I'm not going to toss you into space, Hart," Wilson said. He tapped the outer portal of the airlock, which had among its features a small porthole made of a thick, transparent alloy. "It's just that the airlocks are one of the only places on this whole godforsaken tub where you can find an actual one of *these*."

"Don't let Captain Coloma catch you calling the *Clarke* a tub," Schmidt said.

"She knows it's a tub," Wilson said.

"Yes, but she wouldn't like you to *say* it," Schmidt said. "She'd start the purge cycle on this airlock."

"The captain's on the bridge," Wilson said. "And anyway, she's got a lot of better reasons to space me than me making a crack about her ship."

Schmidt peered at the porthole. "This isn't going to be a very good view," he said.

"It'll do well enough," Wilson said.

"There are lots of monitors on the ship that will give you a better look," Schmidt said.

"It's not the same," Wilson said.

"The resolution on the displays is better than your eyes can resolve," Schmidt said. "As far as your eyes are concerned, it will be exactly the same. Even better, since you'll be able to see more."

"It's not the eyes that matter," Wilson said. "It's the brain. And my brain would know."

Schmidt said nothing to this.

"You have to understand, Hart," Wilson said. "When you leave, they tell you that you can never come back. It's not an idle threat. They take everything from you before you go. You're declared legally dead. Everything you own is parceled out according to your will, if you have one. When you say 'good-bye' to people, it really is for the last time. You don't see them again. You never see them again. You won't know anything that ever happens to them again. It really is like you've died. Then you get on a delta, ride up the beanstalk and get on a ship. The ship takes you away. They never let you come back again."

"You never considered the idea you might come back one day?" Schmidt said.

Wilson shook his head. "No one ever did. No one. The closest anyone ever comes to it are the guys on the transport ships who stand in front of the room full of new recruits and tell them that in ten years, most of them will be stone dead," he said. "But even they don't ever come back, really. They don't leave the ships, at least not until they get back to Phoenix Station. When you're gone, you're gone. You're gone forever."

Wilson looked out the porthole. "It's a hell of a thing, Hart," he said. "At the time, it might not seem like a bad deal. When the Colonial Union takes you, you're seventy-five years old, you've probably had some major health scare and a few minor ones, you might have bad knees and bad eyes and maybe you haven't been able to get it up for a while. If you don't go, then you're going to be dead. Which means you'll be gone anyway. Better to be gone and live."

"It seems reasonable," Schmidt said.

"Yes," Wilson agreed. "But then you *do* go. And you do live. And the longer you live—the longer you live in *this* universe—the more you miss it. The more you miss the places you lived, and the people you know. The more you realize that you made a hard bargain. The more you realize you might have made a mistake in leaving."

"You've never said anything about this before," Schmidt said.

"What is there to say?" Wilson said, looking back at his friend. "My grandfather used to tell me that his grandfather told him a story about his grandfather, who immigrated to the United States from some other country. What other country, he wouldn't say; he never talked about the old country to anyone, Grandpa said, not even his wife. When they asked him why, he said he left it behind for a reason, and whether that reason was good or bad, it was enough."

"It didn't bother his wife not knowing where he came from?" Schmidt asked.

"It's just a story," Wilson said. "I'm pretty sure Grandpa embroidered that part. But the point is that the past is the past and you let things go because you can't change them anyway. My grandfather many times over didn't talk about where he came from because he was never going back. For better or worse, that part of his life was done. For me, it was the same thing. That part of my life was done. What else was there to say?"

"Until now," Schmidt said.

"Until now," Wilson agreed, and checked his Brain-Pal. "Quite literally now. We skip in ten seconds." He turned his attention back to the porthole, silently counting off the seconds.

The skip was like all skips: quiet, unimpressive, anticlimactic. The glare of the lights in the airlock were enough to wash out the sky on the other side of the porthole, but Wilson's genetically-engineered eyes were good enough that he could make out a few of the stars.

"I think I see Orion," he said.

"What's Orion?" Schmidt asked. Wilson ignored him.

The *Clarke* turned, and a planet rolled into view.

The Earth.

"Hello, gorgeous," Wilson said, through the porthole. "I missed you."

"How does it feel to be home?" Schmidt asked.

"Like I never left," Wilson said, and then lapsed into silence.

Schmidt gave him a few moments and then tapped him on the shoulder. "Okay, my turn," he said.

"Go look at a display," Wilson said.

Schmidt smiled. "Come on, Harry," he said. "You know it's not the same."

II.

"This is a bad idea," Colonel Abel Rigney said to Colonel Liz Egan over pasta.

"I agree," Egan said. "I wanted Thai."

"One, you know that it was my turn to pick," Rigney said. "Two, you know that's not what I'm talking about."

"We're talking yet again about the summit between us and the Earthlings at Earth Station," Egan said.

"Yes," Rigney said.

"Is this an official thing?" Egan asked. "Are you, Colonel Rigney, communicating to me, the Colonial Defense Forces liaison to the Department of State, a statement from your superiors that I will be obliged to deliver to the secretary?"

"Don't be like that, Liz," Rigney said.

"So, no," Egan said. "It's not an official communication and you're just taking advantage of our lunchtime to kvetch again in my general direction."

"I'm not comfortable with that assessment of the situation," Rigney said. "But yes, that's basically correct."

"Are you opposed to the summit?" Egan said, twirling her pasta on a fork. "Have you joined the ranks of those in the CDF who think we need to go to Earth with guns blazing and try to take over the place? Because *that* will be an adventure, I have to tell you."

"I think the summit is likely to be a waste of time," Rigney admitted. "There are still too many people pissed at the CDF down there on Earth. Then there are the people who are pissed at the Earth governments for not letting them emigrate or enlist before they die. Then there's the fact there are still a couple hundred sovereign states on that planet, none of which wants to agree with anyone else, except on the subject of being unhappy with us. It will all end up with yelling and screaming and time being wasted, time that neither we nor the Earth really have. So, yes, waste of time."

"If the summit were to go off as originally planned, I would agree," Egan said. "Although the alternative—no summit, the Earth turning away from the Colonial Union, the Conclave waiting in the wings to sweep it up as a member—is considerably worse. Engagement is key, even if nothing gets done, which it won't."

"That's not my actual concern," Rigney said. "If our diplomats and theirs want to talk until they are blue in the face, then I wish them joy. I have problems with the setup."

"You mean having it on Earth Station," Egan said.

"Right," Rigney said. "It'd be better to have it here at Phoenix Station."

"Because there's no environment the Earthlings will find *less* intimidating than the single largest object humanity's ever built," Egan said. "Which incidentally will also serve to remind them just how bottled up we've kept them for the last two hundred years or so." She stuffed pasta into her mouth.

"You may have a point," Rigney said, after a second of consideration.

"I *may*," Egan said, around her pasta, and then swallowed. "We can't have the summit here, for the reasons I just enumerated. We can't have the summit on Earth because there's nowhere on the planet short of the Amundsen-Scott South Pole Station where there wouldn't be riots, either by the people who hate the Colonial Union or by the people who want us to get them off that rock. The *Conclave,* of all people, offered to host the summit as a quote unquote neutral third party at their own administrative rock, which I will remind you is an order of magnitude or two larger than Phoenix Station. We definitely don't want the Earthlings to make any inferences off of *that.* So what are we left with?"

"Earth Station," Rigney said.

"Earth Station indeed," Egan said. "Which we own, even though it's above Earth. And that is in fact going to be a negotiating point."

Rigney furrowed his brow. "What do you mean?" he said.

"We're offering to lease it," Egan said. "The lease strategy was approved this morning, in fact."

"No one told *me* about it," Rigney said.

"No offense, Abel, but why would anyone tell you?" Egan said. "You're a colonel, not a general."

Rigney pulled at the collar of his uniform. "Stab me again, why don't you, Liz," he said.

"That's not what I meant," Egan said. "I wouldn't know about it, either, except that I'm the liaison, and State needed the CDF to sign off on this. This is an agreement far above both of our pay grades. But it really is a masterstroke, if you think about it."

"Us losing our sole outpost above Earth is a masterstroke?" Rigney said.

"We're not going to lose it," Egan said. "We'll still

own it, and mooring rights will be part of any deal. It's a masterstroke because it changes the nature of the game. Right now Earth has no egress into space. We locked up the planet for so long that there's no infrastructure for space travel. They have no stations. They have no spaceports. They hardly have *spaceships,* for God's sake. It will take them years and a few multiples of their yearly global output to gear up. Now we're offering up the one way into space that's already there. Whoever controls it will control trade, will control space travel, will control the destiny of Earth, at least until everyone else on the planet gets their act together. And you know what that means."

"It means we make someone *else* the target and take the heat off of us," Rigney said.

"For starters," Egan said. "And in the immediate time frame also disrupts any united front they may have had going. You said it yourself, Abel. The nations of Earth can't agree about anything except being angry with us. In a single stroke we look apologetic and reasonable, they start fighting among themselves and scrambling to make alliances and deals—"

"And we can pick and choose among the players, play them off against each other and work deals to our advantage," Rigney finished.

"Exactly so," Egan said. "It changes the entire dynamic of the summit."

"Unless they all decide to put aside their petty differences and focus in on us," Rigney said.

"Seems unlikely," Egan said. "I know you and I left Earth fifteen years ago, but I don't think planetary international relations on Earth have reached the 'join hands and sing songs' stage in that time, do you?"

"I guess the right answer here is, 'Let's hope not,'" Rigney said.

Egan nodded. "So now you see why Earth Station is

in fact the very best place for the summit to take place," she said. "We're not just discussing Earth and Colonial Union issues, we'll also be walking the showroom with the floor model."

"Do your diplomats know they've been reassigned to be salespeople?" Rigney asked.

"I believe they're finding out right about now," Egan said. She speared some more pasta.

"They're going to hate this," Rae Sarles said, at the hastily-convened diplomatic staff meeting on the *Clarke*. "We were supposed to be here to have a frank discussion about other matters entirely, and we're changing the agenda literally hours before we're supposed to be under way. This isn't how it's supposed to be done."

Wilson, standing in the back, glanced over to Abumwe and wondered just how the ambassador would step on this particular recalcitrant underling's head.

"I see," Abumwe said. "And will you be making that observation to the secretary herself? Or the leadership of the Colonial Defense Forces, who signed off on this plan? Or to the heads of every other Colonial Union department involved in this policy change?"

"No, ma'am," Sarles began.

"No," Abumwe said. "Well, then I would suggest that you don't spend any additional time on how things are supposed to be done, and spend a little more time on what we have to do now. The representatives from the various Earth governments may indeed be surprised that we are now open to leasing Earth Station. But our job, Ms. Sarles, is to make them be happy by the change of events. I trust you might be able to manage this."

"Yes, Ambassador," Sarles said.

Wilson smiled. *Head squished,* he thought.

"Beyond this, fundamentally, *our* role has not changed," Abumwe continued. "We have been assigned a series of discussions with smaller and non-aligned countries on Earth. These are third-tier nations in terms of power and influence on Earth, but the Colonial Union is not in a position to ignore or discount any of them, and there is some potential for significant advantages for us . . ." Abumwe picked up her PDA to send her underlings their updated mission roles. Each of them picked up their own PDAs as if they were in church, following the lead of their pastor.

Half an hour later, the room emptied of underlings, leaving Abumwe and Wilson. "I have a special assignment for you," Abumwe said.

"Will I be meeting with Micronesia?" Wilson said.

"No, I will," Abumwe said. "As it happens, I am supposed to speak with them about the possibility of establishing a base on Kapingamarangi. It's a negotiation of no small importance, or so I have been assured by the secretary herself. So if you're done condescending to me and my team regarding our assignments, let's continue."

"Sorry," Wilson said.

"Since the Perry incident, the Earth has demanded that no Colonial Union military ships or personnel come to or be stationed on Earth Station or on the planet," Abumwe said. "Outside of an occasional high-ranking individual or two, the Colonial Union has honored that request."

"Oh, boy," Wilson said. "This is where you tell me that my assignment is to guard the *Clarke*'s rivets, isn't it."

"Keep interrupting me and it will be," Abumwe said.

"Sorry," Wilson said again.

"And no," Abumwe said. "Leaving aside anything else, it would be cruel to bring you this close to Earth and keep you confined to the ship. And beyond that, you continue to prove yourself useful."

"Thank you, Ambassador." Wilson said.

"You're still a pain in my ass," Abumwe said.

"Understood," Wilson said.

"The CDF continues to have no formal role in these negotiations," Abumwe said. "However, it also sees your presence as an opportunity to reach out to military organizations on Earth. In particular, we know that the United States will have a small military unit present at the summit. We've alerted them to your presence, and they are receptive to meeting with you. So your assignment has two parts. The first part is simply to make yourself available to them."

"Available in what way?" Wilson asked.

"Whatever way they want," Abumwe said. "If they want you to talk to them about life in the CDF, do that. If they want to talk about CDF military strength and tactics, you can do that as well, so long as you don't reveal any classified information. If they want to drink beer and arm wrestle, do that."

"And while I'm doing that, am I drawing out information from them as well?" Wilson asked.

"If you can," Abumwe said. "You're of low enough rank that the members of that military detail should be comfortable with you as a person. Capitalize on that."

"What's the second part of the assignment?" Wilson asked.

Abumwe smiled. "The CDF wants you to go skydiving."

"Come again?" Wilson said.

"The U.S. military brass heard rumors that the CDF will occasionally drop soldiers onto a planet from a low orbit," Abumwe said. "They want to see it happen."

"Swell," Wilson said.

"You've done it before," Abumwe said. "At least, when I got the assignment for you, it noted that you had done it before."

Wilson nodded. "I did it once," he said. "It doesn't mean I *liked* it. Falling into an atmosphere at supersonic speeds and trusting a thin, fluid layer of nanobots to keep you from turning into a smeary black friction burn across half the sky is not my idea of a fun time."

"I sympathize," Abumwe said. "But inasmuch as it's an actual order, I don't think you have much of a choice."

"There is the minor problem that while I have a standard-issue CDF combat unitard, I don't have the getup for a skyfall," Wilson said.

"The CDF is sending a cargo drone with two," Abumwe said. "One for you and one for whoever jumps with you."

"Someone's jumping with me?" Wilson asked.

"Apparently one of the military detail at the summit has experience with aerial drops and wants to try something more exotic," Abumwe said.

"They understand that the drop suits are controlled by a BrainPal, right?" Wilson said. "Which this other guy won't have. First he'll asphyxiate, then he'll burn up, and then the tiny parts of him will eventually fall to earth as raindrop nuclei. It's not a good plan."

"You will be controlling the deployment of both suits," Abumwe said.

"So if he dies during the jump, it'll be my fault," Wilson said.

"If he dies during the jump, I would suggest it would be politic for you to follow him," Abumwe said.

"I liked this assignment better when all I had to do was drink beer and arm wrestle," Wilson said.

"There is the fact that when you complete your skydive, you will be on Earth once again," Abumwe pointed out. "Which is something you were told would never happen."

"There is that," Wilson admitted. "I can't say I'm not looking forward to that. On the other hand, Earth Station is connected to the planet by way of a space elevator. I would much rather go that way. Much less dramatic, but also much safer."

Abumwe smiled. "The good news is that you will indeed be taking the beanstalk," she said, referring to the space elevator by its less formal name. "The bad news is that you'll be taking it *up*, back from Earth, almost immediately after you land."

"I'll try to enjoy it until then," Wilson said. "What about you, Ambassador? You're originally from Earth. Any interest in going down to the surface?"

Abumwe shook her head. "I have almost no memory of Earth," she said. "My family left because of civil war in Nigeria. It had lasted the entire span of my parents' lives on Earth. My mother and father's memories of the planet are not pleasant ones. We were lucky to have left, and lucky that there was a place to leave to. We were lucky that the Colonial Union existed."

"These negotiations matter to you," Wilson said.

"Yes," Abumwe said. "They would anyway. This is my job. But I remember my mother's stories and my father's scars. I remember that for all of the sins of the Colonial Union—and it *has* sins, Lieutenant Wilson—the Earth would always have its wars and its refugees, and the Colonial Union kept its doors open to them. Gave them lives where they didn't have to fear their neighbors, at the very least. I think of the wars and refugees on Earth right now. I think of how many of those refugees who have died might have lived if the Colonial Union was able to take them."

"I'm not sure the Colonial Union has the same priorities that you have, Ambassador," Wilson said.

Abumwe gave Wilson a bitter smile. "I'm aware that the Colonial Union's main purpose in reestablishing relations with Earth is to renew its supply of soldiers," she said. "And I understand we're no longer able to colonize because of the Conclave threatening to wipe out any new settlements we make. But the planets we have still have room, and still need people. So my priorities will still be served. So long as we all do our jobs. Including you."

"I will fall out of the sky as best I can for you," Wilson said.

"See that you do," Abumwe said. She picked up her PDA to turn to other business. "Incidentally, I've assigned you Hart Schmidt, in case you need an assistant for anything. You two seem to work together well. You can tell him I assigned him to you not because he's unimportant, but because your assignment is a priority for the Colonial Union."

"I will," Wilson said. "Is it really?"

"That will depend on you, Lieutenant," Abumwe said. She was fully engrossed in her PDA.

Wilson opened the door to find Hart Schmidt on the other side of it.

"Stalker," Wilson said.

"Cut it out, Harry," Schmidt said. "I'm the only one of the team without an assignment and you just had a ten-minute one-on-one with Abumwe. It doesn't take a genius to figure out who's going to be your monkey boy for this trip."

III.

"It doesn't seem like much, does it?" Neva Balla said to Captain Sophia Coloma.

"You're referring to Earth Station," Coloma said to her executive officer.

"Yes, ma'am," Balla said. The two of them were on the bridge of the *Clarke*, stationed a safe distance from Earth Station, while the *Clarke*'s shuttle ferried diplomats back and forth.

"You grew up on Phoenix," Coloma said to Balla. "You're used to looking up and seeing Phoenix Station hanging there in your sky. Compared to that, any other station looks small."

"I grew up on the other side of the planet," Balla said. "I didn't see Phoenix Station with my own eyes until I was a teenager."

"My point is that Phoenix Station is your point of reference," Coloma said. "Earth Station is on the smaller side, but it's no smaller than stations over most of the colonies."

"The space elevator is interesting," Balla said, shifting the subject slightly. "Wonder why it's not used elsewhere."

"It's mostly political," Coloma said, and pointed at the beanstalk in the display. "The physics of the beanstalk are all wrong, according to standard physics. It should just drop out of the sky. The fact it doesn't is a reminder to the people of Earth how much more technologically advanced we are, so they avoid trying to get into it with us."

Balla snorted. "Doesn't seem to be working very well," she observed.

"Now they understand the physics of it," Coloma said. "The Perry incident solved that problem. Now they have a wealth and organization problem. They can't afford to build another beanstalk or a large enough space station, and if any one nation tried, the rest of them would scream their heads off."

"It's a mess," Balla said.

Coloma was about to agree when her PDA sounded. She glanced down at it; the flashing red-and-green banner indicated a confidential, high-priority message for her. Coloma stepped back to read the message. Balla, noting her captain's actions, focused on other tasks.

Coloma read the message, punched in her personal code to acknowledge receipt of it and then turned to her executive officer. "I need you to clear out the shuttle bay," she told Balla. "All crew out, no crew back in until I say so."

Balla raised her eyebrows at this but did not question

the order. "The shuttle is scheduled to return in twenty-five minutes," she said.

"If I'm not done before then, have it hold ten klicks out until I clear it for docking," Coloma said.

"Yes, ma'am," Balla said.

"You have the bridge," Coloma said, and walked out.

Minutes later, Coloma eased herself into the chair in front of the command panel of the shuttle bay's control room and began the bay's purge cycle. The air in the bay sucked into compressed storage; the doors of the bay opened silently in the vacuum.

An unmanned cargo drone the size of a small personal vehicle slipped into the bay and settled onto the deck. Coloma closed the doors and repressurized the bay, then walked out of the control room toward the cargo drone.

The drone required identification to unlock. Coloma pressed her right hand against the lock and waited for it to scan her prints and blood vessel configuration. After a few seconds, it unlocked.

The first thing Coloma saw was the package for Lieutenant Harry Wilson, containing a pair of suits and 'bot canisters for his upcoming dive—for which, Coloma noted sourly, he would need her shuttle again. She disapproved of what happened to her shuttles when Wilson was involved.

Coloma pushed the thought, and Wilson's package, aside. She wasn't really there for them.

She was there for the other package, nestled alongside Wilson's. The one with her name on it.

"I'm supposed to be assisting you," Schmidt said to Wilson.

"You are assisting me," Wilson said. "By bringing me beer."

"Which is not going to happen again, by the way,"

Schmidt said, handing Wilson the IPA he'd gotten him from the bar. "I'm your assistant, not your beer boy."

"Thank you," Wilson said, taking the beer. He looked around the place. "The last time I was here, in this mess area, and I think at this very table, I saw my first alien. It was a Gehaar. It was a big day for me."

"You're not likely to see another Gehaar here," Schmidt said. "They're charter members of the Conclave."

"A shame," Wilson said. "They seemed like nice people. Messy eaters. But nice." He took a drink from his beer. "This is excellent. You can't get a good IPA in the Colonial Union. I have no idea why."

"Shall I fetch you some pretzels, O my master?" Schmidt asked.

"Not with that attitude," Wilson said. "Tell me what you found out about the state of the summit instead."

"It's madness, of course," Schmidt said. "They barely got through the welcome session before they ended up throwing out the agenda for the entire summit. The fact the Colonial Union is shopping around a lease on this station has disrupted things before they could even begin."

"Which is exactly what the Colonial Union wants," Wilson said. "Nobody's talking anymore about reparations to the Earth for keeping them down for so long."

"They're still talking about it, but nobody really cares," Schmidt said.

"So who are the early contenders?" Wilson asked. He took another sip from his beer.

"The United States, which is not entirely surprising," Schmidt said. "Although to cover their unilateral tracks, they're talking about roping in Canada, Japan and Australia for a coalition bid. The Europeans are putting their chips together, and so are China and the Siberian States. India is going it alone at the moment. After that it's a mess. Ambassador Abumwe has had most of Africa and

Southeast Asia at her door, trying to schedule time with her in groups of three or four."

"So we'll have four or five days of this, at which point we'll suggest that the Earth diplomats should go back to their home countries, formalize their proposals and present them at a new round of negotiations," Wilson said. "They'll do a first round of eliminations, which will cause a shifting of alliances and proposals, each progressively more advantageous to the Colonial Union, until at the end of it we get most of the planet doing what we want, which is supplying us with soldiers and the occasional colonist."

"That does seem to be the plan," Schmidt said.

"Well done, Colonial Union," Wilson said. "I mean that in a realpolitik way, mind you."

"I got that," Schmidt said. "And what about you?"

"Me? I've been here," Wilson said, waving a hand to encompass the bar.

"I thought you were supposed to be meeting with the U.S. military guys," Schmidt said.

"Already met with them here," Wilson said. "Except for the one who'll be skydiving with me. Apparently he was delayed and will meet up with me later."

"How did it go?" Schmidt said.

"It was a bunch of soldiers drinking and telling war stories," Wilson said. "Boring, but comfortable and easy to navigate. Then they left, I stayed and now I'm listening to everyone who's come in here talk about the events of the day."

"It's a little loud for that," Schmidt said.

"Ah, but you don't have superhuman, genetically-engineered ears, now, do you," Wilson said. "And a computer in your head that can filter down anything you don't want to focus on."

Schmidt smiled. "All right, then," he said. "What are you hearing right now?"

"Aside from you complaining about having to fetch me

beer," Wilson said, "there's a Dutch diplomat and a French diplomat behind me wondering whether the Europeans should let the Russians into their bid for the station, or whether the Russians will let bygones be bygones and join up with the Siberian States and China. Also behind me and to the left, an American diplomat has been hitting on an Indonesian diplomat for the last twenty minutes and appears to be entirely clueless that he's not going to be getting anything from anyone tonight, because he's a complete twit. And directly across from me, four soldiers from the Union of South African States have been drinking for an hour and wondering for the last ten minutes how to pick a fight with me and make it look like I started it."

"Wait, what?" Schmidt said.

"It's true," Wilson said. "To be fair, I *am* green. I *do* stand out in a crowd. Apparently these fellows have heard that Colonial Defense Forces soldiers are supposed to be incredibly badass, but they're looking at me and they don't see it. No, sir, they don't see it at *all*. So they want to pick a fight with me and see how tough I really am. Purely for the sake of inquiry, I'm sure."

"What are you going to do about it?" Schmidt asked, looking over at the soldiers Wilson was speaking of.

"I'm going to sit here and drink my beer and keep listening to conversations," Wilson said. "I'm not worried, Hart."

"There are four of them," Schmidt said. "And they don't look like nice people."

"They're harmless enough," Wilson said. He swallowed a large portion of his IPA and set the glass down, then appeared to listen to something for a minute. "Oh, okay. They've just decided to do it. Here they come."

"Great," Schmidt said, watching as the four men stood up from their table.

"Relax, Hart," Wilson said. "It's not you they want to punch out."

"I can still be collateral damage," Schmidt said.

"Don't worry, I'll protect you," Wilson said.

"My hero," Schmidt said, sarcastically.

"Hey," one of the soldiers said, to Wilson. "Are you one of those Colonial Defense Forces soldiers?"

"No, I just like the color green," Wilson said. He finished the rest of his beer and looked regretfully at the empty glass.

"It's a fair question," the soldier said.

"You're Kruger, right?" Wilson said, setting down the glass.

"What?" said the soldier, momentarily confused.

"Sure you are," Wilson said. "I recognize the voice." He pointed to another one. "That would make you Goosen, I'd guess. You're probably Mothudi"—he pointed at another, and then at the final one—"and that would make you Pandit. Did I get everyone right?"

"How did you know that?" Kruger asked.

"I was listening in to your conversation," Wilson said, standing up. "You know, the one where you were trying to figure out how to make it look like I started swinging at you first, so you could all try to kick the shit out of me."

"We never said that," said Pandit.

"Sure you did," Wilson said. He turned and gave Schmidt his glass. "Would you get me another?" he asked.

"Okay," Schmidt said, taking the glass but not taking his eyes off the four soldiers.

Wilson turned back to the soldiers. "You guys want anything? I'm buying."

"I said, we didn't say that," Pandit said.

"You did, actually," Wilson said.

"Are you calling me a liar?" Pandit asked, agitated.

"It's pretty clear I am, now, isn't it?" Wilson said. "So: Drinks? . . . Anyone? . . . No?" He turned back to

Schmidt. "Just me, then. But, you know, get something for yourself."

"I'll take my time," Schmidt said.

"Eh," Wilson said. "This won't take long."

Pandit grabbed Wilson's shoulder, and Wilson let himself be spun around. "I don't appreciate being called a liar in front of my friends," Pandit said. He took his hand off Wilson's shoulder.

"Then don't lie in front of your friends," Wilson said. "It's pretty simple, actually."

"I think you owe Pandit here an apology," Kruger said.

"For what?" Wilson said. "For accurately representing what he said? I don't think so."

"Mate, you're going to find it in your best interest to apologize," Goosen said.

"It's not going to happen," Wilson said.

"Then I think we're going to have a problem here," Goosen said.

"You mean, *now* you're going to try to beat the crap out of me?" Wilson said. "Shocked, I am. If you had just admitted this up front, we could be done by now."

"We're not going to *try* anything," said Mothudi.

"Of course not," Wilson said. He squeezed the bridge of his nose as if exasperated. "Gentlemen. I want you to notice that there are four of you and one of me. I also want you to notice that I am not the slightest bit concerned that a quartet of clearly experienced military muscleheads such as yourselves are planning to attempt to pummel me into dogmeat. Now, what does that *mean*? One, it could mean that I'm absolutely delusional. Two, it could mean that you really haven't the slightest idea what you're getting into. Which is it? You get to choose."

The four soldiers looked at one another and grinned.

"We're going to go with absolutely delusional," Kruger said.

"Fine," Wilson said. He walked into the wide public corridor directly in front of the bar. The four soldiers watched him walk away, confused. Wilson turned to look at them. "Well, don't just stand there like morons," he said. "Get out here."

The four of them walked out to him, hesitant. Wilson waved them closer. "Come on, guys," he said. "Don't act like you didn't want this. Gather round."

"What are we doing?" Goosen asked, uncertain.

"You guys want a crack at me," Wilson said. "Okay, so, here's the deal. Spread yourselves out any way you like. Then one of you tries to hit me. If you can hit me without me blocking you, you get to hit me again. But if I block you, then it's my turn. I have to hit all four of you without any of you blocking me. If any of you block me, it's your turn again. Got it?"

"Why are we doing it this way?" Mothudi asked.

"Because this way it looks like we're having harmless high jinks rather than the four of you attempting to start a war between Earth and the Colonial Union by randomly assaulting a CDF soldier," Wilson said. "I think that's wise, don't you? So, go ahead now, position yourselves."

The four soldiers spread out in a semicircle in front of Wilson.

"Anytime," Wilson said.

"Harry Wilson?" said a female voice.

Wilson turned to look. Kruger rushed him, arms raised. Wilson blocked Kruger and put him on his back. Kruger exhaled in surprise.

"Attacking while I was distracted," Wilson said. "Nice. Futile, but nice." He hauled Kruger back up and pushed him back into his old position. Then he returned his attention to the woman who addressed him.

"Danielle Lowen," he said. "What a pleasant surprise."

"All right, I give up," Lowen said. She was standing with a man wearing a uniform. "What exactly are you doing?"

"I'm embarrassing these four knuckledraggers," Wilson said.

"Do you need any help?" the man next to Lowen asked.

"No, I'm good," Wilson said, and Mothudi took a lunge at him. Mothudi was on the deck shortly thereafter. "You went out of turn," Wilson said, mildly, to him. He got off Mothudi's neck and let him crawl back into position. Then he looked back to Lowen. "Where are you two off to?" he asked.

"Actually, we were looking for you," Lowen said, and nodded to the man standing with her. "This is Captain David Hirsch, United States Air Force. Also, my cousin."

"You're the one taking the high dive with me," Wilson said.

"That's right," Hirsch said.

"Nice to meet you," Wilson said.

"Hey," Kruger said. "Are we fighting here or what?"

"Sorry," Wilson said to him, and turned back to Hirsch and Lowen. "Excuse me for a minute."

"Take your time," Hirsch said.

"Will take no time at all," Wilson said. He faced the four soldiers again. "Three rounds," he said.

"What?" said Kruger.

"Three rounds," Wilson repeated. "As in, I hit all of you three times each and we're done. I've got people to see, and you probably need to practice breathing through your mouths or something. So, three rounds. Okay?"

"Whatever," Kruger said.

"Good," Wilson said, and smacked each of them

across the face, hard, before they knew what hit them. They stood, holding their cheeks, stunned.

"That's one," Wilson said. "Here comes round two."

"Wai—," Kruger began, and the end of the word was lost in multiple smacking sounds.

"Okay, that's two," Wilson said. "Ready for three?"

"Fuck this," Goosen said, and all four men rushed Wilson simultaneously.

"Aaaaand that's three," Wilson said, to the four, who were all on the deck, clutching their necks and gasping. "Don't worry, guys, your tracheas are just bruised. You'll be fine in a day. Well, two days. Don't rush it. So, we're done here? . . . Guys?"

Kruger vomited onto the deck.

"I'm going to take that as a 'yes,' " Wilson said. He reached down and patted the back of Kruger's head. "Thanks for the workout, kids. It's been fun. Don't worry, I'll see myself out." He stood back up and walked over to Lowen and Hirsch.

"That was impressive," Hirsch said.

"What's really going to disturb you is that I am the Colonial Defense Forces version of totally out of shape," Wilson said. "I've spent the last several years as a lab nerd."

"It's true," Lowen said. "He barely moved at all the last time I saw him."

"I did drink you under the table," Wilson reminded her.

"And ignored the pass I was making at you," Lowen said.

"I'm not that kind of boy," Wilson said.

"I'm not sure I want to be around for this conversation," Hirsch said.

"It's just banter," Wilson assured him.

"Coward," Lowen said, smiling.

"Speaking of which, my friend Hart is back in the bar,

holding a beer for me," Wilson said. "Care to join us?" He jerked a thumb back at the four soldiers, still prone on the deck. "I tried to buy them beers, but they refused. Now look at them."

"I think we'll join you," Hirsch said. "If only out of self-defense."

"Wise," Wilson said. "Very wise."

IV.

"You wanted to see me," Abumwe said to Coloma.

"Yes," Coloma said. "I'm sorry to take you away from your commitments."

"You didn't," Abumwe said. "I had scheduled an hour to eat and relax. This is it. And after forty minutes of a delegate from Kenya explaining to me how that country should be *given* Earth Station, on account of the space elevator having its base in Nairobi, anything you have to say to me will be a stream of clear rationality by comparison."

"I've been drafted," Coloma said.

"I withdraw my previous assertion," Abumwe said. "What do you mean, drafted?"

Coloma showed Abumwe her PDA, open to the order from the CDF. "The Colonial Defense Forces, with permission from the Department of State, has at least temporarily classified the *Clarke* as a CDF ship, and has at least temporarily drafted me into the service. Same rank, and I share a joint designation as captain with the Colonial Union's civilian service, so none of my crew has to be drafted to follow my orders. I've also been ordered to keep this drafting, and the new designation for the *Clarke*, in strict secrecy."

"You're telling me," Abumwe observed.

"No, I'm not," Coloma said.

"Understood," Abumwe said.

"Whatever this is involves you and your people," Coloma said. "Orders or not, you need to know."

"Why do you think the CDF has done this?" Abumwe asked.

"Because I think they expect something," Coloma said. "We sacrificed the *Clarke* at Danavar—the former *Clarke*—when someone set a trap for the Utche. We don't know who. *This* ship was used by the CDF to try to ferret out a spy in their own ranks, unsuccessfully. When the Earth delegation came onto the ship, one of their own murdered another of their own, and tried to frame us for it, for reasons that have never been made clear to us. And then there was the *Urse Damay*, which fired on us when we were meeting with the Conclave, and controlled by forces unknown."

"We're not to blame for any of those," Abumwe said. "Those weren't about us in particular."

"No, of course not," Coloma agreed. "We've been in the wrong place at the wrong time. But in each case some outside, unknown group has been manipulating events for their own purpose. The same group? Separate groups? If separate, working together or apart? And to what end? And now we're here, meeting with representatives from Earth. We know there's still a spy within the CDF. We know that on Earth, someone is also pulling strings."

"And if either is going to make a statement or an action, this would be the time and the place," Abumwe concluded.

Coloma nodded. "Even more so because the Colonial Defense Forces have no ships at Earth Station and no personnel, other than Lieutenant Wilson."

"And now you," Abumwe said.

"Right," Coloma said. "My primary orders are to pay close attention to any incoming ships. They've given me a schedule of every ship, from the Colonial Union or elsewhere, that is expected at Earth Station in the next ninety-six hours. They've also given me access to Earth

Station's flight control systems, so I can track ship communications. If anything looks suspicious, I'm to alert Earth Station and ping a drone they've placed at skip distance, which will immediately skip back to Phoenix Station."

"There's the possibility that the threat might come from Earth, not outside of it," Abumwe said. "The beanstalk to Earth Station has been bombed before. There are riots happening on Earth right now because of this summit and the CDF. Any of that could be cover for an event."

"It's possible, but I don't think that's the CDF's main concern. I think whoever it is that's modeling this over there thinks an attack from a ship is the likely play," Coloma said.

"What makes you sure?" Abumwe asked.

"Because the CDF gave me something else besides orders," Coloma said.

"So what the hell is the Colonial Union really up to?" Lowen asked Wilson. They, Schmidt and Hirsch were on their third round together at the bar.

Wilson smiled and leaned back in his chair. "This is the place where I'm supposed to feign surprise and exclaim that the Colonial Union is acting only from the best and purest motives, right?"

"Smart-ass," Lowen said.

Wilson raised his glass to her. "You know me so well," he said.

"It's a serious question, though," Lowen said.

"I know," Wilson said. "And my serious answer is that you know as much about it as I do." He motioned to Schmidt. "As either of us does."

"We got our new directives about an hour before we set foot on Earth Station," Schmidt said. "We were taken as much by surprise on this as you folks were."

"Why would you do it that way?" Hirsch asked. "I'm not a diplomat, so I might be missing out on some deep-level chess moves, but it seems like you guys are flying by the seat of your pants, here."

"That's what it's *supposed* to look like," Lowen said. "Spring the idea of leasing the station here on the delegations from Earth to disrupt their plans to act in concert addressing legitimate grievances they have with the Colonial Union. Spring it on the actual diplomats from the Colonial Union so they don't have any real authority to do anything other than listen to the Earth delegations grovel for a shot at the station lease. Change the conversation and change the direction of how Earth sees the Colonial Union. No, David, it's supposed to look like confusion. But I'd bet you long odds that the Colonial Union's been planning this little strategy for a long time. And for right now it's working exactly how they wanted it to." She drank from her beer.

"Sorry," Wilson said.

"I don't blame *you*," Lowen said. "You're just a tool like all the rest of us are. Although you seem to be having more fun than most at this point."

"He's been drinking beer and beating up people," Schmidt said. "What's not to like?"

"This from a man who hid at the bar while I was taking on four guys at once," Wilson said.

"You told me to go," Schmidt said. "I was just following orders."

"And anyway, Captain Hirsch here and I will be doing some very important business tomorrow," Wilson said.

"That's right," Hirsch agreed. "Come fourteen hundred hours, Lieutenant Wilson and I will jump out of a perfectly good space station."

"It's the first step that gets you," Wilson said.

"I'm not worried about the stepping," Hirsch said. "I'm mildly concerned about the landing."

"Well, leave that to me," Wilson said.

"I have to leave it to you," Hirsch pointed out. "You're the one with the computer in your head."

"What does that mean?" Lowen said.

"The suits we'll be inside of are controlled by a Brain-Pal," Wilson said, tapping his temple. "Unfortunately your cousin lacks one, and doesn't seem likely to get one between now and the jump. So I'll be controlling the deployment of both suits."

Lowen looked at her cousin and then back at Wilson. "Is that safe?" she asked.

"We're dropping to the Earth from the darkness of space," Wilson said. "What about this is safe?"

Hirsch cleared his throat, loudly and obviously.

"What I meant to say is, of course it's safe," Wilson said. "Couldn't be safer. Safer than going to the bathroom. Lots of people die pooping, you know. Happens every day."

Lowen narrowed her eyes at Wilson. "I'm not supposed to say this, but David is my favorite cousin," she said.

"I'm telling Rachel," Hirsch said.

"Your sister owes me money," Lowen said. "Now shut up. I'm threatening Harry, here." Hirsch grinned and shut up. "As I was saying, David's my favorite cousin. If something happens to him, I'm going to have to come for you, Harry. And I won't be as easy on you as those four soldiers were. I will, and this is a promise, kick your ass."

"Have you ever kicked anyone's ass?" Hirsch asked. "Ever? You were always kind of a girly-girl."

Lowen slugged Hirsch in the arm. "I've been saving my kick-assery up for a special occasion," she said. "This could be it. You should feel honored."

"Oh, I do feel honored," Hirsch said.

"If you're so honored, you can get the next round," Lowen said.

"I'm not sure I'm *that* honored," Hirsch said.

Lowen looked shocked. "I threaten a Colonial Defense Forces soldier for you, and you won't even get me a beer? That's it, you no longer have official favorite-cousin status. Rachel is back on top."

"I thought she owed you money," Hirsch said.

"Yes, but *you* owe me a beer," Lowen said.

"Family," Hirsch said, to Wilson and Schmidt, and then got up. "Anything for you two?"

"I'll get Harry's," Schmidt said, getting up. "Come on, David. Walk you to the bar." The two of them made their way through the crowd toward the beer taps.

"He seems like a good guy," Wilson said, to Lowen.

"He is," Lowen said. "And I'm serious, Harry. Don't let anything happen to him."

Wilson held up his hand, as if pledging. "I swear I will not let anything happen to your cousin. Or at the very least, if anything happens to him, it will happen to me, too," he said.

"That last part doesn't inspire me with confidence," Lowen said.

"It will be fine, I promise," Wilson said. "The last time I did this, people were shooting at me on my way down. I missed having a leg blown off by millimeters. This will be a cakewalk compared to that."

"I still don't like it," Lowen said.

"I sympathize entirely," Wilson said. "This wasn't exactly my idea, you know. But, look. David and I will have to get together tomorrow before the jump anyway in order to go over dive protocols and to walk him through what we'll be doing. In your ample spare time, why don't you tag along with him? I'll give the impression I know what I'm talking about, I swear."

Lowen pulled out her PDA and scrolled through her schedule. "Can you do it at eleven?" she asked. "I have a fifteen-minute hole in my schedule then. I was going to use it to pee, but I can do this instead."

"I'm not responsible for your bladder," Wilson said.

"I'll keep that in mind," Lowen said. She put her PDA away. "At least I have time to pee. There are some people I know who have so many meetings now that they're positively at risk for peritonitis."

"Busy schedules," Wilson said.

"Yes, well," Lowen said. "This is what happens when one party drops a bomb onto everyone's schedule and turns what was going to be an orderly summit into a goddamned mess, Harry."

"Sorry," Wilson said again.

"This goes back to that arrogance thing," Lowen said. "You remember. You and I talked about this before. The Colonial Union's biggest problem is its arrogance. This is a perfect example. Rather than sit down with the nations of the Earth to discuss the ramifications of keeping us bottled up for centuries, it's attempting a sleight-of-hand maneuver, distracting us with this station lease."

"I remember also saying to you that if you wanted someone to defend the Colonial Union's practices, you came to the wrong shop," Wilson said. "Although I'll note, strictly as a matter of observation, that the Colonial Union's plan seems to be working perfectly."

"It's working *now*," Lowen said. "I'm willing to concede it's a reasonable short-term solution. But as a long-term solution it has problems."

"Such as," Wilson said.

"Such as what is the Colonial Union going to do when the United States, China and Europe all say that as a matter of restitution, the Colonial Union should *give* us Earth Station?" Lowen said. "Forget all this leasing crap. The cost of one space station is a substantial discount on the profits accrued from two centuries of essentially free labor and security for the Colonial Union. You'd be getting off cheap."

"I'm not sure the Colonial Union will agree with that theory," Wilson said.

"We don't need you to agree," Lowen said. "All we really have to do is wait. The Colonial Union is unsustainable without new colonists and soldiers. I'm sure your economists and military planners have figured this one out already. You need us more than we need you."

"I would imagine the natural response to this would be that you wouldn't like what happens to Earth if the Colonial Union fails," Wilson said.

"If it was just the Earth, you'd be right," Lowen said. "But there's option B."

"You mean joining the Conclave," Wilson said.

"Yep," Lowen said.

"The Earth would have to get itself a lot more organized than it is at the moment," Wilson said. "The Conclave doesn't like having to deal with fractions of a planet."

"I think we could be sufficiently motivated," Lowen said. "If the alternatives were either a forced alliance with former oppressors, or being collateral damage when that former oppressor falls."

"But then humanity is divided," Wilson said. "That's not going to be good."

"For whom?" Lowen countered. "For humanity? Or for the Colonial Union? They're not the same thing, you know. If there is a human division, in the end, who will be to blame for it? Not *us*, Harry. Not Earth."

"You don't have to sell me, Dani," Wilson said. "So, how is this line of argument going with the U.S. delegation?" Wilson asked.

Lowen frowned.

"Ah," Wilson said.

"You would think nepotism would help me out here,"

Lowen said. "Being the daughter of the U.S. secretary of state should have a perk or two, especially when I'm right. But there's the minor problem that Dad is under orders to tell us to try to hammer out a deal before the end of the summit. He says my points will make a fine 'backup plan' if we don't end up getting the lease outright."

"Does he mean it?" Wilson asked.

Lowen frowned again.

"Ah," Wilson said once more.

"Oh, good, our drinks are here," Lowen said, motioning to Hirsch and Schmidt, who were navigating back, beers in hand. "Just in time to drown my sorrows."

"Did we miss anything?" Hirsch asked, handing his cousin a beer.

"I was just talking about how hard it is to be right all the time," Lowen said.

"You were talking to the right guy about that," Schmidt said, sitting down. "Harry has the same problem. Just ask him."

"Well, then," Lowen said, and raised her glass. "I propose a toast. Here's to being right all the time. May God and history forgive us."

They all clinked glasses to that.

PART TWO

V.

"Captain Coloma," Ensign Lemuel said, "another ship skipped in."

Coloma muttered her thanks to Lemuel and checked her PDA. She had made it a standing order to her bridge crew to alert her when ships arrived or departed Earth Station, without giving them further explanation. The crew didn't question the order; it was trivially easy to track the other ships. The order had been in effect for most of a day now. It was late morning on the second day of the summit.

Coloma's display registered the new ship, a small freighter. It was one of eleven ships floating outside of Earth Station, the other ten arrayed in parking zones. There were four Colonial Union diplomatic ships; including the *Clarke,* there was the *Aberforth,* the *Zhou* and the *Schulz,* each carrying its complement of diplomats negotiating with the delegations from Earth, who came to the station by way of the beanstalk. Three ships, the *Robin Meisner,* the *Leaping Dolphin* and the *Rus Argo,* were cargo freighters from the Colonial Union, which had some limited trade with the Earth. The two remaining ships were Budek cargo haulers; the Budek were negotiating to join the Conclave but in the meantime were fans of citrus fruits.

In her earpiece, Coloma could hear Earth Station's flight controller ask the new ship to identify itself: the first red flag. Colonial Union cargo ships had encrypted transponders that the station would ping as soon as the ship skipped into its space. The fact that control was asking for identification meant it either had no transponder or had disabled it. It also meant the ship was an unscheduled arrival. If it had been scheduled but was without a transponder, control would have hailed it under the expected name.

Coloma had the *Clarke* scan the new ship and ran the data against a specific database of ships given to her by the CDF. It took less than a second for a match to pop up. The ship was the *Erie Morningstar,* a civilian transport and cargo ship that had gone missing months earlier. The *Erie Morningstar* had started its life as a CDF cruiser more than seventy years prior; for civilian use, it was gutted and reconfigured for cargo-carrying purposes.

It didn't mean it could not be reconfigured back into combat.

Earth Station was now hailing the *Erie Morningstar* for the third time, to no response, which satisfied Coloma that the ship was now officially in the "suspicious" territory.

"Captain, new ship skipped in," Lemuel said.

"Another one?" Coloma asked.

"Yes, ma'am," Lemuel said. "Uh, and another . . . two . . . ma'am, I have a bunch skipping in pretty much simultaneously."

Coloma looked down at her display. There were eight new contacts there. As she watched, two new contacts lit up, and then another two.

In her earpiece, Coloma could hear Earth Station control cursing. There was an edge of panic to the voice.

Now there were fifteen new contacts to go with the *Erie Morningstar*.

Coloma's database from the CDF had sixteen ships on it.

She didn't bother running the other fifteen.

"Where's our shuttle?" Coloma asked.

"It just docked at Earth Station and is prepping to return," Lemuel said.

"Tell it to hold and prepare to bring back our people," Coloma said.

"How many of them?" Lemuel asked.

"All of them," Coloma said, ordered the *Clarke* on emergency alert and sent an urgent message to Ambassador Abumwe.

Ambassador Abumwe was listening to the Tunisian representative discuss her country's plans for Earth Station when her PDA vibrated in three short bursts followed by one long one. Abumwe picked up the PDA and swiped it open to read the message there from Captain Coloma.

Big trouble, it said. *Sixteen ships. Get your people out now. Shuttle at gate seven. It leaves in ten minutes. Anyone still there after that stays there.*

"Go back to the beanstalk," Abumwe said, looking at the Tunisian representative.

"Excuse me?" the Tunisian representative said.

"I said, go back to the beanstalk," Abumwe repeated, and then stood up. "Get on the first elevator down. Don't stop. Don't wait."

"What's happening?" the Tunisian representative asked, but Abumwe was already out the door, sending a global message to her team.

VI.

"You look like you're in a unitard," Danielle Lowen said to Harry Wilson, pointing to his combat suit as he and Hart Schmidt came up to her and David Hirsch. The four of them were meeting in an otherwise unoccupied cargo hold of Earth Station.

"The curious reason for that is because I am in a unitard," Wilson said. He stopped in front of her and dropped the large canvas bag he was carrying. "That's what our combat suit is. This one is actually a heavy-duty combat suit, designed for vacuum work."

"Do you engage in dance battles?" Lowen asked. "Because if you did, I think that would be stupendous."

"Sadly, no," Wilson said. "And we're all the lesser for it."

"So I'm going to have to put one of those on," Hirsch said, pointing to the combat suit.

"Only if you want to live," Wilson said. "It's optional otherwise."

"I think I'll choose life," Hirsch said.

"Probably the right choice," Wilson said. He reached into the bag he was carrying and handed Hirsch the unitard within it. "This is yours."

"It's a little small," Hirsch said, taking the article and looking at it doubtfully.

"It will expand to fit," Wilson said. "That will fit you, or Hart, or Dani. One size really does fit all. It also features a cowl, which when I activate it will cover your face entirely. Try not to freak out when that happens."

"Got it," Hirsch said.

"Good," Wilson said. "You want to put it on now?"

"I think I'll wait," Hirsch said, and handed it back.

"Chicken," Wilson said, taking and storing it back in the bag and pulling out another object.

"That looks like a parachute," Hirsch said.

"Functionally, you are correct," Wilson said. "Literally, not. This is your store of nanobots. When you hit the atmosphere, they release and form a heat shield around you to keep you from burning up. Once you make it into the troposphere, then they form into a parachute and you'll glide down. We'll be landing at a football field outside of Nairobi. I understand some of your friends will have a helicopter standing by to take me back to the beanstalk."

"Yes," Hirsch said. "Sorry it won't be a longer stay."

"It'll still be good to hit the home soil," Wilson said. He set down the 'bot pack and reached in for one more object. "Supplementary oxygen," he said. "Because it's a long way down."

"Thank you for thinking of that," Hirsch said.

"You're welcome," Wilson said.

"It doesn't seem like a lot of oxygen," Lowen said, looking at it.

"It's not," Wilson said. "When the combat suit is covering his face, it will sequester the carbon dioxide and recirculate the oxygen. He won't need as much."

"It's a handy suit," Lowen said. "Shame it looks so silly."

"She's right, you know," Schmidt said.

"Don't you start, Hart," Wilson said, and then both his BrainPal and Schmidt's PDA went off in alarm. Wilson accessed his message, from Ambassador Abumwe.

Sixteen unidentified ships have appeared around Earth Station, it said. *Stop what you're doing and head to gate seven. The shuttle leaves in ten minutes. Do not wait. Do not start a panic. Just go. Now.*

Wilson looked over to Schmidt, who had just finished his message. Schmidt looked back, alarmed. Wilson quickly put everything back into his canvas bag.

Lowen caught their expressions. "What is it?" she said.

"There might be trouble," Wilson said, hefting the bag.

"What kind of trouble?" Hirsch said.

"Sixteen mysterious ships suddenly appearing outside the window kind of trouble," Wilson said.

Lowen's and Hirsch's PDAs sounded. They both reached for them. "Read them while walking," Wilson suggested. "Come on." The four of them made their way out of the cargo hold and headed to the main corridor of the station.

"I'm being told to head to the beanstalk elevators," Lowen said.

"So am I," Hirsch said. "We're evacuating the station."

The four of them walked through a maintenance door into the main corridor, and into chaos. Word had spread, and quickly. A stream of Earth citizens, with looks ranging from concern to panic, were beginning to push their way toward the beanstalk elevator entry areas.

"That doesn't look good," Wilson said, and started walking purposefully against the general rush. "Come on. We're going to our shuttle at gate seven. Come with us. We'll get you on our shuttle."

"I can't," Hirsch said, stopping. The others stopped

with him. "My team has been ordered to assist the evacuation. I have to go to the beanstalk."

"I'll go with you," Lowen said.

"No," Hirsch said. "Harry's right, it's a mess, and it's going to get messier. Go with him and Hart." He went in to give his cousin a hug and a quick peck on the cheek. "See you soon, Dani." He looked over to Wilson. "Get her out of here," he said.

"We will," Wilson said. Hirsch nodded and headed down the corridor, toward the beanstalk elevators.

"Gate seven is still a quarter of the way around the station," Schmidt said. "We need to start running."

"Let's run," Wilson agreed. Schmidt took off, weaving through holes in the crowd. Wilson followed, keeping pace with, and making a path for, Lowen.

"Will you have room for me?" Lowen asked.

"We'll make room," Wilson said.

"They're not doing anything," Balla said to Coloma, staring at the sixteen ships. "Why aren't they doing anything?"

"They're waiting," Coloma said.

"Waiting for what?" Balla asked.

"I don't know yet," Coloma said.

"You knew about this, didn't you," Balla said. "You've been having us count off ships as they came in. You were looking for this."

Coloma shook her head. "The CDF told me to be looking for *a* ship," she said. "Their intelligence suggested a single ship might attack or disrupt the summit, like a single ship tried to disrupt our meeting with the Conclave. A single ship would be all that would be needed, so a single ship is what they prepared me for. This"—Coloma waved at the display, with sixteen ships hovering silently—"is not what I was expecting."

"You sent a skip drone," Balla said. "That will bring the cavalry."

"I sent the data to the drone," Coloma said. "The drone is at skip distance. It will take two hours for the data to get to the drone, and it will take them at least that long to decide to send any ships. Whatever is going to happen here is going to be done by then. We're on our own."

"What are we going to do?" Balla said.

"We're going to wait," Coloma said. "Get me a report from our shuttle."

"It's filling up," Balla said, after a minute. "We're missing two or three people. We're coming close to our deadline. What do you want to do?"

"Keep the shuttle there as long as you can," Coloma said.

"Yes, ma'am," Balla said.

"Let Abumwe know we're holding on for her stragglers, but that we'll have to seal up if things get hot," Coloma said.

"Yes, Captain," Balla said, and then pointed at a display that was focused on the station itself. From the bottom of the station there was movement. A car on the elevator was making its way down the beanstalk. "It looks like they're evacuating people through the elevator."

Coloma watched the elevator car descend silently for a moment and then felt a thought enter her head with such blinding assurance that it felt like a physical blow. "Tell the shuttle pilot to seal up and go now," she said.

"Ma'am?" Balla said.

"Now, Neva!" Coloma said. "Now! Now!"

"Captain, missile launch!" said weapons desk officer Lao. "Six missiles, headed for the station."

"Not to the station," Coloma said. "Not yet."

"Stuff them in," David Hirsch said, to Sergeant Belinda Thompson. "Pack them in like it's a Tokyo subway."

The two of them had been assigned to keep order at the elevator cars, which were "cars" in only the strictest sense. Each of the cars was more like a large conference room in size, torus shaped around its cable. The car could comfortably fit a hundred or so; Hirsch planned on jamming in twice that number. He and Thompson shoved people in, none too gently, and yelled at them to go all the way to the back of the car.

A thrumming vibration in Hirsch's soles told him that one of the other elevator cars was finally under way, sliding down the cable toward Nairobi and to safety. *Two hundred fewer people to worry about,* he thought, and smiled. This was not the day he'd been planning to have.

"What are you smiling about?" Thompson wanted to know, shoving another diplomat into the car.

"Life is full of little surpris—," Hirsch said, and then was sucked out into space as six missiles targeting the departed elevator car smashed into the car, destroying it, and into the beanstalk cable, wrenching it askew and sending a wave up the cable into the car-boarding area. The wave tore open the deck, sending Hirsch and several others tumbling into the vacuum and tearing open the deck, crushing the car Hirsch and Thompson had been filling into the hull of the boarding area. The air sucked out of the gash, launching several unfortunates into the space below the station.

The station's automatic overrides took control, sealing off the elevator-boarding area, dooming everyone in it—three or four hundred of Earth's diplomatic corps—to death by asphyxiation.

Elsewhere in Earth Station, airtight bulkheads deployed, sealing off sections of the station, and the people in them, in the hope of stanching the loss of atmosphere to only a few areas and protecting the rest still inside from the hard vacuum of the outside cosmos.

For how long was the question.

VII.

Wilson felt rather than saw the emergency bulkhead springing up in front of him and saw Hart Schmidt on the other side of it. Wilson grabbed Lowen and tried to push his way through the now thoroughly panicked crowd, but the mob pushed him and Lowen back and into their flow. Wilson had just enough time to see the shock on Schmidt's face as the bottom and top bulkheads slammed shut, separating the two of them. Wilson yelled at Schmidt to get to the shuttle. Schmidt didn't hear it over the din.

Around Wilson, the screams of the people near him reached a crescendo as they realized the bulkheads had sealed them off. They were trapped in this section of Earth Station.

Wilson looked at Lowen, who had gone ashen. She realized the same thing everyone else had.

He looked around and realized that they were at shuttle gate five.

No shuttle here, Wilson thought. Then he thought of something else.

"Come on," he said to Lowen, grabbing her hand again. He went perpendicular to the crowd, toward the shuttle gate. Lowen followed bonelessly. Wilson checked the doorway at the shuttle gate and found it unlocked. He pulled it open, pushed Lowen through it and closed it, he hoped, before any of the mob could see him.

The shuttle area was cold and empty. Wilson set down the bag he was carrying and began to dig through it. "Dani," he said, and then looked up after he got no response. "Dani!" he said, more forcefully. She glanced over to him, a lost look in her eyes. "I need you to take off your clothes," he said.

This snapped her out of her shock. "Excuse me?" she said.

Wilson smiled; his inappropriate remark had gotten the response he'd hoped for. "I need you to take off your clothes because I need you to get into this," he said, holding up the CDF combat unitard.

"Why?" Lowen said, and a second later her eyes widened. "No," she began.

"Yes," Wilson said, forcefully. "The station is under attack, Dani. We're sealed off. Whoever's doing this has the ability to peel the skin off this station like an orange. We missed our ride. If we're getting off this thing, there's only one way to do it. We're jumping off."

"I don't know how," Lowen said.

"You don't have to know how, because I do," Wilson said, and held up the unitard. "All you have to do is get into this. And hurry, because I don't think we have a whole lot of time."

Lowen nodded, took the unitard and started unbuttoning her blouse. Wilson turned away.

"Harry," Lowen said.

Wilson turned his head back slightly. "Yeah?"

"For the record, this was not really how I planned to get undressed with you," Lowen said.

"Really," Wilson said. "Because this was how I planned it all along."

Lowen laughed a shaky, exhausted laugh. Wilson turned away, to let Lowen retain her modesty and so she couldn't see the expression on his face as he tried to ping Hart Schmidt.

Earth Station gave a shudder, sirens went off and that was enough for Jastine Goeth, the *Clarke*'s shuttle pilot.

"Buttoning up now," she said, and sealed the door to the shuttle.

"I have two people left," Abumwe said. "We wait for them."

"We're leaving," Goeth said.

"I don't think you heard me," Abumwe said, using her coldest *Don't fuck with me* voice.

"I heard you," Goeth said, as she worked her departure sequence. "You want to wait? I'll unseal the door for you for five seconds so you can get out. But I am *going*, Ambassador. This place is blowing up around us. I don't plan to be here when it breaks apart. Now leave or shut up. You can string me up later, but right now this is my ship. Sit down and let me work."

Abumwe stared at Goeth for several seconds in cold fury, which Goeth ignored. Then she turned, glared one of her staff out of a seat and sat.

Goeth pushed the "Emergency Purge" option on her control panel, which overrode the station's standard purge cycle. There was a bang as the shuttle bay's outside portal irised open with the bay's atmosphere still inside, sucking out through the dilating door. Goeth didn't wait for it to open all the way. She jammed the shuttle through, damaging the door as she went. She did not believe at this point that it would matter.

Schmidt saw the bulkheads go up, saw Harry yell something at him he couldn't hear and then took off running again toward gate seven, which he could see at the far end of the section. Schmidt knew at this point that his time had likely expired, but he still had to get there to see for himself.

Which was how Schmidt saw the shuttle leave, through the wide window of the seating area just as he came up to the gate.

"So close," Schmidt whispered, and could barely

register the words over the screams of those trapped in the section with him. They were all going to die in here together.

He wished they wouldn't be so loud about it.

Schmidt looked at the seating area, shrugged to himself and collapsed onto one of the benches, staring up at the ceiling of the gate area. He'd missed his ride by a matter of seconds. It was sort of appropriate, he supposed. At the end of the day, he was always half a step behind.

Somewhere in the section, he could hear someone sobbing, loudly, terrified of the moment. Schmidt registered it but didn't feel the emotion himself. If this was the end, it wasn't the worst end he could imagine. He wasn't scared about it. He just wished it weren't so soon.

Schmidt's PDA went off; the tone told him it was Wilson. *The lucky bastard,* Schmidt thought. He had no doubt that even now Harry was figuring out some way out of this. Schmidt loved his friend Harry, admired him and even looked up to him in his way. But right now, at what looked like the end of his days, he found the last thing he actually wanted to do was talk to him.

"Two new missiles launched," Lao said. "They're heading for our shuttle."

"Of course they are," Coloma said. Whoever was doing this wanted to make some sort of point about people leaving Earth Station.

Fortunately, Coloma didn't have to stand for it.

She went to her personal display, marked the missiles heading toward the shuttle and marked the ship that had fired them. She pulled up a command panel on her display and pressed a button.

The missiles vaporized and the ship that launched them blossomed into flame.

"What was that?" Balla said.

"Neva, tell the shuttle pilot to go to Earth," Coloma

said. "These ships are firing Melierax missiles. They're not rated for atmosphere. They'll burn up. Get that shuttle as deep into the atmosphere as it can go, as fast as it can go."

Balla passed on the order and then looked back at her captain.

"I told you the CDF was expecting one ship. So they gave me one of their new toys: a drone that fires a beam of antimatter particles. It's been floating alongside the *Clarke* since yesterday. I think they wanted it to have a field test."

"I think it works," Balla said.

"The problem is that it has about six shots to it," Coloma said. "I put a beam to each of the missiles and three beams into that ship. I've got another shot left, if I'm lucky. If there was just one ship out there, that wouldn't be an issue. But there are fifteen others. And I've just made the *Clarke* a target."

"What do you want to do?" Balla asked.

"I want you to get the crew to the escape pods," Coloma said. "They're not firing at us now because they're still trying to figure out what just happened. That's not going to last long. Get everyone off the ship before it happens."

"And what are you going to do?" Balla asked.

"I'm going to go down with the ship," Coloma said. "And if I'm lucky, I'm going to take some of them with me."

VIII.

The first volley of missiles aimed at Earth Station, six in all, destroyed the elevator car and irreparably damaged the beanstalk cable itself. The second volley of missiles, five times the number of the first, violently sheared Earth Station from the cable, severing the two just below their join.

The station and beanstalk were previously under the thrall of impressively high-order physics that kept them where they were supposed to be, at an altitude they should not have possibly been at, constructed in a manner that should not have sufficed. This physical legerdemain was powered literally by the earth itself, from a deep well of geothermal energy punched into the skin of the planet, which took extra effort to reach from Nairobi, situated more than a mile above sea level.

Without this nearly inexhaustible draw of power, the station reverted to life under conventional physics. This spelled doom for it, and for the beanstalk it fed on, a doom that was designed as minutely and purposefully as the station itself.

Its doom was designed to do two things. One, to protect the planet below (and, depending, space above) from falling chunks of a space station 1.8 kilometers in diameter, as well as several hundred kilometers of beanstalk. Two, to keep the secrets of the technology from falling into the hands of Earthlings. The two goals dovetailed into a single solution.

The beanstalk did not fall. It was designed not to fall. The energy formerly devoted to keeping it whole and structurally sound was rapidly and irrevocably committed to another task entirely: tearing it apart. Hundreds of kilometers above the surface of the planet, the strands of the beanstalk began to unwind at the molecular level, becoming minute particles of metallic dust. The waste heat generated expanded gases released by the process, puffing the dust into the upper reaches of the atmosphere. Air patterns and turbulence in the lower reaches of the atmosphere did the same task farther down. The people of Nairobi looked up to see the beanstalk smearing itself into the sky, pushed by prevailing winds like charcoals rubbed by a frenetic artist.

It would take six hours for the beanstalk to evaporate. Its particulate matter treated East Africa to gorgeous sunsets for a week and the world to a year of temperatures one one-hundreth of a degree Celsius cooler than they would have been otherwise.

Earth Station, damaged and cut away from its power source, began the process of killing itself in an organized fashion before its rotational energy could do it chaotically. Resigned as it was to its own death, the station powered up its emergency energy sources, which would keep the now sealed-off segments of the station warm and breathable for approximately two hours, more than enough time to get the remaining people on the station to the escape pods, which now showed themselves by way of pathed lighting and an automated voice system, directing the trapped and desperate to them. On the outside of the station, panels blew off, exposing the hulls of the escape pods to space, making it easy for them to launch once they were filled.

Once all the escape pods were away, the station would dismantle itself, not by the beanstalk method, which required massive, directed energies the station no longer possessed or could harness, but by a simpler, less elegant solution: detonating itself through the use of shaped, high-energy explosives. Nothing larger than thirty cubic centimeters would remain, and what did remain would either burn up in the atmosphere or be tossed into space.

It was a good plan that did not take into account how an actively attacking force might affect an orderly self-destruction.

Because Hart Schmidt was one of the few people in his section of the station not screaming or crying, he was one of the first to hear the automated voice informing the people trapped there that escape pods were now available on the shuttle deck of every gate. He blinked, listened again to confirm he'd heard what he thought he had heard and then gave himself a moment to think, *Who the fuck tells people there are escape pods after they're already trapped and think they're going to die?* Then he picked himself up and headed to the door of gate seven.

Which was stuck, or appeared to be, at any rate; Schmidt's attempts to pull it open were like those of a child attempting to yank open a door held shut by a professional athlete. Schmidt cursed and kicked the door. After he was done dealing with the pain of kicking a door, a thought registered with him: The door was so cold, Schmidt could feel the heat sucking out of his shoe even with just a kick. He put his hand on the door proper, close to the jamb; it was like ice. It also seemed to suck at his fingertips.

Schmidt put his head close to the door, and over the din of people yelling and screaming, he heard another sound entirely: a high, urgent whisper of a whistle.

"Are you going to open that door?" someone asked Schmidt.

He turned, stepping away from the door, and rubbed his ear. He looked over.

It was Kruger and his three buddies.

"It's *you*," Kruger said. His neck was purple.

"Hi," Schmidt said.

"Open that door," Kruger said. By now a small group of people, who had heard the automated message, anxiously stood behind Kruger.

"That's a really bad idea," Schmidt said.

"Are you fucking kidding me?" Kruger said. "The station is blowing up around us, there are escape pods on the other side of that door and you're telling me it's a bad idea to open it?" He grabbed Schmidt before he could respond and tossed him out of the way, hurling him into a bench in the process. Then he grabbed the doorjamb and pulled. "Bastard's stuck," he said, after a second, and prepared to give it a mighty yank.

"There's a vacuum—," Schmidt began.

Kruger indeed yanked mightily, throwing the door open just enough that he might conceivably slide through, and was sucked through so quickly that when the door slammed shut on his hand, it left the tops of three of his fingers behind.

For the first time since the crisis began, there was dead silence at gate seven.

"What the *fuck* just happened?" bellowed Mothudi, breaking the silence.

"There's a vacuum on the other side of that door," Schmidt said, and then saw the blank expression on Mothudi's face. "There's no *air*. If you try to go in there, you won't be able to breathe. You'll die before you get down the ramp to the escape pods."

"Kruger's dead?" asked another of the soldiers, the one called Goosen.

Unless he carries his own oxygen supply, you bet, Schmidt thought, but did not say. What he said was, "Yes, Kruger is dead."

"The hell with this," said the third soldier, the one named Pandit. "I'm going to gate six." He bolted toward the gate at the end of the section, where people had queued to make their way to the escape pods. Mothudi and Goosen joined him a second later, followed by a yelling mass of humanity from gate seven who finally got it through their heads that there might not be enough spaces on the escape pods for all of them. A riot had begun.

Schmidt knew that for survival purposes he should be in the fray at gate six, but he couldn't bring himself to do it. He decided he'd rather die as a fundamentally decent human being than live as the sort of asshole who'd tear out someone's liver to get into an escape pod.

The thought brought him inner peace, for about five seconds. Then the fact that he was going to die bubbled up again and scared him shitless. He leaned his head back against the bench Kruger had thrown him into and closed his eyes. Then he opened them again and looked forward. Into the back of the gate attendant's lectern. Which among other things had a large first-aid box slotted into it.

Schmidt looked over at Kruger's fingertips for a second, snerked and reached over to the box. He pulled it out and opened it up.

Inside, among many other things, were a foil blanket and a very small oxygen kit.

Hey, look, your very own oxygen supply, Schmidt's brain said to him.

"Yeah, well, don't get too excited," he said, out loud, to his brain. "You still can't get that door open without losing your hand."

Gate six exploded.

In the immediate aftermath, Schmidt wasn't sure if he'd been deafened by the pressure blast blowing out his eardrums or all the air in the section that contained gate six and gate seven being sucked out into space, along with Goosen, Pandit and Mothudi and everyone else who had been raging at gate six. Then he felt the air in his lungs seeping out through his lips and nose and decided it just didn't matter. He grabbed at the first-aid box, wrapped the blanket over the top half of his body as tightly as he could with one hand and with the other covered his face and mouth with the mask of the oxygen kit.

The mask immediately fogged. Schmidt gave himself a quick hit of oxygen and tried not to panic.

In another minute, the section was completely silent and Schmidt felt himself start to freeze. He got up from the bench he'd crouched under and went to the gate seven door. It opened with only the slightest resistance.

On the other side of the door was Kruger: cyanotic, fingerless, frozen and looking, in death, extraordinarily pissed. Schmidt sidestepped Kruger's corpsicle and ran as quickly as he could down the ramp, blue fingers clutching the space blanket and the oxygen.

The shuttle deck of gate seven had sprouted what looked like several doors leading to subterranean alcoves: the escape pods. Schmidt picked the closest one and with shivering hands cycled the portal shut. Sealed, the escape pod sensed the vacuum and freezing cold and blasted both oxygen and warmth into the pod. Schmidt cried and shook.

"Pod launch in fifteen seconds," a computerized voice said. "Secure yourself, please."

Schmidt, still shivering violently, reached up and pulled down the padded seat restraint as the escape pod counted off the seconds. He passed out before the voice got to three and missed his launch entirely.

Lowen cried with relief when the automated announcement about the escape pods fired up and then started going for one of them when their egress doors on the deck floor opened. Wilson reached out and held her back.

"What are you doing?" she yelled at him, clawing at his hand.

"We have a way off this station," Wilson said to her. "Other people don't."

Lowen pointed to the escape pods opening up around her. "I'd rather go this way," she said. "I'd rather have something around me when I launch myself into space."

"Dani," Wilson said, "it's going to be okay. Trust me."

Lowen stopped going for the escape pods but didn't look the least bit happy about it.

"When they start launching these things, they're probably going to cycle out the air," Wilson said. "Let's go ahead and cover up." He attached his oxygen apparatus and then covered his head with his cowl.

"How do you see?" Lowen asked, looking at the blankness of the cowl.

"The suit nanobots are photosensitive and send a feed to my BrainPal, which allows me to see," Wilson said. He reached over to help her with her oxygen and to seal her cowl.

"Great," Lowen said. "How am I going to see?"

Wilson stopped. "Uh," he said.

"'Uh'?" Lowen said. "Are you *kidding* me, Harry?"

"Here," Wilson said, and sent instructions from his BrainPal to Lowen's suit. It sealed up everywhere but the eyes. "That should be fine until we go," he said.

"When is that?" Lowen asked.

"I was going to do an emergency purge of the deck," Wilson said. "But now I'll wait for the pods to go before we do."

"And then I'll be blind," Lowen said.

"Sorry," Wilson said.

"Just talk to me on the way down, all right?" Lowen said.

"Uh," Wilson said.

"'Uh,' again?" Lowen said.

"No, wait," Wilson said. "You have your PDA, right?"

"I put it in my underwear, since you insisted I take off my clothes," Lowen said.

"Put the audio up as loud as you can. Then I should be able to talk to you," Wilson said.

From above the shuttle deck, the two of them heard panicked yelling and screaming, and the thundering of people running down the ramp to the shuttle deck.

"Oh my God, Harry," Lowen said, pointing at the rush. "Look at that."

Harry turned in time to see a flash, a hole in the hull where the bottom of the ramp used to be, and people both thrown into the air and sucked out of the hole. Lowen screamed and turned, losing her footing and falling hard against the deck, momentarily stunning her. The suction of the hole sent her tumbling silently into space.

Harry frantically sent a command to her suit to cover her eyes and then leaped into space after her.

IX.

Captain Coloma had been keeping tabs on Schmidt and Wilson, the *Clarke*'s lost sheep, via their PDA and Brain-Pal, respectively. Wilson had been moving about shuttle gate five but seemed fine; Schmidt was at gate seven, having just missed the shuttle, and was largely motionless until the announcement about the escape pods. Then the ships attacking Earth Station started putting missiles into the shuttle gates, intentionally targeting the decks where the people were funneling into escape pods.

"You sons of bitches," Coloma said.

She was alone on the *Clarke*. The escape pods off the ship seemed not to attract attention. At the very least, no missiles were sent in their direction. Not every crew member was happy to go; she'd had to threaten Neva Balla with a charge of insubordination to get her into a pod. Coloma smiled grimly at this memory. Balla was going to make an excellent captain.

The ships targeted and hit the sections Wilson and Schmidt were in. Coloma zoomed in and saw the wreckage and the bodies vomiting out of the holes in the Earth Station hull. Remarkably, Coloma's tracking data told her both Wilson and Schmidt were alive and moving. "Come on, guys," Coloma said.

Wilson's data indicated he had been sucked out of gate five. Coloma grimaced at this but then watched his BrainPal data further. He was alive and just fine, aside from hyperventilating slightly. Coloma wondered how he was managing this trick until she remembered that he was scheduled to do a jump with a U.S. soldier later today. It looked as though he were doing it earlier than he expected. Coloma watched his data for a few seconds more to assure herself that he was good, then turned her attention to Schmidt.

Her data on Schmidt was less exact because his PDA did not track his vital statistics, unlike a BrainPal. All Coloma could tell was that Schmidt was on the move. He had gotten himself down the ramp of gate seven, which the *Clarke*'s shuttle pilot had damaged, meaning it was filled with vacuum. Despite that, Schmidt had planted himself in an escape pod. Coloma was curious how he'd managed that and regretted that at this point it would be unlikely that she would ever find out.

The escape pod launched, plunging down toward the atmosphere.

The *Erie Morningstar* launched a missile directly toward it.

Coloma smiled. She went to her display, tracked the missile and vaporized it with the final blast of her antiparticle beam. "No one shoots down *my* people, you asshole," she said.

And finally, Coloma and the *Clarke* had the attention of the interloping ships. The *Erie Morningstar* launched two missiles in her direction. Coloma waited until they were almost on top of her before deploying countermeasures. The missiles detonated beautifully, away from the *Clarke*, which was now swinging itself around as Coloma plugged in a course for the *Erie Morningstar*.

The *Erie Morningstar* responded with two more missiles; Coloma once more waited until the last minute before countermeasures. This time she was not as lucky. The starboard missile tore into the skin of the *Clarke*, rupturing forward compartments. If anyone had been there, they would be dead. Coloma grinned fiercely.

In the distance, three ships fired on the *Clarke*, two

missiles each. Coloma looked at her display to gauge how long it would be until impact. She grimaced at the numbers and pushed the *Clarke*'s engines to full.

The *Erie Morningstar* was now clearly aware of what the *Clarke* was up to and was attempting evasive maneuvers. Coloma compensated and recalculated and was pleased with her results. There was no way the *Erie Morningstar* wasn't going to get kissed by the *Clarke*.

The first of the new set of missiles plowed into the *Clarke*, followed by the second and then the third and fourth in rapid succession. The *Clarke* went dark. It didn't matter; the *Clarke* had inertia on its side.

The *Clarke* crumpled into the *Erie Morningstar* as the fifth and sixth missiles struck, shattering both ships.

Coloma smiled. Her Colonial Defense Forces orders were, should she engage a hostile ship that attacked either her or Earth Station, to disable the ship if she could and destroy it only if necessary. They wanted whoever was in the ship, in order to find out who was behind everything the Colonial Union was coming up against.

That ship is definitely disabled, Coloma thought. *Is it destroyed? If it is, it had it coming. It went after my people.*

Sitting there in the dark, Coloma reached over and patted the *Clarke* fondly.

"You're a good ship," she said. "I'm glad you were mine."

A seventh missile tore into the bridge.

Wilson couldn't see Lowen but could track her. His BrainPal vision showed her as a tumbling sprite twenty klicks to the east. Well, fair enough. He was tumbling, too, because of his hasty exit from Earth Station; his BrainPal gave him an artificially stabilized view of things. Wilson was less concerned about her tumbling and more concerned about her utter silence. Even screaming would be better because it would mean she was conscious and alive. But there was nothing from her.

Wilson pushed it from his mind as best he could. There was nothing he could do about it right now. Once they were in the atmosphere, he could maneuver himself over to her and see how she was doing. For now, all he needed to do was get her through the burning part of reentry.

Instead of thinking about Lowen, Wilson had his BrainPal turn its visual attention to Earth Station, which floated darkly above him, save for the occasional flare as the missiles struck another area of the station. Wilson did a status check of the Colonial Union diplomatic ships at Earth Station. The *Aberforth,* the *Zhou* and the *Schulz* were all pulling away from Earth Station at speed, with or without their diplomatic contingents. Their captains were probably aware by now that one way or another, Earth Station was going up like a Roman candle.

The *Clarke* was missing or not responding. That was not good at all. It it wasn't there, then it wouldn't matter whether the shuttle got everyone out or not; they would have met their fate on the ship. Wilson tried not to think about that.

He especially tried not to think about Hart.

There was a dazzling light from Earth Station. Wilson focused his attention on it once more.

It was detonating. Not haphazardly, as in the attack; no, this was a planned and focused thing, a series of brilliant flashes designed to reduce an entire spaceship into chunks no larger than one's own hand. Whatever the attacking ships started, the Colonial Union's detonation protocols were finishing now.

A thought flashed into Wilson's head: *Some of that debris is headed this direction and it's going much faster than you are.*

A second thought flashed into Wilson's head: *Well, fuck.*

Wilson's BrainPal alerted him that Lowen was beginning to drag on the Earth's atmosphere. A second later, it told him he was beginning to do the same thing. Wilson ordered the release of the nanobots and immediately found himself encased in a matte black sphere. On the other side of that, he knew, would be several thousand degrees of reentry friction that the nanobots were shielding him from, taking some of the heat from the reentry to strengthen the shield as he fell.

This would not be a good time for Dani to wake up, Wilson thought, thinking about the flat darkness surrounding him. Then he remembered that she would be in darkness anyway because she had no BrainPal.

I'm definitely not a fun first date, Wilson thought.

He fell and fell some more and tried not to think of Lowen, or Hart, or the *Clarke,* or the fact that screaming chunks of Earth Station were almost certainly whizzing past him at ultrasonic speeds and could turn him into kibble if they smacked into him.

This did not leave a whole lot to think about.

There was a sudden fluttering sound and the nanobots tore away. Wilson blinked in the noontime sun. He was amazed to remember that it was still barely after noon, Nairobi time; everything that had happened happened in just about an hour.

Wilson did not think he could take many more hours like this.

Lowen pinged on his consciousness. She was now less than five klicks away and a klick up, still tumbling but less so in the atmosphere. Wilson carefully negotiated his way over to her, stabilized her and, as much as he could, checked her vitals. At the very least, she was still breathing. It was something.

Still, not having her conscious was not going to be a good thing when it came to landing.

Wilson thought about it for a moment, but only for a moment, because the ground was going to become a problem in the very near future. Then he checked how many nanobots he had left, estimated how much weight they were going to hold and then wrapped himself around Lowen, face-to-face. They were going to go in tandem.

That covered, Wilson finally looked around to see where he was. In the close distance the beanstalk still stood, feathering in the wind. Wilson had no idea what that was about, but it meant that he remained somewhere near Nairobi. He looked down, compared the terrain with what he had stored in his BrainPal and realized he could make it to the football field he and Hirsch were originally planning to land at.

Lowen woke up at around three thousand meters and began screaming and thrashing. Wilson spoke directly into her ear. "I'm here," he said. "Don't panic."

"Where are we?" Lowen asked.

"Ten thousand feet above Kenya," Wilson said.

"Oh, God," Lowen said.

"I have you," Wilson said. "We're in tandem."

"How did you manage that?" Lowen asked, calming down.

"It seemed a better idea than you falling alone while unconscious," Wilson said.

"Point," Lowen said, after a second.

"I'm about five seconds from deploying the chute," Wilson said. "Are you ready?"

Lowen tightened up around Wilson. "Let's never do this again," she said.

"Promise," he said. "Here we go." He deployed 'bots from both of their packs so that both of them were tethered into the chute. There was a sharp jerk, and then the two of them were floating.

"We're close enough to the ground and going slow enough that you could use your eyes if you wanted," Wilson said, after a few moments. Lowen nodded. Wilson had her cowl open up.

Lowen looked down and then jerked her head back up, eyes closed. "Okay, that was a spectacularly bad idea," she said.

"We'll be down in just a minute," Wilson promised.

"And this parachute for two won't mess us up?" Lowen asked.

"No," Wilson said. "It's smarter than a real parachute."

"Don't say this is not a real parachute, please," Lowen said.

"It's smarter than other parachutes," Wilson corrected. "It's been compensating for wind and other factors since we opened it up."

"Great," Lowen said. "Just tell me when we're down."

They were down a minute and a half later, the nanobots dissipating into the wind as their feet touched down. Lowen disengaged from Wilson, grabbed her head, turned to the side and threw up.

"Sorry," Wilson said.

"It's not you, I swear," Lowen said, spitting to clear her mouth. "It's *everything*."

"I understand," Wilson said. "I'm sorry about that, too."

He looked up in the sky and watched bits of Earth Station fall like glitter.

X.

"I told you it was a bad idea," Rigney said, to Egan.

"Your continued lack of enthusiasm is noted," Egan replied. "Not that it does us any good at this point."

The two of them sat on a bench at Avery Park, a small neighborhood park in an outer borough of Phoenix City, feeding ducks.

"This is nice," Rigney said, tossing bread to the ducks.

"Yes," Egan said.

"Peaceful," Rigney said.

"It is," Egan said, tossing her own bread at the quacking birds.

"If I had to do this more than once a year, I might stab something," Rigney said.

"There is that," Egan said. "But you said you wanted to catch up. I assumed you meant actually catch up, not just talk sports scores. And right now is not the time to be catching up on anything in Phoenix Station itself."

"I knew that much already," Rigney said.

"So what do you want to know?" Egan asked.

"I want to know how bad it is," Rigney said. "From your end, I mean. I know how bad it is on my end."

"How bad is it on your end?" Egan asked.

"Full-bore panic," Rigney said. "I could go into details, but you might run screaming. You?"

Egan was quiet for a moment while she tossed more bread at the birds. "Do you remember when you came to my presentation for those midlevel bureaucrats and you heard me tell them that the Colonial Union is thirty years out from total collapse?" she said.

"Yes, I do," Rigney said.

"Well, we were wrong about that," Egan said. "It's closer to twenty."

"That can't all be because of what happened at Earth Station," Rigney said.

"Why couldn't it?" Egan said. "They think *we* did it, Abel. They think we lured several hundred of their best diplomatic and political minds into a shooting gallery and then had a fake group of terrorists blow the place apart. They didn't shoot to destroy the space station outright. They went after the elevator car and they waited until people went for the escape pods to put holes in the shuttle bays. They went for the Earthlings."

"They also shot at the *Clarke* and its shuttle," Rigney pointed out.

"The shuttle got away," Egan pointed out. "As did the single escape pod to make it off Earth Station. As for the *Clarke,* how hard is it to make the argument that it was a decoy to throw the scent off their trail, especially since everyone but their captain survived? And especially since fourteen of the ships that attacked Earth Station seem to have disappeared back into the same black hole from which they came. Seems a fine conspiracy."

"That's a little much," Rigney said.

"It would be if we were dealing with rational events," Egan said. "But look at it from the Earth's point of view. Now they have no serious egress into space, their political castes are decimated and paranoid, and they're reminded that at this moment, their fate is not their own. The easiest, best scapegoat they have is us. They will never forget this. They will never forgive it. And no matter what evidence comes to light about it, exonerating *us,* they will simply never believe it."

"So Earth is off the table," Rigney said.

"It's so far off the table the table is underneath the curve of the planet," Egan said. "We've lost the Earth. For real this time. Now the only thing we can hope for is that it stays neutral and unaffiliated. That might mean that seventy years down the road we might have a shot at them again. If they join the Conclave, it's all over."

"And what does State think the chances of that are?" Rigney said. "Of them joining the Conclave?"

"At this moment? Better than them coming back to us," Egan said.

"The consensus at CDF is that the Conclave is behind all of this, you know," Rigney said. "Everything since Danavar. They have the means to plant spies in the CDF and in the Department of State. They have the resources to pluck our ships out of the sky, turn them back into warships and drop them next to Earth Station. All sixteen of the ships that disappeared showed up there. And there's something else we haven't told State yet."

"What is that?" Egan said.

"The ship Captain Coloma smashed the *Clarke* into. The *Erie Morningstar*. It had no crew. It was run by a brain in a box."

"Like the one in the *Urse Damay*," Egan said. "Of course, the Conclave maintains the *Urse Damay* was taken from them as well. Along with several other ships."

"Our intelligence hasn't confirmed those stories," Rigney said. "They could be running that across the trail to keep us confused."

"Then there's the matter of someone out there actively sabotaging our relationship with Earth," Egan said. "And the fact there's a growing segment of the colony population who wants to replace the Colonial Union with an entirely new union with the Earth at the center. That certainly seemed to spring up overnight."

"Another thing the Conclave has resources for," Rigney pointed out.

"Perhaps," Egan said. "Or perhaps there's a third party who is playing us, Earth and the Conclave for fools for purposes we haven't figured out yet."

Rigney shook his head. "The simplest explanation is usually the correct one," he said.

"I agree," Egan said. "Where I disagree is whether making the Conclave the bad guy is the simplest explanation. I think it's clear that someone wants the Colonial Union dead and destroyed, and Earth is the lever to do that. I also think it's possible the same someone has been poking at the Conclave, trying to find the lever that destroys them, too. We almost found one, once."

"I don't think the CDF is comfortable with that level

of shadowy conspiracy, Liz," Rigney said. "They prefer something they can hit with a stick."

"Find it first, Abel," Egan said. "Then you can hit it all you like."

The two sat there, silent, chucking bread at ducks.

"At least you've gotten one thing right," Egan said.

"What's that," Rigney said.

"Your fire team," Egan said. "Ambassador Abumwe and her people. We keep setting her up with impossible missions and she always gets something out of them. Sometimes not the things we want. But always something."

"She blew the Bula negotiations," Rigney said.

"*We* blew the Bula negotiations," Egan reminded him. "We told her to lie, and she did exactly what we told her to do, and we were caught red-handed when she did it."

"Fair enough," Rigney said. "What are you going to do with Abumwe now?"

"You mean, now that she and her team are the only group to survive the Earth Station attack intact, and her captain has become a posthumous hero both for saving her entire diplomatic team and for taking down two of the attacking ships, *and* the sole bright spot for the Colonial Union in this whole sorry mess was Lieutenant Wilson saving the daughter of the United States secretary of state by leaping off an exploding space station with her in tow?" Egan said.

"Yes, that," Rigney said.

"We start with a promotion, I think," Egan said. "She and her people are no longer the B-team, and we don't have any more time to waste. Things are never going back to what they were, Abel. We need to build the future as fast as we can. Before it collapses in on us. Abumwe's going to help get us there. Her and her team. All of them. All of them that are left, anyway."

Wilson and Lowen stood on the grounds of what remained of the Nairobi beanstalk and Earth Station, waiting for his ride, the shuttle that was slowly coming in for a landing.

"So, what's it like?" Lowen wanted to know.

"What's what like?" Wilson asked.

"Leaving Earth a second time," Lowen said.

"It's the same in a lot of ways," Wilson said. "I'm excited to go, to see what's out there in the universe. But I also know it's not likely that I'm ever coming back. And once again, I'm leaving behind people I care about."

Lowen smiled at that and gave Wilson a peck on the cheek. "You don't have to leave," she said. "You can always defect."

"Tempting," he said. "But as much as I love the Earth, I have to admit something."

"And what's that," Lowen said.

"I'm just not from around here anymore," Wilson said

The shuttle landed.

"Well," Lowen said, "if you ever change your mind, you know where we are."

"I do," Wilson said. "You know where I am, too. Come up and see me."

"That's going to be a little more difficult now, all things considered," Lowen said.

"I know," Wilson said. "The offer still stands."

"One day I'll take you up on that," Lowen said.

"Good," Wilson said. "Life's always interesting with you around."

The shuttle door opened. Wilson picked up his bag to go.

"Hey, Harry," Lowen said.

"Yes?" Wilson said.

"Thanks for saving my life," she said.

Wilson smiled and waved good-bye.

Hart Schmidt and Ambassador Ode Abumwe were waiting inside.

Wilson smiled and shook the ambassador's hand warmly. "You have no idea how glad I am to see you again, ma'am," he said to her.

Abumwe smiled equally warmly. "Likewise, Lieutenant."

Wilson turned to Schmidt. "As for you," he said. "Don't you do that again. That whole almost dying thing."

"I promise nothing," Schmidt said.

Wilson hugged his friend, then sat down and buckled in.

"Did you have a good time back on Earth?" Schmidt asked.

"I did," Wilson said. "Now let's go home."

Abumwe nodded to the shuttle pilot. They put the Earth below them and headed into the sky above.

EXTRAS

After the Coup

Author's Note: "After the Coup" is an original story featuring three of the main characters of The Human Division, *written for the debut of Tor.com in 2008. The events of the story take place several months before the events of* The Human Division. *Enjoy.*

—JS

"How well can you take a punch?" asked Deputy Ambassador Schmidt.

Lieutenant Harry Wilson blinked and set down his drink. "You know, there are a number of places a conversation can go after a question like that," he said. "None of them end well."

"I don't mean it like that," Schmidt said. He drummed the glass of his own drink with his fingers. Harry noted the drumming, which was a favorite nervous tell of Hart Schmidt's. It made poker games with him fun. "I have a very specific reason to ask you."

"I would hope so," Harry said. "Because as conversational icebreakers go, it's not in the top ten."

Schmidt looked around the *Clarke*'s officers lounge. "Maybe this isn't the best place to talk about it," he said.

Harry glanced around the lounge. It was singularly unappealing; a bunch of magnetized folding chairs and equally magnetized card tables, and a single porthole from which the yellowish green limb of Korba-Aty was glowing, dully. The drinks they were having came from the rack of vending machines built into the wall. The only other person in the lounge was Lieutenant Grant, the *Clarke*'s quartermaster; she was looking at her PDA and wearing headphones.

"It's fine, Hart," Harry said. "Enough with the melodrama. Spit it out already."

"Fine," Schmidt said, and then drummed on his drink some more. Harry waited. "Look, this mission isn't going well," he finally said.

"Really," Harry said, dryly.

"What's that supposed to mean?" Schmidt said.

"Don't get defensive, Hart," Harry said. "I'm not blaming you."

"I just want to know how you came to that conclusion," Schmidt said.

"You mean, how did I come to that conclusion despite the fact I'm this mission's mushroom," Harry said.

Schmidt frowned. "I don't know what that means," he said.

"It means that you keep me in the dark and feed me shit," Harry said.

"Ah," Schmidt said. "Sorry."

"It's fine," Harry said. "This is a Colonial Union diplomatic mission, and I'm Colonial Defense Forces, and you don't want me seen by the Korba because you don't want my presence to be interpreted as provocation. So while the rest of you head down to the planet, and get to breathe real air and see actual sunlight, I stay up here in this latrine of a spaceship, training your technicians to use the field generator and catching up on my reading. Which is going well, incidentally. I just finished *Anna Karenina*."

"How was it?" Schmidt said.

"Not bad," Harry said. "The moral is to stay away from trains. The point is, I know *why* I'm kept in the dark. Fine. Fair enough. But I'm not *stupid*, Hart. Even if none of you tell me anything about the mission, I can tell it's not going well. All of you deputies and assistants come back to the *Clarke* looking like you've had the crap beat out of you all day long. It's a subtle hint." He picked up his drink and slugged some back.

"Hmm. Anyway, yes," Schmidt said. "The mission isn't going well. The Korba haven't been nearly as receptive to our negotiations as we thought they might be. We want to try something new. A new direction. A new diplomatic tack."

"A new tack that is somehow focused on me getting punched," Harry said, setting his drink back down.

"Maybe," Schmidt said.

"Once or repeatedly?" Harry asked.

"I think that would depend on your definition," Schmidt said.

"Of 'once'?" Harry asked.

"Of 'punched,' actually," Schmidt said.

"I already have very deep reservations about this plan," Harry said.

"Well, let me give you some context," Schmidt said.

"Please *do*," Harry said.

Schmidt produced his PDA and began to slide it over to Harry, then stopped midway through the motion. "You know that everything I'm about to tell you is classified."

"Good lord, Hart," Harry said. "I'm the only person on the *Clarke* who *doesn't* know what's going on." Harry reached over and took the PDA. On its screen was the image of a battle cruiser of some sort, floating near a skyscraper. Or more accurately, what was left of a skyscraper; it had been substantially destroyed, likely by the battle cruiser. In the foreground of the picture, small, vaguely-humanoid blotches seemed to be running from the ruined skyscraper. "Nice picture," Harry said.

"What do you think you're seeing there?" Schmidt said.

"A strong case for not letting trainees drive a battle cruiser," Harry said.

"It's an image taken during the recent Korban coup," Schmidt said. "There was a disagreement between the head of the military and the Korban civilian leadership. That skyscraper is—well, was—the Korban administrative headquarters."

"So the civilians lost that particular argument," Harry said.

"Pretty much," Schmidt said.

"Where do we come in?" Harry asked, handing back the PDA. "Are we trying to restore the civilian government? Because, to be honest about it, that doesn't really sound like something the CU would care about."

"We don't," Schmidt said, taking back the PDA. "Before the coup, the Korba were barely on our radar at all. They had a non-expansionist policy. They had their few worlds and they'd stood pat on them for centuries. We had no conflict with them, so we didn't care about them. After the coup, the Korba are very interested in expanding again."

"This worries us," Harry said.

"Not if we can point them toward expanding in the direction of some of our enemies," Schmidt said. "There are some races in this area who are pushing in on us. If they had to worry about someone else, they'd have fewer resources to hit us with."

"See, that's the Colonial Union I know," Harry said. "Always happy to stick a knife in someone else's face. But none of this has anything to do with me getting *punched* in the face."

"Actually, it does," Schmidt said. "We made a tactical error. This mission is a diplomatic one, but the new leaders of Korba are military. They're curious about our military, and they're especially curious about our CDF soldiers, whom they've never encountered because our races have never fought. We're civilians; we don't have any of our military on hand, and very little in terms of military capability to show them. We brought them that field generator you've been training our technicians on, but that's defensive technology. They're much more interested in our offensive capabilities. And they're especially interested in seeing our soldiers in action. Negotiations up to this point have been going poorly because we're not equipped to give them what they want. But then we let it slip that we have a CDF member on the *Clarke*."

"*We* let it slip," Harry said.

"Well, *I* let it slip, actually," Schmidt said. "Come on, Harry, don't look at me like that. This mission is failing. Some of us need this mission to succeed. My career's not exactly on fire, you know. If this mission goes into the crapper, I'm going to get reassigned to an archive basement."

"I'd be more sympathetic if saving your career didn't require blunt force trauma for me," Harry said.

Schmidt nodded, and then ducked his head a little, which Harry took as something akin to an apology. "When we told them about you, they got very excited, and we were asked by the Korbans' new leader—a direct request from the head of state, Harry—if we would be willing to pit you against one of their soldiers in a contest of skills," Schmidt said. "It was strongly implied it would make a real difference in the tenor of the negotiations."

"So of course you said yes," Harry said.

"Let me remind you of the part where I said the mission is going into the crapper," Schmidt said.

"There is a small flaw in this plan," Harry said. "Besides the part where I get the crap kicked out of me, I mean. Hart, I'm CDF, but I'm not a soldier. I'm a *technician*. I've spent the last several years working in the military science division of the Forces. That's why I'm here, for God's sake. I'm training your people to use technology we developed. I'm not training them to fight, I'm training them to twirl knobs."

"You've still got the CDF genetic engineering," Schmidt said, and pointed to Harry's sitting form. "Your body is still in top physical shape, whether you use it or not. Your reflexes are still fast as ever. You're still as strong as ever. Look at you, Harry. There's nothing flabby or squishy about you. You're in as good a shape as any soldier on the line."

"That doesn't mean anything," Harry said.

"Doesn't it?" Schmidt said. "Tell me, Harry. Everyone else on this mission is an unmodified human. Is there any one of us that you couldn't take in hand-to-hand combat?"

"Well, no. But you're all *soft*," Harry said.

"Thanks for that," Schmidt said. He took a sip of his drink.

"My point is whether or not I'm engineered for combat, I haven't been a soldier for a very long time," Harry said. "Fighting isn't like riding a bicycle, Hart. You can't just pick it up without practice. If these guys are so hot to see CDF in action, send a skip drone back to Phoenix and request a squad. They could be here in a couple of days if you make it a priority request."

"There's no *time*, Harry," Schmidt said. "The Korba want a combat exhibition tonight. Actually,"—Schmidt checked the chronometer on his PDA—"in about four and a half hours."

"Oh, come *on*," Harry said.

"They made the request this morning, Harry," Schmidt said. "It's not like I've been keeping it from you. We told them about you, they made the request and ten minutes later I was being hustled off to the shuttle back to the *Clarke* to tell you. And here we are."

"What is this 'skill contest' they want me to have?" Harry asked.

"It's a ritualized combat thing," Schmidt said. "It's physical combat, but it's done as a sport. Like karate or fencing or wrestling. There are three rounds. You get scored on points. There are judges. From what I understand it's mostly harmless. You're not going to be in any real danger."

"Except for being punched," Harry said.

"You'll heal," Schmidt said. "And anyway, you can punch back."

"I don't suppose I can pass," Harry said.

"Sure, you can pass," Schmidt said. "And then when the mission fails and everyone on the mission is demoted into shit jobs and the Korba ally themselves with our enemies and start looking at human colonies they can pick off, you can bask in the knowledge that at least you came out of this all *unbruised*."

Harry sighed and drained his drink. "You *owe* me, Hart," he said. "Not the Colonial Union. You."

"I can live with that," Schmidt said.

"Fine," Harry said. "So the plan is to go down there, fight with one of their guys, get beat up a little, and everyone walks away happy."

"Mostly," Schmidt said.

"*Mostly*," Harry said.

"I have two requests for you from Ambassador Abumwe," Schmidt said. "And she said for me to say that by 'request,' she means that if you don't do them both she will find a way to make the rest of your natural existence one of unceasing woe and misery."

"Really," Harry said.

"She was very precise about her word use," Schmidt said.

"Lovely," Harry said. "What are the requests?"

"The first is that you keep the contest close," Schmidt said. "We need to show the Korba from the start that the reputation the CDF has is not undeserved."

"Not knowing what the rules of the contest are, how it's played or whether I'm even physically capable of keeping up with it, sure, why not, I'll keep it close," Harry said. "What's the other request."

"That you lose," Schmidt said.

"The rules are simple," Schmidt said, translating for the Korban who stood in front of them. Normally Harry would use his BrainPal—the computer in his head—to do a translation, but he didn't have access to the *Clarke*'s network to access the language. "There are three rounds: One round with Bongka—those are like quarterstaffs, Harry—one round of hand-to-hand combat, and one round of water combat. There are no set times for any round; they continue until all three judges have selected a victor, or until one of the combatants is knocked unconscious. The chief judge here wants to make sure you understand this."

"I understand," said Harry, staring at the Korban, who came up, roughly, to his waist. The Korba were squat, bilaterally symmetrical, apparently muscular, and covered by what appeared to be an infinite amount of overlapping plates and scales. What little information Harry could uncover about the Korban physiology suggested that they were of some sort of amphibious stock, and that they lived some of their lives in water. This would at least explain the "water combat" round. The gathering hall they were in held no obvious water sources, however. Harry wondered if something might not have been lost in translation.

The Korban began speaking again, and as he spoke

and breathed, the plates around his neck and chest moved in a motion that was indefinably strange and unsettling; it was almost like they didn't quite go back in the same place they started off at. Harry found them unintentionally hypnotic.

"Harry," Schmidt said.

"Yes?" Harry said.

"You're all right with the nudity?" Schmidt asked.

"Yes," Harry said. "Wait. What?"

Schmidt sighed. "Pay attention, Harry," he said. "The contest is performed in the nude so that it's purely a test of skill, no tricks. You're okay with that?"

Harry glanced around the gymnasium-like room they were in, filling up with Korban spectators, human diplomats and *Clarke* crew members on shore leave. In the crowd of humans he located Ambassador Abumwe, who gave him a look that reinforced her earlier threat of unending misery. "So everyone gets to see my bits," Harry said.

"Afraid so," Schmidt said. "All right, then?"

"Do I have a choice?" Harry asked.

"Not really," Schmidt said.

"Then I guess I'm all right with it," Harry said. "See if you can get them to crank up the thermostat."

"I'll look into it." Schmidt said something to the Korban, who replied at length. Harry doubted they were actually speaking about the thermostat. The Korban turned and uttered a surprisingly loud blast, his neck and chest plates spiking out as he did so. Harry was suddenly reminded of a horny toad back on Earth.

From across the room another Korban approached, holding a staff just under two meters in length, with the ends coated in what appeared to be red paint. The Korban presented it to Harry, who took it. "Thanks," he said. The Korban ran off.

The judge started speaking. "He says that they apologize that they are unable to give you a more attractive Bongka," Schmidt translated, "but that your height meant they had to craft one for you specially, and they did not have time to hand it over to an artisan. He wants you to know, however, that it is fully functional and you should not be at any disadvantage. He says you may strike your opponent at will with the bongka, and on any part of the body, but only with the tips; using the unmarked part of the bongka to strike your opponent will result in lost points. You can block with the unmarked part, however."

"Got it," Harry said. "I can hit anywhere? Aren't they worried about someone losing an eye?"

Schmidt asked. "He says that if you manage to take an eye, then it counts. Every hit or attack with a tip is fair." Schmidt was quiet for a moment as the judge spoke at length. "Apparently the Korba can regenerate lost limbs and some organs, eventually. They don't see losing one as a huge problem."

"I thought you said there were rules, Hart," Harry said.

"My mistake," Schmidt said.

"You and I are going to have a talk after all of this is done," Harry said.

Schmidt didn't answer this because the judge had started speaking again. "The judge wants to know if you have a second. If you don't have one he will be happy to provide you one."

"Do I have a second?" Harry said.

"I didn't know you needed one," Schmidt said.

"Hart, please make an effort to be useful to me," Harry asked.

"Well, I'm translating," Schmidt said.

"I only have your word for that," Harry said. "Tell the judge that you're my second."

"What? Harry, I can't," Schmidt said. "I'm supposed to be sitting with the Ambassador."

"And I'm supposed to be in a bunk on the *Clarke* reading the first part of *The Brothers Karamazov*," Harry said. "Clearly this is a disappointing day for both of us. Suck it up, Hart. Tell him."

Schmidt told him; the judge started speaking at length to Schmidt, chest and neck plates shifting as he did so. Harry glanced back over to the seating area provided the Colonial Union diplomats and *Clarke* crew, who shifted in their rows. The stands were half-sized for humans; they sat with their knees bunched into their chests like parents at a preschool open house. They didn't look in the least bit comfortable.

Good, thought Harry.

The judge stopped speaking, turned toward Harry, and did something with his scales that caused a wave-like ripple to go around his head. Harry shuddered involuntarily; the judge seemed to take that as a response. He left.

"We're going to start in just a minute," Schmidt said. "Now might be a good time for you to strip."

Harry set down his bongka and took off his jacket. "I don't suppose *you're* going to strip," he said. "Being my second and all."

"The judge didn't say anything about it in the job description," Schmidt said. He took the jacket from Harry.

"What *is* your job description?" Harry asked.

"I'm supposed to research your opponent and give you tips on how to beat him," Schmidt said.

"What do you know about my opponent?" Harry asked. He was out of his shirt and was slipping off his trousers.

"My guess is that he will be short," Schmidt said.

"How do I beat him?" Harry said. He slipped off his shoes and let his toes test the spongy flooring.

"You're not supposed to beat him," Schmidt said. "You're supposed to tie and then take a fall."

Harry grunted and handed Schmidt his pants, socks and shoes. "Am I correct in assuming that there are several species of legume that would do a better job being my second than you, Hart?"

"Sorry, Harry," Schmidt said. "I'm flying by the seat of my pants here."

"And my pants," Harry said.

"I guess that's true," Schmidt said. He looked at the nude Harry and counted the number of apparel he was holding. "Where's your underwear?" he asked.

"Today was laundry day," Harry said.

"You went *commando* to a diplomatic function?" Schmidt asked. The horror in his voice was unmistakable.

"Yes, Hart, I went commando to a diplomatic function," Harry said, and then motioned to his body. "And now, as you can see, I'm going *Spartan* so a midget can whack me with a stick." He bent and picked up his bongka. "Honestly, Hart. Help me out here. Focus a little."

"All right," Hart said, and glanced at the pile of clothes he was holding. "Let me just put these somewhere." He started off toward the human seating area.

As Hart did this, three Korba approached Harry. One was the judge from earlier. Another Korban was carrying his own bongka, proportional to his own height; Harry's opponent. The third was a step behind Harry's opponent; Harry guessed it was the other second.

The three Korba stopped directly in front of Harry. The one holding the bongka handed it to his second, looked up at Harry, and then thrust out his hands, palms forward, making a grunting noise as he did so. Harry hadn't the slightest idea what to do with this. So he handed his bongka to Schmidt, who had just come running up, thrust his own hands forward, and returned the motion. "Jazz hands," Harry said.

The Korban seemed satisfied, took back his bongka, and headed toward the other side of the gym. The judge spoke, and held up something in his hand. "He says that they're ready to begin," Schmidt said. "He will signal the start of the round with his horn, and will use it again at the end of the round. When the round ends, there will be a few minutes while they set up for the next round. You can use that time to rest and to confer with your second. Do you understand?"

"Yes, fine," Harry said. "Let's get to it, already." Schmidt responded; the judge walked off. Harry began working with the bongka, testing its balance and warp. It felt like it was made of a hard wood of some sort; he wondered if it would splinter or break.

"Harry," Schmidt said, and pointed to where the judge stood, horn raised high. "We're starting."

Harry held his bongka in both hands, chest high, horizontal to the ground. "Any last pieces of advice?" he asked.

"Aim low," Schmidt said, and backed off the floor.

"Great," Harry said. The judge blasted his horn and moved to the side of the gym. Harry stepped forward with his bongka, keeping his eye on his opponent.

His opponent raised his bongka, expanded his chest and neck by an alarming amount, emitted a deafening noise somewhere between a belch and a roar, and launched himself at Harry as fast as his little feet could carry him. The Korba in the stands, ringing the gym save for the small section for the humans, cheered mightily in a similar chest-inflating, burping fashion.

Three seconds later Harry was confronted by the fact that he had absolutely no clue what he was doing. The Korban had set on him with a slashing, dizzying array of bongka maneuvers; Harry blocked about a third of them and avoided the rest by stumbling backward as the Korban pressed his advantage. The Korban was whirling his bongka like a rotor blade. Harry realized that having the longer bongka was not an advantage here; it took longer to swing, block and attack. The little Korban had the upper hand, as it were.

The Korban lunged at Harry and appeared to over-extend; Harry swung his bongka overhead to try to tap him on the backside. As he did the Korban twisted inside the arc of Harry's attack; Harry realized he'd been played just as the Korban viciously whacked both of his ankles. Harry went down; the Korban jumped back just far enough to begin enthusiastically tenderizing Harry's midsection as he fell. Harry rolled and blindly thrust his bongka at the Korban; somewhat improbably, it connected, poking the Korban in its snout. The poke fazed the Korban into stopping its attack and taking a step back. Harry poked it back a couple more steps and then stood up, testing his ankles. They complained but held.

"Keep poking him!" Schmidt yelled. Harry glanced over to snap something back, giving the Korban an opening. He took it, whacked Harry hard upside the head, then reapplied himself to Harry's ankles. Harry stumbled but kept upright, wheeling in a drunken fashion toward the center of the gym. The Korban followed, swinging merrily at Harry's already bruised ankle bones. Harry got the distinct feeling he was being toyed with.

Screw this, Harry thought, and stopped, planted his bongka firmly into the gym mat and hurled himself up the staff. A second later he was doing a handstand at the top of it, balanced by dint of his finely calibrated if disused motor control, courtesy of the Colonial Defense Forces genetic engineering.

The Korban, clearly not expecting this tactic, stopped and openly gawked.

"That's right," Harry said. "Come whack on my ankles *now*, you little prick."

Harry continued to feel smug about his plan right until the moment the Korban crouched and launched itself into the air with a push of its powerful legs. The Korban didn't make it as high as Harry's ankles. He did, however, get right on level with Harry's face.

Oh, crap, Harry thought, before the blinding crack of a bongka smashed across the bridge of his nose and robbed him of any further capacity for reaction, commentary or thought. All those things came back to him with blinding pain as Harry's spinal column compressed into the gym mat as he fell. After that there were a few moments of curiously distant sensation as the Korban's bongka dug into various parts of his body, followed by an even more distant blast of a horn. The first round was over. The Korba strutted off to the sound of belching applause; Harry propped himself up on his bongka and staggered over to Schmidt, who had found him a water bottle.

"Are you okay?" Schmidt said.

"Are you dumb?" Harry said. He took the water bottle and squirted some of the water on his face.

"I'm kind of wondering what the thinking was on that handstand," Schmidt said.

"The thinking was that if I didn't do something my ankle bones would be a fine powder," Harry said.

"What were you going to do then?" Schmidt asked.

"I don't know," Harry said. "I was in a rush, Hart. I was making it up as I went along."

"I don't think it worked the way you wanted it to," Schmidt said.

"Well, maybe if I had a second who told me these little bastards could high-jump two meters straight up from a squat, I would have tried something else," Harry said.

"Fair point," Schmidt said.

"Anyway, you want me to lose, remember?" Harry said.

"Yes, but we want you to lose by just a little," Schmidt said. "You need to keep it closer than this. Ambassador Abumwe is glaring a hole through the back of your head right now. No, don't *look*."

"Hart, if I could have made it closer I would have," Harry said. He drank some water and then stretched, trying to find a place on his body that didn't hurt. His left instep seemed the most likely candidate. Harry glanced down and was glad the Korban had not seemed aware that human testicles were especially painful when struck; his had managed to escape injury.

"Looks like they're ready for the second round," Schmidt said, and pointed at the judge, who was standing with his horn. On the other end of the gym the Korban was hopping from foot to foot, loosening himself up for the hand-to-hand combat.

"Swell," Harry said, and handed the water bottle back to Schmidt. "Words of wisdom for this round?"

"Mind your ankles," Schmidt said.

"You're a big help," Harry said. The horn blew and he stepped back onto the gym floor.

The Korban wasted no time fronting an offensive, charging Harry almost as soon as he was on the floor. A few meters out the Korban kicked and launched himself into the air, claws out; he was aiming for Harry's head.

Not this time, you son of a bitch, Harry thought, and pushed himself back and toward the gym floor. The Korban slid just over Harry's head, slashing as he did so; Harry responded by bringing up a leg and delivering to the Korban's posterior a truly excellent bicycle kick. The Korban suddenly accelerated head first into the stands, colliding violently into several other Korba, whose refreshments went flying. Harry arched his head from a lying position to see the carnage, then glanced over to Schmidt, who gave him an enthusiastic thumbs up. Harry grinned and picked himself off the floor.

The Korban burst out of the stands, enraged and refreshment-coated, and launched himself once more and incautiously at Harry. Being suddenly and humiliatingly launched into the stands had apparently simplified the Korban's attack strategy down to *tear the human a new one*. Harry didn't mind.

The Korban approached and wheeled back to deliver a mighty blow, either to Harry's midsection or genital region, whichever was closer. Harry responded by holding steady until the last second and then shot out his arm. The Korban's forward motion smacked to standstill as Harry's left palm met the little alien's forehead. It was like stopping a particularly aggressive eight-year-old. Harry smirked.

The Korban was not amused at what it registered as a condescending defense maneuver on Harry's part; it burp-snarled its rage and prepared to shred Harry's forearm. Harry reared back his right arm to slug the Korban, distracting it, and then quickly retracted his left palm, made a loose fist, and popped the Korban in the face. The Korban snorted in alarm; Harry took that moment to bring his right hook square into the Korban's snout.

The scales and plates of the Korban's face puffed out as if the alien's head were a flower traumatized into blossom; they settled back as the Korban collapsed onto the ground. Harry kept him on the ground by kicking it viciously every time it so much as puffed a plate. Eventually the judges got bored with this and blew their horn. Harry walked off the floor; the Korban's second came and dragged him off.

"I think you might have overdone the kicking," Schmidt said, handing Harry his refilled water bottle.

"You're not the one whose kidneys were mashed into pâté in the first round," Harry said. "I was just giving him what he gave me. He was still breathing at the end of the round. He's fine. And now the contest is closer, which is what you wanted." He drank.

A door opened on the side of the gymnasium and a forklift-like contraption drove in, carrying what appeared to be a large kiddie pool full of water. The pool was set down near Harry; the forklift then retreated, to reappear a minute later with another pool, which it set down near Harry's Korban competitor.

Harry looked over at Schmidt, who shrugged. "For the water combat round?" he ventured.

"What are we going to do, splash each other?" Harry asked.

"Look," Schmidt said, and pointed. The Korban competitor, now somewhat recovered, had stepped into his pool. The judge, standing again in the middle of the gym, motioned at Harry to step into his pool. Harry looked at Schmidt, who shrugged again. "Don't ask me," he said.

Harry sighed and stepped into his own pool; the water, very warm, came up to his mid-thigh. Harry fought back the temptation to sit down in it and have a nice soak. He looked over again to Schmidt. "Now what do I do?" he asked.

Schmidt didn't respond. Harry waved his hand in front of Schmidt. "Hart. Hello?" he said.

Schmidt looked over to Harry. "You're going to want to turn around, Harry," he said.

Harry turned around, and looked at his Korban competitor, who was suddenly about a foot taller than he had been, and growing.

What the hell? Harry thought. And then he saw it.

The level of the water in the Korban's pool was slowly falling; as it did, the scales and plates on the Korban were shifting, sliding against each other and separating out. Harry watched as the scales on the Korban's midsection appeared to stretch apart and then join, as the plates that used to be underneath locked into place with the plates that used to be above, expanded by the water flooding into the Korban's body from the pool. Harry's eyes shifted from the Korban's midsection to its hands, where its digits were expanding by rotating the overlapping scales, locking them together into a previously unknown dance of Fibonacci sequences.

Harry's mind thought of several things at once.

First, he marveled at the absolutely stunning physiology of the Korbans on display here; the scales and plates covering their bodies were not simply integumentary but had to be structural as well, holding the shape of the Korban body in both states; Harry doubted there was an internal skeleton, at least as it was understood in a human body, and the earlier puffing and expanding suggested that the Korban structural system used both air and water to do certain and specific things; this species was clearly the anatomical find of the decade.

Second, he shuddered at the thought of whatever evolutionary pressure had caused the Korban—or its distant amphiboid ancestors—to develop such a dramatic defense mechanism. Whatever was out there in the early seas of this planet, it had to have been pretty damn terrifying.

Third, as the Korban forced water into its body, growing to a size now a square of the size—and some terrifying cube of the mass—of Harry's own dimensions, he realized he was about to get his ass well and truly kicked.

Harry wheeled on Schmidt. "You can't tell me you didn't know about this," he said.

"I swear to you, Harry," Schmidt said. "This is new to me."

"How can you *miss* something like this?" Harry said. "What the hell do you people *do* all day?"

"We're diplomats, Harry, not xenobiologists," Schmidt said. "Don't you think I would have told you?"

The judge's horn sounded. The towering Korban stepped out of his pool with a hammering thud.

"Oh, shit," Harry said. He splashed as he tried to get out of his own pool.

"I have no advice for you," Schmidt said.

"No kidding," Harry said.

"Oh God, here he comes," Schmidt said, and then stumbled off the floor. Harry looked up just in time to see an immense fist of flesh, water and fluid dynamics pummel into his midsection and send him flying across the room. Some part of Harry's brain remarked on the mass and acceleration required to lift him like that, even as another part of Harry's brain remarked that at least a couple of ribs had just gone with that punch.

The crowd roared its approval.

Harry groggily took stock of his surroundings just as the Korban stomped up, lifted its immense foot, and brought it down square on Harry's chest, giving him the sensation of involuntary defibrillation. Harry watched as the foot lifted up again and noted two large hexagonal depressions in them. The part of his brain that had earlier marveled at the physiology of the Korba recognized these as the places where the body would take in water; they would have to be at least that large to grow the body as quickly as it did.

The rest of Harry's brain told that part to shut the hell up and move, because that foot was coming down again. Harry groaned and rolled, and bounced a little as the impact of the foot on the floor where Harry had just been caused everything to vibrate. Harry crawled away and then scrambled to his feet, narrowly missing a kick that would have sent him into a wall.

The Korban lumbered after Harry, swinging at him as the crowd cheered. The alien was quick because its size allowed it to cover distance quickly, but as it swung at Harry, he realized that its attacks were slower than they were before. There was too much inertia going on here for the Korban to turn on a dime or make quick strikes. Harry suspected that when two Korba fought in this round, they basically stood in the middle of the gym and beat the hell out of each other until one of them collapsed. That strategy wouldn't work here. Harry thought back on the first round, where the smaller Korban's size was an advantage—size and the fact it knew its way around a bongka. Now the situations were reversed; Harry's smaller size could work to his advantage, and the Korban, in this size, wouldn't know how to fight something smaller.

Let's test that, Harry thought, and suddenly ran at the Korban. The Korban took a mighty swing at Harry; Harry ducked it, got in close, and jammed an elbow into the Korban's midsection. Whereupon he discovered to his dismay that thanks to their engorgement, hitting the Korban's plates was just like punching concrete.

Oops, Harry thought, and then screamed as the Korban grabbed him by his hair and lifted him. Harry caught hold of the arm lifting him so his scalp wouldn't tear off. The Korban commenced punching him in the ribs, cracking a few more. Through the pain, Harry levered himself on the Korban's arm and kicked upward, jamming his big toe into the Korban's snout; clearly it was the one body part of the Korban's that Harry was having luck with today. The Korban howled and dropped Harry; he flopped down and thudded to the floor on his back.

Before he could roll away the Korban stamped on his chest like a piston, once, twice, three times.

Harry felt a sickening stab. He was reasonably sure he had a punctured lung. The Korban stamped again, forcing fluid out of Harry's mouth. *Definitely a punctured lung*, he thought.

The Korban raised his foot again and this time aimed for Harry's head, taking a moment to perfect his aim.

Harry reached up and grabbed the top of the Korban's foot with his left hand; with his right he formed his fingers into a point and jammed them into one of the hexagonal depressions as hard as he could. As he did, Harry could feel something tear: the fleshy valve that closed to keep the water inside the Korban. It tore, and a spray of warm water pushed out of the Korban's foot and splashed over Harry.

The Korban offered an unspeakably horrible scream as the unexpected pain obliterated any other focus and tried to shake Harry off. Harry hung on, jamming his fingers further into the valve. He wrapped his left arm around the Korban's lower leg and squeezed, juicing the Korban. Water sprayed on the floor. The Korban hopped, frantically attempting to dislodge Harry, and slipped on the disgorged liquid. It fell backward, causing the entire floor to quake. Harry switched positions and now started pushing on the leg from the bottom, forcing even more water out of it; he could actually see the leg deflating. The Korban howled and writhed; he clearly wasn't going anywhere. Harry figured that if the judges had any brains at all, they would have to call the round any second now.

Harry looked over to Schmidt. Schmidt looked at him with something akin to raw terror on his face. It took Harry a minute to figure out why.

Oh, right, Harry thought to himself. *I'm supposed to lose.*

Harry sighed and stopped juicing the Korban, letting the leg go. The Korban, still in pain, eventually sat up and looked at Harry, with a look that Harry could only imagine was complete confusion. Harry walked over and knelt down into the Korban's face.

"You have no idea how much it *kills* me to do this," Harry said, reached out to the Korban's face and made a grabbing motion. Then he stuck his thumb out from between his index and middle fingers and showed it to the Korban. The Korban stared at him, not comprehending.

"Look," Harry said. "I got your *nose*."

The Korban swung a haymaker straight into Harry's temple, and the lights went out.

"That's really not the way we expected you to do that," Schmidt said.

From his bunk, Harry tried very hard not to grimace. Facial expressions hurt. "You asked me to keep it close, and you asked me to lose," he said, moving his jaw as little as humanly possible.

"Yes," Schmidt said. "But we didn't think you'd make it so *obvious*."

"Surprise," Harry said.

"The good news is, it actually worked for us," Schmidt said. "The Korban leader—who, incidentally, you caused to get drenched in fruit juice when you kicked your competitor into the stands—wanted to know why you let your competition win. We had to admit we told you to lose. He was delighted to hear it."

"He had money on the other guy," Harry said.

"No," Schmidt said. "Well, probably, but that's not the point. The point was he said that your willingness to follow orders even when winning was in your grasp showed that you could make short-term sacrifices for long-term goals. He saw you almost winning as making a point about CDF strength, and then losing as making a point about the value of discipline. And since he seemed quite impressed with both, we said those were indeed exactly the points we had wanted to make."

"So you have brains after all," Harry said.

"We rolled with the changes," Schmidt said. "And it looks like we'll come out of this with an agreement after all. You saved the negotiations, Harry. Thank you."

"You're welcome," Harry said. "And I'll bill you."

"I have a message for you from Ambassador Abumwe," Schmidt said.

"I can't wait," Harry said.

"She thanks you for your service and wants you to know she's recommended you for commendation. She also says that she never wants to see you again. Your stunt worked this time but it could just as easily have backfired. All things considered, you're not worth the trouble."

"She's welcome," Harry said.

"It's nothing personal," Schmidt said.

"Of course not," Harry said. "But I like the idea that I had choreographed having the crap kicked out of me down to that level of detail. Makes me feel like a genius, it does."

"How do you feel?" Schmidt said. "Are you okay?"

"You keep asking that same very dumb question," Harry said. "Please, stop asking it."

"Sorry," Schmidt said. He turned to go, and then stopped. "It does occur to me that we know the answer to another question, though."

"What's that?" Harry said.

"How well you can take a punch," Schmidt said.

Harry smiled, and then grimaced. "God, Hart, don't make me smile," he said.

"Sorry," Schmidt said again.

"How well do *you* take a punch, Hart?" Harry asked.

"If this is what it takes to find out, Harry," Schmidt said, "I don't want to know."

"See," Harry said. "I told you you were soft."

Schmidt grinned and left.

Hafte Sorvalh Eats a Churro and Speaks to the Youth of Today

Hafte Sorvalh, alien, walked the Mall in Washington, D.C., toward Antonio Morales, proprietor of Tony's Churros, a small stand parked not too far from the Lincoln Monument. She had completed her morning meetings, had a couple of hours before her afternoon engagements, and had a craving, as she usually did when she was in D.C. for hot Mexican pastries.

Tony had her standard order of a half dozen cinnamon churros ready by the time she approached the stand. He handed them to her in a bag, smiling. "You knew I was coming," Sorvalh said to Tony, as she took the bag.

"You are ten feet tall, Señora," Tony said, using the Spanish honorific because he knew it charmed Sorvalh when he did; Morales had lived in the D.C. area his entire life and struggled through Spanish in high school. "It's hard not to know you are coming."

"I suppose that's true," Sorvalh said, paying for her pastries. "And how are you, Tony?"

"Business is good," Tony said. "But then business is always good. People like churros. Are you happy? Have a churro. Depressed? Have a churro. About to go to prison for embezzlement? Have a churro before you go. Just got out of prison? Churro time."

"Truly, the miracle food," Sorvalh said.

"You come to get them every time you're in town," Tony said. "Tell me that I'm wrong."

"You're not wrong," Sorvalh said. "Although a sentient being cannot live on churros alone."

"Don't be too sure," Tony said. "In Uruguay, they make churros filled with cheese. That's lunch right there. I may experiment with that. You can be my test subject the next time you come round."

"I think I'll pass," Sorvalh said. "I like what I like. I am a creature of habit."

"Your loss," Tony said. "And how have you been, Señora? How is the diplomatic whirl?"

Sorvalh did her version of a grimace at this. Things had not been going well at all; since the destruction of Earth Station, things had been a real mess. Although the Conclave, which she represented, had nothing to do with its destruction, the loss of the station had put the entire planet into paranoid, angry mode at anyone who was not in fact a human from Earth. Consequently, her meetings with human diplomats and officials in Beijing, Moscow, Paris and the Hague were less like discussions and more like therapy sessions, in which her human counterparts vented as she sat there, cramped in their tiny offices (when one is nearly ten feet tall, all human offices are tiny), practicing what she hoped the humans involved would interpret as a sympathetic expression.

"It could be better," Sorvalh admitted.

"That bad," Tony said. He was getting used to reading Sorvalh's physiology, and correctly guessed that there were many things Sorvalh was choosing not to say at the moment.

"It's a complicated world we live in, Tony," Sorvalh said.

"It's a complicated world *you* live in," Tony said. "I make churros."

"And that's not complicated?" Sorvalh asked. "In its own way?"

Tony shrugged. "You know, this is actually my second

job," he said. "I went to school in business, got an MBA and spent ten years being one of those finance pricks who make everyone else miserable. I had a lot of fun at first and then near the end there I felt every day like I either needed to get drunk or start a fight with someone. So I uncomplicated my life. And here I am, with a churro stand. And now I'm happy most of the time. Because no one's unhappy to see the churro man."

"You'll never get rich being the churro man," Sorvalh said.

Tony smiled and opened his arms wide. "I was a finance prick! I'm already rich! And anyway, as I said, business is good. In fact, here come some new customers." Tony pointed down the Mall, where a gaggle of eight-year-olds, herded by a pair of harried-looking adults, were heading chaotically churro-ward.

Sorvalh followed Tony's pointed finger to look at the children. "Hopefully not all theirs," she said.

"I would guess not," Tony said. "More like a school outing to see the monuments."

"Should I step back?" Sorvalh asked. Not every human was comfortable around ten-foot aliens. She didn't want to get in the way of Tony's business.

"You might," Tony said. "If they were all adults I'd tell them to get a grip, but these are kids and you never know how they're going to react."

Sorvalh nodded and walked a bit away, toward a bench near the stand. Her body shape and height wouldn't have made it comfortable for her to sit on, but for some reason it was less awkward for her to unfold and sit on the ground near a bench—a designated sitting area—than it was anywhere else. Sorvalh was sure if she thought about it enough, she could figure out where she had picked up this particular quirk of hers, but the fact of the matter was she was much less interested in that than she was in her now-cooling churros. She started applying herself to them while Tony's stand was overrun with screaming, tiny humans, excited to cram fried dough into their gullets. She looked the other direction for most of that.

After a few minutes of quiet contemplation of her churros, Sorvalh turned to see one of the human children not too far from her, staring up at her solemnly. Sorvalh stopped chewing her churro, swallowed, and addressed the child directly. "Hello," she said.

The child looked behind her, as if expecting that Sorvalh was speaking to someone else, then turned back to her when it was clear she wasn't. "Hello," the girl said.

"Enjoying your churro?" Sorvalh asked, pointing to the churro in the girl's hand. The girl nodded, silently. "Good," Sorvalh said, and moved to go back to her own.

"Are you a monster?" the little girl asked, suddenly.

Sorvalh cocked her head and considered the question. "I don't think I am," Sorvalh said. "But maybe that depends on what you think a monster is."

"A monster fights and wrecks things," the little girl said.

"Well, I try to avoid doing that," Sorvalh said. "So maybe I'm not a monster after all."

"But you *look* like a monster," the girl said.

"On Earth I might look like a monster," Sorvalh said. "Back home on my planet I look quite normal, I promise you. Maybe a little taller than most, but otherwise just like anyone else. On my planet, you would be the one who looks strange. What do you think about that?"

"What's a planet?" the girl asked.

"Oh, dear," Sorvalh said. "What are they teaching you in your school?"

"Today we learned about Abraham Lincoln," the girl said. "He was tall, too."

"Yes he was," Sorvalh said. "Do you know what the Earth is?"

The girl nodded. "It's where we are."

"Right," Sorvalh said. "It's a planet. A big round place where your people live. My people have a place like it, too. But instead of calling it Earth, we call it Lalah."

"Hannah!" One of the adult humans had figured out that the girl had wandered away from her group and was talking to the big, scary-looking alien sitting by the bench. The human adult—a woman—came running up to retrieve her charge. "I'm sorry," the woman said to Sorvalh. "We don't mean to bother you."

"She's not bothering me at all," Sorvalh said, pleasantly. "In fact, we were reviewing basic astronomy facts, like how the Earth is a planet."

"Hannah, you should have known that," the woman said. "We learned that earlier in the year." Hannah shrugged. The woman looked over at Sorvalh. "We really did cover the solar system earlier this year. It's in the curriculum."

"I believe you," Sorvalh said.

"It says it's from a planet called LAH LAH," Hannah said, overenunciating the name, and looking up at her teacher. "It's in the solar system, too."

"Well, it's in *a* solar system," Sorvalh said. "And I'm a woman, just like you are."

"You don't look like a woman," Hannah said.

"I look like a woman where I come from," Sorvalh said. "We look different, is all."

"You're very good with children," the woman said, noting Sorvalh's responses and tone.

"I spend my days dealing with human diplomats," Sorvalh said. "Children and diplomats can be remarkably similar."

"Would you mind?" the woman said, gesturing to her main gaggle of children. "I know some of the other kids would love to meet an alien—is it all right to call you an alien?"

"It's what I am," Sorvalh said. "From your point of view."

"I just never know if it's a slur or something," the woman said.

"It's not, or at least I don't think it is," Sorvalh said. "And yes, you may bring the other children over if you like. I'm happy to be an educational experience for them."

"Oh, okay, great," the woman said, and then grabbed Hannah by the shoulders. "You stay here, honey. I'll be back." She rushed off to get the other children.

"She seems nice," Sorvalh said to Hannah.

"That's Mrs. Everston," Hannah said. "Her perfume makes me sneeze."

"Does it," Sorvalh said.

"It makes her smell like my grandmother," Hannah said.

"And do you like how your grandmother smells?" Sorvalh asked.

"Not really," Hannah admitted.

"Well," Sorvalh said. "I promise not to tell either your grandmother or Mrs. Everston."

"Thank you," said Hannah, gravely.

Presently Sorvalh found herself surrounded by a gaggle of small children, who looked up at her expectantly. Sorvalh glanced over at Mrs. Everston, who also looked at her expectantly. Apparently it was all on Sorvalh now. She suppressed an inner sigh and then smiled at the children.

Some of them gasped.

"That was a smile," Sorvalh said, quickly.

"I don't think so," said one of the children.

"I promise you it was," Sorvalh said. "Hello, children.

I am Hafte Sorvalh. Have any of you ever spoken to an alien before?" There were head shakes all around, signifying "no." "Well, then, here's your chance," Sorvalh said. "Ask me anything you want to know."

"What are you?" asked one of the children, a boy.

"I am a Lalan," Sorvalh said. "From a planet called Lalah."

"No, I mean are you like a lizard or an amphibian?" the boy asked.

"I suppose that to you I might look a little like a reptile," Sorvalh said. "But I'm not really like one at all. I am more like you than I am like a lizard, but I admit I'm mostly not like either. It's better to think of me as my own thing: a Lalan."

"Do you eat people?" asked another boy.

"I eat churros," Sorvalh said, holding up her now-neglected treat. "So unless churros are made of people, no."

"You can't eat churros all the time," this new boy pointed out.

"Actually, if I wanted to I could," Sorvalh said, taking the opposite position of her earlier comment to Tony. "It's one of the perks of being a grown-up."

The children seemed to pause to consider this.

"However, I don't," Sorvalh said. "When I am on Earth, I usually eat your fruits and vegetables. I particularly like sweet potatoes and tangerines. I only rarely eat your meats. They disagree with me. And I don't eat people, because I wouldn't want people to eat me."

"Are you married?" asked another child.

"My people don't get married," Sorvalh said.

"Are you living in sin?" asked the same child. "Like the way my mother says my Aunt Linda is?"

"I don't know about your mother or your Aunt Linda," Sorvalh said. "And I'm not sure what 'living in sin' means here. My people don't marry because that's just not how we do things. The best way to describe it is that we have lots of friends and sometimes as friends we have children together."

"Like my Aunt Linda," the child said.

"Perhaps," Sorvalh said, diplomatically as possible.

"Are you pregnant now?" asked another child.

"I'm too old for that now," Sorvalh said. "And we don't get pregnant anyway. We lay eggs."

"You're a chicken!" said the first boy, and there was laughter to this.

"Probably not a chicken," Sorvalh said. "But yes, like your birds we lay eggs. We tend to do this all at the same time, and then the community cares for them all at once."

"How many eggs have you laid?" asked the latest child.

"It's a difficult question to answer," Sorvalh said, guessing that Mrs. Everston probably wouldn't want her to go into great detail about Lalan reproductive matters; humans were known to be twitchy about such things. "It's probably best to say that I had four children who lived to adulthood, and two of them now have had children of their own."

"How do you speak our language?" asked a girl, close to Sorvalh.

"I practice it," Sorvalh said. "Just like anyone does. I'm good with languages, though, and I study yours every night. And when I go to other countries, I use this." She held up her PDA. "It translates for me so I can speak to other humans and they to me."

"Do you play basketball?" asked another child.

"I don't think it would be much of a challenge for someone of my height," Sorvalh said.

"How do you get into rooms?" asked a different child.

"Very carefully," Sorvalh said.

"Have you met the president?" asked a different little girl.

"Yes, once," Sorvalh said, recalling the event. "I liked visiting the president because I can stand up easily in the Oval Office. It has high ceilings."

"Do you poop?" asked a boy.

"Brian *Winters*," Mrs. Everston said, severely.

"It's a valid question!" the boy said, protesting. He was apparently the sort of eight-year-old boy for whom it made sense to have the phrase "it's a valid question" in his repertoire. Mrs. Everston said something else to Brian while Sorvalh quickly looked up the definition of "poop" on her PDA.

"I apologize for that," Mrs. Everston said.

"Not at all," Sorvalh said, smoothly. "It's not the worst question I've ever been asked. And to answer your question, Brian, no, I don't *poop*. At least not like you do. I do excrete waste from time to time, and when I do, it's otherwise very much like going to the bathroom is for you. Next question."

"Do you know any other aliens?" asked another girl.

"Whole planets' worth," Sorvalh said. "I have personally met people from four hundred different races of intelligent beings. Some of them are as small as that," she pointed to a squirrel running frantically toward a tree, "and some of them are so large that they make me look tiny."

"Do *they* poop?"

"Brian *Winters*," Sorvalh said, severely. "That is *not* a valid question." Brian Winters, unused to being reprimanded by a ten-foot alien, shut up.

"Will more aliens come here?" asked a boy.

"I don't know," Sorvalh said. "More have been coming recently, because my government, which is known as the Conclave, has been talking to the governments here on Earth. But I think a lot will have to happen before they are so common that you don't notice them anymore when you walk down the Mall."

"Are we going to have a war?" asked Hannah.

Sorvalh turned her head to look at Hannah directly. "Why do you ask, Hannah?" she said, after a minute.

"My dad said to my mom that he thinks there's going to be a war," Hannah said. "He said that it's going to be the humans against everyone else and that everyone else wants a war to get rid of all of us. You'll fight us and then when we're gone you'll live where we live and no one will know we were here."

"'A monster fights and wrecks things,'" Sorvalh said. She looked out at the children and saw them quiet, waiting for her answer, the two adults standing silently as well, patient.

"I can't say there will never be a war," she said. "We can't make promises like that. What I can say is that I am a diplomat. What I do is talk to people so we don't have to fight them. That's why I'm here. To talk and to listen and to find a way all of us can live together so that we don't fight, and we're not scared of each other." She reached out and gently touched Hannah on the cheek. "It's my job to make sure that none of us has to see the other as a monster. Do you understand what I mean, Hannah?"

Hannah nodded.

"Good," Sorvalh said. "Then you can tell your dad, from me, that I don't want a war either."

"Okay," Hannah said.

"All right, kids," Mrs. Everston said, clapping her hands together. "Time to say good-bye to Mrs. Sorvalh now. We still have to walk to the Washington Monument."

"Get a picture!" one of the kids said. "No one will believe us if you don't."

Mrs. Everston looked over. "Is it okay? I know we've imposed a lot on you today."

"No you haven't," Sorvalh said. "And yes, it is."

Five minutes later the pictures were done, the children were organized as much as a passel of eight-year-olds could be, and the entire crew was headed toward the Washington Monument. Sorvalh watched them go. As they walked, Hannah turned to look at Sorvalh. Sorvalh waved. Hannah smiled and turned back to her group. Sorvalh looked at the cold remains of her churros, tossed them into a nearby trash can, and went to get fresh pastries.

Tony was waiting for her with a bag of churros already gathered up.

"You are good," Sorvalh said, taking the new churros. She reached for her money pouch.

Tony waved her off. "On the house," he said. "You earned it today, Señora."

"Thank you, Tony," Sorvalh said, and pulled one out of the bag. "I think I did at that." She smiled at her friend and then took a bite.